SECRET BRIDE

THE COMPLETE TRILOGY

ALTA HENSLEY

DEDICATION

To my family who understand just what it takes to finish a book.

NEWSLETTER

ALTA HENSLEY'S HOT, DARK & DIRTY NEWS

Do you want to hear about all my upcoming releases? Get free books? Get gifts and swag from all my author friends as well as from me? If so, then sign up for my newsletter!

Alta's Newsletter

1

THERE'S A FLY IN THE HONEY.

The contamination must be rid.

Please allow him to be the one who gets away.

"Run. Run," I whisper against the glass of the window. My breath fogs my vision, but I can still see. "It's not too late. You still have time. Run."

He can't hear me. They never hear me.

I consider pounding my fists against the glass to capture his attention but know that will only make it worse. If he sees me... he'll continue to come forward in curiosity. He won't run away.

He *needs* to run away. He just doesn't know it yet.

There's a fly in the honey and Hell will be paid.

He's not the first. He won't be the last.

· · ·

Please, please, please allow this man to be the one who gets away.

My heart stops as he points his camera in my direction. What if he sees me? What if I'm in his picture? Will I be to blame for what comes next? I know what's in store. It's always the same.

Although there is something different in this man from the others. His camera looks bigger and harder to use. He has to spin the front of it back and forth as he takes the pictures. He's dressed differently than the ones before him. Hiking boots, khaki pants with lots of pockets, a cream cotton shirt that buttons with sleeves rolled to his upper arms above the elbows. His attire makes him appear more worldly than the others. Like he's on an adventure rather than just a sightseeing day trip.

Yes, he's different.

But he's still the fly in the honey and will have to face the consequences. There's nothing I can do. I know this.

He should have stayed on the beaten path. He should have heeded the warnings of the no trespassing signs. There is plenty to see down the hill. The old, abandoned buildings in the main part of Hallelujah Junction are just as good as the ones up here. The ghost town and main attraction are down the hill.

Not here.

There's an old church, a mercantile, pharmacy, a livery, and even a small jail. All the houses remain standing and preserved. Inside is the left behind furniture of the 1800s residents who built this mining town before they all vacated in a hurry for some unknown reason. History frozen in time. Secrets and whispers of the ghosts mesmerize people from around the world.

Why had the townsfolk left in such a hurry?

Why would they leave their belongings behind?

These were the eerie questions that made Hallelujah Junction become the tourist attraction that it was.

The tourists can see the schoolhouse from the main street. It towers on the top of Cemetery Road meant to look at but never approach. There are several buildings in Hallelujah Junction that are strictly off limits to the public due to safety reasons. The signs clearly mark the prohibited from the welcome.

So why? Why does he ignore the signs? There are just as many worn-down houses and dilapidated pieces of history to take pictures of in the main area. Stay with the tourists. Stay where it's safe. Listen to the ranger and follow the rules. The rules are simple: Stay on the paths. No littering. No destruction of property. *Stay. On. The. Paths.*

The rules are so simple.

Break the rules, and you will pay the price.

I see his shadow first. The ranger.

He has a job.

Enforce the rules.

I should leave the window and walk away. Pine Cone, my cat, rubs along my leg begging for some attention. She knows what is good for me. I should listen to her. I don't need to see this. I shouldn't see this. But I can never look away. This time could be different.

The man is larger than the ranger. His shoulders are broad and his chest wide. It appears as if he could run faster with his long, lean legs. He could resist and win. Maybe that is why he broke the rules. Maybe he knows he can.

But I don't want him to hurt the ranger.

The ranger is my Papa Rich. He's mine. He's all I have.

I hold my breath, not sure what I want to see. Whose side am I on? The rule breaker or my Papa Rich?

"You're trespassing," I hear Papa Rich say. The glass of the window is thin. The air is still.

The rule breaker turns, startled. "Oh sorry, man. I'll be out of your hair in just a second. I'm shooting an article for *Rolling Stone* called 'Find Your Wild.' I want to make sure I capture it all."

"Did you not see the signs?"

"I'll be quick. I saw the schoolhouse up here on the hill and needed to get a better picture up close." He continues taking pictures as if the ranger has no power over what he does or doesn't do.

Papa Rich's jaw tightens. His eyes narrow. I recognize this look. I know exactly what comes next. Papa Rich looks at the old schoolhouse. At me. I'm hidden away in the structure of this trespasser's dangerous obsession.

Can he see me? No. I know the way the sun is angled that the reflection protects me from the eyes of others. I know the times of the day I'm safe from view. Years and years have made me an expert. Papa Rich can't see me but no doubt knows I'm watching. He knows I can see. I can hear. I will learn from this man's mistakes. Another lesson of what happens to those who break the rules.

"The story of the ghost girl in the school window is fascinating," the rule breaker says as he snaps away. "I want to make sure I really get the right images to go with it." He doesn't stop taking pictures. "Have you ever seen the ghost while working here? I'd really like to interview you if you have."

"There's no trespassing up here," Papa Rich repeats.

The rule breaker doesn't look away from the schoolhouse. He should. He really should.

Like so many times before, Papa Rich pulls a thick wooden mallet from his knapsack he carries every day and hits the rule breaker on the back of the head. The sickening crack echoes up the path and stabs at my heart.

Yes, the rule breaker is bigger. Yes, he could run faster. But just like the others, he falls to the ground. The lens of his fancy camera shatters on the desert dirt and scatters beneath the branches of the sagebrush.

I turn away from the window then and finally pet Pine Cone under her chin. I don't need to see what comes next. I know Papa Rich will drag his limp body to the acid pits in the old mill building.

Another tragic accident.

Another careless tourist who didn't pay attention to the danger signs and falls to his death in the pits. It's not like anyone will find the rule breaker. The acid pits will sizzle his flesh and bone until nothing is left.

The fly in the honey will be rectified. Contamination will be cleansed.

2

EMBER

I HATE THE SOUND OF THE DOOR OPENING AND SHUTTING AFTER A trespasser is dealt with. Papa Rich is always in such a foul mood. Without fail, he'll lecture me and cite the Bible as if I am the one who has committed the crime. I'll have no choice but to stare on with wide eyes, nodding on occasion, and give every visual cue I possibly can that I am receptive of his schooling and learning about the difference between good and evil.

Yes, Papa Rich.

You're right, Papa Rich.

He deserved to pay for his crimes, Papa Rich.

You're just acting as the hand of God, Papa Rich. I'll pray for his soul.

But the sounds coming from the front of the schoolhouse sound different. So different, that I consider hiding as I was taught to do if anyone other than Papa Rich were to ever enter the building.

"Ember," Papa Rich calls out. "Ember, get out here."

I pad barefoot against the cool wood floor cautiously. Something is wrong. Something is very wrong. I can feel it. I can hear it in the way he says my name, winded.

I peer around the wall and freeze in my tracks.

Papa Rich has hold of the rule breaker underneath his arms. He's dragging him inside the door.

No acid pits.

No discarding of the body as if it were trash.

The rule breaker lay limp, unconscious and is awkwardly being yanked with all the force Papa Rich can muster. The stranger's dusty from being dragged along the dirt path, and there's a matted patch of blood on the back of his head from where he was hit.

I can't tell if the man is alive or dead.

Am I supposed to be a hand of God today? I don't want to.

I swallow the bile down.

Papa Rich looks up, his blue eyes hold me frozen as he motions me towards him. His greasy hair sticks to his temples as sweat beads down his sun-weathered face.

I watch a small grin curl his lips as he says, "Give me a hand, Ember. Don't just stand there."

I can see the man is too big for Papa Rich. I'm guessing that is why Papa Rich didn't just drag him to the old mill himself. Maybe it was too far. But I don't want to go to the acid pits. I had been there before and begged Papa Rich to never make me do it again. He said if I was a good girl, I wouldn't have to. I was a good girl, but my heart stops in fear that Papa Rich blames me for this man crossing the trespassing line.

His nostrils flare, and the cords in his neck strain. I recognize his hardened emotions and am scared. "Pick up his feet. Help me carry him to the hatch."

His command ricochets through my body. Although having a direct order makes it easy for me to comply. I take hold of the man's ankles and lift while I stumble and shuffle my feet as Papa Rich walks backwards.

He directs his gaze to my shaking hands. "Don't drop him."

My lungs labor for air, and my muscles burn. The man is heavy, and I don't understand why we are taking him to the hatch, but I don't dare question Papa Rich. When he has a plan, we follow it.

I have never seen a dead body up close before and having to touch one makes the taste of vomit linger in the back of my throat.

When we finally reach the hatch, Papa Rich says, "Put him down and rest for a moment."

The thud of the body hitting the dusty schoolroom floor strikes me with a reality I'm not sure I can face.

Papa slides the antique school desk that conceals the hatch across the planked floor. It's our secret. Only ours. The hatch opens to an underground tunnel that connects to other tunnels running beneath all the buildings in Hallelujah Junction. The miners of yesteryear built the tunnels, and Papa Rich made them safer by reinforcing and adding battery-operated lighting. It's how we walk among the tourists undetected. *Like mice*, Papa Rich used to tell me. I never leave the buildings. I never go outside. I only use the tunnels. It's the rule.

I don't move. My gaze is paralyzed on the man's face. I take in the straight profile of his nose, the sharp angle of his jaw, and the wayward brown hairs on his head in desperate need of a trim.

"We need to bring him to the house." Papa's order is sharp and unkind.

A tremor shivers through my heart. My pulse thrashes in my throat. I open my mouth to refuse, but the hard look in Papa's eye changes my mind.

He opens the hatch, silently motions for me to pick up the man's feet again, and I obey. I scan the room for Pine Cone hoping she is near and won't somehow get out of the schoolhouse. Papa Rich had warned me time and time again that there are vicious wild animals outside that would tear her flesh to bits, and I was to never open the doors or the windows if I valued her life. I would normally carry her through the tunnels but know that is not a possibility right now. I will have to come back for her later.

As we awkwardly push the body down the hatch and stand in the base of the tunnel, Papa Rich twists around, scrutinizing the distance of our journey. "Come on. Let's get going before he comes to."

Comes to?

Is he alive?

Not dead?

My stomach cramps, and my heartbeat slams into a rapid staccato at this new piece of information. If he is alive, why are we taking him to our home? We never have guests... well, not really. Papa Rich has a friend named Scarecrow who comes to visit often, but I don't consider him a guest. He's not wanted by me. I wish he never comes, and whenever he does, he leaves a stench of onion and sweat that takes days to rid.

Releasing a heavy breath, I do as Papa Rich says and hurry down the tunnel as fast as I physically can. I bite down on my lip to not cry out as my bare feet scrape against the cold and jagged rocks. I don't have the time to take careful steps as I usually do.

"Come on, we're almost there. Good girl. You're doing so good," he praises as he huffs and puffs with the weight of the unconscious man in his arms.

Tears blur my vision as I stare at the man, hating myself for my part in whatever this is. I don't know why we are doing this. I don't know Papa Rich's plan and how any of this could possibly be a good idea. But I know deep down to the tip of my now bloody toes that something is wrong.

When we finally reach the hatch leading to the main house Papa Rich and I live in, I somehow find the words to say, "Papa Rich, what are we doing?"

When his eyes meet mine, the sinister secret only he knows looms near. A surge of terror scorches through my veins.

"There's a serpent in the garden," he says. "Judas among us." He begins to pull the man up the hatch to our home. "So blood will be shed. Unless... unless..."

I exhale a chest full of air as I do my part in this misdeed. I know it is wrong. My Papa Rich is supposed to be a Godly man. A man I never question. But my soul screams no. No, no, no. Forgive me, God. What do I do? Forgive me, God. Forgive me.

With one final push, the man—the stranger—is now in our home.

Hello, Devil. Nice to meet you.

3

RICHARD

TWENTY YEARS AGO

If a town could be the hairy armpit of the devil, this town would be it. I roll up the cracked window of my pick-up truck to prevent inhaling the fetor of poverty and white trash. If it were possible to avoid this town completely, I would. I hate it. I hate it. I hate it. But I need supplies. As soon as I get them bought and loaded in the back of my truck, I will hightail it back to Hallelujah Junction and not leave again until I have to do another supply run.

Hallelujah Junction... my salvation.

God blessed me the day he found me the job of being a ranger for the infamous ghost town hidden in the hills of Nevada. An old mining town long abandoned by the residents for an unknown reason. The 1800s town's current popularity centers around the fact that every ancient resident left with only the clothes on their backs and what little supplies they could carry. They left everything behind in a hurry to flee. All the furniture, dishes, books, handcrafted items, family heirlooms, hand-stitched clothing, and the hidden secrets of why they deserted their homes remained. It makes the haunted town a living museum of a time long ago. An eerie place turned to stone as if touched by Medusa. Tourists would come from all over the world to see history paused. They wanted answers. Why? Why would the people build a life here, and then vacate so quickly without taking what meant everything to them and what they had worked so hard to gain? Reasons were rumors and speculations only. Plague? Dangers from the daily mining and plundering of the earth such as poisoned water or toxic gases? Impending attack from nearby Indian tribes? No one knew.

I don't care why they left. I'm happy they did. The town is mine. They left me a gift. Yes, I have to share the bottom half of my utopia with the common folk, even though I despise each one of them. But regardless, Hallelujah Junction is my paradise before I reach Kingdom Come.

But the truth remains...

They stink.

An odor of money and materialism.

A redolence of false promises and fake smiles.

They are walking misery cloaked in designer clothes and shoes.

I loathe the air around them.

But I have a job to perform if I want to remain in my paradise. I have to watch over them and enforce the rules that my boss handed me in a weathered pamphlet when he offered me the position. Health codes, environmental mandates, dictates from the government and all the laws I have to not only abide by but guarantee are followed perfectly.

But the upper half of the town is where I live. I was given a house so that I can live on-site. It is the only piece of property that had been outfitted to meet modern day needs. I would have gladly accepted one of the historical houses and live off the grid, but I was handed the ranger's house that has indoor plumbing and electricity. Being a ranger is comfortable, and it pays well—not that I have any real need for paper money other than my monthly run into town for supplies. My wealth comes from the land and my solitude.

And the tourists only come during the warmer weather months. The winter brings snow so severe that the dirt road leading up to Hallelujah Junction is often closed down until the melt. I plan for those months and stockpile my goods. I look forward to those months.

Alone.

No one around me. No one but one other man who lives in isolation even further into the hills.

Scarecrow is like me. He needs no one and chooses to leave society behind. It is because of him that I know so much about the land I thrive on. He's a one-legged bastard who hates everyone but the Lord, and maybe tolerates me. Refusing modern medicine to receive a prothesis for his missing appendage, he chose to stuff the bottom half of his pant leg with straw and call it good. Scarecrow showed me the secrets of Heaven shrouded in the sagebrush-covered hills.

This city I drive through, however, is a Godless city on a flat, dried land. Desert filth all around with no hope of salvation.

And then I see her... again. Poor little girl sitting in her own filth cross-legged in a field of weeds in front of a dilapidated trailer.

Spawn of white trash.

Forsaken.

Every month, I see her. Every month she appears to be alone. Today is no different except that this time I slow my truck so I can get a better look. She's dirty. Dirtier than normal. Her blonde hair isn't brushed and may have never been. Her clothes are too small, and she wears no shoes. Her wide eyes are blue as they look up at me as I lurk by. They scream desperate to me. They holler hunger and need. They shout for help over and over, so accustomed to never being heard. Her eyes. Her sad little eyes.

I drive on. I have to. I can't stay. Sorry, little girl. I can't listen to those eyes. Not today. Not ever.

I get my supplies and drive home. Home. Focus. Get the hell out of this pit of sin. But then I see the little girl again. She hasn't moved. I suppose she has nowhere to move to. So, I stop. God help me. I stop.

Rolling down my window, I say, "What are you doing outside?"

She twists her head to look at the trailer she calls home. She then stares at me and shrugs.

"How old are you?"

She puts up five fingers.

"Where is your mommy? Your daddy?"

She shrugs. Her eyes grow even bigger as if they are screaming louder. So loud.

"Are you alone?"

She nods.

"How long have you been alone?"

She shrugs.

Those eyes of her demand. They command me to get out of the truck and walk over to where she still sits. She smells of urine and neglect.

"What's your name?"

"Ember," she answers with a slight whistle of air escaping from her two missing front teeth.

"Can you show me inside your house?" I say as I extend my hand for her to take.

Without pause, because why would a five-year-old fear anything at all, she places her tiny palm into mine. We walk to the trailer, and I wonder why I am. What do I expect to see? The front door is wide open, but I could see that from my truck.

"Where is your mommy?" I ask again as we enter the dirty tin can.

"She's not here. She left a long time ago. She said her boyfriend was taking her on a trip. I wanted to go, but she said no. She said no kids allowed." Her voice is fragile and so delicate that the timbre nearly splinters my soul.

I glance around the front room. Empty beer cans and discarded needles scatter the stained floor. Flies swarm around crusty plates painted with dried food. I walk straight to the refrigerator and open the door. It's empty although I don't expect to see anything but. I open the cabinets and find them bare as well.

"When is the last time you ate?" I ask.

She shrugs again. Her eyes beg to be fed. Her eyes... her eyes...

"Are you hungry?"

"Yes, please." She's not old enough to be afraid of me, but old enough to have manners. Although by the looks of her upbringing, she was never *taught* how to behave. It just shows that children are born good and pure until corrupted by the evil ways of man.

"Are you all alone?" I already know the answer, but I suppose I need to hear the reply from her tiny, chapped lips.

"Mommy said someone would come and get me soon. She said to just sit outside every day and a person would come." She walks up to me and takes my hand again and squeezes tightly. So tight that I doubted I would ever be able to free my hand again. "She was right. You came."

Dear Lord, drown the bells in my heart. Silence the whispers in my mind.

"Yes, child. I've come."

4

CHRISTOPHER

HEAT FLOODS MY MUSCLES AS I STRUGGLE AGAINST THE CONFINES. A metal, cold shackle surrounds my ankle as if I'm cast back in the days of medieval times. I stifle the urge to scream but don't want to waste the sound without knowing my surroundings. My pulse speeds and alarms blare.

The room is dimly lit by an oil lamp in the furthest corner, too far for me to reach with the short length of chain hooked to the iron cuff holding me captive. I can see a door, a small window toward the ceiling that with my six-foot height I can maybe peer out of if I can get the chain to extend, which based on how long I have tried to free myself, seems unlikely. There is no sunlight shining through the dirty glass, which tells me I have been knocked out for hours and night has already fallen. There are crates against the wall opposite of me, but still too far for me to utilize in any way to aid in my escape. The dank, dusty air, the dirt-covered floor, and the cool temperature of the room leads me to believe I'm in a cellar or a basement. The painful pounding on the back of my head reveals the story of how I ended up chained to the floor in a foreign place.

But where is my attacker?

Why am I here?

The unknown answers are nearly as terrifying as my current situation.

I can stand and take two steps before the chain stops me. I sit down and tug on the chain some more, but it is anchored into concrete. My ankle is bloody from all the fruitless effort rubbing it raw.

I need to regain my senses. I need to stay level-headed and focused. It's clear that I won't be able to break free from my constraints on my own, so I need to find another solution.

Footsteps approach the other side of the aged and discolored wooden door. Standing again, I widen my stance to prepare. When the door opens, I ready myself for war. A man walks in who, after a few moments, I recognize as the ranger of Hallelujah Junction. He's the last man I spoke to before... before...

He still wears his uniform of tan khaki with a state forestry patch on the shirt, or I wouldn't have come to the realization so quickly. On his heels is a thin, tiny blonde woman, though I have to question if she's truly a woman or a girl. I do see breasts, however, barely visible beneath her oversized, dirty, floral dress that hangs on her like a child playing dress up with her mother's clothing. Her eyes are wide, her cheeks sunken slightly, and her long blonde hair hangs down her back weaved in a braid.

Neither of them seems surprised to see me awake. The shadows of the room conceal the finer details of both of their appearances, but I can now see who are responsible for me being shackled to the floor. The ranger stares at me directly, but the woman does not. She fixes her eyes at the ground before her, biting her lip and wringing her hands.

"Christopher Davenport," the man says as they fully enter the room.

I reach for my back pocket and notice my wallet is missing.

"115 57th Street, New York, New York. Staff photographer for *Rolling Stone Magazine*. Chiefly known for his portraits of the rich, the infamous, and the powerful but also freelances with additional photo credits in other magazines like *National Geographic*. Son of wealthy socialite Louisa Davenport and only heir to the Davenport textile empire," the ranger says as if reciting a book report. He clearly has researched me based on my I.D. he now possesses.

"What the fuck do you want?" I rasp. My hands are free from restraint. He will soon regret that decision.

Take a step closer, motherfucker.

Come on. Step closer.

Is this a ransom situation? When traveling overseas and in dangerous countries, the reality of something like this happening is a possibility and one I am always aware of. But not in the United States. Not in Nevada off the beaten path.

"You've traveled a long distance to be here," the ranger says as he stands in front of the crates directly before me. The woman is still near the doorway as if entering the room is too dangerous.

"I don't know why you did this, but if it's money you want—"

"Money is the root of all evil," the man interrupts. "That is the last thing that my daughter and I want."

I track my eyes to his *daughter* and question those words. She doesn't look anything like the man, nor does she seem particularly comfortable in his presence. The dim light of the room, the calmness of the man speaking, the fear visible in the stance of the woman, have the tiny hairs on my nape standing on end.

"Then what the fuck do you want?" My voice snaps through the still and stagnant air.

He bends toward me, his face closer—but not close enough for me to reach out and strangle—and cast in haunting shadows. "Well, the first thing I want from you is for you to watch your language. There's a lady present, and I expect you to show some respect."

My fist twitches.

Everything inside of me threatening to boil to a point of epic disaster if I don't control my emotions. I must stay calm. I must use my mind, because I have no doubt I am smarter than the man in front of me. Outwit over force considering there is a metal chain restricting me from escaping.

I glance at the woman again. She swallows, licks her lips, and continues to stare at the floor, her weakness causing my blood to boil even more.

"I am a man who believes in asking and thou shall receive," the ranger says. "My daughter, Ember, is of marrying age. Some would say a few years past. It's my responsibility to arrange a suitable and Godly partnership for her. Up to this point, I have failed her in this regard. But I suppose you could say that I'm picky. I don't believe in love at first sight, dating, playing the field and all the other foolish and sinful ways of today's belief. The only love that needs to exist for union, is the mutual love for God."

He holds his palm out to his daughter, waiting.

Something flickers in her blue eyes as she stares at him.

Comprehension.

Fear.

Reality.

She eventually moves to take his hand and twists her body to face me head on. We share a look, and in that moment of time, I have hope. She doesn't want to be here. She doesn't want *me* to be here.

I can see it.

I can feel it.

"Although you are not prepared to be her husband yet. Far from worthy in the eyes of the Lord. But I do believe I can groom you during the courting of my daughter," he continues, though his words are not entering my mind as they should. I can't make sense of the madness spewing from his lips. "And though Ember has no momma to guide her, she is a good girl and can learn quickly."

"Papa Rich," Ember says tentatively, "I don't—"

"Silence!" His lip curls as he seethes his venom. He reaches out and strikes her upside the head, causing her to tighten her fists in front of her, focusing on the floor in complete silence. He straightens his shoulders as he takes a deep breath. "My apologies. My daughter is usually much more submissive and obedient. She normally does not talk out of turn. But I assure you I will school her in the ways of being a proper bride as I groom you in your duties as a husband. I give you my word as a man I will take my responsibilities seriously."

Ember's face reddens with a quick glance my way, and she stares back down toward her hands as her brows pull together.

"You want me to marry your daughter?" I ask. Even saying the words seem unreal. I feel as if I am floating in muddy water, suffocating, struggling to hold on to life.

Ember peers at me through her thick lashes. Her face is now a sheet of white, her chin quivering in anticipation of what can possibly come next. I wonder if she is a mirror, reflecting my internal struggle with my new reality.

"Not immediately," he says casually. "I do believe a proper time is required for courting."

"You hit me over the head, knocked me out"—I lean toward him as a raging fire erupts inside of me—"to marry your daughter?"

I have never killed a man. Never considered it before now. Now... I will.

"Correction," he says, crossing his arms under his chest. "I hit you over the head as a consequence for your rule breaking. You were trespassing. But then, God spoke to me. Rather than dragging your body to its death, I spared you. I am offering the hand of my daughter to you. You should be grateful."

I lurch forward, determined to inflict pain and massive amounts of blood. "You sick motherfucker!" The chain prevents me from reaching him, throws me off balance, and forces me to my knees.

The ranger charges me in instant retaliation but freezes in his tracks. I brace myself for the punch to the face, in fact, I welcome it. Something, anything but this insanity I'm thrust into. I slam my fist down, hard enough to make Ember gasp and scurry toward the door.

"You want to kill me?" I shout. "Go for it, you sick fuck."

He straightens to his full height and takes a few steps back. Without removing his eyes from mine, he crooks a finger at Ember. She wipes away traces of tears from her eyes and walks back to where she once stood by his side.

"I'm going to leave you and Ember for a while so you both can become acquainted with each other better. I don't feel your initial meeting should be with me hovering over you both."

"You can't keep me down here," I begin. "People know where I am. It's just a matter of time until the authorities will be combing every inch of this fucked-up town looking for me."

A slow-growing smile forms on his face. "It's a shame that you fell to your death in the acid pits. It happens every year, sadly. People get careless as they take pictures and not pay attention to all the warning signs. It's a dangerous, dangerous place here in Hallelujah Junction. You should see the amount of paperwork it causes me, but the local police are aware it's just part of our environmental hazards. But then again, if you had only followed the rules, you would still be alive. I did recover pieces of your camera near the pits, however. So, your family may be able to have some sense of closure, though we will never know if you tripped, or if a beam or floorboard gave way. No real way of knowing considering the shoddy condition the old mill is in. And a body will never be found of course, not with the way the acid will fry your flesh and bone to nothing. But your poor, poor mother. I'm sure she was always worried your job was too dangerous. I'm sure she always wished you would have just taken over the family business. If only she had not bought you your first camera when you were a child." His smile never leaves his face. "Shame. Shame. Another young soul has lost his life. Shame."

"You plan on keeping me locked up down here forever?" I ask.

Cords twang in his neck as he looks over his shoulder at Ember. His smile never deflates. "Of course not. I have a plan, son. A plan for our future."

"Plan?"

"No worries to you both. I'll be a good father-in-law. I know kids these days need a leg up, and I'll provide this to the both of you." He puts up his palm to stop me from speaking. "And yes, I know you aren't quite a kid. You are older than my Ember, but I do believe she is an old soul, and though she is only twenty-five, she will be able to match you as a partner. And I'm old fashioned. I believe having an older man to help guide his wife is beneficial to any union."

"I don't care what you do to me, but I won't do this," I say as I sit back as if the air has been punched out of me. I wish I sounded stronger. I should be standing. I should be acting as if the man should fear *me*. But I can barely breathe.

"But you will," he states. He walks to the frightened woman and pats her on the head. "I'm going to leave you alone for now. You watch over him like a good girl, you hear?"

She hesitates, her eyes locked on me, but then she nods.

"Welcome, Christopher. My name is Richard, this here is Ember. We'll be your new family. Your only family."

He leaves. The door closes.

I lower my voice for only her ears. "You need to help me get out of here." I lift my leg to show her the metal cuff. "Do you know where he keeps the key?"

Her forehead pinches and her lips part. "Don't anger him."

"Okay, listen to me. I know you're scared. But we need to act fast while he's gone." Hysteria, anxious need, and downright fear have me pleading with the girl to listen.

She remains in place.

"Ember is it? You need to help me. To help yourself."

Deep breath. Deep breath. Reason with her. Don't scare her.

"I don't want to get into trouble," she says.

"You won't get into any trouble. You didn't do this, and I will tell the police that. But you need to help me escape."

"Papa Rich will get mad if he knew you were talking like this." She takes a few steps away from me, her eyes locked on the door.

I want to strangle her yet rescue her at the same time.

Deep breath. Deep breath. She's a wild animal. Afraid.

"We both can leave here together. I promise I won't let anything happen to you." I stroke her with my words. Hoping. Praying.

"Why would I want to leave?" she asks. "This is my home."

"He's crazy! This is pure insanity. He kidnapped me. Don't you see that?"

She tenses and changes her breathing. "He didn't kill you like I thought he would. So, that means he must like you. It shows he really means what he says and wants you to be part of our family."

Oh. My. Fucking. God.

She is as crazy as he is.

I stand again, hoping my height and dominant presence might intimidate her enough for her to at least fear me a little. "You need to get me out of here." The words are harsh, forceful, unforgiving. They are delivered like a rapid firing of a gun.

"Please stop asking me to," she says. "Even if I could..." Whatever drifts through her mind distracts her to silence.

But then... it appears that she considers.

Her footsteps approach. Not close enough for me to reach out to her, but close enough that I could see the tremble in her lip, the tears blurring the blue in her eyes, and the wisps of blonde curls framing her face. She's so much shorter than me, her head only reaching the height of my shoulder, and her bare feet don't give her any added height from the addition of shoes.

"Papa Rich is a fair man," she says. "As long as you don't fight him, and you follow his rules, everything will be all right. He won't harm you."

"He can't keep me here. He wants to force me to marry you. He's crazy and dangerous. You have to see that."

"He's my father..."

"I understand how hard this must be," I say softly, hoping I can reason with her rather than forcing her to run away from me. "But he needs help. If you let me go, we can do whatever it takes to get him the kind of help he needs. We can all be happy."

"He just wants me to be married. Isn't it part of growing up?"

"Ember!" Her name is shouted from outside the room. It's muffled but loud. "Come join me upstairs. We have company!"

Her eyes dart to the door, and then back at me. "I have to go. But I promise when I return, I'll make you comfortable. I'll do good by you. I promise."

"Wait! Don't leave," I say as I desperately reach out to her but come nowhere close to actually touching skin on skin.

She runs to the door leaving me standing there in my own despair.

"I'll be back as soon as I can, Christopher. I know you don't like this, but I'll make it all better. Somehow I will." She leaves the room and softly closes the door behind her.

5

EMBER

THE STENCH OF CHEAP WHISKEY, SPOILED ONION, AND BODY ODOR roots me in place.

Scarecrow.

He's here.

He never announces his arrival, and we never know how long between visits, but it does seem as if he was here not that long ago. Why Papa Rich likes him, when he hates all other people, baffles me.

Papa Rich sees me in the doorway of the kitchen and motions me to enter. "I was just telling Scarecrow that we have a houseguest."

I don't want to look at Scarecrow, but his heavy breathing and thumping of his crutch against the planked floor forces me to. His agitated state confuses me.

"This isn't right, Richard, and you damn well know it. She was promised to me," Scarecrow says.

Papa Rich calmly leans against the wooden counter we prepare all our meals on. It's scarred with years of neglect and abuse, but clean and built well. The counter will forever hold his weight. "I never made the promise she would marry you."

"You did!" Scarecrow snaps.

"I said if I could not find a suitable husband for Ember, I would *then* allow you to marry her. But as I have just informed you, I have found a suitable man who will take her hand in marriage. You won't be needed to step in."

My pulse spikes, but at the same time, relief cascades down my spine. I didn't realize any such deal had been made between them. The thought of marrying Scarecrow makes me ill. He's greasy, stinky, and meaner than a trapped and provoked hornet.

"Who?" Scarecrow asks as spittle escapes from his chapped and canker sore-riddled lips. "You know that she's different. *We* are different. And she should marry me!" He slams his crutch against the floor again, and our teacups and china plates I have stacked on a shelf to the right of the sink rattle.

I worry they will fall to the ground and shatter, and then we will be without. Papa Rich won't replace the pretty things. I have one chance to keep the pretty close, or the practical will take over. But I won't approach Scarecrow to save them from falling either. I see he has something crusty and dark on his flannel shirt. I can't tell if it is dried blood or fecal matter.

The man is contamination in all ways.

"I will help you find a proper wife," Papa Rich says. "God will speak to the both of us and let us know who that woman will be."

"Who do you think you are speaking to?" Scarecrow leans forward, and the movement causes loose straw to fall out of his pant hem that is tied with a mud-stained piece of rope. His hay-stuffed leg sways back and forth with the movement. "*I* am the preacher in these parts. Don't you start speaking about the Lord to me. Not to *me*!"

"I understand you're disappointed."

"We had an agreement. A handshake."

Papa Rich nods but still remains calm regardless of the rage before him. "I have not gone against my word. I said from the beginning that if I didn't find a proper husband who—"

"Who is this man you consider better than me?" Scarecrow bellows. "Show him to me."

"In due time."

"Where is he?"

Papa Rich resettles his weight from one foot to the other but never breaks his steady positioning. "When I feel the time is near, I'll send word to you. I do ask you, my friend, to preside over the wedding. It would mean the world to me to have your pronouncement forever bind them together."

Scarecrow crosses his arms against his chest and huffs. "You have some nerve."

Papa Rich chuckles. "Call it what you will, but I want the best for my daughter."

Scarecrow shoots angry eyes my way for the first time. "Is this what you want, girl?"

I say nothing. Does he expect me to declare I want Scarecrow as my husband instead of Christopher? Those words will never leave my mouth.

Scarecrow redirects his attention back to Papa Rich and points with a dirty, mangled finger missing a nail. "You better make good on your word and find me a bride, Richard. You better make good."

Banging from downstairs, followed by the shouts for help from Christopher pull all of our attentions to the stairway.

My heart skips, my fingertips flutter against my lips. I worry for the man below. He's not listening to Papa Rich. He's not following the rules.

I also worry for me. If Papa Rich gets angry and takes Christopher to the acid pits, then it means I will have to marry Scarecrow instead.

I would rather throw myself in the pits than even touch the vile man before me.

Scarecrow shakes with laughter. "Is this the groom you speak of? The man hollering for help?" He wipes at the spit escaping his mouth. "I think you've lost your damned mind, but I'll be a good friend regardless." He looks directly at me. "But if you change your mind and want a Godly man who can provide as a husband of yesteryear once did, then I'll always welcome my home and bed to you. I give my word on that."

He could have punched me in the gut, and the same effect would occur. I have to actually focus on not doubling over as the air seems to rush out of me.

Christopher continues to shout his demands from downstairs. I feel sorry for him. If he thinks that Scarecrow is the kind of man who would actually care or help a person chained up against his will in a cellar, then he is sorely mistaken.

Scarecrow shakes his head in disbelief and moves toward the door to leave but stops and looks over his shoulder at Papa Rich. "How long do you plan on keeping the man locked up down there?"

"That decision is up to him," Papa Rich answers simply. "In time, the man will be just as eager to marry Ember as I am to have her married."

"And if you're wrong?" Scarecrow challenges.

"This isn't about me. God spoke, and God is never wrong."

Limping past the threshold and finally leaving our house, Scarecrow says, "I hope you listened correctly, and it was actually God speaking and not the Devil. Evil is alive and well, and it's ravenous as hell."

Help! Is anyone up there? Help, I'm down here! Help!

"Ember, go downstairs and quiet the man up," Papa Rich orders, but he still remains calm. I'm grateful that I don't see him angry... yet.

"Papa Rich?" I begin, risking not following his command right away. "Were you really going to have me marry Scarecrow?" I nearly whisper the words in fear that Scarecrow is still in earshot.

I truly had no warning, or even an inclination that it was a possibility, and I feel a sense of betrayal because of it.

He approaches me and strokes my cheek. "My sweet Ember. I would never make a decision that is not right for you. Nor would

God. It's why that man downstairs was brought to us. I prayed the right person would someday come, and he did."

"I didn't know you wanted me to get married... now."

He continues to stroke my face like I stroke the head of my cat, Pine Cone. "It's time. No father wants to see his little girl grow up, but the day will always come."

"You want me to leave you?" I ask, sadness filling my heart. We never discussed this. I had always assumed... my place is with Papa Rich.

"Never, my girl. Never. Hallelujah Junction is your home and will forever be your home. But you are such a beautiful girl and have so much to offer that we can't waste that gift."

"But you just *took* him."

"Yes, that is true. But God spoke to me. And even though the man downstairs doesn't know it yet, he is destined to be your husband. To join our family."

"Are we to live here in the main house? Married? Downstairs? My room? What if he says no? He can't stay chained up forever."

"Shh..." He still caresses my face. "These are my worries to carry. Not yours."

"But I don't understand."

"You will," he says, finally ceasing in his constant petting. "For now, I need you to focus on learning how to be a wife. You need to woo Christopher just as he woos you. Yes, many unions happen by arrangement only, and that is still a possibility if the Lord chooses that path for us. But I do want love for you. I would like to see that occur between the two of you if at all possible."

"Love?" Thoughts of all the romance novels I read and fantasize about in the schoolhouse rush in. I never thought love was a possibility as I turned those pages lost in the fairytale of true happiness. I am in hiding. I can't leave. I can't find love.

But did love find me?

"It will take time," he says as he leans against the counter as he had been while speaking with Scarecrow. "He may be resistant at first, and you may not know how to love anyone other than me. But I feel like it can happen if you both work hard enough."

His talk of love wraps around me like a warm hug. I want it. I want it so badly. More than anything in my entire life.

A husband.

A man to love me like the men in all the books love their women.

I want the happily ever after too.

Papa Rich is finally giving me a gift. A gift of love.

"Thank you, Papa Rich. I'll work really hard on being good and making Christopher want me as his wife."

Papa Rich nods his approval. "I know you will, child. I know you will."

The hollers come again from downstairs, followed by more pounding on the wall or ground, and even the rattling of the chain.

"But I won't ask you again," he says, his tone changing from light to dark. "Go silence him before he works my last nerve."

6

CHRISTOPHER

THE TINY WOMAN ENTERS THE ROOM AGAIN, AND ANY HOPE someone will hear my shouts for help is deflated. Someone was upstairs, and clearly did not hear me. Or maybe they did, and they were killed or tied up somewhere in their own prison.

"You have to be quiet," Ember says as she places her thin finger to her lips.

"Who was up there?" I'm sitting but consider standing to bulldoze her fragile state of mind with my stance but choose to wait and see how she reacts. I don't want to chase her away, because I truly feel she may be my only chance at escape, as thin as it is.

"Trust me," she says as she closes the door behind herself. "The man upstairs will not help you in any way. You don't want him down here." Her lips pinch, and her nose wrinkles.

I watch her walk completely across the room and light another lantern on a small table in a far corner. It reveals another door I hadn't seen before.

"There's indoor plumbing in the main house unlike the rest of the buildings in Hallelujah Junction," she says, pointing to the door. "There's a bathroom here, although the water heater doesn't work very well, so most likely the water will be cold." She glances at the chain around my ankle, restricting me from even going near the door. "I'm sure I can convince Papa Rich to give you a longer chain or something so you can use it."

Her voice is so soft. So delicate. Almost melodic.

"How long have you been here?" I ask as she sits on one of the crates before me—still out of reach.

Her eyes widen, and she tilts her head. "What do you mean?"

"He's not your father, is he?"

"He is."

I shake my head. "I don't believe he is."

She swallows hard and looks down at her fingertips. "He saved me. He's my father in the eyes of God, and that's all that matters."

The way she recites the sentence tells me that she's been fed the line of crap for so long she actually believes it. I can't help but feel she is a lost lamb about to be devoured by wolves. Hell, she's already their evening meal.

"How long has he been your... father?"

"My mother left me when I was five. Papa Rich took me and raised me as his own." Her eyes lift and she stares at me head on. "I've never discussed this with anyone before. Actually... I've never discussed anything with anyone. You're the first person— besides my father's friend, whom I hate—that I have ever spoken to."

"Why?" I ask, feeling like I must get this woman to open up to me if I have any shot at convincing her to find the key to my shackles.

"I have to stay hidden," she says so softly, I have to lean forward to read her lips to help make sense of her words.

"Hidden?"

She looks at the door, pauses for a moment, and then refocuses her attention on me. "My mother is dangerous. If she knew I was here, she would come get me. My life would be at risk with her.

Even now as an adult, she would still want me for revenge purposes alone. I'll never be safe. Papa Rich says she has people looking for me, and we can't trust anyone. No strangers. No one. So, my only chance of staying alive from the power and evil she has, is to stay hidden. He keeps me safe in Hallelujah Junction far away from most. He doesn't think she would ever look for me here, but we have to make sure by not allowing me to ever be seen by anyone."

Ember can't possibly believe the words she says, but it appears she does. She truly does.

"So, you came here to live when you were a child? How old are you now?"

"Twenty-five. But we don't celebrate birthdays. I read about them in books, but Papa Rich says that materialistic things are the root to evil, and birthdays are about presents, and we don't partake in the ways of modern man. We're different."

This poor woman. She was kidnapped twenty years ago and has been brainwashed by the crazy man upstairs. She's a victim just like me.

She just doesn't know it.

"So, you live in this house? Were you ever chained up like me?" I ask, trying to make sense of her situation. Speaking to her is like putting a puzzle together one piece at a time.

She smiles warmly and nods. "My father is the ranger in Hallelujah Junction. They give him this house which is up the road behind the schoolhouse. The visitors can't come up here where we actually live." She pauses and looks at my ankle shackled in metal. "Well... visitors aren't supposed to." She takes a deep breath and then looks back into my eyes. "There are underground tunnels that connect many of the buildings. They were built years and years ago by the miners who founded this town. Papa Rich trusts me to walk them so I can visit more buildings than just our home. The schoolhouse is my favorite because I like to read, and that's where we keep boxes of old books. My father teases me and tells me that someday, I'll read them all, but I still have a long way to go. I haven't opened all the boxes yet."

"Are you never allowed outside?" I rub my ankle, knowing that forcing my way out from these restraints is futile. But this woman... this woman can be my ticket to freedom.

"Not during tourist season." She glances at the door again. She's scared my captor will hear her. I can see it. Mental note: this *daughter* does fear her *father*. I can use that fact to my advantage. "But during the wintertime, the road up to Hallelujah Junction is usually closed due to the snow. So then, the entire town is ours. Papa Rich allows me to go outside then. I love it. We build snowmen, and even snowshoe for exercise. Winter is my favorite season because of the..."

Freedom, I want to answer for her but remain silent.

"I only visit the buildings that the tourists can't in the busy season," she adds.

An eerie realization dawns on me. "You're the female ghost in the schoolhouse window that makes Hallelujah Junction so famous, aren't you?"

She plays with the ends of her hair and nods. "It was an accident. I didn't know I could be seen. When Papa Rich found out that people saw me, he was so angry. He told me I had to stay here in the cellar like you. It was a long time before he let me out."

I exhale a lungful of air I didn't realize I was holding.

She twists her hair around and around her index finger. "But he eventually let me out of this room. He taught me when it was okay to be in the school window and when it wasn't. He said my accident actually protects me even more. Because if I am somehow seen again, he can blame the ghost and folklore getting in the minds of people hoping to see the schoolhouse haunting."

I reposition my body, and as I do, I see this woman in a completely different way.

The darkness of the room that drips and oozes with diabolical acts drowns by the warmth in her voice. "I'm the ghost of

Hallelujah Junction," she adds, and I can't tell if that last statement makes her proud or sad.

I carefully consider how I proceed with Ember. My earlier attempt of trying to reason with her didn't work. Whether I understand it or not, she loves her kidnapper. I can't expect her to give up years and years of believing the man is her savior by simply telling her she's wrong. He has earned her trust, devotion, and loyalty. My only chance is somehow overpowering those feelings and emotions with her own toward me. How? I am not sure. But somehow.

"Are you hungry? Thirsty?" she asks.

"Not yet." I can't accept the fact that I will be down here long enough to even consider food and water.

"I'm a good cook. Or at least Papa Rich says so. I found several old cookbooks in the schoolhouse that I use, although I have the recipes memorized now. Is there anything special you like to eat?"

Her smile is slow building, but when it fully forms, her appearance completely changes. She doesn't appear nearly as haunted as before.

Jesus. She's so hopeful she can actually please me in my current situation.

"Ember..." I proceed with caution. "Have you ever wanted to leave Hallelujah Junction?"

"My mother—"

"If you could be protected from her," I cut in, validating her concern. "If *I* could protect you from her."

"As my husband?" she asks almost whimsically. Like I was her found Prince Charming and could slay all the dragons.

I can't say yes, but I also don't want to lose her. "I would protect you."

Ember hops off the crate she is sitting on and takes a few cautious steps toward me. I wouldn't reach out and grab her even if I could. I can already tell this process of convincing her to release me will take small baby steps.

"What can we do to make you more comfortable?" she asks. "I can get blankets and pillows if that helps."

I bite back the bubbling fury building inside of me. I want to snap, to yell, to shake sense into her that no amount of pillows or blankets are going to make me comfortable, but she will run. I know she will run.

"A chair," I say, shaking off my frustration. "So, I don't have to sit on the ground."

Her eyes light up, and that smile of hers returns. She quickly runs around a crate and drags a wooden chair from behind it. She doesn't pause before reaching me this time, which I take as a good sign. If I wanted to, I could grab her and snap her neck with my bare hands. But she is unaware of that fact which tells me the trust level is beginning.

She places the chair beside me, and I stand. She still doesn't move or take any steps backwards. She doesn't even flinch.

"Thank you," I say softly.

We are close enough now that I can see more defined features of her appearance. Though I had originally thought her dirty based mostly on her attire and our surroundings, I could now see she is very clean. Oddly so, considering she was barefoot in a dirty cellar. Her nails are short, but no dirt caked underneath them. Her blonde hair shines bright as if freshly washed. Even her dress isn't dirty... worn... but not dirty.

Her eyes are bluer than any eyes I have ever seen. They stand out the most on her nearly angelic face. She's smaller than most women, and skinnier but not necessarily malnourished or starving. *Stunted*, would be a word best to describe her. Almost as if her body is brainwashed—just like her mind—to believe she is an innocent child even though she is a grown woman.

"Ember." Saying her name feels odd. "Did your father tell you what his plans are?"

"In regard to our wedding?"

I nod as I take the seat and twist my body so I am looking right at her. "Or about me in general."

She takes a deep breath and closes her eyes for a brief moment. "He hasn't told me much. I didn't know he wanted me to be married. I didn't know this was the plan. He's told me to allow him to worry about all the details and to just focus on... us."

"Us?"

"On falling in love," she says with over-bright eyes filled with foolish beliefs.

I think up to this point, I never actually felt true panic. Not until this very moment.

Panic.

Fucking Hell...

Love? Love? *Love?*

The word seems absurd. The emotion seems deranged. Love and madness is my new reality, and all I can do is drown in my wave after wave of hysteria.

"I should really go and start supper," she says as she steps away from me for the first time since bringing me the chair.

I wonder if she can see the lunacy in my eyes. Can she see how it has finally hit me like a brick that I am held captive and may never escape? In a matter of hours, I will be dead to all who know me. They will have no reason to doubt the ranger that I fell to my death. They know I would always go the extra distance to get the perfect picture, even if it meant falling to my death in a pit of acid.

"I was going to make stew... if that is alright with you?" She wants my approval. She is nearly begging for it with those eyes of hers.

I have nothing left in me to continue on. Not now, and maybe not ever.

Jesus fucking Christ.

"Stew is fine," I mumble.

Fuck. Fuck. Fuck!

7

CHRISTOPHER

I HATE THE FACT I ACTUALLY ALLOWED MYSELF TO SLEEP LAST NIGHT. I even hate myself more for eating the stew Ember made and settling into the pillows and blankets she brought me as a dutiful hostess would do.

I should fight more. I should not allow any acceptance of this situation.

The bright light shining through the window only reminds me it is now official. In the real world, I am a missing man.

My editor will be waiting for me to send photo proofs. I'm pretty sure I have a lot of unread emails, unreturned text messages, and missed phone calls. My mother won't be particularly worried yet, since she has become accustomed to me not speaking to her every day. Although my sort of girlfriend, Marissa, will no doubt think I am banging some other chick and currently be in the middle of a stream of texts ranting about what an asshole I am and how my failure to commit to her only proves I am a spoiled, silver spoon-fed momma's boy with no hope of ever finding true happiness. It's likely some will assume I'm on a bender, though not my work. No matter what, the workaholic in me has forced me to show up every day, meet every deadline, and act in the utmost professional manner. Odd, that it will be my employer who will notice my disappearance and find it concerning before my mother or my... well... the woman I sleep with, will.

If any one of them knew I'm actually chained up, in a cellar, held captive by a psychopath grooming me to marry his physically and mentally stunted kidnapped pretend daughter, they wouldn't believe it. Who could believe this? I'm struggling to grasp the reality myself.

I wonder if Richard is reading all of my texts and getting pleasure in watching my life implode one angry message at a time.

My poor mother, and not for the reasons one would think. This will be all the gossip and really hurt her socialite status. The pity in the eyes of all her lunch date besties will truly eat her alive. The hushed rumors, the well wishes laced with hidden agendas just to dig for more gossip. Her invites to parties will decrease because no one wants a dark cloud to attend a gala. And of course, she won't be able to hold a proper funeral for me where she can wear a ten-thousand-dollar designer black dress and dab her eyes with a handkerchief once belonging to some queen of another country and considered a priceless antique. She will not be able to have all eyes on her as she throws her body over my open casket declaring she doesn't know how she can go on without her only son.

She will feel cheated that there is no body for her handsome son. I'm sure I would make for a very attractive corpse in an expensive, custom-fitted suit.

Oh yes... my poor mother.

I rub the sleep from my eyes and find it odd I'm still a little groggy.

The stew...

There must have been something in the stew Ember cooked to knock me out. No way could I have slept through the night on a cold cellar floor without some sort of sedative. Especially since I can't remember the last time I went to bed without several glasses of whiskey and two or three sleeping pills. My nighttime cocktail is my way of life, and I don't judge myself nor do I give a shit who does.

I do me. Do I drink more than mother dearest would approve of and pop pills like a child in a candy store with free samples? Damn straight. And when this entire nightmare is over, I will throw myself a true rager to attempt to erase the awful memories of this medieval dungeon from my mind. It may take me never being sober again to forget this ordeal.

But for now, all I can do is get off the ground to sit on my chair of dignity. It's how I see this chair. At least I am not on the floor like some animal.

My throne.

For I am now the king overseeing the demented, the unhinged, and the stark raving madness of this depraved empire.

I notice the chain to my ankle cuff is longer. A lot longer.

This must have happened while I slept in a drug-induced stupor.

Standing up and testing the length, I can see this Richard fuck is smarter than I give him credit for. I can make it to the bathroom, which I use instantly, and I can make it around the room for the most part. But I can't reach the doorway to escape at all. Richard will be able to stand by the door, and I can't reach him to strangle him to death. I can also reach the wall with the window, but barely. There isn't enough slack for me to stand on a crate or chair to look out of it. It's like this asshole measured every single inch of this room and read my mind on what I would do once I knew he gave me enough slack to move more freely.

"How did you sleep?" I hear a soft voice from behind me ask as I stare up at the window. I didn't notice Ember enter the room.

"I think you know the answer to that since you drugged me," I say as I walk back to my chair.

"Papa Rich said it would make you more comfortable." She takes a few cautious steps toward me and points to the chain. "He said if I sprinkled the stew with the powder, he would give you more length so you can use the restroom."

I don't say anything but take in her appearance instead. She's wearing another floral dress that seems to fit her better. The fabric is still worn, and the hem that reaches below her knee is frayed. She is still barefoot, her hair remains in a braid down her back, but her face seems to have more color. More life. The rosy color in her cheeks only brightens the blue in her eyes more. She is actually a very pretty woman, especially considering she clearly gets no assistance from salons or plastic surgeons like all the women I'm used to seeing in New York.

Her wide eyes are full of worry, and her fingertips touch her collarbone. "Are you mad at me?"

Such a simple question.

Such a normal question.

"There are a lot of people worried about me right now," I say, examining her closely to see how she reacts to my statement.

She looks to her feet. I see guilt. Good.

"Do you have a big family?" She lifts her eyes and looks at me through long eyelashes. "Brothers and sisters?"

"No brothers or sisters, but I have a mother who I'm close with. I have friends and coworkers who no doubt are scared." I consider telling her of Marissa too, but I do worry that if Richard finds out, he may just kill me and find another poor fool to go through this absurd *courting*. I need to stay alive long enough to somehow figure out a way to escape.

"Being an only child is lonely," she says as she walks to the same crate she sat on yesterday. Sitting, she crosses her legs, leans forward, and locks her stare on me.

"I suppose so."

"What is *Rolling Stone*? Papa Rich says that's where you work."

I swallow hard to force down the growing frustration. She's acting like we are on a date learning about each other when what a normal woman would be doing is helping me come up with a plan to run away.

"It's a magazine. I take pictures for it." I have no idea if she even knows what a magazine is.

"I saw your camera when you first arrived." She weaves her fingers together and looks down at them. "It broke when Papa Rich—"

"Can you stop calling him that?" I snap. "You aren't a child. It makes you come across as..." I take a deep calming breath. "You do realize you are a grown woman, right?"

Her eyes narrow, and I see her breathing change. She stiffens her spine, and the rosy hue in her cheeks pale. She stands. "I'll go cook you something for breakfast. Pap—my father has already left for work down the hill, so it's just us today."

She goes to the door, and I try to stop her. "Wait. I'm sorry. I didn't mean to sound so mean. It's just that—"

She opens the door and leaves without saying another word.

I look around the room and consider all options again and again. I could try to break a crate and use the splintered wood as a weapon. But against who? As frustrating as Ember is, I'm not going to harm the woman. I really feel deep down that she is just as much a captive as me. I haven't seen Richard since the first meeting, and I can already tell the man is smart. I highly doubt he will come close enough for me to use any form of violence in my favor. Not only isn't the chain long enough to allow me to climb on a crate to see through the window, I'd never fit through the rectangular opening if I were to break the glass. I already screamed for help, and that got me nowhere.

Fuck. Fuck. Fuck.

There is a high possibility a search party would be called to look for me. Unless somehow the crazy man is actually able to convince authorities I fell to my death like he claims he can. But without being able to see out the window, I won't know when to shout and make as much ruckus as I can. I'm not foolish enough to be at it all hours of the day. Pushing the patience of an unstable man isn't wise, and I would rather not be killed for testing the limits too far.

Ember.

She's my only chance of getting out of here—I know this, and I keep telling myself this and yet, I'm failing at actually listening. And I just successfully pissed her off. She wants to trust me. She wants to like me. I can see she wants to prove herself to her fucked up Papa Rich and be the perfect wife in this sick world they live in. She desperately wants me to be the Prince Charming she reads about in her books in that haunted shack of a schoolhouse.

Fucking with a woman's mind is not how I roll. It never has been. I have always said it like it is, to the point where I can be considered an asshole. But I have always preferred to be a straight forward asshole rather than a slimy, lying prick. I don't do pick-up lines. I don't tell a woman what she wants to hear just to get in her pants. I don't bang chicks for the mere sport of it.

But here I am.

I have no choice but to fuck with this poor woman's mind if I ever want to escape. I have to play this demented chess game. Except in this game, I'm nothing but a weak pawn.

Fuck. Fuck. Fuck.

My hands shake and my head pounds. I need coffee. Actually, I need a shot of whiskey, a few uppers to help me face my day, but I'll settle for coffee to try to take this edge off.

I look at the door and figure that Ember will be returning soon with breakfast. I need to do a better job and can't scare her away anymore. I need her on my side.

Getting up and walking to the bathroom to clean up, I mentally prepare for what will no doubt be the hardest thing I will ever do in my life. I know I am highly intelligent—an attribute that has always benefitted me in my life. I'm also a fighter—another quality that has served me well. Yes, I'm chained in a cellar in an old mining ghost town, soon to be presumed dead. But I'm not going to throw in the towel. Not yet.

Richard will regret the day he chose me to marry his daughter. I'll make damn fucking sure of it.

8

EMBER

CONCENTRATING ON NOT DROPPING THE TRAY OF FOOD, I SOMEHOW open the door and enter with Pine Cone close at my heels. She's not used to ever being without me, nor all my attention not being focused on her. I keep my eyes on the scrambled eggs, bacon, and toast, not really wanting to look directly at Christopher. He makes me uncomfortable, and I don't know if I am scared of him, like him, hate him, or feel bad for him. All I know is my knees want to buckle as I enter the room.

"I wasn't sure how you liked your eggs," I say as I reach back with my foot and close the door shut.

"Please tell me what's inside that mug is coffee," he says which makes me look up and see he has a smile on his face. He also has washed off the dirt on his exposed skin and has rinsed the matted blood from his hair.

"It's black, but I can get cream or sugar if you want."

I hope he doesn't want sugar because I have very little of it, and I want to save what I do possess so I can make a cake later as a special treat. Papa Rich doesn't make a supply run for a few days, and I doubt he will make any exceptions.

"Black is perfect. So is scrambled. I'm not picky."

I let out the breath I'm holding, and hand him the tray. Not sure if I should remain in the room or not, I look for my cat. She has jumped up on the crate I sat on last time I was in the room. It's like she is making the decision for me. So, I sit.

"I didn't put anything in the food," I inform, although I quickly regret saying it as I see his body tense. But I also don't want him doubting every bite as he eats.

"What's your cat's name?" he asks as he drinks from the coffee first.

"Pine Cone," I answer as I pet the top of her gray head, needing the sound of her content purr to ease my discomfort. I'm not used to sharing air space with another, especially during the day while Papa Rich is at work.

"I'm sorry," he says with a mouthful of eggs. "I didn't mean to snap at you like I did. I'm sure you can understand my frustrations."

"I do. I was down here for a long time once. And... I sometimes have to come to the cellar and be very, very quiet during inspection times. My father wants to make sure that I'm not spotted by anyone during the yearly State inspections."

"How long until they do another inspection?"

I know why he is asking, but I don't blame him. "They were just here about a month ago. So, another year is when we can expect a visit. They don't deviate from the schedule... or at least not since I've lived here."

"While you were upstairs cooking, I was thinking."

I don't say anything but run my fingers through Pine Cone's fur to soothe me. This man makes me nervous, and I need any help I can not to start shaking exactly where I sit.

"So, if we get married"—he takes a drink of coffee—"*when* we get married, I will need to still work and provide for our family." He looks at me seriously, the steam from the coffee circling around his face as he sips. "I can't do my job from here. My office is in New York, and I travel a lot to get the pictures I need. You understand that once we are wed, I can't stay here. *We* can't stay here. Right?"

My heart skips and the overwhelming... euphoria... nearly closes my airway. He wants to provide. He said the word *family*. He is talking marriage and our future.

"I'm sure Papa Rich has—"

"Let me tell you something about men. It's in our nature to provide." He bites into the bacon and pauses as I see his eyes search my face. "A strong man wants to lead his family. I understand that your father is the head of the household for you currently. But, when we get married, that role changes. *I* will be your husband. *I* will have to make decisions that are best for us. You understand that, I'm sure."

Did I? I suppose it makes sense that Christopher would want to be the one in charge. Not my father.

"We don't have to make a final decision right now," he says, which puts my swirling mind at ease a little. "I just want to plant the seed. That we do have to discuss our future and my career eventually. I can't provide for you financially and keep a roof over our heads unless I work. And I can't do that here."

"I don't think Papa Rich will allow us to leave," I say, scared that I will upset Christopher again because I like this new side of him I'm seeing.

But rather than his eyes darkening, and his jaw tightening like I am getting used to seeing, he smiles again. "We can plan all that later. It's always hard for parents to let go of their children and allow them to go and spread their wings. I get that. We don't have to tell him our plans yet. Let's just wait on that. Let him get used to the fact that another man is about to *steal his daughter away...* so to speak. Even though he wants you to get married, this is still going to be really tough for him. So, we can keep all our marriage talk between us for now."

"But what about Hallelujah Junction, and my mother?"

"I promise you that your mother will not be an issue. No matter where we go, she won't be. I give you my word. I come from a family with a lot of money and a lot of resources. On top of all that, I make my own income and can hire the best security and guarantee that you never have to hide again. As for this town, well..." He takes the last bite of food and chews it slowly before continuing. "Just like the miners who built this town. They all had to leave their homes and their families to start anew. It's part of life and has been happening since the beginning of time. I'm sure you've read about it countless times in all those books of yours."

True. I have. He has a very good point.

"I've never been to New York." I glance down at Pine Cone who is asleep by my side. I briefly remember simpler times when it was just my pet and me together in our isolation as we waited for the hours of the day to tick by. My face heats with shame as I add, "I've never been anywhere."

"You'll love it. It may take some getting comfortable to the idea since it's so different than what you're used to, but we could build a great future together. I'll buy you a home, and you can decorate it however you want to." He points to Pine Cone as he leans over and places the tray on the floor, keeping the coffee cup in his hand. "You can bring your cat, of course."

"She's my best friend," I admit.

"Which is sad," Christopher says, harsher than how he's been speaking. He quickly smiles to conceal the momentary... judgment of my situation, but I saw it. I saw the flash in his eyes before he could hide it from me.

The euphoria I was feeling only seconds ago is suddenly suffocated by something much darker.

Skepticism.

Doubt.

Suspicion.

I tilt my head and examine how easily Christopher crosses his legs and leans back in the wobbly wooden chair. He cups the mug of coffee and appears so... calm. Night and day difference from the man this morning.

This isn't real.

He isn't real.

An act. And I should know all about acts. I have gotten very good at them.

"Why are you lying to me?" I ask, hating that the words have to come from my lips. I want to believe. So badly, I want what he says to be true. "I'm not stupid, Christopher. I know you must think I'm dumb, which I can understand. I can believe you hate me. I can believe you can't stand that I'm sitting in this cellar and doing nothing to help you. But what I can't believe is what you are telling me now." I lean forward and bite the quiver out of my lip. "You don't have to lie to me."

For the first time since arriving with breakfast, I see an honest emotion in his eyes that he doesn't bother to enshroud in false promises and impossible dreams.

Hatred.

I clearly see hatred.

"Ember, what the fuck do you want me to say?" He swallows the last of his coffee and glares directly into my eyes. "Do I have a god damn choice? Huh? Daddy Dearest has declared we're getting married. So, it's a done deal."

"But you don't have to lie to me. You don't have to tell me I will someday have a home I can decorate, or how we'll someday have a family. If you don't mean it, you don't have to say it."

"Bullshit!" He throws the coffee cup across the room, and it shatters to pieces.

I jump and cower backwards but resist the urge to flee. He has the right to be angry. At least now, he's being honest. This is what I want. I don't want deceit. I want the real Christopher, no matter how awful the man could end up being. No matter how painful his words may be, I want them to at least be true.

He stands up and storms over to where I sit. The chain is long enough now. He can hurt me if he desires, but he stops inches from me with fisted hands.

"Do you want me to tell you I want to kill you? Because I don't. Do you want me to tell you I want to hurt you? That would be a lie too. I've already told you the truth. You know I want out of here. You know I want your help... that I *need* your help. I've already told you the fucking truth. Where has that gotten me?" He leans even closer, but his hands remain at his sides. I can feel his warm breath on my face. I feel his inner demons rage out of control, but his composed demeanor keep them at bay. "Huh? Tell me!"

He's shouting now, and though I want to run out of the room, scurry through the underground tunnels and retreat to my schoolhouse sanctuary, I feel I owe it to him to remain in place. I can't ask for the truth and then flee from it.

"What's going on here?" A voice I recognize well, slices through the tense air. Pine Cone snaps awake and darts behind the crates. She fears Papa Rich and has never warmed up to his presence.

Christopher remains where he's at but turns his head to face Papa Rich who stands in the doorway.

"We're just talking," I answer softly. I don't know why he's home from work. He rarely leaves the lower level of the town during open hours.

"It sounds like fighting," Papa Rich says, but he does not enter the room. His eyes are glued on Christopher as a stare down begins.

I'm surprised when Christopher breaks the tense connection and walks back to the chair and sits. "We were just discussing the future. You wanted me to get acquainted with my future bride, correct?" Venom drips from his words, but his body is casual and relaxed as he leans back and crosses his ankles as if he is at complete ease.

"I know the situation down here in the cellar is not ideal," Papa Rich says. "I understand why you look at me with such hate in your eyes. I don't blame you at all. But soon, you'll see why I've done what I've done."

"Is that what you think?" Christopher asks as he leans forward.

"It's what I know."

"You're wrong, madman. Wrong. You're going to have to kill me in here, you know that, right? Either that, or I'll escape. Somehow I will. Death or escape are my only two options and there is nothing you can do to change that. You may think you have all the control, but you're wrong." Christopher glances at me and adds, "You can't make me marry your daughter. You can't force this plan on me. I'll refuse. I'll choose death over letting you get your way."

"Tough guy I see," Papa Rich says calmly, but I'm barely breathing as I wait for his explosion of rage.

Christopher shrugs which I know is meant to infuriate Papa even more. "I speak the truth. You might hate hearing it, but it's reality. Are you prepared to kill me? Because that is what you'll have to do."

Papa Rich motions for me to stand by him, which I quickly do. I can feel something bad is brewing. I don't know what, or how, or when, but the hairs on my arms stand on edge in warning.

"Have you ever heard of the phrase *whipping boy*?" Papa Rich asks Christopher as I stand right by his side.

"I suppose I have."

"Good. But just to be certain you do, let me clarify. The whipping boy was used in the past to great effect. Corporal punishment was used on the unfortunate soul to keep a prince or a member of royalty in line who could not be disciplined themselves due to their status. To beat a dog before a lion. Watching another be beat for your transgressions would hopefully prevent you from doing the action again."

Papa Rich reaches for the buckle of his belt and begins to unfasten it. I've seen him do this before, but I have always done whatever it takes to avoid this action. For the most part, I succeed, and I worry about why he is removing his belt while his eyes are pinned on Christopher who hasn't moved an inch.

"Ember," Papa Rich begins, "lift your dress, bend over and touch your toes." He frees the belt completely, folds the belt in half, and snaps the leather.

My heart stops as confusion swamps my senses. "But, Papa—"

"Now, Ember."

I know better than to make Papa Rich repeat himself. The punishment will only be worse if I resist or beg for him not to. I also assume since there is an audience, he will have to prove a point if I am to embarrass him with my disobedience.

I am to show respect at all times. I know this.

Closing my eyes so I don't have to see Christopher as I bare myself, I do as directed. I hope the belting will be swift and not because of the pain but because of the embarrassment and shame of having to do such an act in front of Christopher.

"You are a strong man, Christopher." Papa Rich's voice is calm but stern. "I can see that in you. So strong that if it became a battle of pure brute strength between us, it's likely you would win. So, there is only one solution to solve any *issues* between us. Ember will now be the whipping boy for you. If you break the rules, if you test my patience, or if you do anything I feel is worthy of correction, Ember will suffer the consequences as you watch. She will take the whipping *you* deserve for you." Papa Rich repositions my body by turning me around so my bare bottom is facing Christopher. "How severe, and how often your whipping boy is utilized is up to you."

I remain in position feeling the cool air of the room on my exposed flesh. I am not wearing panties and regret that decision. But the two pairs I do own are so tattered and thin they wouldn't have provided much coverage anyway.

I desperately want the lashing to begin. Stinging pain would be far better than the intense degradation I am feeling now. I may never be able to face Christopher again after this punishment. What must he think?

"You are a sick, sick man," I hear Christopher say.

"I am a man of conviction."

"You're insane for even thinking of this. And a coward. Who's to say I even care what you do to her?"

"You care," Papa Rich says. "No man would want to see an innocent girl pay for their crimes. I have a feeling it will just take a couple of lessons to truly keep you in line. Just know each whipping will be worse." The leather touches my skin, and then I can sense the belt is being raised behind me to prepare for the first strike. "But just to prove my theory that you'll make sure your whipping boy doesn't suffer my wrath often, let us begin."

9

CHRISTOPHER

Jesus fucking Christ. What do I do?

Do I try to stop him? But even if I charge him, I already know the chain doesn't reach where they stand. I'm also wise enough to realize storming toward them may help ease my conscience that I at least tried to stop this cruel act, but it will also only anger him more, and my *whipping boy* will pay for it rather than me.

"You want to whip someone, be man enough to try to whip me." I attempt not to look at the bare skin of the woman bent over for my viewing. She's owed her dignity, and I won't gawk at the display, yet at the same time, I feel I owe her the respect of not ignoring the situation by simply looking away.

I want to close my eyes, cover my ears, and scream from the top of my lungs, but I know it will only intensify the situation. I can't give this psychopath what he wants. He wants to break me. He wants me weak. He wants to see my fear.

The first strike lands firmly on her upturned ass. She squeals but holds her position even though her thighs quiver.

"I rarely have to punish Ember," Richards says as he raises his arm to prepare for the next assault. "You'll be a lucky man in that regard. You won't have to discipline her often, if at all."

This man...

He speaks as if it is completely normal to spank a grown woman.

This woman...

Remains in place and doesn't put up a fight as if she too believes this is the way of society.

Although a quick glance around at my nightmarish surroundings makes it quite obvious I'm trapped in a morphed reality. This is their world. Their twisted and distorted ordinary.

He whips her again, this time a cry escaping from her trembling frame.

I can't watch as he does it again and again, but I have to. I fear what will happen if I look away.

The whipping boy.

The cruelest torture imaginable.

I watch a poor girl get a belting that would have anyone pleading for mercy, and yet she remains mute. She whimpers, she cries out with each contact of leather against flesh, but she never begs.

I'm helpless. I can't do anything to help her. I want to grab that belt and beat the living shit out of the monster. I want to wrap the leather strap around his neck and suffocate the life right out of him. With every wallop, my desire to kill the man grows. I want him dead. I want to murder another human being. I want to become the monster he is but even worse. I want to make him pay. Pay in the most agonizing way possible.

"Enough!" I shout.

Richard doesn't stop. Instead, he looks at me with an evil grin and snaps the implement on her twice as hard as he had been doing. Ember howls into the musty air of the cellar but does not collapse even though her knees wobble.

"Stop! Stop! You cruel bastard!" I stand from the chair, though I know my actions mean nothing to this man.

His venomous smile grows. His whipping intensifies.

"For the love of God, fucking stop!"

I have to do something. Think. Outsmart. Otherwise he will beat the girl within inches of her life just to prove a point to me and make me suffer.

Ember screams this time as the belt cracks against her, and I nearly vomit.

"She's mine!" I yell, which has him pausing mid swing. "She's my fiancée, and I demand you stop touching her in this way. She's not your concern to discipline in the eyes of God. She's now *mine*!"

My words seem to work because he lowers the belt, and then pulls Ember's dress back over her red and raw ass. He reaches for Ember's midsection and helps her to a standing position.

"You're right," he says, his sinister eyes glaring at me. "This should be *your* duty." He hands Ember the belt. "Ember, go to your future husband, present yourself for punishment, and allow him to finish the task."

She holds the belt in her tiny fist and slowly walks toward me. Her eyes are downcast, which I'm grateful for because I wouldn't be able to look her in the eyes either. I blame myself for her pain and humiliation. I curse myself for not being able to take control of the situation and save her. My body aches far worse than it would had Richard beat me with the belt himself.

"The punishment is over," I try to dictate.

"No," Richard states simply. "Five more lashes before it's complete. Either you do it as your duty, or I'll step in and do it myself. And if I have to, your whipping boy will suffer the consequences for your weakness in being a man."

"I'm sorry," I hear Ember say so quietly I doubt her father hears her. She hands me the belt, turns around, bends over at the waist, and touches her toes.

She is in position.

I have never struck a woman or even so much as desired to.

I glance at Richard and know that if I refuse, he will teach me a lesson with my already sore and trembling *whipping boy*.

Fighting back the bile and rage that wants to erupt from my gut, I lift her dress up as I know will be expected of me.

Five. Just five.

I raise the belt and bring it down on her red ass cheek. The weight, the gravity, and my inexperience has me hitting her far harder than I planned. Ember remains stoically quiet, and part of me feels she is doing it for my benefit.

Four. Just four.

"Harder," the sick asshole directs.

Wanting to get this ordeal over with as fast as I can, I bring the belt to her skin again. I feel the contact in my hand, in my soul, and I shatter as I hear a tiny mewl release from her lips.

Three. Just three.

I strike again, and her mewl turns into a sob. I want to hold her. Comfort her. I want to promise her that all will be okay, and I will never let anyone hurt her again.

But I am the one hurting her! Two... just... I can't count anymore. I can barely breathe let alone attempt to cope.

She cries out as I whip her again, and a part of me dies.

I stare directly into Richard's eyes as I deliver the final blow and silently vow to make the man suffer. Revenge will be mine. For Ember.

From this moment on, if there was one thing I would do, it will be to save this woman. Never, never will this woman suffer again while I do nothing to stop it.

I quickly cover her with the fabric of her dress and instinctively pull her into my arms. She needs comfort. I know this. She deserves this.

At first, Ember is stiff, but when I press her head into my chest and gently stroke her hair, she relaxes in my hold. I bring my lips to her ear and whisper, "I will never allow that to happen again. Never."

I know Richard is watching. I know he's considering if he is all right with this unexpected and surprising act of affection—even to me—but I don't care. He will have to come to where we stand to pull Ember away, and I'll kill him with my bare hands before I'll let her go back to him.

"It's not easy being the head of the household," he says as he leans against the doorframe showing he has no intent to stop me from holding his daughter, nor does he plan to leave the cellar.

I have nothing to say in response because I feel I have nothing left inside of me. I can only concentrate on the trembling girl who now clings to my shirt in a silent desperation for more.

More what?

What can I offer?

I have no answers.

Richard won this battle in this war of mine. He decimated his enemy leaving me in nothing but shattered pieces. If this was his intent, then he succeeded.

"Ember is a good girl. I hope she doesn't have to suffer again," he says. "I'm going to go back to work and will be home in plenty of time for an early supper. Ember..."

She lifts her head from my chest and turns to face him. "Yes, Papa Rich?"

"You be a good girl, you hear?"

"Yes, Papa Rich." Her voice is so soft. Delicate. Not an ounce of hate or disgust. How can she remain almost angelic in response when the man just... how the fuck does she do it?

He leaves, and for the first time since he arrived, I feel like I can fully breathe. I still hold Ember and neither one of us seem to want to pull away. I think if we do, it means we have to face what happened and neither of us are ready for that moment. I don't want to have to look her in the eyes. I don't want to have to see my reflection which I can only imagine appears like a monster.

"I don't blame you," she mumbles against my chest as she seems to press herself even closer. "I know that wasn't easy for you."

If this had been an hour ago, I would be pushing her to help me escape. Demanding that she see the man she calls Papa Rich as the fucking sick perverted man he is. Frustration would be growing in me at her lack of action. I would want to strangle her for not seeing the way I did.

But not now.

Now, I understand. I get it.

I will never blame Ember again. I will never expect this broken child trapped in a woman's body to be whole. She's splintered, and I can see that. I can feel that. All it took was one taste of the man's poison for me to fall into her deep and dark hole myself.

I understand.

"I'm so sorry, Ember."

I close my eyes and inhale deeply. I smell strawberries.

I kiss the top of her head and squeeze her tighter; not for her but for me. I can't think. I can't plan. I can't plot a way out. All I can do is smell strawberries in the wisps of her blonde hair.

10

EMBER

CONVICTION.

Papa's conviction is thick like blood. I can see he has no intention of letting Christopher ever leave Hallelujah Junction. And though I know that fact to be true, I still have no idea what he has planned for us. When do we get married? What happens once we are? I have so many questions but no answers.

I want to ask him. I should be able to ask him. I'm his daughter, and yet I fear him now. He's not the same. Or maybe I'm not. Maybe I'm seeing him through Christopher's eyes rather than my own.

If Papa Rich knew the thoughts I have been thinking...

He can never know. Never.

But today I choose happiness. I stir the batter of the cake I have been wanting to make for Christopher since day one and focus on joy. I use the last of our sugar and flour, but I know Papa is going into town for supplies today and I added them to the shopping list. I don't always get everything I want, but if I don't ask, then I have no chance of getting. Usually Papa is willing to give me the essentials for baking, but not always.

"Now what do I see here?" I hear the question behind me, and

I instantly tense and breathe from my nose. I don't want to smell him. I don't want to see him. I don't want Scarecrow here.

But he's here. It's been four days since his last visit, but I shouldn't be surprised. He always has Papa Rich get supplies from town for him.

"I'm baking a cake," I say, not breaking from stirring in hopes that he sees I'm busy and leaves me alone.

He hobbles to where I'm at, by the sink, and leers over my shoulder at the bowl of batter. No matter how hard I try not to, I smell feces. Scarecrow is dirtier than normal, and his stench is overwhelming. Without warning, he dips his filthy finger into the batter and puts it into his mouth.

"What a treat," he says as he licks his finger clean of the raw cake. "Who's the cake for?" His hand is crusty, scaly in brown and yellow flakes.

My heart sinks as my stomach churns. No way can I serve Christopher this cake now. It's contaminated with the touch of Scarecrow. I'd rather feed Christopher poison than to feed him the disgusting grime of the man standing inches from me.

The cake is ruined.

"For you," I lie. "To thank you for agreeing to marry Christopher and me."

In the corner of my eye, I see Scarecrow beam a toothless and decayed smile.

"For *me*?" His voice is pitched higher than normal. "I've never had a cake made just for me." He leans closer to the bowl and inhales. "My very own cake."

I can't stand the air I breathe for another second, so I walk across the room with the cake batter and make it appear like I'm looking for some ingredient in a nearby cabinet. I've yet to look Scarecrow in the eyes, and I hope to keep it that way. My hope is he will leave due to my lack of engagement.

"I'll have it ready for you when Papa Rich comes back with your supplies this afternoon," I say, trying not to grieve what should have been Christopher's cake.

"Where's your pa now?"

"Down the hill. I think he's waiting for you there." I don't know that he is, but I decide to lie again in hopes that Scarecrow will leave to find him.

I hear the sound of his crutch hitting the wooden floor behind me as he walks to the door. "I'll go find him. And... Ember..."

I know I have to turn to face him. He's waiting. "Yes?" I say as I spin around and offer a weak smile.

"You'd make a mighty fine wife. If ever this man in the cellar doesn't work out, I plan to make good by you. If need be."

I give a slight nod, and go back to the cabinet, moving spices around in my fake attempt of being busy.

I hear him leave and release the breath I had been holding. I quickly finish the spoiled cake and put it in the oven. I may not be able to offer it to Christopher as planned, but I still have the flowers I picked earlier to try to lighten up his gloomy space. Maybe the little bit of color will cheer him up some.

As I enter the cellar, I see Christopher awkwardly leaned back in his chair, attempting to use his belt buckle to cast a shining light through the window across the room from him. He doesn't even try to hide what he's doing from me.

"I wish you wouldn't do that," I say as I place the mason jar full of jasmine next to where he sits.

He doesn't stop but instead focuses on aiming the shimmering light toward the window.

"No one is out there that can see it," I inform. "And if Papa Rich sees you doing this..."

He stops and stares at me, then at the flowers. "And what am I supposed to do?" he asks. "It's been days. Days!" He raises his voice, but I'm not afraid of him. I can feel his anger is not directed at me.

He's frustrated, and I don't blame him. Caged animals want to be free.

I point to the flowers. "I picked the last of the jasmine for you. The first snowfall is coming soon, and things will change."

"How?" he asks as he repositions himself on the chair, giving up on his attempt of escape by belt buckle.

"You haven't angered Papa Rich since... well since last time. And everything gets better here when it snows. The tourists leave, the town is closed, and the road here becomes impossible to travel without a truck and chains, and even then, it's difficult."

"How is that better?"

I glance down at the chain on his ankle. "I think I can eventually convince Papa Rich to remove the chain. To allow us to move freely in the other buildings. Maybe you and I can stay someplace besides the cellar. Maybe the schoolhouse can become our home... after we're married." I feel my heart flutter and my mouth dries. "Papa Rich is less strict in the winter. And well... I choose to have hope the upcoming snow storm means good for you... for us."

Christopher smirks. "I seriously doubt he'll ever take this chain off. I'd run, and he knows it. And if I could get close enough to him, I'd kill him. He knows that too. I'd do whatever I could to escape this hell."

"You can't run in the winter. It's impossible."

"How so?"

I point as his bare feet and then at mine as I wiggle my toes. "There's a reason we don't have shoes. I've never worn a pair of shoes in my life except for snow boots when I'm allowed to go snowshoeing, but Papa keeps those with him. We'd get frostbite and lose our toes before we'd even make it to the gate. If somehow you made it to the gate, there are cameras and alarms to let Papa Rich know of trespassers. He'd be down the road in his truck before you'd get far. And even after the gate, there are miles of dirt road before reaching the town. No shoes, means no escape."

"Cameras. Gate. Escape. Do you hear yourself? Is this a normal conversation for you? You must see how wrong this is.

Your father has kidnapped me. He's holding me here against my will. Surely you see the insanity in this."

"It's just the way it is," I say softly, not necessarily disagreeing with Christopher, but not wanting to agree either. Because if I agree, what does that mean?

Is my Papa Rich the monster that Christopher believes him to be?

He reaches out and takes my hand. His eyes connect with mine and I see sadness. "Ember," he says slowly. "The fact you're telling me all these details means you've thought of running away. It means you know deep down you're a captive here just as much as me. You know this don't you?"

I shake my head. "No. I'm not a captive. I'm just telling you what Papa Rich has told me. He told me that if I ever get curious and want to go to town, that it would be impossible. He was telling me this for my own good. Just in case I wanted to go to the store myself to buy sugar or a book."

Christopher squeezes my hand, but not hard. "You've never had a pair of shoes?"

I shake my head as I look down at his fingers intertwined with mine. I like the connection. I like the feel. His fingers are cold due to the temperature of the room, but mine are warm, and I enjoy knowing I'm heating his with the touch.

"He doesn't allow you to wear shoes, so you won't run," he says.

"It's for my own good. Curiosity killed the cat, right?" I smile in hopes to lessen the tension I'm feeling.

"Don't you ever want to leave Hallelujah Junction?" he asks with the softest of voice. "You've spent your entire life here. Don't you ever want to see what's out there? Wouldn't you like to go to the store yourself? Wouldn't you like to wear a pair of shoes?"

These questions...

I never gave myself the luxury of thinking this way in the past.

If Papa knew we were having this discussion...

"We all have different paths in life," I say as I release

Christopher's hand. I need space and walk to the crate that has become my chair as of late.

"And yours is to stay locked up in a schoolhouse forever?"

I don't like this conversation. It makes my heart beat hard and my stomach tighten. I glance to the door and hope that Papa Rich isn't within earshot.

"We need to be good," I nearly whisper. "If we keep being good, Papa Rich will reward us. I know it. He'll give us more freedom. And once he does, you'll see just how special Hallelujah Junction is. I have so many places I want to show you. There are so many secrets here." I give a big smile to him and feel my cheeks heat in excitement for future possibilities of happiness. "I don't believe in ghosts... not really. But at the same time, you can nearly hear them speak in the walls of these buildings. If you listen real close."

"And I have special places I'd like to show you," he says. "But they aren't here. There's so much more than *here*."

Delusion is easy.

Reality is hard.

But I still want to ask the next question.

"If you could leave here, would you really take me with you?"

"Would you be willing to leave with me?" he asks.

Papa Rich had always taught me to answer every question asked of me honestly, but I can't in this case. Because I don't know.

"This is my home," I say because that is the only truth I know.

He nods in understanding. "But this isn't mine."

I criss cross my legs and settle in. I have a bit of time before I have to take Scarecrow's cake out of the oven and start making lunch. I want to spend the time with Christopher and to continue to learn about this man.

"Tell me about your home," I say, hoping he'll open up to me.

He swallows hard but then smiles. "New York is about as polar opposite of this place. It's loud, it's busy, it's full of life and energy and I love it. You can feel the life of others sizzle in your blood."

"I've read about it."

"Words and stories can't give it justice. You really have to live it."

"Do you have a big house there?" I try not to picture Christopher and me living in New York together as husband and wife, but the thoughts force their way into my imagination. The fantasy of what could…

"An apartment. There aren't a lot of houses in the city. I grew up in a fairly large townhouse in the Upper Eastside with my mother, but square footage is usually limited when it comes to living space unless you're really wealthy." He looks at me and smiles again. "You'd like my place. It has a view of Central Park, and at night, the lights of the city truly are magical. I could sit and stare out the window for hours."

"Are you wealthy?" I figure he is because of his conversation with Papa Rich when he first arrived, but I don't know for sure.

He chuckles. "I suppose so. My family has a lot of money. But I do pretty good for myself as a photographer. I never had to work, but I wanted to. It was important for me to earn my own way. To be my own man. I love what I do. My career is very important to me. So much so, that I suppose it consumed me in all ways. I chose work over all else. Passion has a way of doing that." He pauses and then asks, "What about you? Isn't there some sort of career you would want to do? What did you dream of being when you were a little girl?"

Another question I don't have the answer for.

I don't dream of things like this.

I don't dream at all.

Passion is a foreign thing to me. It doesn't exist in my world.

"I like to draw. I like to read." As soon as I say the words, I realize how small and hollow they sound.

"But no dreams of a future?"

He doesn't seem like he's judging me, or even has pity which is what I have felt from him since his arrival. He seems interested, and for the first time, I feel he really wants to know the person I am.

Christopher is easy to read. I think he believes he's not, but his eyes and the way he shifts his jaw reveals all. I've seen his rage, his sadness, his fear, and his acceptance. I've also seen how he views me. He doesn't hate me like he hates Papa Rich, but he's sad for me. His heart breaks for me. I see it all. I feel it all. But today... right now... I feel a different emotion from him.

Curiosity.

He's trying to figure me out. He's trying to understand how I think and what I feel. He wants to know. Not just because of escape possibilities, but for something more.

I can feel it. Christopher is trying to see me as I have been trying to see him.

I shake my head and focus on the ground before me. "I wake up each day and live the now. Dreams can also be nightmares, so I avoid both."

11

CHRISTOPHER

FIVE DAYS.

Five fucking days.

How long am I going to be expected to live in a cellar, chained to a wall? This can't be my life now. This can't be my normal, and yet, I'm starting to realize that my only chance of escape rests with a psychopath and his terrified daughter.

I'm fucked.

I might as well be dead.

Oh yeah... in the eyes of my family and friends, I am dead.

"Good morning," Ember says as she walks into the cellar with a breakfast tray full of eggs, bacon and toast. Her cat is close behind her feet, and I can see such happiness in her eyes. A stark contrast to my despair.

I can't even bring myself to say anything to her or even bother to get off my pile of blankets I sleep on. Why bother?

She places the tray next to me on the floor and walks over to the small window across the room and looks up. "It's snowing."

Part of me wants to strangle the smile right off her face.

Great... snow. Snow means the tourists will soon stop arriving and any chance of being heard, being seen, or being rescued will be gone forever. Snow suffocates hope.

"Not a big storm yet," she continues. "Papa Rich can't close Hallelujah Junction yet, but soon." She spins on her bare feet to look at me with the same warm smile that hasn't left her face since entering the room. "And when he does, I really think I can convince him to give us some more freedom. You've been good."

"Good?" I say, raising an eyebrow as I do. "What choice do I have in the matter?" I jiggle the chain around my ankle that has nearly rubbed the flesh of my ankle raw. "Not like I can be anything but 'good'."

She crawls up onto the crate she sits on daily, and her cat cuddles up next to her. It's what she does every single day. Every single day of the five days I've been in this hell. It's our routine. It's our life. We sit and talk. She breaks the awkward chit chat by going to make meals. We then sleep. Repeat. Repeat. Fucking repeat!

She points to the untouched breakfast. "Aren't you hungry? Are you not in the mood for eggs?" Worry marks her tiny face. "I can make something else if you want."

I sigh deeply and run my fingers through my hair. It takes everything inside of me not to lose my absolute shit on this poor woman. I go from moments of pure rage, frustration, and fury to pity, sympathy, and even genuine concern. I feel for this girl. As I'm starting to hear more and more about her life here, I can clearly see just how much of a victim she is. She doesn't see it for herself, however, and though I try to get her to see the reality of her situation time and time again, she refuses. Her wall is so high around her feelings toward Richard I realize I may have no chance of ever breaking down the evil foundation that's been built by a madman and his delusions.

"I need a change of clothes," I say. I struggle to keep my voice calm and even gentle because I'm discovering just how easy Ember spooks. "I appreciate being able to clean myself in the bathroom, and the towel you gave me, but I can't keep wearing the same clothing."

I have never been so filthy in my life, which was really saying something considering some of the adventure photoshoots I had been on in my time. I can't smell myself yet, but it's just a matter of time until that happens. Ember had given me soap, a toothbrush and even a comb. But sleeping on the floor in a dirty cellar, not to mention being dragged in here had me covered in grime that's getting worse by the day.

Nibbling the bottom of her lip and circling her blonde hair with her finger, she says, "You're taller and bigger than Papa Rich. Plus, most of his attire is his ranger uniform."

"Am I expected to live here and be your husband in the same clothes forever?"

It's an asshole move to bring up our fucked up impending matrimony with Ember. It instantly makes her jump to action and get me whatever I want. She aims to please, and I know it. Now if only I can figure out how to manipulate her enough to get me out of this place. I want her to jump up and find me a key to my shackles, but I know I have to take baby steps with her if I have any chance at all.

She hops off the crate and rushes to me. "But I have a washer and a dryer upstairs. I can wash your clothes and bring them right back down to you."

I can see how excited she is at the thought of serving me in this way.

Not wasting a moment, I strip off my shirt without the least bit of embarrassment or shame. I don't care if she sees me nude. I've never been ashamed of my body and, considering I had already lost all sense of dignity being chained to a wall like a mangy mutt, I have nothing left to lose.

When Ember sees what I'm doing, her face reddens, and she quickly turns her back to me. "I'm sorry... I..."

"Why are you sorry?" I drop my pants and underwear to my ankles and just stare at her.

I can see she doesn't want to turn around and see me, and the asshole I am, decides it's time to mess with her head some.

"I'm going to be your husband," I say. "You're going to have to see me naked. A lot."

Her body tenses, and she peeks over her shoulder at me. I see her eyes drop down to my dick and then a small gasp escapes her lips.

"I take it you've never seen a penis," I say, already knowing damn well she hasn't. Unless her kidnapping father is more sadistic than I already knew he was.

She shakes her head and turns completely away from me again but reaches her hand out so I can give her the clothing. When I move to completely remove them, I realize there is no way to fully take my pants and underwear off with the chain around my ankle.

"Slight problem," I say, shaking the chain for emphasis. "Unless you have a key, I'm not able to hand these to you."

"Oh no," she says softly as she glances over her shoulder and looks at the chain. She shakes her head. "I don't have the key, and Papa Rich won't…" Her voice fades away as she studies the chain, glances at my pants, and then back at the chain.

"I guess you won't be doing my laundry after all."

She bites her lip and turns to face me, still staring at the chain as if trying to come up with a solution. Suddenly, her eyes light up. "Hold on, I have an idea." She quickly runs out of the room.

I feel ridiculous standing naked with my pants pooled around my ankles, so I pull them up and actually hate the idea that I may never truly be clean again.

As I get ready to sit in my chair of dignity—filthy—I'm stopped when Ember comes running back into the room with a pair of scissors in her hand.

"I'll cut them along the outside seam and then sew buttons on them so we can take them off you easily from now on. I know how to sew, and I have a jar of buttons upstairs." She pauses and then shrugs. "The buttons won't all match, but I guess it doesn't really matter."

She doesn't wait for me to answer, but instead kneels at my feet and begins cutting along the fabric. I don't stop her, although I'm not sure how having buttons up my entire leg will work, but it's not like I have a lot of options either. At least she's trying, and I have to give her an A for effort.

When she reaches my underwear, she asks, "Do you want me to sew buttons on these too?" I can see her face is bright red. "I mean... do you want to keep them? I don't mind... I just, I just want you to be comfortable."

"Go ahead and cut them off. I can go commando from here on out."

As sick as it is, I struggle to not smile. The poor girl is extremely uncomfortable having to be so close to my privates, and the fact that my clothes are just a few snips away from falling off of me, with her face right in front of my groin area... well, the humor is not lost on me. I grant her some mercy and help her lower my pants off me completely. She tries her best not to look at me, but I also know there is no way she didn't get an eyeful.

"I'll be back as soon as I can," she says as she scurries out of the room with my soiled clothes in hand and doesn't even bother to close the door behind her.

Being trapped must be getting to me, because I actually have to fight back the urge to laugh. The absurdity of my situation. The fact that I'm sitting on wool blankets in a near dungeon being held captive by a lunatic and about to marry a waif of a woman who would kiss my feet if I ask, is something no one would ever believe. This is a nightmare I can't wake up from.

Wrapping a blanket around myself, I settle against the wall, pull the breakfast tray to me, and begin eating. I notice the slices of oranges on the plate are perfectly peeled as if Ember had painstakingly pulled every little piece of pith on the fruit off. She wants so desperately to be the good wife she has read about in books or what she has been told by Richard. I can see how hard she tries to please in her domestic duties. And yet... I wonder if I ever have a chance of convincing her to help us run away. I wish it's easy trying to reason with her.

But there's no reason in lunacy.

I take a sip of cold coffee and wish for a shot of whiskey to add to it.

Five days.

Five days with no booze. No pills. No sex. No life.

The shakes are subsiding with each new morning, but it makes me realize just how dependent my body is on my lifestyle. The cravings make this entire situation even worse. Detoxing in a twisted medieval horror story is about as bad as it can get.

Eventually Ember reenters the room with my clothes folded nicely in her arms almost as fast as she had left. "I was able to get most the dirt out, I think. There's a hole in the leg that I can mend later if you want, but since I took so long with the buttons, I didn't want to keep you waiting any longer."

I stand up on full display. Since she's walking toward me, there is no way she can turn her back on me now. I want her to see me. I want her to face me. I want her to see the reality of what is right in front of her.

Bold, bare, and stripped.

Once she sees me, her eyes quickly dart to the floor. Funny how my nudity causes more discomfort in her than seeing me chained to a wall against my will does.

"Thank you," I say, deciding to give her some mercy and get dressed quickly. That and my balls were damn near freezing off with the chill in the room. Although it's not easy pushing the buttons through each hole that run from my ankle to waist.

I notice as I'm dressing that her cat never leaves her side, it follows her around wherever she goes. Instead of walking to her crate, as I expect her to do, Ember moves toward my pile of blankets and begins to fold and position them into a nice little bed again. She then grabs the tray from breakfast and brings it over to the doorway. She then walks to the bathroom, and I can hear the water running as I guess she is cleaning that area the best she can.

Quite the dutiful woman she is.

"What's going on in here?" Richard booms from the doorway. "Sinners!" he seethes.

I spin around and see wide eyes full of hate directed my way. I'm only wearing my pants as I haven't had time to put my shirt on yet due to how long the buttons took on the pants, and I smirk. I know what he's thinking.

Think it, motherfucker.

Imagine me fucking Ember as she cries out my name.

He takes a step into the room as I know he wants to charge toward me and strangle me with his bare hands, but he halts... not a stupid man. He remains in the doorway out of reach.

"Papa Rich..." Ember says, coming out of the bathroom. Her eyes glance at my bare chest, her mouth drops as her lower lip begins to tremble. She knows what he's thinking too.

"Get over here now!" Richard demands. He points to the spot right beside him and as Ember quickly moves to obey, I stop her.

Placing my hand in front of her and pushing her behind me, I say, "No. She'll be staying right where she is."

"Ember, now!" he shouts as spittle spews from his chapped lips and his face reddens.

"I said no," I repeat as I grab Ember by the arm in case she decides to try to make a run for it toward her father. Although, I also assume she isn't thrilled about the idea of being within her father's reach at the moment.

Regardless that I'm enjoying knowing the thought of me having sex or even being inappropriate with Ember is making the man go insane with anger, I also am not going to allow him to whip her again.

"I had to wash his clothes," she tries to explain.

"Ember, you have two seconds to get over here, or I will blister your ass raw."

"Come and get her," I taunt. "Or are you afraid to face me like a man?"

I can feel Ember try to pull away, but I know the man will beat her as I'm forced to watch. No way will I ever allow that to happen again if I can help it. Plus, it feels damn good to have some control over a situation again.

Richard wants Ember.

He can't have her.

An evil grin spreads across Richard's face as he takes a step backwards. "All right... if you two want to be together so much, then fine. Ember, you can stay in here with our guest. It's high time you both get closer anyway since the wedding day is coming."

He quickly turns around, storms out of the room, slams the door shut. The sound of keys on the other side, and then a click tells me all I need to know.

He locked Ember in the cellar with me.

Ember breaks from my hold and runs toward the door and tries to open it to no avail. She bangs on it and screams, "Papa! I'm sorry. I was only doing his wash. I swear! Nothing happened."

His voice comes from the other side of the door. "Pray, Ember. Pray for forgiveness for your sinful ways. God will forgive. And when he does, I'll return. Until then, pray."

"Papa, I didn't sin. I swear! I swear!"

No answer.

"Papa! Please!" She jiggles the handle again, but there's no opening it.

She turns and looks at me wild-eyed. "It's locked. He's gone."

I smirk and open my arms wide. I shouldn't make light of the situation. I shouldn't allow my sick sense of humor to take over. But I can't help myself. "Welcome to my prison, my dear."

12

EMBER

THE CHAINS OF SIN STRANGLE MY SOUL. I DIDN'T MEAN TO BE THIS way. I didn't mean to cross the bridge where the Devil sat.

"I'm sorry," I say to Christopher.

"For what? Doing my laundry?"

"For sinning and bringing you down the hole with me."

Christopher finally puts his shirt on and then sits down on the chair looking at me still standing by the door. "You didn't sin."

"I did."

He tilts his head and his eyes narrow. "Because your father told you so? Is that why you think you sinned?"

I make my way to the crate feeling deep shame. "Papa Rich knows. He could see it. Feel it."

"See and feel what?"

"I looked at your... I saw your..." I try to confess but can't say the vile word.

He smirks. "My what?"

He's going to make me say it.

"My what?" he asks again.

"Your manhood," I blurt. "I saw it. I sinned."

Christopher chuckles and shakes his head. "I can't believe you said 'manhood'." He laughs again but then quickly steadies his emotions. "And yes, Ember, you're going to see my *manhood* if we're going to be married. It's not a sin. It's part of life. It's normal. Sex is normal and will be part of our life." He pauses. "Unless you don't want to get married?"

I quickly shake my head, worried that I offended him with my words. "No, that's not it. I want to marry you. I mean... I have to marry you."

"You don't have to marry me if you don't want to. I can help you. I mean it when I say I'll protect you. And if you choose to, we can run away together, and you don't have to marry me or face my *manhood* ever again."

Not wanting to discuss this further and feeling as if my face is several shades of red, I turn my attention to finding my cat.

"Pine Cone," I sing out, looking behind the crates. "It's okay. You can come out."

"Your cat hates your father."

I nod. "She's afraid of him. Always has been."

"What about you?" Christopher asks. "Are you afraid of him?"

I don't want to answer the question, but I have a feeling Christopher will insist that I do.

"Sometimes," I mumble, not seeing Pine Cone but knowing she is most likely in the furthest corner of the room behind the larger crates where I can't reach her.

"Do you think that's normal? For a daughter to fear her father?"

I shrug, really not wanting to discuss this further. "I'm like my cat. I scare easily."

"He locked you in here with a stranger. He was going to whip you again if I didn't stop it, and he did all this for what? You did nothing wrong. Do you feel this was fair or the actions of a good man?"

I give up looking for Pine Cone and instead walk over to the empty breakfast tray that is still by the door. I take a bowl that I used to put the slices of oranges in and make my way to the bathroom. Once there, I fill up the bowl with water and then go put it by the crate I usually sit on with Pine Cone. I want her to have fresh water when she finally gets the courage to come out.

"I hope Papa Rich allows me out soon. I don't want Pine Cone to be hungry. There's no food for her."

"I'm sure there's plenty of mice down here for her to hunt. She'll be fine," he reassures. "But that doesn't exactly help us."

"He won't let us go hungry. Whenever he gets angry, he calms quickly, "I say, hoping this situation would be like the ones of my past. "He just needs a day or two."

"A day or two?" He shakes his head and then stares at the ceiling as he inhales and exhales loudly. "Ember, I'm finding it really difficult to stay patient with you. I know your heart isn't evil. I know you aren't like him, but at the same time, what you're doing is wrong. Don't you see that? I know you know the difference between right and wrong. I know you do, and you have to be feeling this is wrong. Me being here is wrong."

I sit on the crate and cross my legs. I refuse to answer. I refuse to think about his words. I refuse.

"Your father speaks of sin, but he's the sinner. He's killed people in those acid pits, right?"

Nodding, I admit, "He has. I hate when he does. I hate it so much, but he says God makes him. God gives him permission."

"Do you believe that? Truly believe that?"

"Why would Papa Rich lie?"

"Because he's a bad bad man, and I think you know this, Ember." He points to the area where Pine Cone is hiding. "Your cat knows this." He tilts his head, pauses and then asks a question that feels like a punch to the belly. "Have you seen him kill people?"

I don't want to answer.

"You have, haven't you?"

"He's protecting me," I try to defend. "He says it's only the people who don't follow the no trespassing signs. They're getting too close to me, and if they do and see me, I'm at risk. He's doing it out of love."

"Do you really believe that?" Christopher asks. "Do you agree with that? Do you think the people he's killed deserve it?"

"No," I answer truthfully. "I hate it. I hate it so much." I feel tears burn the back of my eyes. "I've begged him not to. But..."

"He's a sick and demented man, Ember. Deep down you know this."

"He makes mistakes," I mumble. "But all humans do. It's the nature of man."

Christopher extends his arms and motions around him. "Is that what this is? A mistake?"

As if Papa Rich can hear us talking about him, the door opens, and he takes one step inside. He has a box of crackers, two apples, and a container that is full of what I know is last night's chicken. He places them by the door and then pulls out a newspaper from his back pocket.

I quickly run toward him and kneel at his feet. I need to make this right. "I'm sorry, Papa. I'm a sinner and will repent however you deem necessary. I don't want Christopher to have to suffer for my misdeeds."

Kissing the top of his boot, the dust of the Nevada desert coats my lips, but I continue on to kiss his other boot. I steal a glance up and see he's not looking down at me but instead at Christopher.

He tosses the newspaper down to me and says, "Read this to your future husband."

I scramble to my feet and do as he asks. I can see exactly what he wants me to read. It's an article about Christopher and his so-called accident.

I clear my throat and begin.

Christopher Davenport, son of the textile heiress Louisa Davenport, has suffered an accident and is now presumed dead. While on a photoshoot in Nevada, he never returned to his Jeep and was reported missing. After conducting an investigation, it was determined he suffered a tragic and fatal accident and fell to his death while trying to capture pictures for an article he was working on about the mysterious ghost town of Hallelujah Junction.

I pause and look at Christopher, my heart breaking for him as he is forced to sit and listen to this. He's pale and his mouth is slack in what I can only assume is disbelief.

"Keep going," Papa Rich demands.

My hands shake as I hold the paper, but I do as I'm asked.

Mr. Davenport isn't the first to suffer such a tragedy in Hallelujah Junction. When the ranger who oversees the historical landmark of a town was asked to comment, he said, "We've had this happen several times in the past. We post warning signs and no trespassing signs to warn of the dangers, but some curious tourists take the risk anyway. The mining pits and old tunnels are extremely dangerous around here. There are acid, toxic gases, hidden shafts, and other lethal elements that make this area deadly if you're not careful. It's a shame he thought a picture was more valuable than his safety and ultimately his life."

Christopher was a well-known photographer for Rolling Stone Magazine *and also had many prestigious photo credits in* National Geographic *and other adventure magazines. His funeral services will be held at St. Joseph Presbyterian Church on November 2nd. The family asks that you respect their privacy during this difficult time.*

I fold the newspaper as I say the last word, and I don't want to see Christopher's face. I know I will see pain. I will see heartache, and I'm not sure I can handle it.

"You sick son of a bitch," Christopher says as he stands from his chair and walks toward us like an animal stalking his prey. He's slow, each step is deliberate and the hatred in his eyes takes my breath away.

Papa Rich remains in the doorway unfazed and crosses his arms smugly. "I told you. I knew it was just as simple as telling them that you are just another careless victim of the acid pits. Bones and flesh sizzled to nothing. No way to know really, but what else could have possibly happened?"

Christopher makes his way to where we stand and extends

the chain as far as he can but it's not long enough. "I dare you to enter this room," he nearly hisses. "Face me. Rather than standing in the doorway like the coward you are, face me. Face me!"

Papa Rich doesn't move. He doesn't seem angry or frightened in the slightest. "They were here. Feet from that window." He points to the narrow cellar window. "They searched high and low for any sign of you. Sadly, they found your camera near the pits. Boot marks with your shoe size near unstable beams that were broken from a heavy weight. Sad. Sad. Sad." He shakes his head in mock mournfulness. "Such a shame. If only he followed the rules or the posted signs."

"Not everyone in my life is going to believe that," Christopher says. "More will come. They'll find me, and when they do, I'll kill you with my bare hands."

Papa Rich shrugs. "Your mother is quite the entitled bitch. She had the nerve to call me and demand to know how this 'incompetence' can occur. She even threatened to sue the State Forestry Department for the unsafe conditions of the town. Not that I care really. Not my problem. Other than the fact I've been asked to post more signs and to gate off the old mill. Not that it will help any. The curious tourists will still come... and they will still die."

Christopher screams in frustration and yanks the chain around his ankle as hard as he can. And for a split moment I wonder if he'll be able to break free with all the pent-up rage inside of him.

"Ember, your fiancé is upset. Which is understandable. It's not easy to hear about your own death." He pushes me toward Christopher. "Comfort your man. Ease his pain as a good wife would do."

My heart skips because I don't know what he means. Of course I will love if there is a way to comfort Christopher, but I don't know how. I don't want to disappoint Papa Rich in not following his order, but I also fear whatever I do will be wrong.

"Kiss him," Papa Rich commands.

"Fuck you," Christopher spats. He turns and makes his way back to the chair. "Sick motherfucker. Chicken shit."

Papa only continues, "Go to him, Ember. Kiss him and offer comfort."

I've never kissed anyone before. I don't know what to do. I can't. How?

My thoughts must be written on my face because Papa Rich says, "Unless you want me to take away this food and not come back for days, you will do as I say. Kiss him and I'll be back in one day's time." I see him look at Christopher who is now standing by his chair. "Kiss my daughter or you both will starve down here."

Christopher spins on his heels and his face is bright red as his eyes seem to bulge from their sockets. "What is wrong with you? You are completely insane. Insane! And I swear to your fucked up God that I will kill you someday. I will fucking kill you."

Papa Rich inhales and very calmly says on exhale, "Kiss. Now."

I know that he doesn't like to repeat himself, and he's already done so more than I've ever heard him do. So, not wasting any more time, I pad across the cold floor to Christopher and stand before him. I look up into his eyes and silently beg for him to listen and comply. Papa will starve us. I have no doubt in this if we don't listen.

I stand up on my tiptoes and place my hand on Christopher's chest to steady myself.

"Please kiss me," I whisper, hoping only he can hear my plea.

Christopher places his hand on the back of my head and lowers his head to mine. Our lips make contact, and I wonder if he's stealing all my air because I can't breathe. My legs feel weak, my heart beats hard, and my stomach flips.

He smells like the soap I gave him, but also something else—earth and spice. I can feel the heat from his body, and his palm on the back of my head seems to nearly scorch my skin. The hair on his face that has grown since arriving pricks my skin, but the roughness sends a shiver to my toes.

My eyes are closed in fear of what I'll see. I don't want Christopher to hate me. I don't want him to be disgusted. I don't want him to think I'm evil. I just want to block it all out and focus on what's happening.

My very first kiss.

My very first intimate touch of any kind.

My very first time feeling... I don't know what I feel.

Is this the Devil that tingles inside of me?

Is this sin that makes me not want to stop?

Good Lord show me the way.

Is this kiss opening the door to evil and will cease any salvation?

My very first kiss...

The sound of the door closing broke the spell of seduction. We both pull away and look at the door as we hear the key locking us inside.

I touch my lips as I step away from Christopher, embarrassed and ashamed by just how much I like the kiss.

Christopher doesn't say anything but sits in the chair and places his head between his legs. His eyes are closed tightly, and I see such a deep sorrow that I struggle to ward it off myself. I want to cry the tears for him. I want to howl at God for such injustice and scream out in agony. I want to take his pain. I want it all. I deserve it. Not him.

"Your father just killed me. And you stood and watched as he did so."

He's right.

I watched a monster emerge from my father just now. He enjoyed seeing the pain in Christopher's eyes. He fed off it like a carnivore tearing the flesh from his bones.

My Papa Rich...

Who is my Papa Rich?

13

CHRISTOPHER

WE REMAINED IN SILENCE FOR SEVERAL HOURS AFTER THE KISS. I sat and stared at the words on the newspaper in disbelief. I had held out hope that no one would believe the ramblings of a madman and truly believe I had fallen to my death.

But they all believe.

They all are mourning my death.

I'm dead.

I'm nothing but an empty coffin being lowered into the ground.

"Would you like some crackers and chicken?" Ember finally asks. "You haven't eaten any today. You must be hungry. The chicken's cold, but I'm sure it won't taste bad."

"Have you ever lost someone? Anyone die in your life?" I ask as I look up to her for the first time in what feels like ages.

She shakes her head. "No."

"It's an awful feeling. The pain is indescribable. My mother, my friends and other family are all suffering right now."

Ember pulls her legs up to her chest on the crate and lowers her dress to cover her ankles and feet. It's getting colder by the hour, and the falling snow outside doesn't help matters. I can't see our breath yet, but I have a feeling it's only a matter of time.

"I know you think I can help you," she says as she pets her cat that finally has crawled up on the crate to join her. "And if I could... and knew it would work... then maybe I would. But I know my father. I know this area. I know our reality. I don't want to see you dead."

"Being dead would be better than this."

"Maybe for you," she says. "But I don't want to feel that indescribable pain you speak of. I know it's selfish, but I don't want you dead. Not for real."

"I'll never be happy here," I say.

"Then I'll lend you some of mine. You can borrow my happiness anytime you'd like."

"And are you really happy, Ember? Truly?"

"Not all the time," she admits as she wraps her arms around her tiny frame. "But I hope that I will always be someday. I'm hopeful. And hope gives me some happiness. Sunshine is within reach."

"Then give me some hope," I say. "I need this sunshine because the darkness is pretty fucking thick right now. Tell me you'll at least consider helping me escape if there comes an opportunity. Tell me you will at least consider it. Give me hope."

"I don't know that I can do that."

Pressing on, I say, "I promise you, Ember. I promise if you help me out of here, I won't leave you behind. I won't abandon you no matter what. I'll take care of you, I'll keep you safe, and you'll never be left alone. If you can make a promise, then so can I."

"I don't want to be alone anymore," she admits softly.

"You won't be."

She remains quiet but then finally nods. "If there comes a time I can help you, I will. I promise."

And just like that, there is a small spark of light in the dark cave of misery I have thrust myself in. Ember is right. Hope does give some happiness. She at least lends me a small grain of sand of hope, and that little bit allows me to breathe again.

"But I know my father," she adds. "He plans everything out. He doesn't make mistakes. And he's determined..." Glancing up and out the window at the falling snow, she moves a piece of her golden hair from her face. Her profile is quite striking in a raw and natural way. "I'm sorry, Christopher. I wish I were stronger. I often wish this, and if I could..." She turns to stare at me, her wide blue eyes are glassed over in pain. "I wish I could save you."

"Come over here," I say as I watch how she shivers beneath the thin fabric she wears. "Come sit by me in the blankets. I can see you're cold."

"That's your bed," she says, but I can see she's eyeing the blankets.

"It's going to be *our* bed for the time being." I pat the pile of faded wool blankets and settle in to make room. "It's cold in here, and it's only going to get colder."

"My cat might follow me," she says as she hops off the crate. "If that's okay."

"I think we'll need all the heat we can get." I glance at the window and see the snow isn't letting up in the slightest. "Your father doesn't care that you could freeze down here?"

"Penance," she says more to herself than me.

I can see she's uncomfortable approaching me. "I don't bite. Come on, let's get warm."

I adjust the blankets so we have one to sit on, one to wrap around our bodies and then use the third one for our laps while we remain sitting. When we sleep, we'll have to make do with piling two blankets on us and hope it's enough to get us through the night.

Ember kneels down beside me, but I can feel her awkward discomfort.

"I'm not going to hurt you," I say as I move toward her and wrap a blanket around her, pulling her to my side.

She snuggles up closer to me. "I don't think you will."

"Then why do you seem afraid?"

"I think that's just how I am."

"Afraid?"

"Yes. In one way or the other. Fear is always knocking on my door I suppose."

"That's sad." I secure the blankets around us and actually find a sense of comfort having her next to me.

Maybe fear is knocking on my door as well.

"I know you pity me. I wish you wouldn't." Her voice is soft, not angry, not even sad. Just soft.

"I can't help it," I admit honestly. "I see your truth and reality, and I see a nightmare. And what I pity is you can't see it for yourself. You're a victim and too blinded by that fear you speak of to know it."

"Papa Rich loves me."

"Maybe so. I won't argue that. Although at the same time, why would a man who loves you lock you up in a cold cellar with a complete stranger chained to the wall? How does he know I won't harm you in retaliation? How does he know if you'll be all right? Wouldn't a father be concerned if his daughter is cold at the very least?"

"He's a strict man."

Ember keeps her eyes focused straight ahead, but I'm a little surprised she isn't trying to pull away or give some space between us. Our bodies are pressed snugly together, and though she is tense, she is remaining close. I don't want to keep pressing her on her father because I could end up pushing her away, so I decide it's best to change the subject if possible. Although there is another part of me that still wants to shake some sense into this girl. A violent urge to grab her by the throat and strangle her just to teach Richard a lesson. Just to hurt him as he's trying to hurt me. To make him pay for his lunacy.

If I kill Ember—which would be so easy to do right now— would I destroy the man as I so desperately want to do?

But does she deserve to die?

Is this her fault?

Taking a deep breath and trying not to let the dark thoughts take over, I say, "I'm sorry about the kiss."

"Sorry?" Ember turns her head to look at me, her beautiful eyes being the only thing I could see.

"You deserve better. Your first kiss should have been so much better. I'm assuming it was your first kiss, right?"

She nods and turns her attention straight ahead. "It was. And it was nothing you should apologize for. I... I liked it," she confesses as she looks down at her fingers which grip the wool blanket. "Is that bad to admit?"

Christ. This woman is as pure and genuine as an innocent child. It's hard to see her as a grown woman. Nothing in life has turned her into a broken and shielded person who would never admit or allow herself to be so vulnerable. I have never had a woman state so simply that she liked a kiss from me. That would make her weak and give me the upper hand.

New York dating laws 101. Don't reveal your true feelings.

"No, it's not bad to admit."

"I've always fantasized about my first kiss. It was nice." I see a smile paint her face and her cheeks pinken.

"Your first kiss should not have happened by force," I say as I reach for a piece of her hair that is hanging in front of her face and tuck it behind her ear. "When you have memories of your first kiss, your father should not be in the picture."

She shrugs, but her smile fades as she does so. A shiver runs through her and spreads to me. Sitting up against the cold wall isn't going to keep us warm for long, and I know I have to make a change.

"Let's lie down," I say.

She doesn't resist and lies down in front of me on her side. I position the blankets so they will be on top of us and spoon her from behind. Her frame is so tiny I worry the weight of my arm over her will be too heavy.

"Are you comfortable?" I adjust my body until I'm as close to her as I can get and try not to focus on the fact her body is curved against mine and we fit like a perfect glove.

Nothing about this situation is perfect, and yet, Ember's body is warm, and I feel a sense of comfort I haven't felt since being hit over the head by a madman. I also feel this overwhelming need to protect. I like knowing Ember is safe in my arms and no harm can come to her.

I don't want to let her go.

For Christ's sake... why don't I want to let her go?

My eyes dart back to the window. "Ember? Tell me about where we are right now. Where in the town are we?"

"Up the hill from the main street. The ranger's house is hidden by the schoolhouse so the public can't see it. It was designed that way to not alter the ambiance of stepping back in time. They didn't want to see lights on or signs of life from the main area. You were walking toward the house when—"

"What are the chances of someone walking by that window?"

"Rare. And if someone does... it won't end well."

"Because of your father? He'll kill them?"

"Yes, in the acid pits at the mill. You were lucky to not be dead."

I nearly laugh. I am far from lucky right now.

"What about the key to my chain? Do you know where that is?"

She shakes her head and her body tenses against me. I may be pushing too far, but I need to try.

"What about a cell phone? A phone of any kind? Is there a way you can get to a phone once he lets you free?"

"We don't have a phone. There's a ranger's radio, but Papa Rich keeps that with him."

My mind runs wild with ways of escape now that I have Ember—even faintly—open to answering my questions.

"What about that man who was upstairs on the first day? You said he wouldn't help, but who is he? Maybe he would."

Ember shivers and I pull the blanket higher over her shoulder. "Scarecrow. He's a bad man. He won't help. Trust me."

"Scarecrow? His name is Scarecrow?"

"He's missing a leg. Instead of getting a fake one or just doing without, he stuffs his pant leg with straw. He lives further up in the hills by himself. A disgusting hermit who only comes to Hallelujah Junction to visit us. He's vile. He stinks. He's an awful, awful man. And he's also Papa Rich's best friend. If he had his way, he'd be marrying me instead of you. So, if anything, he'd just throw you in the pits himself so he can have you out of the way."

"And you never see anyone?" I continue, not wanting to give up. There has to be someone. Some way…

"Just from afar. I watch the tourists down below. That's it."

"And you said that there are underground tunnels, right? Your father allows you to walk them from building to building?"

"Right."

Okay… this will be a long game.

A fucking twisted and fucked up game.

I will have to play it. I will have to play along so I'm given that moment… the brief moment… to find my opportunity of escape. But it will happen. Not by force, but by wits.

"And when I marry you…" I say as I inhale the strawberry essence from her hair, "you believe your father will let us live freely as you once did?"

"I hope so. I know he has a plan, and I'm sure you and I being able to live a normal life as husband and wife will be part of it." She inhales deeply and then lets it out slowly. "I really hope so."

We lie in silence as I hold her and scan the room looking for anything to give me an idea of escape. I stare at the window and pray to see boots walking by. I eventually settle in and know I have to think bigger picture. The cat finally joins us and cuddles up against my leg for warmth. I can see my breath now, but I at least feel warm next to Ember.

She's putting off heat in this cold hell.

"Thank you, Christopher," she says as she presses her body even closer to mine. "I know you want to hate me. So, thank you for fighting that emotion off."

"I don't hate you."

"But you have to fight for that. So, thank you."

14

EMBER

"Wake up. It's your wedding day." Papa Rich's voice bellows off the cold, dank floor and walls.

I shoot up from the ground and stand as quickly as I can. I pray that Papa doesn't consider my sleeping with Christopher under the blankets in such close proximity as a sin. But I had no choice. If it weren't for Christopher's kindness and sharing the blankets, I'm not sure I could have made it through the night. Even with the wool over me and the heat off of Christopher's body, I still remained cold and uncomfortable for most of the night.

Christopher is much slower in getting off the ground, but he does reach out and grab my arm, no doubt refusing for me to be able to run toward Papa and be within his reach. Although I will gladly take another whipping with his belt over spending another night in the cold cellar.

Papa Rich glances down at the untouched food he sent. We had been too cold to go eat once we found the smallest amount of warmth with our body heat.

"You didn't eat." He looks at me, and adds, "Go make some breakfast for you and your fiancé and make quick work of it.

Scarecrow has blessed us with his presence before the next big storm. We think winter's coming fast and furious this year, and he wants to preside over your wedding before it becomes impossible for him to make his way here."

"Today? You want me to get married today?" The words didn't seem real.

"Snow-covered ground, eagles flying overhead in search of prey, and the good Lord's grace deeming it so. What better a day to wed?"

I glance at Christopher, not sure what I will see on his face. Will he storm to Papa Rich in rage again?

"If the Lord deems it so," Christopher says as he shakes out the blankets and folds them nicely and... in such control.

Papa's brow raises and a smile masters his face. "Well lookee here. Isolation has chased the Devil right out of your body." He looks at me and his smile grows even move. "Go on, girl. Get busy. You have to get dressed and ready for your big day, and we don't have a lot of time. Scarecrow wants to head on home before it storms again."

My head spins in uncertainty and confusion. Chaos bangs destruction inside of me. Both men seem... off. Both are unusually happy and at ease when they were both nearly homicidal only hours ago. But at the same time, I'm not going to risk upsetting either, so I quickly run out of the room toward the kitchen with Pine Cone underfoot. And Papa is right... I don't have a lot of time because the smell of onion and sweat tells me that Scarecrow is here and waiting.

When I enter my room after making and serving Christopher breakfast, I am surprised to see a white lace dress spread on my bed. It's not new, and actually quite old based on the discoloration, but it's still beautiful. Long sleeves, delicate buttons that go up the back to the high collar, and such intricate design in the lace fills me with an excitement I have never felt in my life. I've never worn anything so pretty and worth so much money before. I've never received a gift, and for my first one to be so beautiful...

"Do you like it?" Papa Rich asks from behind me.

I pick up the dress and hold it against me. "Where did you find it? It's beyond anything... Oh, Papa Rich." I spin and face him, not being able to control the tears that fall from my eyes. "Thank you. It's perfect."

"My daughter only gets one wedding day."

There's kindness in his eyes. I see it. For the first time since Christopher arrived, I see a small glimmer of my Papa Rich. He's not a bad man... not always. Not always.

He approaches me and reaches into his pocket as he does. "I got these for the both of you too." He pulls out two gold bands and places them in my palm. "Something for you both to wear forever symbolizing your love and unity. And hopefully"—he looks down at his feet and fidgets for a moment—"you remember just how much I love you when you look at it on your finger. I know I have a hard time showing it. I know I'm broken down to the bone, and though I've tried so hard not to show you just how jagged my spirit is, I know you've seen. You're a wise woman. Extremely wise. You see with eyes of a woman far older and experienced than your years. You see me... and for that, I'm often disappointed."

I don't know what to say, but the tears continue to fall. I love him. Christopher may not understand why, and I get that. But right now. This very moment. I love my father. I can't control my heart. I can't control my feelings. And though I should... I can't help but slip back into time and remember that little girl who was so desperate for love and security.

Papa Rich gave me that.

He saved me.

He loved me.

He kept me.

"You deserve the best," he says as he steps away from me and gives me the space I need to process. "True love does not find you.

You have to find it. You have to fight for it. And though your nature is not one of a fighter, it's time you learn how. You will have to have an inner strength to be married and to hold that love near at whatever cost."

I look down at the gold in my palm and picture the rings on my and Christopher's fingers. The weight of the bands are heavy with hidden tales of my future. They nearly burn.

What is ahead for us?

Once we become husband and wife... then what?

"You go on and get ready, and then I'll help you with those buttons on the back of your dress," he says. "We don't want to keep Scarecrow waiting long. A storm's brewing and we don't want him getting caught up in it."

He leaves my room, and the sense of warmth I briefly felt is suddenly replaced with a deep chill that runs up my spine. But I do exactly as he commands and dress for my wedding.

15

CHRISTOPHER

THERE'S A CHAIN AROUND MY ANKLE.

There's a chain around Ember's ankle.

We are connected by this chain.

And we are about to be wedded standing before a one-legged pastor who leans on a crutch. The sound of hay rustles beneath his denim pants with the slightest move, and I think it's fair to say I have never seen a more disgusting creature in my life.

I have officially entered a new phase of Hell.

"Good Lord, bless us on this day," the pastor known as Scarecrow begins. "Brother Christopher and Sister Ember stand before the Almighty to be crowned under the union of matrimony."

He looks at Richard who is actually wearing something besides a ranger uniform, although his faded black pants and wrinkled black shirt are far from what I consider fancy.

"Who gives away this woman?" Scarecrow asks.

"I do with the blessing of God. Her father."

Scarecrow raises his arms up toward the ceiling of the schoolhouse, and I see the sweat stains under his pits. His stench nearly makes me as sick as the act of being forced to marry a woman while literally chained to her. This is my wedding day. No guests other than a madman father, no flowers, no best man or bridesmaids. It's my wedding day and I wear the same dirty outfit I arrived in—minus the shoes.

Ember, however, is beautiful in a haunted, captivating way. Her long hair hangs down her back and shines beneath the sunlight that invades the room we stand in. The dress she wears is ancient in appearance but still seems to fit her personality and size perfectly. I feel as if I have stepped back in time, trapped in a bleak and dark vortex, yet Ember does offer some light. The blue in her eyes sparkle with happiness.

My heart breaks over her happiness.

She's happy even though she's chained to me.

She's happy to be marrying me even though it's not by her choice.

She's happy...

We stand inside her favorite place. The schoolhouse is our church for this day. At least getting here allowed me to see the underground tunnels Ember told me about. Getting outside the cellar allowed me to take mental notes on every step of the way. Richard was smart, however, which I expected him to be. When he showed up with a pistol in his hand and another chain in his hand, I knew what he planned before he even said a word. Shackling me to Ember would make it next to impossible to run unless we somehow mastered running together in a cadence and step that would take careful practice and discussion.

"Now you will feel no rain, for each of you will be shelter for the other. Now you will feel no cold, for each of you will be warmth to the other. Now there will be no loneliness, for each of you will be companion to the other. Now you are two persons, but there is only one life before you. May beauty surround you both in the journey ahead and through all the years. May happiness be your companion and your days together be good and long upon the earth. May you both walk under God as dutiful servants. We honor fire and ask that our union be warm and glowing with love in our hearts. We honor wind and ask that we sail through life safe and calm as in our father's arms. We honor water to clean and soothe our relationship—that it may never thirst for love. With all the forces of the universe you created, we pray for harmony as we grow forever young together. Amen."

Ember and Richard both say, "Amen," but I can't bring myself to speak.

Scarecrow nearly chants the words, and they sound more satanic than holy. And now it dawns on me why when you see pictures from old backwoods weddings in the Appalachian Mountains or some other small town, the people never smiled. They stood side by side with the look of death on their faces. Dark circles under their eyes and sunken cheekbones.

This is me. I'm the ghostly man in these pictures. I completely understand.

If someone could take a picture of me now, what would they see?

I'm trying to tell myself this is not real. This is an act. This is all a game so I can win in the end.

I'm not really getting married.

This Scarecrow man can't be a real pastor, and even if he is... this isn't real. I'm chained to my bride. I'm fucking chained.

I'm not really holding the hand of my bride—soon to be my wife.

This isn't real.

Scarecrow opens his dirty hands before us, and resting in his palm are two gold bands. I take the smaller one, and Ember takes the larger.

Oh Jesus, this is getting more real by the second. Wedding bands. Something for me to wear every single day. Will it choke the life out of me?

I'm fucking getting married!

"Brother Christopher," Scarecrow breaks my thoughts. "Do

you take Sister Ember to be your bride, to honor, to cherish, and to walk under God's eyes together as one?"

"I do," I somehow say as I slide the ring onto Ember's finger.

I have to. I have to stay focused on the plan. The only way to escape is to marry her. At least in this fucked up world I'm locked in.

"Sister Ember." Scarecrow has spittle spewing from his chapped lips, and I force myself to look at the woman before me which is a far better sight. "Do you take Brother Christopher to be your husband, to honor, obey, and walk under God's eyes together as one?"

"I do," she says softly as her eyes connect with mine. She wants this so badly. I can see it in the way her face nearly beams like an angel. I can feel it.

The band slides on my finger and actually fits perfectly even though I wonder if it will blister my skin with the evil it's laced with.

"I now pronounce you husband and wife. You may kiss your bride."

I actually *have* to kiss her. It's the only thing to keep me standing as my entire being is swirling in complete chaos. I need a grounding force, and the lips of this sweet and pure woman before me are all I have to cling to.

As gently, and as lovingly as I can muster, I bring my lips to hers. She deserves a wedding kiss to remember. She deserves a memory that isn't blanketed in thick darkness. I want to give her that gift. I want her to look back on this moment and remember how happy I truly believe she is.

My lips touch hers and I feel her release a breath. I inhale in hopes that her innocent view on life will help me chase away the horror flowing through my veins. I need her strength. I need her optimism. Otherwise, I'll be swallowed up whole just as if I had been thrown in the acid pits.

"Ember   Davenport,"   Scarecrow   says.   "Christopher

Davenport." His words break our kiss. "You are now joined as one under God."

As I look upon this delicate flower, I want to make my own wedding vows to her.

I want to promise her we will find a way to leave this Hell.

I want to make a vow that she will never have to live this existence again.

I want to offer my words for a future that will be better, safer, and normal.

On this land, in Hallelujah Junction and in the eyes of all who stand and look upon me, Ember is my wife.

She is my captive bride.

16

EMBER

I DREAMED OF THIS DAY.

When hopelessness surrounded me, that my existence would be nothing more than being the ghost of Hallelujah Junction, I had dreamed of a Prince Charming arriving from afar who would kiss away all the bad and bring me only good.

I stand before my Prince Charming.

My husband.

I know this isn't what he wants. I know he wants to be free. I know he wants my father dead. But I also know fate has brought him here for a reason. Maybe he simply doesn't know it yet. Maybe it's my job to show him.

I know I can make him happy if I work really hard.

I know I can give him love and tenderness.

I can be a good wife. I know I can. I just have to convince him of that fact.

Papa Rich and Scarecrow leave us alone in the schoolhouse. The act alone shows that the marriage changes things. We aren't going to have to spend our wedding night in the cold cellar. Papa Rich only had one dictate, and one that I am prepared to follow.

"You will lay this white sheet beneath you as you

consummate the marriage. God will expect to see the signs of the union."

He wanted proof of Christopher taking my virginity.

But I will do that. I will do anything if it means Christopher can remain in my private sanctuary.

Christopher and I hadn't exchanged any words since our vows, but now that we stand in the schoolhouse alone, I feel it's my duty to break the ice. "This is where I spend most of my time. I have a room in the main house, but I still prefer this place." I point to the windows. "There's a lot of sunshine." I point to the old wood-burning stove. "And we can use this to heat the place in the winter. Not while there are tourists or they'll see the smoke, but we can soon when the tourists leave."

Christopher slowly meanders to the window that overlooks the town. The same window I was at when I watched Papa Rich hit him upside the head.

Because of the chain, I have no choice but to go with him.

"The ghost of Hallelujah Junction." He smirks and then looks at me. "Is now my wife."

My face heats and I look down at the floor at my bare feet. They are dirtier than I like, but I haven't been able to keep up on the cleaning of the floors since I was in the cellar and I was busy with Christopher even before that.

He refocuses his attention outside the window. "When I took this assignment, to capture the sights of the ghost town known as Hallelujah Junction, I actually worried it would be too boring. I almost declined the job. I mean, who cares about an old mining town anyway? Who would read about that, and who would want to look at pictures of run-down dilapidated buildings? Boring." He laughs more to himself than anything. "If I only knew."

We stand there in silence, and I have no idea what to say. I know he's in pain. I know he's sad and angry. I want to make it better. I want to make it all go away.

"I don't know how to be a wife," I confess, feeling like I have to be honest.

He chuckles, still looking outside. "Oh, I can pretty much guarantee I have no idea how to be a husband either."

I swallow against the lump in my throat and glance over my shoulder at the mattress on the floor with the bedding piled on top of it. The white sheet on top of the other blankets brings me back to the reality of what's going to occur soon.

He's going to take my virginity.

"Papa Rich said that tonight is going to hurt."

Christopher turns his head and looks at me with confusion. "What are you talking about? What's going to hurt?"

"When you claim me," I say softly, not being able to look him in the eye as I say the words. "He said it's my duty and that I must just endure the pain. I'm scared," I confess.

"Jesus," he says as he runs his hands through his hair and looks out the window again. "I'm not going to claim you. I would never hurt you, and I sure as hell wouldn't take what isn't given. He can force many things, but he sure as fuck can't force me to have sex with you."

"But we have to consummate the marriage," I say, feeling my heart sink. I don't want to fail at being a wife on day one.

"What he knows or doesn't know is none of his business. We don't have to tell him what we do. Make him believe whatever makes him happy. I don't give a shit."

"Christopher..."

He spins to face me directly. His eyes are filled with anger. "I'm not going to take your virginity. I'm not that kind of man!" He moves his cuffed leg a little. "I may be chained like a damn animal, but that doesn't mean I'll behave like one."

"You don't want to have sex with me?" My lip trembles as I ask the question, and I struggle to hold back the tears that threaten to fall. I look down at my dress. "Am I not desirable?"

He grasps my chin and forces my head up to look at him. "First of all, you're beautiful. Don't ever feel you aren't. You have a true and genuine beauty I've never seen before in another woman. There's an angelic purity to you that you have somehow maintained even though you live in the absolute pit of despair."

"Then why are you angry?" I ask. "Why is the thought of having sex on our wedding night getting you upset?"

"Because you deserve better!" he snaps. He glances at the mattress on the floor. "Your first experience should be romantic. It should be special. It should be an experience you want and have been looking forward to. I don't want you to have sex because your father demands it."

"But he does," I say, pointing at the white sheet. "He told me he will expect to see proof of it tomorrow morning."

"Motherfucker!" Christopher shouts as he punches his fist against the wall of the schoolhouse.

I jump back, but I can't fully retreat without falling to the ground as the chain holds one foot in place.

Christopher sees my reaction and instantly softens and pulls me into his arms. "I'm sorry. I'm sorry." He takes a deep breath in. "I don't ever want to scare you."

I pull away just enough so that I can look into his eyes. "Please don't fight him on this. He'll whip me if we refuse, and he'll lock us back in the cellar." I glance around the schoolhouse and add, "I know this may not be your apartment in New York, but it's better than sleeping on the cold floor of the cellar. And I promise I'll try to fix it up real nice. I'll try to make it feel like our home." I glance down at my feet. "Just don't give Papa Rich reason to take it all away. He will. He doesn't bluff."

Christopher lifts my chin so I have to look up at him. "Where I come from, the woman chooses to give her virginity away. It's a gift. And it's not something I'd just take."

"You aren't taking. I'm giving."

"It shouldn't be like this."

"We're husband and wife now. It's what's supposed to be done. And..." My face heats and I divert my eyes in shame. "I'm way past the age. I know this. I shouldn't be a virgin anymore. I don't want to be. I want to be... normal. Or at least as normal as I can be in my setting."

"Your setting?" I see hope in his eyes. I know he wants me to think the way he does. He thinks I live in denial, and maybe I do.

"I know I'm different. I know a normal woman doesn't grow up in a ghost town hidden from the world. I know I'm sheltered." Saying the words out loud actually stabs at my heart. "I'm aware of my circumstances and how they look to you. I also know you *pity* me."

"I wouldn't use the word *pity*," he says. "But I see the truth, and I'm not sure you do."

"What's the truth you see?"

"Your father keeps you here against your will."

I look down at my feet and then back up at him. "You're right. That is my truth."

"Then why don't you want to escape?" he asks.

"It's not a matter of want or not. It's a matter of reality. I know we can't escape. And I also know what the consequences could be. And even if I do escape...if *we* escape. Then what? What do I do? Where do I go? I don't know anyone or anything. I have no idea what is outside of Hallelujah Junction."

"I already told you," he says. "I promised that I would help you. I wouldn't just abandon you."

"And that is *pity*."

"No. That's human decency. I would help you."

"Because you have to? Because we're now husband and wife? Because—"

"Because I'd want to," he interrupts. "I feel this need to protect you, and it's not going to go away just because we leave this town. I promise you that."

He looks over my shoulder at the mattress with the white sheet. His brow furrows, but he doesn't speak anymore. He takes a deep breath, runs his fingers through his hair and then pulls my head against his chest.

"I wish I could rescue you from this place tonight," he says softly. "I wish I could introduce you to a normal life. I wish I could show you life as it's supposed to be. I wish I could give you a romantic wedding night."

I inhale his scent and close my eyes, savoring the fragrance. "You're my husband. Being in your arms, I feel... safe. That's all I need and all I'll ever ask for."

"But you aren't safe. As long as we're here, you'll never be safe."

He's right. I know this deep down. I love my Papa Rich, but I know that one wrong move by Christopher or even me, and his temper could attack. He seems so unhinged, and it's growing deeper and deeper by the day.

I break away from the hold and walk to the mattress. I begin unfolding the sheet and covering the bed with it, taking extra care to smooth out the wrinkles and tuck the corners in snuggly. I want our wedding bed to be as perfect as it can be.

I try to ignore the fear sizzling through my veins. Papa said it would hurt, and he'd never lied to me before, so I believe every word. But I also know it's my duty as a wife, and one that I want to do well. I can't give Christopher true freedom, but I can do whatever I can to make him happy and well cared for. It also shames me that a big part of me is curious and even excited for what's to come. I want another kiss. I want more tender caresses and holding. I want the love. God, how much I want the love.

Not wanting to discuss this further, not wanting to beg for Christopher to comply, and not wanting to wait on anxious breath anymore, I lie on my back and slowly open my legs. I'm not wearing panties because I have none that were fancy enough for such a special day and night.

"I'm ready," I nearly whisper, not sure what else to say. My voice cracks as I say the words.

I stare at the ceiling and wait to hear the slightest noise from Christopher. The first thing I hear is the release of a deep breath and then his footsteps approaching the mattress.

"I can't do this," he says as he towers over me, looking down with sorrow in his eyes. "This isn't me. It feels wrong."

I sit up and reach for his hand. Pulling him down to the mattress, I say, "Please. I know you think it's dark now, but it can get so much darker. We must obey."

"I don't care what he does to me. He can't make me lose who I am to my core."

"He'll hurt me, Christopher," I say softly. "Protect me. As my husband, I'm asking you to please keep me from harm."

I lie back down and close my eyes tightly, preparing myself for what is to come... or at least what I hope is coming.

17

CHRISTOPHER

"Open your eyes," I say firmly. "It won't be like this. I won't have your first time be a memory of you grinning and bearing it because you think it's your wifely duty. If we're going to have sex, then you're going to allow me to make it as special as it can be considering our circumstances."

"Special?" She opens her eyes and looks up at me.

The protective need coursing through me right now is beyond powerful. I don't know why. I don't know why I feel this overwhelming need to give this woman the best that I can, and if that means something as simple as making her first time having sex as pleasant as possible, then so be it.

I position my body so I'm beside her. I look into her eyes and say, "All you have to say is stop, and I will. Ask me to slow down, and I'll listen. Your voice will be heard. Do not suffer through this. Understand?"

She nods and licks her lips as her eyes look at mine.

I lean forward and press my mouth to hers and am surprised when she willingly kisses me back. A bolt of desire shoots through me from the simple act, and I can't resist but to press my tongue past her lips and caress it with hers. Rather than pulling back, tensing, or flinching like I expect her to do, she instead lets out a gasp as she dances her tongue with mine. Our kiss grows in intensity, and a passion I haven't felt since I was a naive young boy who believed in puppy love, causes my cock to harden.

I need to block out all else and focus on Ember. Focus on giving this poor girl a memory that is good. I don't want another first to be stolen from her. I don't know why that is so important to me, but it is. She didn't get the firsts in life, and now that I get to be part of one, I am determined to make it a good one.

And as we kiss, my body awakens, and I want to be inside of her. But I refuse to rush this.

I run my hand over her breasts with the finest touch. I keep my eyes open as I do, watching her face for any sign of distress. But instead, I see her eyes close, her lips open, and ever so slightly, she arches her back to meet my touch. I then trail my fingertips down her belly, inching my way to the space between her legs. I want to see how far I can go before she panics and asks me to stop.

She never does.

Her body's hungry. Needy for touch and affection.

I look at the dress and have no idea how to go about removing it. The buttons are on the back.

"Can you help me get you out of this dress?" I lean down and kiss her softly one more time to try to calm any nerves in her body with the idea of getting naked in front of me. "I'll take my clothes off too."

I need to remove all the barriers because I know she doesn't have the experience or confidence to do it herself or even aid me. She watches me with wide eyes as I lift my shirt over my head revealing my bare chest and abs.

I pause before I move to my pants. "Are you okay with this?"

She nods with more enthusiasm than I've seen and licks her lips again. I try not to smirk and reveal that her face is easy to read. She'd be an awful poker player.

I unbutton and remove my pants completely and kneel before

her on the mattress. Her eyes refuse to look down at my dick, and I consider making her but remember how she believed she was so sinful before for stealing a peek. Instead, I turn her around so that I can begin unbuttoning the line of pearl buttons that run from neck to waist.

"You looked beautiful in this dress," I say as she holds up her hair so I can see each pearl.

"Thank you," she says softly.

When the buttons are undone, I lower the fabric slowly off her shoulders and kiss a trail as I do. I haven't kissed a woman's shoulders as I undress her ever before.

I'm not a gentle man in bed. In fact, I can be downright aggressive and nearly primal. The women don't complain, in fact, they can be just as animalistic as me.

But with Ember, I want to be easy and soft.

I want to treat her like the candle of bright light she is, and make sure I don't put out the flame. The flicker of heat from her skin, connecting with my lips nearly makes me explode with a hunger to claim her as mine.

I don't want anyone else to touch her. I don't want anyone to harm her, or scare her, or abuse her in any way. I want to hold her close like fine china to be handled with the utmost care.

Once all our clothes are shed, I lower her back to the bed and place my body over hers. I don't want to frighten her with too much foreplay and foreign acts that she may not be aware of yet. But I also know she isn't ready for me to just take her.

"I don't want this to hurt," I say as I lower my mouth to her lips and kiss her again. "So, I'm going to get you ready with my fingers. I'm going to touch you in a very intimate way if that's okay?"

Would I ever say these words to a woman I was dating or hooking up with? Hell no. In fact, it would probably kill the mood. But Ember was different. She needed this. She needed the steps and the instructions, or I was going to scare the living shit out of her.

I reposition my body so I can reach between her legs more comfortably. I plan to really take my time allowing her body to wake up to arousal. When my fingers touch her pussy, I'm surprised to find her wet. Her tiny moan gives me the permission I need to start massaging the delicate flesh.

"I'm going to put my finger inside of you," I say as I kiss her neck and slightly nibble.

She doesn't answer but nods as I take notice that her breath is coming out more labored and her body tenses as my fingers stroke and spread her lips wide.

I place my finger at her entrance and ease my way in, knowing this is the first thing that has ever been inside of her. Her hips lift and her breath hitches. She places her hands on my back but doesn't stop me. I push my finger deeper inside and her breath turns to a moan.

"Does that feel good?" I ask.

She closes her eyes, bites her lower lip, and nods.

I pull out my finger only to push it back in— a little deeper this time.

"It feels so... it feels so full," she says.

And that is going to be the problem. My dick is far from small, and if my finger is snug in her tight little hole, then this is going to hurt, and I don't want that. Determined to try my best in getting her body accustomed to the stretch, I begin adding the tip of a second finger to open her hole just a little wider. Luckily her juices flow freely, and I have no friction or need for additional lubrication. Her body responds to my touch which has my own body lighting up with fire.

What had started as feeling like I had no choice but to fuck her, has turned into me not being able to picture anything but. I want her. I want Ember possibly more than I have ever wanted anyone before.

"I'm adding a second finger. I need to get you prepared for my size. If this hurts, tell me."

When I add the second finger fully and begin pumping it in

and out, Ember opens her eyes and looks at me. "I like it. Is that bad?"

I lean down and kiss her softly on the lips, fingers still inside of her. "That's very good. I want you to like this. I want you to love this."

"Can we do it now?" she asks softly. "I'm ready."

I pull my fingers out and position myself on top of her, nudging her legs further apart with my knees. I make eye contact with her as I position my cock at her entrance. "Are you sure?"

She nods and holds on to my back as I slowly press inside. Once I get the tip in, I pause so she can adjust to the feeling.

"Take me," she says as she pulls me closer to her with her hands and lifts her hips up to force me deeper inside.

With one fluid motion, I press on, feeling the pop of a barrier as she cries out. I pause and kiss her as passionately as I possibly can to distract her from any pain. She kisses me back with just as much desire, and I know I can continue on.

I pull out slowly and then push back in, not feeling the resistance like before. Over and over, I thrust, kissing her as I do. When I pull away just enough to look into her face, I see tears in the corners of her eyes.

"Are you doing okay?" I ask.

"I've never felt so... so close to anyone." A tear falls from her eye as she lifts her head and presses it into my neck.

She holds me tight as we make love for the first time. And though I am taking great care in preventing any discomfort, I still worry. I want her to enjoy this. I want her to look back at this moment and feel nothing but love and tenderness.

"I feel alive," she murmurs against my neck. "I feel free."

In and out, I move, feeling my own level of connection that I struggle to process. This woman in my arms needs me. This woman wants me. This woman is truly giving herself to me. She isn't holding back, or protecting her heart, or thinking of anything else but me. I can feel it. I can feel how wholeheartedly she is giving herself to me.

I feel it.

"Christopher," she moans.

"It's okay, Ember. Allow those feelings to rush in. Don't be afraid."

Her moans deepen and her breath speeds up. Her fingers dig into my back as her body spasms beneath me.

"Come for me," I say as I push my cock deeper inside of her. "Release it all."

Her inner walls milk my cock, and I know I don't have long at all. As she releases a delicate mewl, her head falls back on the mattress, and her eyes are closed in completion.

Not being able to hold back any longer, I pull out of her quickly as a rush of come leaves my body and splatters on her belly. As my body spasms every last bit of completion, I look down on her face and see true bliss. She appears almost spiritual in the way her smile lights up her face.

Very slowly, her eyes open up and she stares up at me with the most perfect blue I have ever seen.

"Thank you," she says. "Thank you."

18

EMBER

I AM FAILING MY HUSBAND.

I know I am, and I don't know what to do about it. I try to cook the best meals I can, although Christopher has to stand by my side and watch as I do since the chain gives us no space. He offers to chop or stir, but I feel as if it's my wifely duty to do it all.

I try to clean our schoolhouse floors and dust all the Nevada desert away, but again, Christopher is right there and feels he needs to help too, or is convincing me I'm being silly trying to clean a prison cell.

I try to make him happy. But he isn't. And each day that passes, I see the dark circles under his eyes intensify and the hollow of his cheeks seem to sink deeper and deeper each hour of our time together.

The man is fading away.

Hallelujah Junction is killing him.

"It's snowing outside," I say as I look out the window. Christopher is simply staring off into space, and I'm desperate to snap him out of the funk he's in.

"Great," he mumbles.

"Papa Rich closed the town to tourists. Which means he may let us out of the schoolhouse soon. We can explore the outside."

Papa Rich had left the two of us alone in the schoolhouse for the most part. He occasionally would enter the room, look around, and then leave as quickly as he came. He didn't seem to taunt Christopher like he did before. If anything, he seemed to be giving us our space so we could get to know each other better.

Christopher leans against his arms on the mattress and stares out the window. "So, now we're really trapped. No people coming. No chance of hope."

Winter also means less visits by Scarecrow which gives me another reason to love this season, so I won't let Christopher bring me down.

"I have something to show you," I say, wondering why I haven't thought of it sooner. It would have helped with Christopher's sour disposition. How could it not?

I move to get off the bed, and Christopher groans as he joins me. I make my way to a storage closet and pull out an old record player that was left behind from a previous ranger before Papa took over the town. Next to the record player are my prized possessions. Records that fill my heart with love and joy, and in my darkest times can always make me smile.

"Sunshine on my shoulders makes me happy," I say as I set up the player and put a John Denver record on it.

Christopher watches what I'm doing with curiosity. It's the first time today he shows any emotion at all, and though it's not a smile, I'll take it. I'm at least shaking the numbness out of him.

I put the needle on the record where I know my favorite song will start.

I begin humming along and then sing out, "If I had a day that I could give you, I'd give to you a day just like today." I begin swaying back and forth with my eyes closed and just listen. Just feel.

And then I feel Christopher's arms around me. He takes my hands in his and begins to slowly dance with me to the music. I had always dreamed of a day I would dance with a man in a grand ballroom somewhere, but this... this right here, dancing with Christopher, is far better than anything I could dream of.

He kisses the side of my head as he pulls me against his chest. Step by step we dance. His heart beats next to mine. His breath blends with mine. And for the first time since our wedding night, I feel close. I feel Christopher. I haven't lost him to the shadows. Not yet.

"You said you would lend me your happiness," he says against my hair. "I feel I need that right now. I feel myself slipping into a deep, dark hole."

"I'd give you anything," I say, my heart breaking for how sad he is.

"I'm not like you," he says. "I can't shake off the cold chill in my bones like you. I can't see the silver lining. I just see four walls closing in on me."

"I've had practice," I admit. "I know how to fight the demons."

"Well, you're going to have to teach me how."

We keep dancing through song after song on the record player as the snow blankets the ground outside. Our wood-burning stove keeps us warm, but it could be a blizzard inside, and I'd still be warm in Christopher's arms.

I put my hand on his face and giggle. "You have a beard now."

He chuckles. "If my mother could see me now, she'd die of a stroke." His smile quickly fades, and sorrow takes over again.

"I can shave it for you," I offer. "I can borrow a razor from Papa Rich."

"I'll keep the beard," he snaps. He stops dancing and pulls away.

I know me mentioning Papa Rich by name causes Christopher to always lose his temper. I should try to do better and avoid his name at all cost.

I leave the music playing but follow Christopher back to the mattress where we sit.

"I want to make you happy," I say, feeling defeated.

He shifts on the mattress so he can see me directly. "You're a good woman, Ember. You are by far the kindest, most genuine person I've ever met. You don't make me unhappy. It's not you."

"You want to leave."

"I want to leave this place. Yes."

"What about me?" I ask, not sure I want to hear the answer. "What do you feel about me?"

He takes me by the hand. "Confusion, to be honest. A part of me tells me I shouldn't have any feelings for you considering I'm here against my will and chained to you. Another part of me feels this almost neanderthal feeling to protect you and make you mine forever. And whenever I start to allow feelings to form for you, I feel like something's wrong with me. Like I'm sick in the head."

"But aren't I yours forever?" I ask. "We made vows. We're married."

"Ember..." I see pity on his face. "We were forced to marry. You know that right? We were married by a crazy one-legged man. Our marriage isn't even legal. It's not real beyond this town."

"It's real to me!" The words come out much harsher than I want, but I can't help it. And for the first time since being chained to Christopher, I really feel trapped. I snap my hand out of his and cross them protectively against my chest. I want to leave. I want to walk through the tunnel and go to the kitchen so I can get some fresh air that is not also breathed by Christopher, but I can't. "I know we come from different places," I say much calmer. "But vows mean something to me." In a tiny voice as I look at my feet, I add, "You mean something to me."

He reaches for my hand again. I don't want him touching me, but I don't really have a choice. I can't run. I can't even cross the room to be alone.

"I didn't mean to upset you," he says. I look into his eyes and see sincerity. "I can't explain all the feelings I have. I feel weak. I've never felt so weak and out of control in my life. I don't want to give up on my plan for escape, and yet... as each day goes by, I find myself doing exactly that." With his free hand, he moves a piece of my hair behind my ear. "You mean something to me too, Ember. I didn't mean to make you feel otherwise. You mean a lot to me. In fact, I don't think I could have gotten by each day here without you. Your sunshine is the only light in my world right now. I need you."

"I need you."

He leans forward and kisses me softly. His hands cup the sides of my face as if he's afraid I'll pull away.

"I want to please you," I say against the kiss. "I want to please you in all ways."

I lower my hand to the button of his pants and boldly unfasten. I wait for him to stop me or tell me I'm doing it wrong, but he only deepens the kiss. When the pants are loose, I lower my hand and touch his hardness. I take hold of it and feel the weight against my palm. I'd never been so daring before nor sinful—but is it a sin if he's my husband?

I fight against the awkwardness of his clothing and the restriction. As if reading my mind, he lifts up enough so that I can lower everything down, freeing his sex. I glance down, but then feel my face heat.

"This isn't wrong," he rasps out.

I know he's right, and I fight the feelings of sin threatening to suffocate me. Instead, I lower my mouth and kiss the tip of his penis. Unsure, I look up at him. "Is this all right?"

He closes his eyes and leans back. "More than all right."

Feeling a sense of accomplishment that I have brought a smile to his face. I kiss a trail from the head all the way to the base and then lick my way up. The salty musk sends a shiver down my spine. My own sex pulsates in need for him to enter me. I want him again. I want to feel that level of closeness and connection again.

On exhale, he says, "Put me in your mouth. Suck me up and down."

His command forms moisture between my legs, but I do

exactly as he asks. Opening my mouth wide, I crawl up on my knees to get a better angle so that I can take all of him.

His hand grips my hair, and he guides my head down and then tugs me back up. We repeat this action several times with his moans growing in intensity with each time. I drag my tongue along his flesh and love the power that I have. I'm giving him pleasure and I know it. I love it. I love the control.

I realize I can tighten my lips and he groans. I can go deeper into the back of my throat and his hips buck. His actions are the result of mine. I'm finally feeling like a wife who can please my husband.

"Ember," I hear Papa Rich call from the tunnel.

He doesn't usually give warning, but thank goodness he is. I jump up and when I see that Christopher isn't moving in the slightest to pull his pants back on, I panic. He's going to push Papa's buttons. I can see it in his eyes.

"Please," I beg, tugging his pants up the best I can.

Christopher sighs, rolls his eyes, but pulls up his pants right as Papa Rich enters from the tunnel.

He stops and looks at me, then Christopher with that suspicious eye I know of his. "Christopher, it's nice to see you look as if you're getting comfortable in your new home."

Christopher smirks and remains leaned back on the mattress. "Very."

Papa Rich looks at me and I know my face must be several shades of red. "And are the two of you getting along good?"

"Extremely," Christopher says with a twinkle in his eye.

I see Papa's jaw tighten and his eyes narrow.

I hold my breath. I don't want Papa to think we're sinners and feel we have to pay penance for our actions. Christopher doesn't seem concerned at all. His hardness is still very visible beneath his pants, and I wonder if tossing a blanket over him will be too obvious.

"I'm running into town," he says to me as he clears his throat.

"I saw your usual grocery list on the fridge. Is there anything else you need?"

"Yes, actually." I say softly. "Is it possible to pick up a razor for Christopher? In case he wants to shave his beard."

I figure that Christopher should have the option, and I know that him borrowing anything from Papa was out of the question and even angered him. At least this way, he will have something of his own.

Papa Rich nods. "Anything else?" He actually looks at Christopher and waits for him to answer.

"Yeah. How about a bottle of Jack?" Christopher says with a cocky grin.

Papa surprises me when he says, "I don't see why not. I'll add it to the list."

I see the cocky look on Christopher's face disappear and something unfamiliar takes its place. He's angry. He knows Papa is playing his game right back. Two men who have fury bubbling up inside but neither will show it.

"Sugar," I add, hating the tension in the room. "I'll make us a cake."

Papa nods again and then goes back into the tunnel.

"You drink?" I ask, knowing Papa Rich rarely did.

He shrugs. "I used to drink a lot. Maybe too much." He chuckles. "This place has been the worst detox known to man."

"Why?" I ask. "Why too much?"

"Life," he says almost sadly. "In some crazy way, being here made me realize that I was in some sort of prison of my own in New York. I think I was self-medicating."

"Booze is a medicine?" I know I'm sheltered from all the things in the outside world, but I have never heard of alcohol being medicinal.

"Just a saying. But it did seem to make me function better. Pills and whisky were my go to." He looks at me. "Like I said though, this place broke me of that habit cold turkey."

"Do you miss it?"

"No." Christopher hops off the bed and walks to the window, jerking me alongside him. "How often does he go to town in the winter?"

"Not as often," I say.

"How long is he gone when he does?"

I shrug. "I'm not sure. A couple of hours with good weather, but the snow slows him down."

Christopher's face lights up and he looks at me. "He's gone for hours?"

I nod. I know what he's thinking. What he's hoping.

He's wrong.

There's no way out of here.

There's no way.

"Is there any other vehicle here? Another ranger truck? Anything?"

I shake my head.

Christopher stares out the window waiting for Papa Rich to leave. The glass fogs up with our breaths, and he wipes at the glass for a better view. "What about the ranger's office? A phone? There has to be a phone."

"Papa has a radio, and he takes it with him. I told you this. No phone. No way out."

"How do you know there's no phone? How do you know? We need to go see for ourselves."

I reach for his hand to try to soothe his wild mind. "I know, Christopher. There's no phone, he locks everything, and he's thought of every possibility. Trust me. I know."

I hate that I'm stealing his hope. I can't stand that I'm the reason his face is falling from excited to despair.

I so desperately want to be the good wife.

I want to please. I want to please more than anything.

"We can look if you want."

Although I already know it will be useless, he needs to see for himself. He needs to walk down the path of hopelessness on his own. I can only hold his hand and be by his side as he does so... as a dutiful wife.

19

CHRISTOPHER

I REFUSE TO GIVE UP HOPE. DAY AFTER DAY AND I REFUSE. THE snow is thick, the air heavy with evil, and all I can do is sit and wait. There will be a time. There will be an opening of opportunity, and I will take it.

I have to hand it to Richard.

The man is smart.

There is no phone, no way to reach the outside world. Ember is right about that.

I have no idea where he hides his keys to the truck even though I look around the kitchen every time we are there to prepare meals. I know I will have one shot, and I don't want to be reckless or foolish when I make the move. I have to be patient. The time will come. I know it will.

"We should start prep for supper soon. I want to make a special recipe of mine for you," Ember says as we sit near the wood stove.

I give her a smile because I know how hard she tries to keep me happy. I wish she could meet the real me. I wish she could see the man I truly am when I'm not shackled and captured against my will. I think she'd like me better. I think she'd feel more loved because I would have more to offer. I would have a soul that wasn't shattered into a million pieces. I am barely hanging on in here. I feel as if the monster of this place is eating me alive, and though I try hard not to take it out on Ember, I know I do. I see the pain in her eyes when I snap. I see her desperate need to fill my days with the rainbows and flowers she imagines, but I just can't. I know she wants me to be the Prince Charming she had always fantasized. I know I should be better.

I just can't.

Not while being here.

Not here in Hallelujah Junction. But if we ever leave... if we ever leave, I'll be a better man.

Movement outside the window catches my eye. I'd seen deer, rabbit and squirrels before, but something in my gut tells me this time is different. This time I need to pay attention.

"Come to the window," I say, not wanting to just drag Ember with me to get a better look.

We make our way to the window, and my heart stops.

Two people snowshoeing in the town below.

"They aren't supposed to be here," Ember whispers. I hear the fear in her voice, but I can't help but feel a sense of excitement that nearly paralyzes me.

My instinct is to bang on the window and start screaming, but I also don't know where Richard is. I don't want to reveal our guests by making a commotion.

"We need to go outside," I say, spinning around and nearly causing Ember to fall because she's not ready.

She reaches for my hand. "Christopher, we can't."

I glare at her so she knows I mean business. I don't want to be mean to her, but I will if I have to. "This is our chance. I'm not going to stand here and miss it."

"If Papa Rich sees us leave the schoolhouse, he may lock us in the cellar and never allow us to come back here again. We'll lose his trust." She looks around the small structure that had become our home with tears in her eyes. "We were just getting comfortable."

"Now, Ember. Now." No patience or understanding is left in my body. "Now."

I take a step forward with my chained leg, and if I have to drag her along, I will.

She walks beside me, but I can sense her internal struggle.

"Pine Cone. Where's my cat? I can't leave her."

"We'll come back for her. I promise," I say, not wanting to waste time hunting down her cat.

"Please don't make me do this," she begs softly. "He'll find us. He will."

"We just need to get to them before he does."

"He knows they're here. I'm telling you, Christopher, he knows." There's urgency in her voice, but I don't care. This is our shot. It could be our only one.

I open the door to the schoolhouse, and even that defiant act has Ember gasping.

"We're barefoot," she states. "We can't just walk out there in the snow."

"We can, and we will."

If I have to, I am willing to lose both my feet to frostbite if it means escaping. I hope I don't have to, and I most certainly don't want that for Ember, but if the sacrifice has to be made, then so be it.

There isn't a lot of slack in the chain connecting us, but I believe I can pick Ember up if need be. It will be awkward but can still be done. But not yet. We need to reach the couple before they get too far away. I need Ember to run at the same pace as me.

"Just focus on running and keeping your foot at the same speed as me. We'll worry about the cold effects later."

We don't have time to plan, and we don't have time to discuss this further, so I jerk her out of the schoolhouse and begin running as fast as Ember's footing can go.

The couple comes into sight and I consider screaming at the

top of my lungs. But they are still far enough away that for them to hear me, means that I have to be loud enough for Richard to also hear me. So, instead, I begin waving my arms frantically in hopes they see us coming.

"A little faster," I say as I wrap my arm around Ember to keep her close at my side and to prevent her from stumbling.

"It's too cold," she says. "We're going to lose our toes. We should go back before it's too late."

I ignore her complaints just as I ignore any discomfort in my feet. Escape is so close.

So close.

We are getting close enough now that I can actually see their expressions on their faces. They're happy, they're excited to be spending their day playing in the snow. They have no idea what they are about to see. They are both in their twenties and give off the puppy love vibe. So innocent. So free from worry. So in love without a care in the world.

Then the boy sees me. His expression turns from joy to confusion.

The girl sees me next, and her smile morphs to a look of fear. She sees the chain around our ankles and backs behind her partner for protection.

"Help us," I call out as we approach. "Help."

The male fully steps in front of the female as a shield, and though we are the ones asking for help, I can imagine what kind of sight we must be.

"You have to get us out of here," I say, still hobbling up to them with Ember at my side. "There's a crazy man here who's kidnapped us. Call 911 now, but we need to get to your car. Now."

"What the fuck?" the man says as he looks down and sees that Ember and I are both barefoot, nearly ankle deep in the snow that we keep sinking into with every step.

"Oh my God," the woman says as her body visibly trembles. "You were kidnapped?"

"We don't have time to talk. Where's your car?"

The woman is pulling out her phone with wide eyes. She looks down at the screen and frowns. "There's no signal."

"We need to get out of here now," I say, while the man nods in agreement.

He points to our right. "We're down the hill some. The snow made it too hard for us to drive to the parking lot. We're going to have to hike a bit to our Jeep." He looks back at our feet. "You can't make it barefoot."

"Here," the woman says, as she takes off her gloves. "Try to put these on your feet."

She hands her gloves to Ember and bends down to help cover her feet. The man does the same with his gloves and gives them to me. Anything is better than nothing, and I'm grateful for the idea and the offer.

The woman then takes off her coat and gives it to Ember. "Don't worry," she says. "I have warm winter clothes on underneath."

The man follows her and does the same, giving me his coat. "Come on," he says. "Let's get you both out of here."

I see Ember look around with panic in her eyes. She's searching for Richard, and I just pray we get out of here fast enough.

"Hurry," I say as the four of us start running in the direction of the Jeep.

The gloves make it difficult to run, but the chain around Ember's and my ankle make it near impossible. I decide to try to pick her up which causes the cuff around my ankle to dig into my flesh, but I ignore the pain. She clings to my shoulders to try to hold on as I plow through the snow with a mission to survive. I can nearly feel the breath of Richard behind me.

He's coming.

I know he's coming.

We just have to get out of the town and down the hill to the Jeep before he reaches us.

Run.

Run.

Run faster.

The couple are running in their snowshoes which allows them to be ahead of me, but they both keep turning and looking over their shoulders to make sure we're close behind. The snowshoes carve a path for me which helps. I'm not sinking down nearly as much in the packed-down snow they create.

"We're almost there," the male says.

I'm afraid to look over my shoulder. I'm worried that if I do, I'll see Richard charging forward with evil and vengeance in his eyes. He'll kill me if he catches us. I have no doubt he will. He'll kill me and he'll torture Ember. He'll also kill this innocent couple who are only trying to help us.

Run.

Run.

Ignore the cold.

Run.

Even if Richard doesn't see us yet, it won't be hard to track us. I can see blood coming from both my and Ember's ankle. The metal cuff has nearly rubbed us both raw and down to the bone. Our path of blood we leave behind is our own personal bread crumb left for the witch who will boil our bodies alive if found.

Ember is silent.

She hasn't said much since we left the schoolhouse. I want to soothe her. I want to comfort her in some way. I want to tell her everything will be all right, but I don't want to lie. I have no idea if this escape attempt will be successful, and until we're in the back seat of the Jeep heading down the road, I won't issue a single word of reassurance. I know she's scared... but I can only focus on marching through the snow one step at a time.

And then I see the Jeep.

Oh Jesus Christ, I see the Jeep.

Freedom is on the horizon and we are nearly there.

My heart skips, my blood boils with renewed energy and

determination to pick up my speed. Safety. We are so close to safety.

We're going to get the hell out of Hallelujah Junction!

"That's it," the man says as he and the woman keep shoeing ahead. "Hurry up. We're almost there."

The male opens the back door to the Jeep and helps me and Ember into the back seat while the woman crawls into the front seat. The man then runs around to the driver's side of the Jeep.

I remove the soaked gloves from my feet which somehow had stayed on and begin massaging feeling back into my feet. Ember is frozen in place and doesn't move.

"Try to get your feet warmed up," I say, but notice she doesn't budge.

"He's going to find us," she says softly which has the girl turn her head to look at her in fear.

"Who?" the girl asks. "Who is going to find us? Who kidnapped you?" She reaches for her phone again, but when she puts it back down, I know she still has no signal.

"We're safe now," I say, taking hold of Ember's foot and removing the glove.

Her foot looks red from the snow, but doesn't look like any frostbite is present, which is the same for my feet.

And just as hope begins to warm my frozen body, the sound of the Jeep *not* turning over happens. The Jeep won't start.

"Come on!" the man says as he keeps trying but nothing.

"Why won't it start?" the woman beside him screeches in terror.

I glance toward the road and know there is no way that Ember and I can make it down the road wearing nothing but gloves on our feet. The couple maybe can...

"You both need to get out of here, now," I say, feeling like I can hear the sound of boots crunching on the snow. "He'll kill you. You need to run."

"We can't just leave you," the man says as he keeps trying to start the Jeep.

"Get down the hill and call the police," I order, scanning the area for any signs of Richard.

The woman hops out of the Jeep and turns and looks at us. "I promise we'll come back for you."

Ember doesn't say anything but removes the woman's coat and hands it to me. I remove the coat given to me and hand both of them to the woman.

"Run as fast as you can. This man, Richard, is insane. He's extremely dangerous."

The couple doesn't waste any time and start snowshoeing down the hill. Ember and I crawl out of the back seat and hobble our way to the driver's side of the Jeep. I jump into the seat and try to start the vehicle myself. It's making no sound at all. It's not even trying. I get out of the Jeep and open the hood of the engine. I'm no mechanic, but maybe Lady Luck will shine down on me, and I'll see something that's an easy fix.

"We need to go back to the schoolhouse," Ember says. "Maybe if we get back there before Papa Rich notices we're missing, then this will be like nothing happened."

I stop staring at all the guts of the Jeep and look at her in the eyes. She has a point. If the couple makes it down the hill and is able to reach the authorities, then it's just a matter of time until we're rescued. But if we show our hand, and we have Richard chasing after them... Maybe trying to get back to the schoolhouse undetected is a good idea.

"Okay," I say, nodding. "Let's get back."

I never thought I'd be going *back* to the schoolhouse if I ever got my chance of escape, and yet, here I am.

We quickly run back to Hallelujah Junction, scanning the area for any signs of Richard. Excuses were running through my head as to what we will tell him if he catches us outside. I decide to remove the gloves from both of our feet and bury them in some snow just in case we are detected. Maybe I can convince him that Ember and I were going stir crazy and had to get out... barefoot or not. I know it's a stretch, but I have to tell the man something. Ember, however, doesn't have a lying bone in her body. The chances of her getting away with a lie is about as impossible as escaping this godforsaken town.

"If your father notices the tracks in the snow," I say as we get closer and closer to the school, "tell him we wanted to play in the snow."

"He'll know the truth," she says. "He always knows everything."

"Ember," I snap. "You need to listen to me. Tell him we went for a quick walk. Nothing else."

A new fear forms. Ember.

If she tells Richard about the couple, he may try to hide us or even relocate. He may go on the run and take us with him to avoid authorities. Hell... he may kill us both to hide any evidence of kidnapping.

"We went for a walk to get some fresh air," I reiterate. "Are we clear?"

She nods, but I don't really believe her. And as we open the door to the schoolhouse—our prison—I just pray to a God I don't know that I believe in any longer that the couple is reaching civilization and getting help quick.

20

EMBER

I SEE OUR PRINTS ALL OVER THE TOWN BELOW. IF I CAN SEE THEM, then I know Papa Rich can too. There are so many, and two sets have snowshoes. There is no way to explain this. There is no way out.

"Shit," Christopher sees what I do outside the schoolhouse window. "We need to somehow hide all those."

It's snowing but not hard enough. Not fast enough.

Mother Nature is not on our side.

We both have our feet wrapped in a blanket from our bedding, warming them up. I can't imagine going back into the snow now.

"I don't see how we can," I say.

"Okay..." Christopher begins. "We tell him that you and I went for a quick walk outside to enjoy the fresh air. When we were down there, we saw the snowshoe tracks, but saw nothing else. We need to keep to this story."

I nod for Christopher's sake, but I already know we are doomed. Papa Rich knows. I know he knows.

"We just have to buy enough time for them to reach the authorities," he says. He turns to look at me with a look of determination in his eyes. "If he finds out, or if he tries to move all of us, we have to fight him. Do you hear me? We have to do whatever we can to fight the man."

I shake my head as tears well in my eyes.

"Ember, I need you to be strong. I need you to listen to me."

"Christopher—"

"I'm your husband!" he shouts. When I flinch, he softens his facial expression. "I'm sorry for yelling. But I'm your husband and you need to trust me. You need to have faith that I'm going to get us out of this. You just have to be on my team. *My* team."

"I'm scared," I admit.

"I know. But we're so close. We just need time."

Father Time is not on our side either.

Because the next voice I hear is Papa Rich's. "Trust," he begins as he slams the door to the tunnel. "Trust is something that should never be abused."

He knows.

He knows.

Christopher turns to face him without the slightest show of fear. "Let me guess," he begins as he crosses his arms against his chest. "You're annoyed that Ember and I went for a walk? Are we expected to never go outside and see the snow? Ember said that when the tourists leave, we can move about the town more freely."

"Very true," Papa Rich says calmly.

"So then why are you standing there as if we did something wrong?" Christopher asks.

I stare down at my feet when Papa Rich looks into my eyes. I can't face him. I can't lie, and he knows it.

"I know you think that you are the head of the household now that you are married to Ember. That you make the rules," he begins. "But not in Hallelujah Junction. I make the rules here. I oversee this kingdom."

Christopher sighs. "Note taken. We'll remain inside. Anything else?"

"Ember?" Papa Rich says, forcing me to look up at him. "We talk about consequences all the time. You know all about them."

I nod. "Yes, sir. But like Christopher said, we just went for a walk. It was quick because of the snow on our feet."

I had never lied to my father before, and it surprises me how easily the words flow from my mouth.

An evil grin forms on his face as he pulls out his pistol and points it at Christopher.

"Papa!" I scream. "No! Don't kill him. Please!"

Christopher calmly puts up his arms in surrender and says, "Richard, you need to think this through. You don't want my murder on your hands. Who will take care of Ember when you go to jail? You think she can survive out in that world without you *and* me? Think of Ember right now." He glances out the window and then back at the gun. "You know the police are coming. You know this. So, think about the bigger picture. Think about what happens if you kill me. What happens to your daughter?"

"Both of you walk," he demands as he points toward the front door of the schoolhouse. "Don't try anything stupid, son," he warns. "I'll shoot your dick off before I kill you. I won't make your death quick. Listen to every command I say or else."

"Papa, you have this all wrong," I try to lie again, but I walk beside Christopher toward the door as I do.

"Out," Papa demands as we exit into the snow. "To the mill," he says, stabbing the gun into Christopher's back.

The mill?

No!

He's going to push Christopher into the pits! That's the consequence. That's what we get for trying to escape. Even if the couple reaches the police, it will be too late. Christopher will be burned alive by the acid. He'll be dead! No!

The chain rattling between our ankles remind me that there is no chance of running. The gun stabbing Christopher's back as we shuffle our way through the snow brings me to a reality I can't face. There's no hope. No hope. I also know that once Papa Rich has his mind set on something, there is no convincing him otherwise.

Christopher has failed him.

Consequences must be given.

Blood must be shed.

The Devil must be conquered.

No!

I reach out and hold Christopher's hand. My last connection. My last touch of the man I have grown to love. He doesn't deserve this and yet... he will pay for his act. I know there is no way out. No way will Papa allow this crime to go unpunished.

"Papa," I begin, but then stop speaking as we enter the mill. I know my breath is wasted. I've been here before. I know what happens.

"In the garden of evil, someone must pay," Papa says as he leads us to the dangerous acid pit that sits in the middle of the mill.

We walk past the warning signs and even yellow caution tape. We maneuver around the broken planks that hang all around us. It's Hell we have entered.

It's dark.

It's cold.

And as we approach the pit closer, I see what the Devil has waiting for us.

"You son of a bitch," Christopher says, as he sees what I do. "You're sick. You're evil."

"I'm merely the messenger of God. Someone must pay for our sins," Papa Rich says.

On the other side of the pit is the couple we met tied at the ankles and wrists. They are also tied to a wooden beam, helpless and afraid. Their mouths are gagged though I don't see the point in that. No one is around who can hear their screams. When they see us, they both try to struggle against their binds with absolute terror in their eyes. It's almost as if they hope we can save them.

We can't save you.

"Trespassers must be punished," Papa Rich begins like he has in the past when he's about to push guilty tourists to their death.

"No!" Christopher shouts. "Let them go! They did nothing."

Papa Rich gives a slanted grin. "Did you think you would get away with it? Did you think I didn't know they were here? Did you think I'd allow for you to steal my daughter and drive away in that Jeep?" He shakes his head. "No. Amazing how fast you can disable a vehicle with a few pulls of some cables. And shocking how trusting the two were when I pulled up beside them in my ranger's truck. They thought I was there to help." He laughs. "You all underestimated your opponent, and now must pay the price."

He reaches down to a bunch of bags by his feet with the gun still pointing at Christopher. Pulling out rope, he begins to wrap it around our ankle chain and then ties us to another beam directly across from the couple.

"Put out your wrists," Papa demands.

Christopher, who appears stunned as his eyes remain pinned on the innocent couple across the way, puts out his wrists. I do the same and Papa ties us both with the rope. It's tight and rubs our skin raw almost immediately.

Now we are as trapped as they are.

"First, we punish you," he says to Christopher. He pulls out a switchblade and opens it to reveal the blade.

"When you weep upon their graves, you may someday be forgiven, but first you must pay your penance."

Papa shoves us both to the ground where we are sitting among the ancient wooden boards. He takes hold of Christopher's foot and slashes the bottom of it with the knife.

Christopher closes his eyes and hisses out in pain, but does nothing more to fight it.

Papa slices again, and again. Striping the bottom of Christopher's foot with one bloody cut after another.

"Thou shall not run again," Papa Rich says as he reaches for Christopher's other foot and begins slicing the flesh on that one as well.

Blood trickles down Papa's wrist as he holds Christopher's foot up, carving his penance into his body.

I see the pain on Christopher's face, but he never cries out. He remains stoic in his punishment. And though I want to scream out and beg Papa to stop, I also feel a sense of hope. If this is Christopher's only punishment, then maybe he will be spared from the pits. Maybe he won't be sacrificed for our sins. Maybe Papa will have mercy. Maybe Christopher will have to bleed but not stop breathing.

Finally, Papa stops, puts away his bloody switchblade and stands. His dark eyes stare me down. "You've been bad, Ember. So very bad. And what happens next is your punishment. It will be your worst discipline yet."

Now that we are unable to run or attack Papa, he tucks the gun into his belt and walks toward the couple. I watch him as he is careful where he steps because one wrong or careless move and it will be Papa Rich in the acid pit instead of them. I used to hold my breath in the past, fearful that Papa Rich would fall, and I would lose him forever. But now...

Now I watch him in hopes that he will slip.

He needs to join the Devil. His time has come.

God help me, I know his time has come.

"Have no fear," he says to the couple as he nears. "Either God will guide you to the gates of Heaven, or the Devil will be there to pull you into the depths of Hell. I am not the one to judge. Your maker will do that. Pray that you have done enough good in this world to help make His decision easy."

Both begin squirming against the ropes and screaming behind the gags. No one faces death with bravery. Everybody I've watched fall into the pits have fought and screamed until the very end.

Papa Rich turns and points his finger at Christopher and me. "You both did this. Their deaths are on you. Your hands drip with their blood. May God forgive you."

"He's really going to do this," I hear Christopher say under his breath. "A madman."

I can only imagine the thoughts and horror going through Christopher's mind. I still remember the first time I watched someone fall to their death. And though it never gets easier, the one thing that has changed for me is that I know there is nothing I can do to stop it. I've begged in the past, swore to do anything I could. I thought I could recite the Bible or try to reach Papa's heart somehow in the past.

Nothing.

This will happen no matter what we say or do.

Papa pulls out his gun again in case the man or woman get any ideas to try to fight him off as he unfastens the rope. They should fight. They should take the bullet over what will come next. They should choose a fast death over the pits any day, but none of them do. They all comply in some foolish hope that Papa Rich won't follow through if they just be good. If they do as he asks, he will save them.

They are all wrong.

As the couple stand side by side, Papa Rich removes their gags. He always removes the gags because he likes to hear them beg. He likes to hear them scream as their flesh sizzles from their bones.

"Please," the man says first. "We'll leave here and pretend we never came."

"Don't do this," the woman says between sobs. "Please. We won't say a thing. Just let us go."

"Richard!" Christopher shouts. "Let them go and punish me. This is all on me. They did nothing wrong but be in the wrong place at the wrong time. Take me."

"They trespassed. There are signs. They are the rule breakers and must be punished."

Not waiting another moment, Papa Rich shoves the girl and then the man with enough force to make them fall over the edge into the pit of water. Oily, black, mineral-based, and full of acid that no one can survive.

Both scream on the way down, followed by a splash. Then an ear-piercing howl as their bodies struggle to climb the walls as the liquid eats at their skin.

Christopher leans forward which also forces me to. I know he wants to see for himself, although his soul is screaming for him to close his eyes and block it all out. But it's impossible. I've tried. Oh how I've tried.

Looking the other way only makes you see it over and over in your nightmares instead. You must face the horror head on as your blood turns cold and your inner self melts along with the poor souls dying below.

The screams rattle the rafters above and dust falls down upon us.

Their sounds of agony will forever be with me. I will forever be the keeper of their charred and stolen spirits. They are locked inside of me with all the others.

Papa Rich stands and watches. He's proud. He's done what he considers his Godly duty. He always looks the same.

Dark eyes, firm jaw, and arms at his side. And then when the last gurgled scream happens, he raises his hands to the sky as if in offering to God.

21

CHRISTOPHER

"WHAT HAVE YOU DONE?" I HISS AS I STRUGGLE TO HOLD ON TO sanity.

Richard walks toward us slowly. "It's what *you've* done, son. You did this. Those poor people are dead because of you."

My eyes dart to Ember who has tears running down her face, but she seems to have a look of acceptance. There is no outrage, or even fear. She just sits with her head down and in silent sorrow.

And if I didn't understand her fear and how controlled she is by Richard before, I do now. If she has had to witness this awful... Fuck... if she had to watch this before... I can't even—

It isn't just having to watch two people die in the most horrific way possible that has my mind reeling. It's also the knowledge that any chance of escape is crushed and will forever be. The burning in my feet from the wounds is nothing to the pain in my entire core. Defeat and loss of hope is far worse than a cut of a blade.

"And now, Ember, it is your time to suffer your consequences," Richard says as he walks past us.

I position my body in front of Ember to the best that I can considering the ties. "You leave her the fuck alone."

I'll die before I'll let him touch her. I will follow that couple into the pits before I will let Richard harm her in any way.

He ignores my threat and leaves the mill.

I pull Ember closer. "I won't let him hurt you."

She looks up at me with tears in her eyes. "I'm sorry, Christopher. I'm sorry."

"Don't ever apologize for that man. He's not you. You have no control over that crazy."

"Those poor people..."

"*You* didn't do that. *I* didn't do that," I lean forward and kiss her cheek.

"I knew what would happen. I knew. I should have never let us leave the schoolhouse." She looks at the pit. "Now they're dead." She looks at my bloody feet. "How much pain are you in?"

Before I can answer, Richard reenters the mill holding Ember's cat in his arms.

Ember instantly cries out and starts shaking her head.

"No, Papa. No. Please no!"

"You are to blame for this, Ember," Richard says as he approaches the pits with the cat. "It broke my heart watching you try to run away from our home. Our home! You allowed sin to enter our home! You know better. I raised you better."

"I'm so sorry. I truly am. I'll do anything. Just please let Pine Cone go."

The cat tries to break free from Richard's grasp and meows in distress as she does. He only holds tighter and shakes his head.

"You must be punished."

Without another word, Richard tosses the cat into the pit and the sound of Ember's scream mixed with the hissing and screeching of the cat nearly drives me mad. It's the worst sound I have ever heard in my entire life. Pain of the animal mixed with agony of its owner nearly destroys me.

I hold onto Ember as she lurches toward the pit, ripping her skin with the rope and chain. If it weren't for her confines, I have no doubt Ember would throw herself into the pit in hopes of saving her cat.

"No!" she wails. "No! No! No!"

"Hear your cat suffer, girl. Listen to your beloved pet pay for your crimes. Listen to the suffering it must endure."

Ember collapses against me and cries out in the most heart-wrenching and devastated way imaginable.

I kiss her head. I hold her close. I hold her ears so she doesn't have to hear the cat struggle.

I try to soothe her as she claws at me in a desperate need to be free. But I refuse to let her hear. I refuse to let her experience this any longer if I can ease it at all.

"Pine Cone!" she cries out. "No, no, no."

And then the room grows silent.

No more victims.

No more deaths.

All that remains are the ghosts of the murdered haunting us all.

Finally, Richard speaks. "I will untie you now. I trust you to find your way back to the schoolhouse. I have to finish cleaning up the mess you both made and hide the Jeep and all signs of the couple."

He moves toward us with pistol in hand in case I choose to do anything. And if it weren't for the gun, I'd plow into his body, driving him into the pit myself, not caring if he pulls me with him.

"I will burn down your entire world. I swear this," I spat at him, not caring about the consequences. How much worse can they be? What I just witnessed was far worse than anything a sane person could imagine.

He nods, pats an inconsolable Ember on the top of the head. "What I did was harsh," he says. "I had to in order to make sure that the two of you don't ever make this foolish mistake again.

God expects me to watch over the two of you. My family. Always my family."

The man needs to die at whatever cost.

But for now, as the rope is removed and Richard leaves us, I focus all my attention on the broken woman beside me who hasn't stopped crying. She can barely breathe between her body-wracking sobs.

"Come on, Ember. Let's get back," I say softly as I lift her to standing. Devastation has weakened her, and I worry if she'll be able to walk at all. "It's freezing, and we need to get back to where it's warm."

I somehow get us back to our four-wall prison, though we both walk in a daze. I wonder if Ember will ever stop crying, and I wonder if I will ever feel like a human again.

Did I do this?

Am I to blame for the deaths?

I want to say no. I want to blame Richard, but I'm the one who forced Ember to leave. I brought my crisis to the innocent couple. I made their problems my own. I expected them to help even though it cost them their lives.

She hiccups, chokes on her tears, and then starts the morose melody all over again. She allows me to rub heat back into her feet by the wood burning stove, but doesn't speak, doesn't make eye contact, doesn't acknowledge me at all.

Her blonde hair hangs in her face, covering her red-blotched, tear-soaked face, and I have never wanted to hold someone as much before. I also want to scream and rage against Richard, but I don't know where Ember's breaking point is, and I worry one more harsh word will send her over the cliff of sanity never to return again.

"Pine Cone," Ember moans as she curls up on the mattress after I stoke the fire. "My Pine Cone."

I crawl up behind her and spoon her body next to mine. Wrapping my arms around her, I kiss the back of her head and try to comfort. "I'm so sorry, Ember. So sorry."

"Why would he do this? Why?" Her cries intensify.

"Because he's a bad man. He's crazy." I'm careful not to allow my rage to show through and manage to keep my voice even and calm.

I want her to face the facts, but I know I must be easy and tentative in getting there. The only thing good that could come from this nightmarish incident is that Ember may finally see her father for the psychopath he is. She may not resist me so much in planning our escape. She may even become a willing participant once her nearly paralyzing grief subsides some.

Her body shakes as her sobs fill the empty space of the room.

"I promise you; I'll get us out of here. I promise."

She spins away from me and sits up with outrage in her eyes. "Like last time?" she screams. She points at me accusingly. "You didn't listen! I told you what would happen. I told you that we'd get caught. I warned you!"

Fury blazes in her eyes and her sobs blend with her screams.

I reach out to her calmly. "I'm sorry. If I could take away your pain, I would."

She snaps her arm away and turns so her back is to me. "You didn't believe me when I told you there is no way out. He knows everything. I've watched for years how he works. I know you think I'm weak and scared. You thought that because you are stronger than me you could outsmart him." She spins her face to glare at me. "You were wrong! If you had just listened, those people would still be alive. My cat would still be here with me!"

"Hate me if it takes away your pain," I say. "Blame me. Crucify me in all ways. I'd prefer anything else but to know you hurt."

"I don't hate you," she says softly between sniffles. "I just feel so... lost. I feel like I'm sinking and drowning in a hole of despair. I wish Papa Rich would have just pushed me in the pit. I'm so tired. So tired."

I inch to her and take her into my arms from behind. She tenses but doesn't push me away. "I love you, Ember. I love you and wish I had no part in causing you this misery."

She slowly turns her head to look at me with red-rimmed eyes, wipes at her nose, and asks, "You love me?"

I pull her close. "I do. I love you and will do whatever I can to make sure this never happens to you again."

She begins to cry again, harder. "There's nothing you can do. This is our forever, Christopher. Fake happiness, false hope, and nothing but dark and evil. I lied to you when I told you that you could borrow from my happiness. I never had any. I know only sadness and loneliness. I'm a liar. I'm a liar and God finally punished me today. This is all my fault."

"No, Ember." I stroke her hair and squeeze her to me. "There's one person to blame, and he'll pay someday. He'll pay."

"Face reality, Christopher. Trust me. It's the only way."

Broken.

My captured bride now finally reveals just how shackled she is.

"I'll save us. I will."

I lower her down to the bed and hold her close as she cries herself to sleep.

Closing my eyes, I see the couple.

Haunted. I will forever be haunted.

22

CHRISTOPHER

I WAKE TO EMBER HOLDING MY FOOT AS SHE EXAMINES IT. SHE notices I'm awake and says, "We need to get these cuts cleaned up. I'm worried they'll get infected. We shouldn't have gone to sleep with them like this." She furrows her brow and looks at the bed. "We got blood and dirt on our bedding. I'll have to do the wash today."

If it weren't for her puffy and blood-shot eyes, I wouldn't know she had nearly died of a broken heart last night. She almost seems like my normal Ember again.

I sit up and cup her cheek. "I'm not worried about my feet. I'm worried about you."

She gently pulls away from my touch. "I'm fine. I'm not the one with gashes on my feet."

She reminds me of my mother right now. When my father died, my mother gave herself a mere twenty-four hours to mourn and cry, and then it was as if she locked all the emotions inside, never to reveal where the key was. No mention of my father again, all pictures and memories stored away, clothing boxed and donated. She simply wiped him away. Not a single tear was shed again.

Survival.

Ember knows how to survive.

No time for tears in survival.

Knowing that Ember will not be happy until she can tend to my feet, I hobble over to the pitcher of water by the wood stove.

"We'll wash it up first. But I may need to go to the main house to get antiseptic and bandages." She begins to wipe at my feet and focuses on her mission. "Yes, we need to get to the main house. I can't clean these enough with what I have here."

I consider asking her if she's okay but see that she doesn't want to relive yesterday. She's moving forward as if nothing horrific happened, and I need to allow it. I need to allow her to cope with tragedy however she does. Clearly, she is an expert at it.

Instead, I need to focus on what happens next for us.

We need a plan.

I don't think going back to the main house is a good idea. I don't want to face Richard yet, and I don't think Ember should either. The homicidal thoughts in me are strong, and I'm not sure I'd be rational when facing the man so soon after his monstrous acts. But I also know that is where the food is. I'm also half expecting for him to arrive today and force us back into the cellar.

He should.

He should expect that I will only try to escape again with more vengeance.

The only lesson he has taught me is that I need to get out of here now. There is never going to be the right time. He's a smart man who I didn't give enough credit to. I thought I could outwit him, but now... I know I have to just force the hand. I have to *make* the escape happen at whatever cost.

Leaving us in the schoolhouse with only a chain around our ankles will be his biggest mistake. Underestimating our level of fear and that it will control us from this point on, is a crucial mistake. I don't fear the man will kill me. No... my true fear is that I will spend the rest of my life in Hallelujah Junction. And after yesterday... I will die trying to escape rather than spend more time here. He should have pushed me in the acid pits. He will regret that he didn't.

And it's not just about me anymore. Ember is in the mix. I meant it when I told her last night that I loved her. I do. What that means, and what that looks like, I have no idea. Nothing is normal with her and me, but that doesn't take away the emotions I have for her inside. Were they forced upon me? Yes, but regardless how they came, they still exist.

If I can only make one captive vow, it will be to save this woman.

It is no longer about me.

I will save Ember until my last breath.

I prefer to end up in the pit of acid before accepting our life here.

"He'll avoid us today," she says as if reading my mind. "He always avoids me for days after... after consequences."

"He won't be at the main house?" I ask.

She shakes her head. "Maybe he's ashamed." She swallows hard. "He should be."

"Where does he go?"

She shrugs. "Sometimes off into the hills to see Scarecrow. Sometimes to town. Sometimes... I don't know."

My mind runs wild again with ideas. He's gone...

"Let's get your feet bandaged and then we can figure out breakfast," Ember says with a warm smile. She appears as if she's aged overnight, but at the same time, her youthful joy is slowly returning. "I don't like you walking through the tunnel barefoot, but we'll clean them good in the bathroom."

When we get to the main house, we oddly both head to the cellar rather than the main living area. I don't know if it's because we both worry Richard is still near and, in a way, we are hiding from him. Or maybe it has an odd feeling of safety and familiarity. Regardless of the reason, we go to the cellar and I carry my old chair of dignity to the bathroom and sit down so Ember can tend to me.

"There's so much dried blood, that it's hard to see," she says as her brow furrows. She reaches for a lantern and matches and lights it so she can see better.

"I think they were surface cuts," I say, looking around the room, thinking.

Thinking.

I won't stop thinking until we are out of here.

She opens the medicine cabinet and pulls out peroxide and bandages. The sight of blood doesn't seem to bother her which fascinates me. Although after what we both watched last night, a few bloody cuts on the bottom of a man's feet seems like child's play.

She reaches for the handle in the shower and starts the water. "I think it's best for you to shower and really get the feet clean," she directs. "Do you want me to wash your clothes again?"

I shake my head. "You just did."

I know she wants to keep busy. My mother always tried to keep busy too after Dad's death. I recognize this tactic. But I do get up, undress and get into the shower to rinse off all the blood, the dirt, and the memories of the mill. Ember has to stand right next to the shower with only the curtain separating us due to the chain. It's how we've showered up until this point, which seems silly, but I respect her discomfort with nudity and being near me in that way.

"What about you?" I call out as I begin to lather up with soap. "A shower might make you feel a lot better too."

I'm surprised when the shower curtain is pushed to the side and a naked Ember joins me under the stream of water.

"Hold me," she says. "I just want to forget that yesterday even happened." She looks up into my eyes and brings her lips to mine. "Help me forget."

I'm taken aback by her boldness, but I do exactly as she asks. I move her body so that she is in the stream of water completely. If there is a way to wash away our misery, I would. She presses her forehead to my chest and releases a shaky breath.

"I want to leave here," she says. "I want to leave and never look back again."

Words I had been waiting to hear.

Finally... finally...

"Then we will," I say as I tighten my hold on her as warm water covers our bodies in a cascade of hope.

"You won't leave me?"

"Never," I say as I tilt her face up to me and press my lips to hers.

My body becomes alive, and I realize I need her as much as she does me to forget. For a moment in time, I need to just feel comfort and hope.

I run circles along her heated flesh, dipping my hand lower between her legs. My fingers run along her silky folds, spreading signs of her arousal all over her pussy, mixing with the stream of water from the showerhead. She attempts to clamp her legs together to conceal her arousal.

I nudge her thighs wider with my hand. I dip my finger back to her soaking pussy, move my finger to her clit, and caress it ever so gently.

Ember tenses and looks at me with wide eyes. The hunger in her eyes nearly changes her appearance. From innocent and afraid, to sexual vixen in seconds.

"Do you like that?" I ask.

She nods and then places her head on my chest again as she moans out in pleasure as I continue to massage her clit.

Heat radiates off her body, and my cock throbs in need.

Leaning down and kissing her lips, I murmur against them, "I need to be inside you."

I flip her around and press her palms against the wall of the shower. I spread her legs and pull her hips out so her ass is on full display for my viewing. I consider that I may be being a tad too aggressive or harsh for her still sexual inexperience, but I can't help myself. My own needs take over, and like she said to me... I need to forget as well. Right now, I want to think of nothing more than being with this woman. I want to pretend that we aren't in a cellar. That we aren't chained together. I want to block out the Hell that I am in and focus on the only shining beacon I've had this entire time.

Taking hold of my cock, I guide it to her pussy and press in with one thrust. I pause when I'm buried balls deep inside of her so we can both adjust to the sensation. She gasps and her breathing increases in speed, and I love watching her delicate fingers splayed against the tile.

Not being able to control my urge to fuck her hard, I begin doing exactly that. Over and over, I pound into her. I wrap my arm around her waist, pulling her into me, and I use the other hand to support my weight against the wall.

"Yes," she pants as tiny moans blend with the sound of the shower cascading around us.

Her pussy is tight around me, and I know I'm spreading her wide with every forceful drive of my cock.

"Release," I command as I push even deeper, hearing her mewls intensify.

Being the perfect obedient wife, I feel her body tense beneath me, and the walls of her sex tighten around my dick. She presses her forehead to the tile and cries out as her body nearly vibrates against mine.

It's all I need to feel my own orgasm near. Pumping in and out a few more times, I take hold of my cock and pull out as I shoot come all over her ass. Not wasting a second, I spin her around, kiss her with the same desire that demanded I take her, and I hold her in my arms as I rinse her body from my passion.

"I love you, Christopher," she says as she looks up at me, eyelashes fluttering, and with blue eyes I can get lost in.

I tighten my hold of her and kiss her on the top of the head. "I love you. I don't know what the future looks like, but I'm never going to let you go."

"I won't ever let you go." I feel her thin arms squeeze around my waist, and I know she means every single word.

What does our future look like?

I have no idea.

Are we to be trapped for the rest of our lives in this prison? Will there now be two ghosts of Hallelujah Junction? Will I become folklore as well?

A husband and wife forever bound in love in the afterlife.

Stories will be told. Sightings will occur. A man and a wife side by side staring out of the schoolhouse to the people below.

Is this my future?

I don't want to be a ghost. I want to pull Ember from the underworld and bring her back to life. I want a life. A real life for the two of us. A renewed energy surges through me. I'll save us. *We* will save us.

23

EMBER

"Papa Rich is gone," I say to Christopher as I stare out the kitchen window. "I see his snowshoe tracks leading up to the hills. He's off to see Scarecrow and pray. He does this after he feels he's... gone too far."

Christopher leans over my shoulder to see for himself. "Where does Scarecrow live?"

"I've only been to Scarecrow's place once. It's far up in the hills. There was once another mining town that barely stands that he calls home. He lives in an old church that he's made his home. It's one of the few buildings that are left standing. The other structures have really been abused by the elements and aren't inhabitable. Not that Scarecrow would want to have neighbors. He likes to live out there by himself. Although he is on the hunt for a wife."

"Jesus, how many mining towns are there?"

I chuckle. "A lot actually. They are splattered through the Nevada hills and desert and go into California. Some are preserved by the states and some aren't."

"How long is he usually gone when he goes and visits Scarecrow? Are we talking hours? Days?" Christopher pushes.

"He'll be gone all day for sure. Papa Rich rarely spends the night there. If weather comes in, maybe..."

Christopher spins me around so I have to look at him. "Ember, did you mean it when you said you want to leave?"

My heart skips and nausea rolls through my stomach. I nod slowly. "Yes, but... I can't bear another consequence if we do something foolish and get caught."

"We have to try to get out of here. This may be our only chance," he says as he glances out the window again. "Can you show me his room?"

That request seems simple and harmless enough. What Papa Rich doesn't know...

I lead us down the narrow hallway and stop before his door. There is a split second I consider turning us around. I'm so programmed to obey and do nothing against my father, and yet, with Christopher by my side, I feel I can break the rule of never entering his room.

I turn the door handle with shaky hands and the door opens. It's the first time I've seen his room in all my life. This is his special place. His sanctuary. I'm invading his space, and I begin to panic.

"What if he knows? He always knows," I say with a weak voice as my knees begin to tremble. I yank on Christopher's arm. "There's nothing in here we need. Let's go."

"I only need a couple of minutes to look around."

I see his single bed which is nicely made. The rest of the furnishings are basic. There is a dresser, a nightstand and a chair. No paintings, no decorations, nothing that makes the room special. But Papa Rich never believed in materialistic things.

Riches are the root to evil.

"We're going to be gone before he returns," Christopher announces as he leads the charge into the room. "He won't ever know we were in here."

Christopher goes straight to the closet door and opens it. The first thing we see is Papa's ranger uniforms hanging nicely in a row. No other clothes are hanging with them. Christopher smiles when he looks to the ground and sees a pair of hiking boots, and my goloshes that I got to wear when Papa and I went snowshoeing together before... well... before he stole Christopher. He picks them up, hands me my shoes, and leads us back to the chair and sits down and starts putting the hiking boots on.

"They're tight, but better than nothing." Christopher's smile grows. "He fucked up. He really didn't think before he left. Did he really think we'd do nothing?"

I can now see what Christopher is thinking. He plans to have us try to hike out of here again, but at least this time we won't be barefoot.

"It's far," I say. "Even with shoes, we may not get out of here and into town before he returns and hunts us down with the ranger truck." I'm not just telling this to Christopher out of fear, but out of reason. Christopher has underestimated my father before, and I refuse to let that happen again.

Christopher moves on as if I didn't say a single word. He helps me put on my boots and then turns his attention to the dresser. He begins pulling out clothing in search for something warm. Satisfied when he finds some sweaters, he quickly pulls one over his head and then dresses me in one as well which dwarfs my body in wool.

"Do you think he has coats anywhere?"

"There's a hall closet with his ranger coats. I'm sure he has his thick one on now for his hike." I know he has a rain coat and a lighter jacket as well.

Christopher reaches for the quilt on the bed and pulls it off. He bundles it in his arms and leads us out of the room.

"Even if we are warm enough," I begin. "It's about how much time we have. It will take us hours to get down the hill. We will be racing against the time it takes for him to return and him jumping in the truck. You know he'll come after us."

"What about the truck?" Christopher asks. The mention of

the truck only fuels his exit plan ideas more. "Is there any way we can find his keys?"

"He'd not leave the keys. He isn't that stupid," I say, not even having to look to see. Although I point to a drawer. "If they are anywhere, they are in that drawer."

Christopher nearly has us sprinting to see, and I watch his face fall as he finds the drawer empty as I expected.

I look outside and see that it's snowing again. The thought of hiking down a hill to the town is daunting. Especially chained together. We struggle to walk comfortably, let alone try to run while shackled. In fact, it feels near impossible. It will be cold. We can die of hyperthermia, shoes or not. And if we get caught...

Papa Rich will torture Christopher right in front of my eyes. He can't take anything more from me now that Pine Cone is gone, but he can kill Christopher. He can make me live the rest of my life without him. I also know that Papa Rich will make me marry Scarecrow as my penance, and I prefer to die in the acid pit over that.

"I think we need to think this through," I begin.

Christopher takes my hand and brushes my hair away from my face. "I know you're afraid. I know warning bells are going off in your head, but I need you to trust me. I need you to give your all. We can escape here if we stick to my plan. I need you not to fight me. I need you to work with me on this. We'll be free, Ember. I swear to you, we will be."

I want to do what Christopher asks. I want to be a good wife. But more than that, I want to be free.

Yes, free.

I don't even know what that word really means. Away from Papa Rich, I suppose means free. Not having to ever see Scarecrow again means free. Leaving Hallelujah Junction and not having to walk amongst the tunnels or be forever locked in a schoolhouse would be free.

But then what?

Where will I live? What will I do?

Who will I be?

Will I be Ember the Hallelujah Junction ghost forever?

I don't know what the world looks like. I don't know what people will say or do. I don't know how to live and breathe in another world. I may be in a cage now like an animal, but I'm fed, I'm protected...

"My mother," I say to Christopher. "If I leave here, who will protect me from my mother? She could find out I'm alive and where to find me. Papa Rich warned me that leaving here means she can find me."

Christopher places his palms on both sides of my face and stares at me in the eyes. "It's a story," he begins. "Richard made this up to scare you and to explain why he would never let you leave this town. The real reason he keeps you hidden from the world is because he'd go to jail if anyone found out about you. You aren't his. You never were. He kidnapped you, Ember. He kept you locked here in his own manipulative way. I know that's hard to hear, but it's the truth. He stole you."

I shake my head, not wanting to hear the words that deep down I know to be true.

"Why?" I swallow hard and divert my eyes from Christopher's stare. "Why would he do that to me? Why would he want to keep me locked up? He's my father. He loves me."

"Ember..." Christopher leans forward and kisses my forehead and then embraces me. "He's a sick man. I can't give you a reason for why he does what he does. He's killed people. Only monsters and demons kill people. He's not your father. He's nothing but darkness, and you have to escape that. You believe we have to get away, right?"

I nod against his chest. "Yes."

I begin to cry, and I don't know why. Is it because I'm scared? Is it because I'm leaving Papa Rich and it's breaking my heart thinking about what I will do without him? Am I sick like him because a part of me doesn't want to leave? Part of me wants to stay... why?

But the sane part of me screams to my soul. I know we have to leave. Not just because of my freedom but because of Christopher's. He can't spend the rest of his life chained to me in a place that isn't his home.

This isn't right. It's never been right.

"And if by some chance," Christopher adds, "you do have some crazy mother out there who wants to harm you, I'll protect you with my life. You have nothing to worry about."

"Then we should go," I say with a sudden spike of courage. "If we try to run, we may beat him before he returns."

24

CHRISTOPHER

EMBER'S RIGHT. WE CAN TRY TO RUN AS FAST AS WE CAN IN THE snow, but it will take time. Time we might not have. And I can't risk us being caught again. This is our one shot, and if I don't plan this out perfectly, then Richard will win again. I can't have that happen.

"We need the authorities to come to us," I say.

"I told you there is no phone or radio. Well there is, but I know Richard has that on him," Ember says.

I freeze for a second realizing that Ember has called her Papa Rich by his full name. She's morphing before my eyes. Courage looks good on her, and I've never been prouder. I know this can't be easy for her. I can't imagine how terrified she must be. And not just because of the fear of being caught. But I also know she's afraid of what happens if we actually do escape. She has no idea what awaits her on the other side.

And her thoughts are valid.

Can Ember survive in the world I live? This is a girl who has never worn shoes or watched television. Electronics and the Internet don't exist in her mind. She doesn't know what it's like to have the constant buzz of sound in her ears from city life. She doesn't even know what a city is. I'm the third person in her life she has ever spoken to since she was taken. She's been a caged bird that has been raised in captivity. Is it fair to throw her out to the wild?

She has no idea what modern society is like, and I'm about to toss her into the lion's den if we do manage to escape. The thought of what happens next for Ember is almost as terrifying as Richard finding and stopping us.

We will be free from the evil of Richard, but not necessarily free from evil in general. The world is hard and brutal at times, and it can chew up a normal human being. But Ember... she's different. She's fragile. And the world could engulf her. Life could be harder for her outside this town than it is inside it, but no matter how hard, anything is better than the hell of Hallelujah Junction.

"I have an idea that is going to help us," I say. "We will bring the authorities to us."

I lead us down to the cellar where we have left the lantern still lit. I pick it up and look at the small flame, knowing exactly what I have to do. Ember looks at me with confusion.

"We're going to catch the town on fire before we leave," I say, reaching for the matches as well.

"What? No. We can't." Ember tugs at my arm and shakes her head furiously. "It's been here for decades. Long before us. We can't burn it. The history... we can't. It's my home."

"It's not your home." I try to take a deep breath and soften my voice. I know I have to be gentle with Ember even if I grow frustrated. I have to put myself in her situation, but at the same time, I know we are running against the clock.

"Christopher, I don't—"

"We have no other choice," I defend. "You're right in saying that Richard might reach us before we get all the way to town. But if the authorities see the smoke and come, they will meet us halfway down the hill. They will get to us before Richard. The fire will be our own S.O.S."

"But if he sees the smoke before he reaches Scarecrow, he may return quicker than planned," she points out.

I pause and consider her words. "True. But it's a risk we have to take."

Not wanting to wait another second, I take the lantern over to the pile of dirty blankets that I spent my first week sleeping on. It will be therapeutic in a twisted way to watch the soiled material burn. The cellar should be the first place in this town to burn to the ground.

When they ignite almost immediately, I know we have crossed the line of no return. I lead us to the bathroom and yank the bottle of rubbing alcohol out of the medicine cabinet and begin splattering it all over the floor to help aid the flames in mastering the room.

We both stand for several minutes and watch the blankets burn and the fire spread across the floorboards, making its way to the wooden crates. I know that once the flames lick the wood, it won't be long until the fire takes over completely.

Taking Ember by the hand, I lead us upstairs to the kitchen to grab the quilt and the coats Ember pulled out of the closet. I put the heaviest coat on her and then also wrap her tiny frame in the quilt. I pray she will be warm enough. We don't have to last long... just until help comes from the fire department.

I also grab the bottle of Jack Daniels that Richard bought me to help ignite the fires I will set. Once we have everything in hand, I turn on the gas stove and allow the gas to run without a flame. It will help ignite the fire even more when it reaches the kitchen.

"I'm hoping there's a sprinkler system on the buildings below," I say, thinking that there may be in some of the buildings.

I'm pretty sure the Forest Department would want that, but then if that is the case, there may also be automatic fire alarms that go straight to a company notifying of a fire emergency. Either way, my intent is to start them all aflame. But first... the fucking mill must burn to the ground.

It's easier to walk to the mill wearing shoes, even if they are so tight that they border on painful, but at least my feet aren't freezing in the snow.

"I don't want to go back there," Ember says, tugging on my arm and stopping in her tracks. "I don't want to go anywhere near it."

I don't blame her, but this is still something I feel I must do. "Only for a second," I say with the lantern in my hand. "We're burning the fucker from existence."

She nibbles her lower lip and stares ahead as if seeing ghosts I can't see. Knowing how painful it was for me to watch that couple die in the most gory and disgusting way, I can only imagine all the memories Ember must have of the mill. She had to watch death after death of innocent people, not to mention her precious cat. I'm sure she wants to see it forever vanish from her mind as well.

"We need to do it for all who died there," I say. "It needs to never exist again."

Appearing satisfied with my answer, she continues on toward the mill. When we get there, I smell sulfur and other minerals, but I also feel I smell death.

The mill is the shallow grave of many, and it reeks of their sizzled bones. If there is an entrance to hell, then this mill is it, and I feel it my duty to burn it to the ground and allow the poor souls to rest in peace with their ashes being all that remains.

I notice a piece of wood that I feel I can use as a torch that I can light and then throw into the building without having to actually go inside. I agree with Ember on not wanting to have to see the inside of the gut of the Devil again. I don't want to risk seeing the ghosts of the couple who had wanted to help us. I don't want to see their eyes looking at me, accusing me of causing their deaths. I don't want to hear the howls of their misery as the sounds forever haunt the mill.

Tossing the lit torch inside, and then lighting all the spare wood on the outside of the mill, Ember and I stand hand in hand as the structure lights. I take a swig of the last of the Jack in celebration of seeing this building ignite. My face heats from the fire, and I know we must move on to another building. As much as I would like to stand before it and watch it melt before me, I know we have little time.

As we walk to the schoolhouse, Ember shakes her head. "Burn down all the other buildings. But not that one. Leave that one."

I don't want to leave a single building of this awful town. I want nothing but charred earth when done, but I have to take Ember's feelings into consideration. This isn't just about me. It's about her. This nightmare is one she has lived her entire life and if anyone gets to make the call, it's her.

I squeeze her hand that I haven't released and agree. I tighten the quilt around her to try to ease the shivers I see wrack her body. "If that's what you want."

"I don't want to see it die. Not because of me. It deserves to stand on that hill. It was my safe place. It protected me. I need to protect it now."

We make our way to the other buildings that are part of the tourist section. I look over my shoulder and see the main house is completely engulfed in flames, and the mill is as well. I have never seen a more morbid and beautiful sight in my life. Even if Richard catches us... there will be no Hallelujah Junction to return to. Nothing but ash. Nothing but embers. Nothing but the ghosts with no place to call their own any longer.

The old wood lights up fast, and I'm pleased to see that the ranger's office appears to be hardwired to an alarm. My hope is that by now, the authorities have been notified of a fire, and help is coming.

"Oh my God," Ember screams as she points up toward the mill. "He's coming! Richard is coming!"

I snap my head in the direction she's pointing and see Richard running as fast as he can in his snowshoes down the hill. His strides are wide, and his arms propel him faster down the hill than I think is possible. His body charges forward with a mission to save, with a goal to capture his prey, and a determination to be victorious.

He's watching everything that has ever meant a thing to him go up in flames. He has to witness it all disappear before him.

I warned him that I would see his world burn.

Burn.

Burn!

By God I am burning it all to the fucking ground.

He's still a distance from us, and I know if we act fast, we can still get away. I also know it's likely he has his pistol on him, and after what he sees we are doing to his precious town, he will no doubt aim the gun right between my eyes and pull the trigger.

I still have the lantern with me, and I run Ember and me toward his truck which is parked by the ranger's office. I don't want to wait for the flames to reach the truck on their own in case Richard gets to the vehicle before they do. I decide I need to speed up the process. I run to the gas tank and open it. I then rip a piece of fabric from the hem of Ember's dress and stick it in. I then pull out the gas-soaked material, stick in the clean side, and then light it.

Not waiting to see the truck light, and concerned it could explode, I take Ember by the hand. "Run. Run as fast as you can. He's coming, but he's not going to catch us."

I've already decided in my mind that if he does catch up with us, I will fight to my death. I will strangle the man to death if I have to. I will kill him at whatever cost.

I can hear the fire burning behind us, and with a quick glance over my shoulder, I see the truck light up in flames. Now it will be a matter of if Richard can outrun us. Yes, we are chained together, but we have a head start. He's still a ways away from the mill, and he has a long distance to even get where we are.

"Run!"

Ember and I begin hobbling side by side as if we are running a potato-sack race. Step after step, we make our way out of the burning town. When we hit the parking lot, I pause just enough to see if I can view where Richard is. I see him run into the main house, and by the sudden stop of our run, Ember must see the same thing.

"No! He's going inside! The fire! It will burn him alive," she screams.

I have no idea why he's running inside the burning building. Maybe to get the pistol I incorrectly assumed he was carrying. Maybe there is something valuable inside he can't live without. Maybe he thinks he can save it.

It's Ember...

He doesn't see us. He doesn't know Ember is outside on the run.

He thinks she's inside burning to death, or at least could be. He's running into the burning building to save his daughter. He'll die to save her. He won't allow her to die.

Monster or not... he's still a father.

And because of that... the flames with swallow him whole.

"Christopher! He's going to die in there."

There's nothing we can do, and even if we could, I won't. I know I can't allow Ember to break down now or try to foolishly insist we return to help.

"Don't look. Run," I order, and thank God, she obeys.

I can only imagine what watching the only world she has ever known burn around her is doing to her sanity. But Richard can emerge from the fire any second and catch up to us. "We need to keep running, Ember. Run. Our lives depend on it."

The mill is collapsing, the main house with the cellar underneath is completely engulfed, and the rest of the town is turning into an inferno. It won't be long until nothing is left at all. But the schoolhouse... the schoolhouse on the top of the hill remains untouched. The only thing different about the schoolhouse is that the ghost of Hallelujah Junction is no longer inside. She's beside me. She's my captive bride. She's mine and will never return to her eternal damnation.

Ember looks over her shoulder again, hesitates for a moment, but then allows me to tug her forward. I see tears running down her face, and my heart breaks for her.

We run down the hill with every last bit of energy we have. I feel evil breathing down my neck, but I plow forward. I know the Devil is reaching out with his claws to pull us back in, but I refuse to let it happen. I don't look back in fear of what I will see.

I just hold on to Ember and emerge from the flames.

The snow bites at our faces, and yet we power on. With my wife by my side, I know we are close. We are so close to breaking free. One foot after another.

One foot after another.

Goodbye Devil... goodbye Hell...

"What is that sound?" Ember asks, still running as fast as she possibly can.

"Our future, Ember. That's the sound of our future."

Click here for KEPT BRIDE.

Thank you for taking the time to read all about Ember and Christopher. But their story doesn't stop yet. The Secret Bride Trilogy follows them in the next two books, KEPT BRIDE and TAKEN BRIDE. I hope you continue on with their journey.

KEPT BRIDE

THE SECRET BRIDE SERIES - BOOK TWO

DEDICATION

To my husband. I'll be your Kept Bride forever.

PROLOGUE

CHRISTOPHER

FLAMES IN THE SKY, SMOKE IN OUR EYES, AND BLINDING LIGHTS—WE are no longer alone.

I thought I'd seen fear before, but nothing measures up to what I see in Ember's eyes now. She's trapped in a terror I can't save her from, though I try.

"It's okay," I shout above the sirens of the firetrucks and the police cars. "We're going to be okay." Even as I repeat the words, I don't know what "okay" looks like. "Help is here."

I hold her hand in mine as I wave down the speeding vehicles with my other.

It becomes a blur after that. So many questions, so many people, so many curious eyes looking.

We're emerging from the ashes, and yet it still feels as if the devil takes hold.

I keep waiting for Richard to march from the smoky landscape, take us both prisoner again, and the chain to never be removed.

I want a gun to defend myself but know there isn't a single police officer who will give me one.

I want to run up to the burning main house with the

firefighters just so I can see the corpse of the monster, known as Richard, sizzle to ash. I want to see his death with my own eyes, but I'm also aware that is not a possibility.

For now, I have to be content that we are saved.

Saved... but not necessarily *safe*.

Because what does *safe* really mean?

1

CHRISTOPHER

"I don't know how many times I have to answer the same questions," I say, leaning back in the metal chair, feeling it dig into my achy back. "I need to see Ember."

"Just a few more questions," Detective Jackson says. "She's still being questioned too, so if you can just be patient, we—"

"I've been patient enough," I snap. "I told you all that I know, and I also told you that Ember has to be terrified right now. She's not used to people, and I need to be by her side. It's been hours, and I'm exhausted. I don't know what more I can offer. I told you all about that psychopath, about me being chained to a goddamn wall and forced to marry his daughter. I told you every last sick detail. What more do you want from me?"

Detective Jackson looks down at his notes as if he didn't listen to a word I said and asks, "So, this Ember woman... you said she claims she's been there since she was a child?"

"Yes," I say on a heavy exhale. "She's as much a victim as I am." I stand up, place my palms on the table, and stare down the detective. "Do I need to ask for my attorney? Because I'm starting to feel that way."

Detective Jackson leans back in the chair and crosses his arms. "Do you feel there is a reason to have an attorney?"

"You tell me," I say and then look at the mirror in the room, trying to see whoever is on the other side. But instead, all I see is my reflection.

Wearing clothing they give to inmates, with matching shoes, I look like a stranger. My hair is long and hangs in my face. I look like I've lost weight while I was losing months of my life. I suppose I should be grateful for the dry clothes they gave Ember and me when we arrived, but it only reminds me of just how much of a prison I've been living in.

"Just a few more questions," Jackson pushes on.

"Unless you're going to charge me or Ember with anything, we're leaving. So please take me to her. Now."

"I understand your frustration," he says. "But the Feds just arrived and are asking Ember more questions."

"I need to see her. I need to be with her. And like I said, unless you're arresting us, I expect to be taken to her now."

Ember hadn't said a word to me since the rescue. She answered all the questions the medics asked as they tended to our wounds around our ankles caused by the chains. And although she was polite and was free with her answers, it seemed as if every syllable hurt her. I knew she hadn't spoken to a single soul other than her father, me, and Scarecrow. I knew she had to be so scared, and to be without me had to have her even more so.

I'm hating the interrogation from the police, so I can only imagine how she must be handling it.

"I'll make a deal with you," Detective Jackson says as he joins me in standing. "I'll bring you to her, but only if you can stay a little bit longer to allow the Feds to get what they want."

I know I don't have to agree to anything, since we aren't under arrest, but I also want to help put this nightmare to an end.

I nod and follow him out of the room and down the hall to another interrogation room.

When I enter, I see Ember looking so tiny and frail on a chair that seems to nearly swallow her up. Her wide eyes lock with mine, and her lower lip trembles the minute she sees me.

I rush to where she sits and kneel at her feet, looking up at her. "Hey," I say softly. "I'm here now. I'm not going to leave your side again." I take her hand, which is cold from the chill in the air of the sterile room. "Are you doing all right?"

Her eyes dart to the man in front of her and then to me. She nods. "They keep asking me about Papa Rich and Scarecrow, and—"

"I know," I interrupt as I get up and take the seat next to her. "It's almost over." I look directly into the men's eyes as they sit across from us. "Correct? Do you have what you need?"

The man looks at Detective Jackson, who motions for him to join him outside. As the two men leave the room, I position my body so I can look at Ember head-on.

Taking both her hands into mine, I say, "We're going to get out of here soon. I promise."

"And then what? Where will we go?" she asks, which makes sense. The only home she has ever known has just burned to the ground.

"I called my mother," I begin. "After nearly causing the woman to have a stroke from hearing from her *dead son*, I made arrangements."

Ember shakes her head. "I don't understand. Arrangements?"

"My mother is in Palm Springs with some of her friends for a vacation. Hearing that we're here... alive... she chartered a private plane so we can get back to New York as fast as possible. She's on her way now to pick us up."

"New York?"

"That's where I live, remember?" I prompt softly, understanding this has to be a lot for Ember to take in. "It's where we will both live now."

Her hands shake in mine, and all I want to do is sweep her up into my arms, get her as far away from Nevada and Hallelujah Junction as I can, and never speak of Papa Rich and this hell ever again. But as the detectives reenter the room, I know I can't have everything right away.

"If you don't mind, we have a couple more questions," Detective Jackson says. "This is Federal Agent Martinez."

"Go ahead," I say, deciding I will answer all the questions I can to avoid them from asking Ember. I can feel in my gut that the poor girl is reaching her max on what she can take.

"So, there are some things you both have said that don't exactly add up. You said you saw this *Papa Rich* run into the burning house?" Agent Martinez asks.

"Yes," I say as I squeeze Ember's hand in reassurance that I have this handled. "I think we've both told you this multiple times."

"No body was discovered in the house," Martinez tells us. "In fact, no bodies have been discovered anywhere in the structures.

I feel Ember's hand go limp in mine. The gut-punching news has me swallowing hard but not wanting to believe the words.

"We saw him go inside," I say. "The house was engulfed in flames."

"But you also both say you continued running and never looked back. Neither of you know if he left the house or not. Correct?"

"Papa Rich is alive?" Ember's shaky voice cuts in. A single tear falls down her face, and I don't know if it's from relief or fear.

Martinez and Jackson both glare at Ember. "You said you don't know where his friend 'Scarecrow' lives. Are you sure you've never visited or heard any details that could help us track this fellow down?"

Ember shakes her head. "He always came to us, or Papa Rich went to him without me. I know he's in the hills somewhere, and it's not exactly close. It takes all day to go back and forth from his home to Hallelujah Junction."

"Did either of you see Scarecrow during the fire?"

"No," I answer. "Are you telling us that you think Richard is still alive? Maybe hiding out with Scarecrow?"

"We're exploring all possibilities right now. All we know is there are no signs of Richard dying in the fire like you both claim."

Ember gasps and looks at me with renewed terror in her eyes. "He's going to find us. He's going to punish us. He won't give up until he does."

I run my hand over the side of her head, caressing her soft blonde locks. "Shh," I try to soothe. "He's not going to be able to find us. And *if* he's alive—*if*—then these men right here are going to find him and lock him away for life." I continue stroking her hair, trying to pet her anxiety away. "We're safe now. I promise you. We're safe."

I glare at the men, pissed that they are only adding to Ember's fear. "If he's not dead, find the sick asshole. You're both wasting time by asking us the same questions over and over."

Detective Jackson looks down at his notes and papers. "Ember, we also looked into the report you gave about how Papa Rich found you and brought you to Hallelujah Junction. The story of being picked up in a nearby town and rescuing you from your mother. We went back and looked up if there were any reports of kidnapping around that time, which there weren't necessarily. But there are records of a young girl who Child Protective Services visited in the area who suddenly turned up missing with no notice from the mother or forwarding address. The child's name was Amber Jennings. Amber... not Ember." He takes a moment for the words to sink in. "We believe Amber Jennings is you." He pushes a file toward us. "There's a picture in there. It looks like a younger version of you."

Ember opens the file and stares down at a picture that no doubt is of her as a five-year-old. You can see the familiarity in the eyes. Such big, blue, and haunted eyes.

"Amber?" she questions more to herself than anyone else. "No, my name is Ember."

"Is that picture you?"

She nods. "But my name is Ember. Not Amber."

"Maybe now... but you were once Amber Jennings."

Tears fill her eyes, and she asks, "What about my mother? Will she know where I am now? Papa Rich told me that she'd kill me if she ever found where I was."

I reach over and close the file, feeling as if this is all too much for her. "It doesn't matter. You're Ember now. And you're safe. The past is the past. Your mother can't hurt you. No one can hurt you."

"We pulled up information on your mother, and I'm sorry to say—or maybe in your case, happy to inform you—she died thirteen years ago."

"Thirteen?" Ember parrots, and without even having to hear the words, I know what she's thinking. She's been safe for thirteen years from all the horror stories Papa Rich told her about her mother coming to hurt her if she ever discovered her location. She could have left the walls of the schoolhouse living as the ghost of Hallelujah Junction had she known the woman didn't exist anymore.

"We've also pulled up every report of missing people who have visited Hallelujah Junction with the belief that their cause of death is due to the acid pit and the old mill," Agent Martinez says. "We have found a report for a couple who matches your description of the victims you witnessed pushed into the pit." He slides over the paper with their photos on it. "Are these the people you encountered?"

I glance down and nod as I rub Ember's back. On the surface, Ember is holding it together. And maybe she is. But I can't help but feel we are walking a very dangerous tightrope, and she's about to come crashing down any second.

"We weren't aware they went to Hallelujah Junction," Detective Jackson says.

"They were trying to help us," Ember murmurs.

"As for the others," Martinez continues, "Ember, did you help your father kill those people?"

I stand up and hit my hand on the table. "That's enough! Unless you both plan to charge Ember or me with anything, we are leaving. We've been here voluntarily for long enough. My wife and I have nothing left to say unless a lawyer is present."

Ember reaches for my arm and gently pulls me down. "It's okay, Christopher. I don't mind answering." She looks at the detective and agent. "All I know is I didn't stop it."

"You *couldn't* stop it," I boom.

"And I will have to live with that and their deaths for the rest of my life," she adds.

"The man was sick!" I shout, but then lower my voice to add, "More than you can imagine. He kidnapped and had me locked in a cellar. Chained to a wall like a rabid dog. I watched as he killed that couple with zero remorse, and there was nothing I, or Ember, could do to stop it. There is absolutely no way Ember had anything to do with those deaths. Not at all. And I'm not going to sit here with my wife and allow this conversation to go in that direction. Are we clear?"

Rather than answering my demand of a question, Martinez asks, "If your father were to run and hide somewhere, where do you think he'd go? Other than this Scarecrow man, does he have any other family or friends?"

Ember shakes her head with a deep sadness in her eyes. "We had no one. We were alone. We only had each other."

"And where do you both plan to go now? If we have any more questions." Agent Martinez looks at us with zero emotion in his eyes. I want to punch the fucker. We just went through this awful ordeal, and he has the nerve to accuse *us* and question *us*.

"We'll be heading home. New York."

"I'd rather you stay in town," Detective Jackson pipes in. "In case we have any further—"

"We'll be flying out within the hour," I interrupt. "Unless I need to call my lawyer, that is."

Agent Martinez stands up, and Detective Jackson follows. Agent Martinez glances at Ember, then at me and says, "That's all for now. I'll be in contact if we have any further questions."

"Mr. Martinez," Ember calls to him as he begins to walk out of the room.

He turns to face her but doesn't answer.

"Is it possible for me to have that photo of me as a child? I don't have any photos. I don't have anything."

I am prepared to lunge for the man and rip the file with her photo right out of his hands if I have to, but luckily, he nods and hands it to her.

"Thank you," she says as she stares down at the picture I'm sure she doesn't truly even recognize.

My heart breaks for what Ember must be feeling. In a matter of hours, she has lost everything. She's been told her mother, who she has feared her entire life, is dead. She's also been told that the father she was forced to live with in captivity could now possibly be alive.

Her eyes remain on the photo as she says, "I've never been on a plane before."

The number of firsts coming up for her are sure to be staggering. All I can do is try to help her muddle through them.

"Well, the good news is, my mother insisted on a private jet, so we won't have to deal with all the crowds. It will be more comfortable too. We can have something to eat on the plane and get some sleep. You look tired." I know I sure as hell am.

Finally breaking her gaze from the picture, she looks up at me with eyes that could tell a lifetime of horrific tales. "You called me your wife," she says in a monotone voice with zero emotion on her face. A blank pallet that leaves me wondering what she's thinking.

"Because you are," I say.

I don't have the mental bandwidth to dive into what our future looks like beyond getting on a plane and getting the hell out of here. I need distance from this nightmare before I can even think. I need clean clothes, shoes that fit, and a goddamn drink. I need normalcy. I fucking need a minute where I feel ordinary.

"I'm scared," Ember admits, but I don't need to hear the words to know that she is.

I pull her up out of the chair and embrace her tight. "We're going to figure this all out. I don't have all the answers now. I don't know what happens next. But you and I will figure it out."

2

EMBER

"OH MY GOD. OH MY GOD. OH MY GOD. OH MY GOD," AN OLDER woman who has the same facial bone structure as Christopher says as she walks toward us, stunned with her mouth wide open. "Oh. My. God." She places her fingers on her lips as a floodgate of tears releases from her eyes. "You're alive. You are really alive. You're really here! Oh my God."

"I'm alive," Christopher says as he approaches and pulls her into a hug. "I'm alive, Mom." He looks up at the sky, then inhales deeply, closing his eyes briefly as he does.

I can't look away, even though I feel as if I'm invading their privacy by observing this twisted reunion. What it must be like to embrace a ghost. To hold your dead son in your arms, only to feel the warmth of life and the breath of the living.

"I know I heard your voice on the phone, but to see you." His mother pulls away from the hug and looks Christopher over from head to toe. "You're really here. I can't believe you're really here. How did this happen? How?"

"There's a lot to tell you," Christopher says as he then turns away from her and reaches out his hand for me to take. "But first, I want to introduce you to Ember. She was with me in Hallelujah

Junction, and we escaped together." When I cautiously approach and take his hand, he adds, "Ember, this is my mother, Louisa Davenport."

Louisa glances down at my hand intwined with her son's and then paints a smile on her face as she gives a slight nod in acknowledgement. She then reaches her hand out to me. I'd never shaken a hand before but know what to do from all my reading. It's odd to touch someone else—a complete stranger— but I want to be polite. I want Christopher's mother to like me.

"Nice to meet you, Ember," she says as she grips my hand firmly.

"Nice to meet you, Mrs. Davenport." I make eye contact with her and notice she has hazel eyes beneath very thick eyelashes against heavily gray-eyeshadowed lids. I've never worn makeup before and wonder if Louisa will someday show me how to apply it like she does.

She is still smiling, but her upper lip twitches, and her eyes seem to bore right through me. I reposition myself from one foot to the other as I feel the weight of her assessment on my shoulders pushing me down and making me feel small.

I need to escape, and yet I have no place to go. No place to run to.

I also don't want to stand on the pavement near the large jet any longer. I wish I could flee and go hide in a corner somewhere out of sight. I need to breathe someplace that is all my own, and yet I can't. I release Christopher's hand, which oddly briefly frees me from the stare of Mrs. Davenport when I do.

"You both look like prison inmates," she says with a wrinkle of her nose as if we possess an odor.

Rather than being offended, Christopher chuckles, and for the first time, I see laugh lines around his eyes and a look of genuine... glee. It's foreign to me, and that fact smacks me hard with what our reality was and what it is now.

"Fitting, since we both were in a prison of sorts for months."

I don't like Christopher referring to our life in Hallelujah

Junction as a prison. I understand why he does, but it doesn't sound right. It doesn't feel right. And even though we are both dressed in clothing given to us by the police, I don't like being compared to an inmate either.

She looks at Christopher, finally breaking her searing stare on me. "Is she coming with us?"

I look at Christopher for an answer as well. Am I?

Christopher swallows hard and nods. "There's... something... that happened while I was held captive." He looks at me and places his palm on my lower back, which gives me a sense of comfort. "The man holding me there forced me to marry Ember. She's my wife, Mom. We're married."

Her fingertips flutter to her lips as her eyes widen. "Your wife? He forced you to marry? You can't be serious."

He nods. "There's a lot I have to tell you about my nightmare, but right now, Ember and I really need to get on the plane, eat something, and get some rest. I also really want to get the hell out of Nevada and never step foot in this godforsaken place again. I can tell you everything once we're in the air. I'm sure you have a lot of questions, but I could sure use a stiff drink."

I look at the jet with the door open and stairs leading up to it, beckoning us to enter. I can't imagine how something so big and what looks so heavy can possibly get in the air and not fall out of the sky.

"Ember?" Christopher prompts as he breaks me from my thoughts. "You ready?"

Without waiting for an answer, he leads me to the plane and up the stairs. His hand stays touching some part of me the entire time, and I realize just how much I need it. I cling to it. I focus on it to try to calm the flutter in my chest and tone down the ringing in my ears. My legs feel weak as I walk up every single stair, and when we enter the jet, I try not to focus on the thin metal walls that surround me. It's as if I've been swallowed up, and it suddenly seems harder to breathe.

"It's going to be just fine," he says softly from behind me. His lips are near my ear, and it takes all my might to keep walking forward to some seats he's guiding me to. "I know this is all new and maybe scary, but it's going to be fine."

"You've never flown before?" Mrs. Davenport asks as she takes one of the leather seats.

"Mom, I told you. Ember was held captive just like me. She grew up in Hallelujah Junction. Richard—the man responsible for my kidnapping—held her there since she was a young child."

I want to correct Christopher. I wasn't captive. I wasn't held there. Papa Rich is my father. Hallelujah Junction is my... *was* my home. But I remain quiet. Mrs. Davenport is glaring at me again, and I can't help but get the feeling that the woman doesn't care for me. By the way her eyes keep darting to Christopher's touch on me, I can clearly see she doesn't like him touching me one bit.

As we take our seats directly across from his mother, Christopher reaches over my lap and buckles a seat belt over me. Mrs. Davenport doesn't like seeing this either. I miss the smile she had painted on her face before. She's not even trying to hide her distaste now.

"So let me get this straight," she finally says as the plane starts to move. "The man who kidnapped you—Richard—forced you to marry Ember, who he also kidnapped?"

"Yes," Christopher says as he reaches for a shelf that stores glasses and some decanters of colored and clear liquid. He looks at me. "Do you want a drink?"

I shake my head. I worry I won't be able to hold down what is in my stomach once this plane actually lifts off into the sky.

Christopher pours his mother a drink without asking if she wants one and then pours himself one. "The man was called Richard, and he normally kills anyone who trespasses," Christopher begins. "I guess I should consider myself lucky he deemed me the one to marry his daughter... or who he considered his daughter... even though Ember is just as much a victim as I was. He made it look like I died in an accident, which sadly is how many other people actually died, and he kept me chained in the basement."

I bite the inside of my cheek to stay quiet. I'm not a victim. I don't like being referred to as one, but I also don't feel it's appropriate to correct Christopher in front of his mother. Instead, I look out the window at the passing scenery and try to not let the panic setting in overtake me.

"They told me you died while taking pictures. That you fell to your death in an old mining pit of acid. I had no idea. I just assumed that— I had no idea." She shakes her head and breathes deeply. "What kind of sick man would do this?"

"There is no way you could have known I was still alive."

"And you both escaped? Where is this Richard now?" she asks as she takes a long swallow of her drink. She leaves red lipstick marks on the glass, and I am once again reminded of the makeup I lack.

I wonder what this woman must think of me.

I feel plain and simple.

I also feel dirty and wrong.

I'm out of place, and I don't belong.

"I waited until the perfect time. We started a fire that burned down the town. We thought Richard died in the fire, but the police just told us that might not be the case. Regardless, we are free from him forever. If he is alive, he's a wanted man and will have to hide in holes until someone eventually finds him."

"I think I'll get us some security just in case," she says as if it's just as simple as that to make any threat of Papa Rich go away.

"If that makes you feel better," he agrees as he reaches for my hand and holds it in his.

We take off into the air, and my belly drops and then flips. A cold sweat covers me, and I instantly want off the plane. I want to go home. I want the schoolhouse. I want my books. I want... I want the way it was.

I lean as close to Christopher's ear as I can and whisper, "I don't feel very good."

He quickly leans forward to the shelf of drinks and opens a can of soda. "Here, drink this. It's ginger ale and should help. Just close your eyes and take some deep breaths."

I take a sip and do exactly as he says, and I do start to feel better as the plane evens out.

"And now what?" Mrs. Davenport continues.

"Ember will be staying with me in New York. We have a lot to figure out and what the future has in store, but she'll be comfortable in my apartment and—"

"I sold your apartment and everything in it," Mrs. Davenport blurts. "I thought you were dead. You know how fast real estate goes in the city, and... I thought you were dead."

"Shit," Christopher says, leans his head against the headrest, and closes his eyes.

"I'm sorry."

"I understand. Like you said. You thought I was dead."

"It doesn't matter," Mrs. Davenport says in a cheerier voice than she has used before. "My townhouse has plenty of room for you. And considering all you've been through, I don't think you should be alone anyway. Your old room is still set up, and Ms. Evans will love having someone to cook for again, since I rarely seem to be home anymore with all the recent social engagements I've been busy with."

"*We*," Christopher says, looking at me with a reassuring smile, "would like that for now. At least until I find us a place to live."

Mrs. Davenport looks at me, back to Christopher, and then back at me. "Ember, do you not have any other family or friends? I'm sure they will be wanting to see you as soon as they can."

"No," I state softly. "My mother is dead, and Papa Rich... well... he was all I had."

A woman who stood by the door as we entered emerged from behind a curtain carrying a tray of sandwiches and bags of potato chips. "When you boarded, I know you said you were hungry. We don't have a lot on the plane," she begins, "but I do have these." She pulls out a table that comes from the shelf of drinks, and it serves as a centerpiece between Christopher and me and his mother. She places the food on the table, and Mrs. Davenport waves her away. She then walks away before any of us can say anything to her.

"So, you want Ember to stay with us?" Mrs. Davenport asks with a look on her face that seems as if she's tasted something bad.

"Mother," Christopher snaps. Then in a calmer voice, he adds, "I told you. She's my wife. So, yes, she'll be staying with me... with us."

"Well, she isn't exactly your wife. Not legally. I'm sure there was no marriage license, and even if there was, you were married under duress. This isn't legal or binding in the slightest. No one would blame you for thinking it wasn't. I'm sure Father Antonio wouldn't blame you one bit, and I seriously doubt we would even have to go forward with an annulment."

"Mom," Christopher says in a tone that rings of warning. "We can discuss this further later. But right now, my *wife* and I need to eat. We need to process. We need to not talk about what happened while we were there. I know you have a lot of questions, and I promise I will answer them soon. But for now, we need some peace. Please."

3

EMBER

Somehow, I manage to fall asleep using Christopher's shoulder as a pillow. I had tried to eat some, but my stomach and nerves wouldn't allow it. But sleep at least came, although it doesn't last for long.

I can hear Christopher and his mother talking as I go in and out of consciousness. He's telling her the story from the minute he was hit upside the head and shackled in the cellar, the deaths of the poor people trying to help us, our marriage, our escape... everything. I try to ignore the words and sleep. I don't want to hear what happened again. I don't want the images to flash in my mind, even though they seem to be forever seared in my memories.

"This is insane, Christopher," his mother says as I keep my eyes closed so they both think I'm asleep. "I understand why you feel responsible for this girl. I do. But you can't be expected to take care of her forever. You most certainly don't have to be married to her!" Her words are low, like a hiss from a snake.

"Shh!" Christopher snaps, and I feel his body tense beneath my cheek. "She might hear you."

"I don't care," his mother hisses again. "This isn't anything I wouldn't say to her face."

"I know you can't understand why I'm doing this. But Ember and I grew really close while we were trying to survive. I care for her, and in no way would I ever abandon her. So you need to get that out of your mind right now."

"She's going to have a lot of issues I don't think you're equipped to handle. What about your career? You are far from marriage material at this stage of your life."

"Yeah, she's got a lot of damage. But we both do. You don't think this experience fucked me up? Frankly, Ember is the only person who will ever truly understand me. That place changed me. Maybe for the worse, or maybe for the better. I can tell you I sure as fuck appreciate freedom and life right now."

"Jesus, what are people going to say? Everyone thought you were dead, when in fact you were kidnapped. But then you want us also to tell people you're married! Can you imagine the gossip this is going to cause? It's unreal!"

"Mom, lower your voice," Christopher whispers as he softly runs his hand over my head. "I don't want you to wake her. And I don't care what people say."

"Maybe you don't, but I do! And what about your job? Your reputation. You don't want to be a spectacle or thought of as some broken person."

"Maybe I am a bit broken. Have you considered that? And I understand Ember is too. Which is why we will stay together and figure this all out. I'm not going to leave her, and I'm not going to fight with you on this either. You need to trust that I'm doing what's right for me and what's right for her. I get it; I know we aren't married legally, but in my heart and in my mind, this girl is my wife. Something happened in Hallelujah Junction that will forever connect us and form a bond that can't be severed. So I need you to accept this. I need you to welcome Ember and make *her* feel accepted."

"I would never be rude to a guest. You know that."

"She's going to be more than just a guest, Mom, and you know it. I need you to be there for her. I need you to be there for the both of us."

I hear her release a heavy breath, but she says nothing more. The momentary silence allows me to fall back asleep. I dream of Hallelujah Junction. I see flames, I see Papa Rich, and I see the schoolhouse. Home. I see my home.

I wake up with a start when the wheels of the plane connect with the ground.

Christopher pats my lap in reassurance. "We're here safe and sound."

I blink away the sleep and notice Mrs. Davenport is staring at me once again. I try my best to not pay attention to the fact and instead run my fingers through my hair, wishing I had a brush.

"I arranged for a limo to pick us up," she says as she reaches for her purse and pulls out a small mirror and lipstick. She applies it with such skill and precision, and I'm once again envious.

"Shit!" Christopher says as he looks out the window.

I look over his shoulder and see cars and people all around the plane as it comes to a stop.

"The media," Mrs. Davenport says. She looks at Christopher and me and what we're wearing. "Oh my God."

"Someone at the police station must have tipped them off. Sold a story," Christopher says as he leans his head back against the chair, closing his eyes. "Paparazzi is not how I wanted to be welcomed home."

Mrs. Davenport pulls her mirror from her purse again and looks over her appearance once more. She then looks at me, reaches into her purse, and pulls out a small brush. "You may want to brush your hair, dear."

"Thank you," I say as I reach for the brush, grateful.

"Fuck. It's a goddamn madhouse out there," Christopher mumbles as he looks out the window again. "There's no avoiding them. I see the limo, but it's surrounded."

"I really wish you two were wearing something else," Mrs. Davenport says, shaking her head with disgust on her face. "I don't want these to be the first pictures people see."

Christopher turns to face me. "There's going to be a lot of flashing cameras, loud voices, and a million questions coming at us. I'm going to lead us through it as fast as I can, but just keep staring straight ahead, and don't say a thing. I've got this handled."

"What are you going to say?" Mrs. Davenport asks. "Should we prepare a speech before we get off the plane?"

Christopher shakes his head as he runs his fingers through his hair in frustration. "I'm not ready to give any kind of speech. I just want us to get to the limo as fast as we can. We'll deal with the media on another day. I'm sure this won't be the last we'll see of them."

"Why are they here?" I ask, my voice cracking from not using it for so long.

"Because of who we are," he answers. "My family's name keeps them interested in us."

"And because of what happened," Mrs. Davenport adds. "If they got wind of the story... this is going to be huge news." She reaches for her phone and starts hitting buttons. "I'm calling Jason. He'll help guide us through this."

"I can handle it," Christopher snaps as he unfastens his seatbelt and stands. I do the same, although my knees feel weak, and I worry I might fall.

"We pay Jason a lot of money to handle issues like this for us," she says, ignoring her son and his wishes completely.

I wait for him to get angry and demand respect as Papa Rich would do, but instead, Christopher leads me toward the exit of the plane. It appears his mother and he have an unknown language I'm not privy to.

He takes a deep breath as the woman who brought us the sandwiches waits for his signal on when to open the door. He looks at me one last time before we exit. "They're going to be taking our pictures. They are going to want to capture us and paint this story in the most glorified, horrific way. Don't give them any reason to make this worse than it is. Stare ahead. Keep your emotions at bay. Just focus on walking to the limo as fast as we can." He leans in and kisses me on the forehead. "It'll be over fast. I promise."

He seems afraid, and it doesn't take me long to know why. The minute we exit the plane, there is a wave of sound that nearly causes me to stumble down the steps. There are so many questions that all I hear is just a solid block of sound. Lights are flashing everywhere to where I nearly feel blind from them. I hear some questions, but they are all the same.

"Were you really chained in a basement for months?"

"Is this the famous Hallelujah Junction ghost? It's rumored your name is Ember. Is that true?"

"Were you really forced to marry the ghost while chained?"

"Were you held captive by the Hallelujah Junction serial killer?"

"How did you both escape? Is it true you burned the town to the ground?"

I try to look forward. I try not to show my fear. I try to do everything Christopher told me to do as he forces our way through bodies of people either shouting questions or taking our picture. I can't see the limo, but Christopher is tugging me along.

"Christopher, what's it like to come back from the dead?"

"Did they catch the serial killer? Is he still on the loose?"

I'm not sure where Mrs. Davenport is, but I assume she's close behind us, because I hear questions directed at her as well.

"Louisa, what's it like to have your son back after believing he was dead?"

"Is seeing your son like seeing a ghost?"

"What do you think about the ghost of Hallelujah Junction walking hand in hand with your son?"

I'm reminded of the desert thunderstorms of Hallelujah Junction. Ninety-mile-per-hour winds, lightning, thunder, and the smell of impending destruction. This is what I'm walking through.

Complete mayhem and chaos.

The purpose to break down our fragile walls as the weather would try to do to the old structures of the ghost town.

I can see the limo in the distance, and the driver is trying to make a path for us as we approach.

It's then that Christopher surprises me when he finally answers all the questions. "It's good to be home," he says with a smile and a wave.

It's the one and only thing spoken as we both duck into the limo, followed by a calm and composed Mrs. Davenport. Both Christopher and his mother seem nearly relaxed, as if they hadn't just marched through a tornado. I, on the other hand, can barely breathe. The air of the limo seems thick and weighs heavy on my lungs.

"I left a message for Jason," his mother says as we begin to drive through the crowd of reporters. "He'll know what our next step needs to be."

"Our next step is getting home, getting showered, and trying to forget everything about Hallelujah Junction," he says as he leans his head back and closes his eyes.

He's not holding my hand anymore, and I realize I need it. I need it more than I've ever needed anything. Knowing I would earn another glare from his mother, I resist the urge to reach for it but instead clasp my fingers together in my lap.

I look out the window at the passing scenery and think about home. I think about Papa Rich and wonder if he's truly alive and hiding with Scarecrow. I think about when things were simpler, with my books and my cat, Pine Cone. I don't want to forget like Christopher does. If I forget, it will be as if I never existed. Hallelujah Junction might be Christopher's nightmare, but it's all I had. It's me.

I'm a walking nightmare Christopher brought along as a constant reminder.

Tears well in my eyes, but I blink them away.

How can I forget?

How can I move on?

What does moving on even look like?

So far, all I've seen are bright lights and shouting faces.

I'm nothing but the ghost of Hallelujah Junction stuck in a different kind of purgatory.

4

CHRISTOPHER

I'M NOT SURPRISED TO SEE MORE MEDIA WAITING OUTSIDE THE front of my mother's Upper East Side townhome. This circus isn't going away anytime soon, and I can't say I blame any of the reporters. Hell, if it weren't me being the object of fascination, I might be one of the photographers on the street myself in hopes of capturing the perfect picture for *Rolling Stone Magazine.* I understand their need to follow the story—it's a fucking unbelievable story—but I still hate seeing them flock around our shelter like vultures.

Luckily, the walk to the front door isn't far, and we can just usher right past them as fast as we can. An iron fence around the stoop is more welcomed now than ever before. It will offer us some protection from the masses.

I'm proud of Ember. I worried when we landed that seeing all the reporters all at once would cause her to have a panic attack of some sort and make a scene. I wouldn't have blamed her one bit, but instead, she remained steadfast and focused on just walking with her head held high and her shoulders back. Regardless how ridiculous we look in our hand-me-down outfits, the woman still appears stunning in my eyes. I am pretty sure there isn't a single picture that was captured that caught her in a bad light. She truly reminds me of an angel, and no doubt her essence will be seen by all who see these pictures.

"Ms. Evans is waiting for us. I told her to open the door the minute we approach," my mother says as she reads the texts on her phone. She hasn't looked away from the screen for even a second since getting in the limo. I am pretty sure every person she knows is texting her and wanting to get the scoop on her son being back from the dead before anyone else. In a sick way, I'm pretty sure my mother is loving every minute of it. Attention whore is a job description of a socialite.

"Ready?" I ask Ember. "Just like when we got off the plane. Just keep walking."

Her eyes dart to the reporters, then to me, and very slowly, she nods. "Ready."

The rush of blurred sound nearly drowns us. I've found myself on *Page Six* a time or two in my life, and I've been captured by the paparazzi a few times with my celebrity friends, but absolutely nothing could have prepared me for this insanity. It's louder and more aggressive than at the airport. Maybe because they know that once we are inside, we're safe and may never come back out. Regardless of how relentless they are in trying to get the best picture and to force me to answer their questions, we charge forward to the door that Ms. Evans now has opened for us.

When the three of us enter and the door is slammed behind us, it's as if we just escaped a blizzard and finally found shelter. I wrap an arm around Ember and kiss her on the forehead. I can't imagine how that had to feel for her, and yet she remained strong through it all.

"Christopher, it is so good to see you... alive!" Ms. Evans says as she stands before me, face pale, eyes wide, and mouth slightly ajar. "When your mother told me.... What a true blessing this is."

"Thank you, Ms. Evans. It's good to be home. Really good."

"Christopher?" I hear a shaky but familiar voice to my right.

I turn my head and see Marissa standing there. I realize she's been there all along, is watching me stand there with my arm around Ember, and is having to absorb the fact that her boyfriend she thought was dead is far from it. Out of respect for her, I take my arm off Ember and step away just to give a little more distance.

"Marissa," I say, but I have no idea what else to follow it with.

She closes the distance between us and hugs me. "When they told me you were dead...."

She starts sobbing against my shoulder, and I rub her back in comfort. I don't know what to do. I don't know what to say. I can feel Ember's eyes on me, but I don't have the courage to meet them.

"What happened?" she asks but doesn't pull her head away. "*How* did this happen?"

"A sick man knocked me out, kidnapped me, and made it look like I died. It's a long and twisted story I don't even know how to tell, to be honest."

"All that matters is that you're back," she mumbles against me, tightening her hold. "You've come back to me."

"Marissa," I say again, swallowing down the awkwardness I'm feeling, knowing I have to take this situation by the balls whether I want to or not. "I need to introduce you to someone." I break the embrace and take a few steps back so that I'm closer to Ember than I am to Marissa. "This is Ember. She was with me in Hallelujah Junction. We were held there together before we escaped."

Marissa looks at Ember and offers a weak smile as she wipes at the tears on her cheeks. "Ember, it's nice to meet you. I'm so happy Christopher didn't have to be alone while there."

"She's my wife," I blurt, not knowing how to say it gently and in a way not to hurt Marissa. I have to rip off the Band-Aid. She deserves to know the bitter truth as soon as possible.

Marissa takes a stumbling step back as if I just punched her in the face. She scans Ember from head to toe and then looks at me. "Your wife? What are you talking about?"

"The man—Richard—who held me captive forced me to marry Ember. He considered Ember his daughter and... well, I was kidnapped with the intention for me to marry his daughter."

"Christopher was *forced* to marry her," my mother chimes in. "He had no choice. He was chained to a wall, and after that, he was chained to this girl."

I still can't look at Ember. I should. I should stand by her side and hold her hand in solidarity, but at the same time, the pain that is now on Marissa's face is killing a piece of me slowly. I don't want to hurt her. Hell... I don't want to hurt anyone. But there is no way I can walk away from this situation without someone's heart getting decimated.

"You're married now?" Marissa asks in disbelief. "Why would you...? Married?

"Not really. Not legally," my mother tries to reassure as she looks at Ember with a level of disgust on her face I've never seen before. "He was kidnapped. He had to do what he had to do to survive."

I finally look at Ember, who is staring at Marissa with just as much confusion and shock as Marissa has painted on her face.

"What about us?" Marissa asks. "What about *me*?"

"I know this is hard," I begin, trying to find the right words. But what the fuck can I say? In Marissa's eyes, I died, I came back to life, and now I'm married. All without a formal breakup or closure.

Do I break up with her?

Isn't the situation obvious?

I run my fingers through my hair as my head spins. What is the fucking situation? I don't even know it myself.

Ms. Evans tries to cut through the awkward air. "Can I get anyone anything to eat or drink?" I don't blame the woman one bit for wanting to flee to the kitchen.

"No, thank you. I think Ember and I need to go get showered and some rest," I say, knowing I too want to flee this room, but I understand I can't just run from my problems. "Marissa... I understand this is a lot to take in. I wish I had all the right things to say, but I don't know what they are. All I know is that right now, I have to take things one minute at a time. I need to shower. I need to process. I need to breathe. I also understand that you have questions. Lots of questions. But can we discuss this all tomorrow? It's been a really long day after months of even longer days. Can you give me that?" I look to my mother. "Can you both give me that?"

"I've prepared your old room for you, Christopher, and I also prepared the guest room for Ember," Ms. Evans says.

"No need for the guest room. We'll both be using mine," I inform everyone.

"Christopher!" my mother says with a loud gasp as she takes a step toward Marissa in a sign of camaraderie and loyalty. "I think that's far from appropriate. I think Ember will be perfectly comfortable in the guest room."

"I'm not going to leave Ember alone right now. I made a promise, and I'm going to stick to it."

I know I'm hurting Marissa. I know I'm upsetting my mother. But as I take Ember's hand to lead her upstairs, I also know I have a responsibility to Ember... to my wife.

"Christopher," my mother calls to me as we are at the top of the stairs. I prepare to spin on my heels and snap her head off. I'm losing patience, and I am in no mood to have her argue with me as to where Ember's going to sleep. "I'll give some of my clothes to Ember until we have a chance to go shopping. We look like we are close in size. I also had some of your old belongings boxed up. Ms. Evans pulled the clothes out for you."

Surprised by her act of kindness to a woman who I can clearly see she dislikes, I look over my shoulder and give her a smile. "Thank you, Mom. I appreciate that." I glance at Marissa, who has tears in her eyes and a blotchy face. "We can all meet and talk it out tomorrow. Goodnight."

When we enter my room, I release a deep breath I didn't realize I must have been holding. It's odd to see my old room, not that it really was my room from my childhood. My mother completely remodeled it when I went off to college, so it's really just another guest room with a queen-sized bed, dressers, and nightstands imported from Paris. She was so proud of the room, but it wasn't my taste at all. I much preferred clean, modern lines over the antique feel, but it made my mother happy.

When I close the door, Ember speaks for the first time. "Who is Marissa?"

Jesus, I need sleep and don't feel like talking anymore, but I also know Ember deserves her questions answered. "She was my girlfriend before."

"Why didn't you tell me?"

"There's a lot about me and my life prior to meeting you that you don't know, Ember. You have to understand that. But should I have told you I had a girlfriend? Yes. And I apologize. I should have prepared you for this—although, in all fairness, I didn't think she'd be waiting for me the minute I arrived home. I thought I'd have some time."

"You had a girlfriend? But you married me?" she asks softly, and although I'm growing frustrated with the situation—it's not like any of this is my fucking fault—I try to keep my calm. Ember doesn't deserve my wrath.

"I didn't have a choice in marrying you." The minute the words leave my mouth, I regret them.

Ember nearly wobbles to the edge of the bed and sits down, looking down at the oriental rug. She kicks off her shoes and wiggles her freed toes.

"I understand that," Ember says as she then looks up at me. "But we're married now. I know your mother says we aren't. But I believe we are. Under God, we are. In my heart and soul, we are. How do you feel?"

Her blue eyes so full of truth stab me in the heart. She's calm, she's collected, and she seems so wise and in control. In a whirlwind of chaos, standing in this room with Ember is the first time I feel a sense of grounding.

"You're my wife," I say. "I don't care what anyone says; you *are* my wife."

"And Marissa?"

"I will need to handle the situation delicately. I don't want to hurt her. I don't want to hurt you. But I can't think right now. I'm tired. I need a shower. *We* need a shower. Tomorrow is another day, and we can face this nightmare then." I point to the closed door. "You can have the shower first. I'll go see about some of my mother's clothes while you're in there."

Ember stands up and walks to me. Inches from my face, she tilts her head up so she can look directly into my eyes. "I'm sorry, Christopher. I'm sorry you have to go through all this. You don't deserve this."

I run my hand down the back of her head and pull her into an embrace. "You have nothing to apologize for. I'm sorry for both of us. This situation is so fucked up."

"Do you regret taking me with you?" she mumbles against me.

"Never," I say, pulling her away enough so that I can kiss her lips. The act of intimacy feels foreign, as if I shouldn't be kissing my wife. "Yes, we made wedding vows, but I made my own vow to you that has nothing to do with being married. I'm never going to leave you, Ember. I'm here for you through all of this." I kiss her one more time, determined for the sensation to not feel wrong, but it still seems off in the light of normalcy and no longer being chained together. "I'm not going to lie to you and tell you this is going to be easy. It's not. It's going to be fucking hard. Really fucking hard."

"But we'll get through it," she finishes for me. "Together."

God, I fucking hope so. I do.

"Christopher?"

"Tomorrow," I interrupt, having reached my max. "Tomorrow."

"But—"

"Ember... I need to... tomorrow."

I know the tone in my voice is harsh. I know I should hold her. I should make promises and reassurances to her. I should put her feelings first.

But right now, all I can do is shut down. My mind says enough. My heart splinters with every sign of my past life muddling my current. The situation is swallowing me up, and I worry I can't be who I need to be and do what I need to do.

Bells are ringing in my ears. Flashes of insanity are approaching.

"Tomorrow," Ember finally says, her voice pulling me from the depths.

5

EMBER

IT SMELLS DIFFERENT.

It sounds different.

It feels different.

This isn't my home. This isn't Hallelujah Junction.

And though I'm lying in bed next to Christopher, I don't recognize anything. Not even him. The man last night was different than I've ever seen. *Everything* is different.

The borrowed nightgown I wear feels too soft—like butter. It slides on my skin, and I feel molested by cloth that's not mine. The sheets feel that way as well. Rich and luxurious but suffocating.

I don't belong here, but regardless, I am here. Where else can I go? Even if I wanted to go back to Hallelujah Junction, it is burned to the ground by my own doing.

"Did you sleep well?" Christopher asks huskily as he rolls over to face me. His eyes sparkle in the sunlight peeking through the curtains.

"No." I don't want to lie to Christopher. I'm not a liar... yet. Maybe this place will change me.

He stretches and yawns. "I know this is a lot to get used to. It'll take time."

With a small groan, Christopher gets out of bed and pads barefoot over to the window, opening the curtain. He's wearing nothing but underwear, and I'm surprised when a stirring in my sex ignites at the sight. I try to divert my sinful eyes, but I can't. He looks down below and curses. "Shit. They're still here."

"The reporters? Why?" How can we be so interesting that people choose to camp outside?

"They know we have to come out someday. They are hunters waiting for their prey.

"I'm scared," I confess.

He looks over his shoulder at me and offers a warm smile. "You don't need to be scared. They seem scary, but they're harmless. Remember, I'm a photographer myself... or I was."

"Not of them," I clarify. "But what if... if we're on television or the newspapers, then *he* can find us. Papa Rich. If he's alive, he'll know where we are."

I sit up, feeling as if I have to in order for the thick mattress not to swallow me up.

"That's not possible."

"How can you be so sure? I know Papa Rich. And if he's alive, he'll want me back with him. He'll want us both. He won't give up until that happens. He's always claimed to be a determined and driven man. He says God gave him the gift of fortitude."

Christopher takes two large strides toward me with a firm jaw and narrowed eyes. His voice is low and terse. "Don't ever be afraid of that man again. You hear me? He's had enough control over our lives for a lifetime. I will not allow him to control another minute any longer." He sits down next to me on the bed and takes my hand in his. His voice softens as he adds, "I'm never going to let you be in danger again. If he's alive... *if*... he better stay away. Because I won't hesitate to kill him myself. He's never getting you again. You aren't his to take. You're mine now."

"Am I yours?" I ask, liking the way it sounds but not truly believing him.

"Yes, mine."

"It doesn't feel that way," I admit. "Your mother is right. You were forced to marry me. She doesn't see me as your wife. No one will." I look out the window and see the blue in the sky. "I'm not even sure you see me as your wife."

"It doesn't matter what others think," he says, rubbing a circle on my hand with his fingertip. "It's about what you and I feel. And right now, I feel more connected to you than I do anything else. My life feels out of control right now. But you are my one grounding constant. You are the one person who truly understands what I went through and what I'm feeling now. I don't care about the term 'wife' or all the legalities. We're together. I'm not leaving you, and that's all that matters." He brushes a lock of hair behind my ear. "You're my wife, Ember. Block out all the noise that says anything different."

He leans forward and places his lips to mine. It's not like last night's kisses. It's different. I hear his breath. I feel his breath. And when he pushes his tongue into my mouth, I taste his breath. It's laced with hunger and need that matches my own.

He pulls away just enough to whisper, "I'm not letting you go. I know you're afraid I will, but I swear to you, you're mine. My wife. My future."

The kiss continues and deepens even more as he lowers me back down to the mattress, mounting me as he does so. Effortlessly, he pulls down his underwear, and it dawns on me that this is the first time we have been able to do this action without a chain to our ankles. We're free... at least from the metal constraints.

Christopher doesn't waste any time removing my clothes fully but instead pushes my nightgown up over my breasts. I'm not wearing any panties, so there is nothing getting in the way of his sex and mine. He nudges my thighs wider, making room for him as he lowers his mouth to my neck and nibbles a trail of lust.

With one hard push, he enters inside, spreading me wide with his thickness. I inhale deeply as my pussy adjusts to his size. He pauses for a moment as he's rooted deep within.

I welcome the connection even more than the feeling. I *need* him in me. I need to feel us as one when I feel he's slipping away. I groan when he pulls out of me, but then I cry out when he thrusts back in. The slickness of my desire makes it easy for him to push and pull at a speed that brings me to climax faster than I had ever been able to before. It's easier this time. I'm not worried about pleasing him and being a good wife in the schoolhouse as the smell of ghosts and secrets surrounds us.

Right now, it's just about having the man I love deep inside me and never wanting him out. We're safe here. We're one. No one can hurt me, or him, or *us*.

The feeling of fear is replaced with a feeling of passion and sensuality. I move my body with his as his moans intensify. His nibbles turn into a bite, and then another. But I like the pain. I like the sting as it reminds me of where I am. It grounds me and puts me beneath the weight of Christopher.

"Harder," I whisper.

A growl emerges from deep inside him, and he hikes my leg up on his hip and drives himself into me farther. He's so deep it feels as if he's nearly bruising my body where only he can touch. The discomfort is almost punishing but also primal in my need for more. I want the discipline of his cock to remind my body and soul that he will never leave me. He will never release his duties of husband and protector. I need his dick to beat the reminder inside me. Over and over. Harder and harder, I need it. *I need it!*

This is *my* Christopher. *My* husband.

He's having sex with *me*. He's claiming *me*.

Me.

Not Marissa.

Not anyone else.

Me.

His wife.

Christopher thrusts even deeper and harder now as if he can feel my hunger for the biting erotic pain. He palms my breast now as he drives forward, with a deep moan following. I feel a second wave of electricity building inside as he pinches my nipple. His eyes connect with mine, and I like that I can see them darken and nearly blur. He's present but also far away. I can feel his own climax is nearing, and as I jerk my hips up to meet him thrust for thrust, his deep roar blends with my own moans of completion.

The weight of his body is on top of me now, and his rapid breathing is slowing as it matches cadence with mine.

"I don't ever want you to doubt me," he whispers against my hair. "I'm committed to you. I'm committed to us."

I cling to his ass with my fingers, holding him inside me. I don't want his dick to leave my pussy. I like it there. I want it to remain always, but I also know we can't hide in this bed forever.

"What happens today?" I ask, truly having no idea what life is like now that we are free from the ghost town.

Rolling over, Christopher stares up at the ceiling for several moments. "I don't know. I really don't. I have to somehow figure out how to get my life back. My job, a place for us to live. I also need to figure out a statement to give the media. They won't go away until I deal with it." He turns his head and looks at me. "What do *you* want to happen?"

I don't know the answer.

I shrug. "I don't know. I try to picture tomorrow, and it's blank. I can't see what's ahead of us."

"I get that," he says, looking sad for a brief moment. "But we'll figure it out."

"How do I get your mother to like me?" I ask. I might be naive in a lot of ways. I know that. But I'm not so naive to know that his mother doesn't like me one bit, and I want to change that.

He sighs loudly. "Give her time. This is a lot for her to process too. This isn't how she wanted it for me. My mother would have thrown a huge wedding that would have been the party of the year. There would have been engagement parties, rehearsal dinners, and basically anything that would mean her planning a special event. She loves that kind of stuff."

"Was she going to do that for you and Marissa?" I ask, leaning up on my elbow so I can look at Christopher better.

"Marissa and I were not discussing marriage or anywhere near that level. We were dating, having a good time, but very casual." He pauses. "For me at least. I'm sure she would have liked to be more serious, but I was far from marriage material. My life wasn't conducive to being a husband."

"But you're a husband now."

He closes his eyes briefly and then looks at me with a seriousness I'm not familiar with seeing on him. "I am now, which means I have to figure out a life where it's conducive."

"I wish you would have told me about her," I admit. I wanted to tell him this last night, but he cut our night short, which I didn't blame him for.

"Would it have made a difference?" he asks softly.

Feeling a twinge of shame, I shake my head. "I suppose not." Papa Rich had planned for us to be married no matter what. And if Christopher refused, Papa Rich would have killed him. I know this. Christopher knows this.

"My mother is not an easy woman," he says as he sits up and reaches for his underwear. "Deep down, she means well. I know she loves me. But she's not easy." He looks at me and nods at my disheveled nightgown. "I'm surprised she gave you that. She also gave you a dress to wear to breakfast. As soon as we can figure out what's in store for us today, we'll get you some clothes, shoes, undergarments, et cetera, for you of your own." He leans down on the bed with his hands and gives me a kiss. "I'm new at all this stuff. So, I'm going to need you to tell me what you want or don't want. I need your input, okay?"

I nod and smile, happy I recognize Christopher again. "Okay."

"We better get downstairs. I'm sure they're waiting for us with a million questions."

"I'll make us breakfast," I offer. "I don't know what's in the pantry, but I'm pretty good at making do. Is there anything your mother doesn't like to eat?"

Christopher chuckles. "Cooking is not a good idea. Not if you want to keep your hands. Ms. Evans will hack them off if you dare."

"She makes the meals?" I've never eaten anything that I haven't made myself. I've always done all the cooking.

"She cooks and cleans for my mother. She has for years. She's like family around here."

"Can I help?" I don't like the idea of having some other woman do all the work. I had read about servants in books, but is Ms. Evans a servant? Shouldn't we all pitch in to help?

"For right now, I think you need to just focus on getting settled in to this new way of life. You and I are going to be busy figuring everything out. Let Ms. Evans worry about the basics."

I must have a look on my face revealing just how uncomfortable I am with the idea of not earning my keep.

"Don't worry," he adds. "When you and I have our own place again, you can make all your famous recipes that I grew to love." He reaches over and pats my leg. "Come on. Get dressed. I'm hungry, and I can hear the thoughts of my mother now. She's pacing the floor. I can bet anything on that right now."

Not an easy woman, Christopher says.

Not an easy woman.

I guess Papa Rich wasn't an easy man.

I've had practice.

6

EMBER

IT'S LOUD WHEN WE WALK DOWNSTAIRS. I HEAR VOICES, AND THE first thing I see is the television on with both Christopher and me on the screen. I'm on television. My face is on television.

Christopher walks straight to the TV and stands in front of it. I stay near him, because I feel I need to in order to be defended against the storm about to hit, but I divert my eyes from the screen. I don't want to see it. I don't want to stare the devil that was our past straight in the eye.

"Fuck," Christopher says under his breath.

"Oh good, you two are finally up," Mrs. Davenport says as she enters the room followed by a man in a suit and tie, his hair slicked back, and black glasses that seem to barely balance on the edge of his nose. "Jason and I've been waiting. He's come up with some good ideas for us to get ahead of this situation."

"Looks like the situation is already moving along full force without us," Christopher says, still watching the news on the television.

"As I was telling Louisa," Jason says, "I've started to work on a statement for you to say. Right now, the media sees you both as victims, which means they are going to be sympathetic to your need for privacy during this difficult time. At least on the surface. Everyone will want to get the full scoop, so we need to decide who we're giving the story to."

Christopher turns away from the television and sighs. He then places a hand on my lower back and starts to lead me out of the room. "At least allow Ember and me to get some breakfast in us before we start planning for battle."

Louisa chimes in, "We need to listen to Jason. He knows how to handle—"

"I get it, Mom," Christopher snaps, and I suddenly see the man from last night that I don't recognize. I instantly want the man I was just in bed with to return.

The phone rings as we both take our seats at a long wooden table. An elegant chandelier hangs above us, and the glass is reflecting beams of light around the room. I don't feel comfortable. I don't want to touch the table in fear of leaving fingerprints on the shiny surface.

Ms. Evans pokes her head out from a door. "Oh good, you are both here. I'll have your breakfast out in a second. I hope you're hungry."

I start to get up to help her, but Christopher places his hand on my lap to signal for me to sit. Remembering the conversation from earlier about Ms. Evans not wanting help in the kitchen, I remain in place and... wait. I've never had someone bring me food before when all I do is sit at a table. I don't like it. I like to feel useful. I like to serve the ones I love. I want to be Christopher's wife and cook him a breakfast I know he'll love. Ms. Evans isn't his wife; I am. What would Papa Rich say if he knew I'm just sitting here doing nothing?

"Christopher," Mrs. Davenport says from the threshold of the doorway. "The phone's for you. It's your editor at *Rolling Stone*."

"I'll be right back," Christopher says to me as he gets up from the chair, takes the phone from his mother, then walks to the other room.

Mrs. Davenport then redirects her attention to me, walks up to the table, and stares down at my bare feet.

"We wear shoes at the dining table in this house," she says between clenched teeth and low enough in tone that only I can hear her.

I glance down at my toes and then back at her, embarrassed I've clearly displeased her. "I'm sorry. I don't know what happened to the slippers the police gave us. When I got out of the shower last night, everything was gone."

"Christopher had everything thrown away. I can't say I blame him. He'll want to forget every part of his horrible ordeal, and I'll do my best to make sure he can."

So, if she knows my shoes were thrown away, why would she question that I don't have any shoes on?

Ms. Evans enters the dining room with two plates of breakfast. "I wasn't sure how you took your eggs, so I made omelets just to be safe for today."

"What size shoe do you wear?" Mrs. Davenport asks, still towering over me.

"I don't know."

"What do you mean, you don't know?"

"I didn't wear shoes before."

Her mouth opens wide, her eyes even wider. "What do you mean? You never wore a pair of shoes in your life?"

I steal a glance at Ms. Evans, who just stands motionless with the plates in her hands. I then look at Mrs. Davenport, resentful that I have to discuss this memory that I'd rather not. "Papa Rich didn't allow me to wear shoes."

"You poor girl," Ms. Evans says softly as she places the plates of food in front of me and Christopher's chair.

Mrs. Davenport clutches her neck for a moment and then gently massages the skin. "Well... Ms. Evans, can you go upstairs and try to find a pair of shoes that might fit her of mine. Her foot doesn't look too different than my own." She looks at the dress I'm wearing. "My dress seems to fit you fine enough."

I nod, looking at the pale pink dress, and force a smile. "Thank you. It fits perfectly."

When I got dressed this morning in the dress and walked out of the bathroom to Christopher, his nose wrinkled, and he told me that we would need to get me my own clothes immediately. He obviously didn't like seeing me in his mother's clothing. I wonder what he will think seeing me wear her shoes.

"I think you should follow Ms. Evans upstairs to receive the shoes," she continues. When I look at my breakfast, she says, "Your meal will still be here when you return. Plus, it would be rude to eat before Christopher returns to the table."

Her tone of voice reminds me of Papa Rich's when he feels I don't do something Godly. I know better than to ever question that tone.

Without saying another word, I scoot my chair out, stand up, and follow Ms. Evans up the stairs barefoot. I can almost feel Mrs. Davenport's stare singeing the flesh on my back.

Mrs. Davenport's foot is a little bigger than mine, but not by much. Ms. Evans finds a pair that she feels will do. "This pair is a bit smaller," she says. "Mrs. Davenport will suffer for style and squeeze her feet into shoes that are a bit too small if she has to. Lucky for you."

I reach for the black heels and wonder if they will be considered too fancy, but I also know I don't have a choice. And looking around Mrs. Davenport's closet—which is as large as a bedroom—I don't see any simple shoes or boots. Everything seems so... expensive and luxurious.

"I'm sorry I didn't help with breakfast," I say, feeling the need to apologize regardless of what Christopher said. The woman seems so kind, and I want her to know how I feel.

"Sorry? Why would you say such a thing? There's nothing to be sorry about."

"I did all the cooking before. Before...."

The smile and cheery disposition she had seem to melt off her face. A sadness appears to wash over her. "I understand how all this has to be really scary and different. It's a completely different world you're now in."

Tears prickle the backs of my eyes, but I refuse to allow them to surface.

"I can't imagine what you and Christopher went through." She waits for me to place the shoes on my feet and then helps me find my balance as I wobble on the heels. "Is what they're saying on the news true? Where you kidnapped as a child and forced to live hidden in a schoolhouse, never to see another soul?"

I take a cautious step and then another. "I never saw it that way growing up." I take another step and worry I may twist my ankle if I'm not careful. "Papa Rich was my family."

"He sounds like a very sick and demented man."

I wonder what the news is saying about him. What are they saying about me?

"I don't know," I say. "I don't know."

"Were you happy there?"

"No," I admit. "No, I wasn't happy. But then I met Christopher."

The woman doesn't say anything for several awkward moments but then finally breaks the thick air by saying, "Well, let's head downstairs. Your breakfast is getting cold."

Making my way downstairs is no easy task. Shoes are hard enough to get used to, but heels are a different beast within themselves. They hurt my feet, make my ankles tired, and my calves seem to be tense at all times. I somehow get to the dining room without falling at the same time Christopher is getting off the phone and taking his own seat at the shiny table.

"Is everything okay?" he asks me with a look of confusion as to why I was gone.

"We just got her a pair of Mrs. Davenport's shoes to wear," Ms. Evans says with a warm smile.

Christopher glances down at my feet and then at his mother, who is now sitting at the head of the table, sipping from a teacup.

"Really, Mother? You can't give her a little grace? Heels?"

Mrs. Davenport raises an eyebrow and then places her teacup on the matching saucer below. "A lady only wears heels."

I take my seat and place my hand on Christopher's lap as he did with me when I tried to stand up to help. "Thank you, Mrs. Davenport. I appreciate you lending me the shoes."

"You can call her Louisa," Christopher says as he takes a bite of omelet. "No need for formalities."

"Well, we don't exactly know each other," Mrs. Davenport cuts in.

"She'll be calling you *Louisa*," Christopher says with a warning voice.

His mother must know when to not push any further when it comes to her son, because even though her lips purse together and wrinkles furrow her brow, she nods curtly and says, "Very well. Yes, please call me Louisa, dear."

I don't know this woman one bit, but I do know she doesn't mean a single word she says. But I also know it's Christopher's wishes, and I'll do as he asks just as his mother will.

"What did your work have to say?" she asks while she watches Christopher and me eat.

"They want me back," Christopher says between mouthfuls. "Jason is on the phone with them now about giving them an exclusive with me and Ember. We need to give it to someone, so why not *Rolling Stone*? He's working out all the details."

"That's excellent news," Louisa says. "It will do you good to get your old life back as soon as possible."

"We're going to start looking for an apartment as soon as possible too," he adds.

"Do you really think that's a good idea?" she asks. "With everything going on, and with the media circus, you may be better off staying here." She looks at me and then paints a smile on her face that makes the corners twitch. I'm learning this smile. I see the fake laced in it. "Think of Ember. If you go back to work with *Rolling Stone*, it will mean Ember being left alone. At least by you two staying here for a bit, she'll never be alone. Ms. Evans will be here."

I notice she doesn't say *she* will be here for me, but instead the servant doing the job of a wife and now the new caretaker. I don't want to be alone at all, but I also don't feel welcomed here regardless of what Louisa is saying.

"You have a point," he says as he takes large swallows of his orange juice. I notice it's not freshly squeezed. I would have squeezed it myself this morning before pouring him a glass.

Jason enters the room and pauses until all eyes are on him. "I have a statement written up for you," he says. "I think it's best for you to do it now. I also spoke with *Rolling Stone*, and all the details are ironed out for you."

Christopher wipes his mouth and stands. "Thank you, Jason, but I can handle the statement myself."

He then looks at me. "Are you done with breakfast? You barely touched your food."

My stomach churns with nerves, and I worry about keeping down the little food I did eat. "I'm done. I'm just nervous."

Christopher helps me out of the chair and says, "Let's get this over with. Just stand by my side, and I'll handle the rest." He takes my hand in his and walks us to the front door. "Remember, it's going to be loud, aggressive, and there will be a lot of flashing lights. Just do what you did yesterday. I saw us on television, and you looked great. You're really photogenic and controlled your emotions perfectly."

Christopher's praise doesn't make me feel any better, but I give him a weak smile. "I'm ready."

When the front door opens, the roar of chaos returns. I can't make out individuals in the crowd, because the flashing lights are so intense. I stay by Christopher's side as he lifts his arm to signal to the horde that he's about to say something.

"I'm happy to be home," he begins. "As you can imagine, this is a lot for me and my family to process. The ordeal I went through was not an easy one or one I wish for anyone to experience. What I witnessed and endured by the hands of a mad man is frankly, unbelievable. But we are home now, and we're safe." He looks at me. "While in captivity, I met this wonderful and courageous woman standing next to me. Although I was living a nightmare, Ember became my one light that got me through it all. Yes, she is what you are all calling the ghost of Hallelujah Junction, but she is made of flesh and bone and feelings. So please take that into consideration with your reporting. The two of us have a lot to adjust to with our new freedom, but we know that with time and understanding from all, we will recover and move on. I ask for our privacy as we take things one day at a time."

"Christopher!"

"Christopher!"

"Christopher!"

So many questions are shooting out at rapid speed. I can't make out any of them and wonder if Christopher can. I hear my name, I hear his name, and I hear Richard being called out. But what the sentences are exactly, I can't tell.

"Ember and I will be answering all your questions soon enough. For now, I ask for our privacy. Thank you."

Jason walks in front of us and calls out, "The family will be issuing a formal statement later today. But right now, Christopher and Ember need time to heal and recover."

He then tightens his grip on mine and turns us around to enter the house once again.

Safe.

But I feel anything but.

7

CHRISTOPHER

"I HAVE A SURPRISE," I TELL EMBER AFTER A LONG DAY FIELDING phone calls.

The FBI had been relentless, asking to speak to both Ember and me several times throughout the day. They kept asking the same questions over and over, and it was enough that I finally decided to hire an attorney. Although no one had gone straight out and said as much, I got the feeling they were questioning whether Ember was an accomplice in the murders Richard committed. I need to make sure they don't paint that picture or somehow trap Ember into saying something that could hurt her.

Jason—which then means my mother as well—doesn't like the optics of us hiring legal counsel, but I have to put my wife first. They keep saying that *I* didn't do anything wrong. And that *I* was a victim. But not once do they say *we*—including Ember. And if they didn't necessarily feel Ember is innocent, then who knows what the authorities and even a judge and jury will believe. It's time to lawyer up. No doubt about it.

Ember lifts her eyes to me, the blue nearly being swallowed up by the dark circles underneath. Her knees are pulled up to her chest, and she rests her head on them. She hasn't said much unless she has to answer direct questions. And though I feel like I've really gotten to know a lot about her with all our constant time held captive together, there is still so much I don't know. I wish I could read her better. I wish I could hear her thoughts.

"Surprise?"

"Come on. I just got off the phone with a really good friend of mine who is doing us a favor. It means we're going to have to make a run for the car I just ordered, but once we do, it's going to be fun from then on."

My mother is standing by the couch, nervously spinning the diamond rings on her fingers. "You aren't really going somewhere, are you? With all those reporters out there? It's not safe, Christopher. Security isn't arriving until tomorrow morning."

"We won't need security. Don't worry. I got this handled. I'm taking Ember shopping."

"Shopping!" she spits out with shock. "You can't be serious."

"I am. I just got off the phone with Christina, and she's shutting down her boutique for us. We're going to come in from the back alley. Even if we're followed or seen, her doors will be locked while we shop." I look at Ember and smile. "We'll have the entire place to ourselves."

Rather than being afraid as I had expected from Ember, she instead seems curious and even happy to have a chance to get out of the house. I can't blame her. It does feel as if the walls are closing in on us.

Watching the town car pull up to the front, I reach for Ember's hand and help her up off the couch. I don't wait for my mother to object or for Jason to tell me that I'm about to create a PR nightmare. This isn't about anyone but me and Ember.

We need to breathe.

We need to be free.

We need to have a moment where we aren't trapped in the house just like we were trapped in Hallelujah Junction.

As we walk to the front door, I can hear my mother mumbling

under her breath, but it's quickly replaced by the roar of the reporters and photographers as we bolt toward the awaiting car.

Once we are safe and driving off, Ember speaks for the first time. "Are you sure we'll be safe?"

"I'm sure." I pat her leg reassuringly and add, "Besides, you can't wear my mother's clothing and her ridiculous heels for long. And I need new stuff as well. It's time we get our lives started."

"I've never been shopping before," she says as she stares out the window at all the scenery passing by.

I can't imagine what it all must be like for her. To see such tall buildings and bright lights. Everything is new for her. Unknown. To do something as simple as shopping for the first time at twenty-five years of age... it's still unbelievable to me.

Every time I find myself about to completely lose my shit— which is often since arriving home—I pause and remind myself that no matter how bad I have it, Ember has it worse. When I want to punch my fist through a wall, or scream out in frustration, or tell everyone around me to go fuck themselves... I look at Ember. Just like in the schoolhouse of a rundown ghost town, she is still my beacon of light. She is still what keeps me sane. She is still my grounding force in all this madness. The least I can do is try to keep my cool and return the favor by at least appearing strong for her.

"My friend Christina has an excellent clothing store. We'll be able to get whatever you want there, and she's anxious to meet you. She said she's already pulling out items she thinks you'll love."

I have to hand it to the driver; he somehow manages to quickly take side streets and loses all the media. I know it's only momentary until they somehow track us down, as they have a scent for a good story like a hound dog for a hunt, but for right now, we have peace. Ember and I are both able to walk into the back door of Christina's without anyone there snapping a picture or asking a million questions. I'm happy to see my friend covered the front glass windows so no one will be able to see us from the front.

"You were able to lose them," she says with a smile as she ushers us in the door.

"Not sure for how long," I reply.

She gives me a long, hard hug, then pulls away to make eye contact that tells me all I need to know. She's happy I'm alive and well. She doesn't say anything, which I'm happy for. I need a break, and oddly... Christina seems to know it.

When we make our way to the main part of the store, she gives the warmest smile to Ember and extends her hand. "You must be Ember. I'm Christina. I've heard a lot about you."

Ember reaches out and shakes her hand, and I'm happy to see her return the smile right back. I haven't seen Ember really smile since the escape—at least not a genuine one.

"It's really nice of you to open your store for us," she says as she glances around at the rows and rows of clothing that flank the walls.

"Christopher is an old and dear friend. There isn't anything I wouldn't do for him." She turns to me and says, "Michael is also shutting his restaurant down an hour early tonight so we can go have dinner without curious eyes."

"You don't have to do that," I say, shaking my head. "You've already done enough for us by allowing us to shop in privacy."

Christina waves her hand and rolls her eyes. "It's done. Don't even try to argue. You're both having dinner with us, and that's it. Michael would kill me if I didn't make it happen. Once we max out your credit card, the least I can do is have my husband cook you both a great meal." She winks at me before looking Ember over from head to toe. "I think I have some great options for you that are going to fit absolutely perfect." She places her arm around Ember's shoulders and leads her to a rack of dresses. "Let's go break Christopher's bank."

Ember glances over her shoulder at me for reassurance that all is fine, but her smile is still present and even brighter than before. I nod and then turn to the side of the store that carries the men's clothing. "You ladies do all the damage you want. Ember has an empty closet that needs to be filled."

I appreciate that Christina doesn't treat either of us like a pity case. She doesn't ask us questions, even though I know she's dying to. I also love that she is being so welcoming and kind to Ember. She's the first person to truly do so since we escaped, unless you count Ms. Evans, but even Ms. Evans stared at us as if we were walking ghosts. Not Christina. She sees me as her friend, and she sees Ember as the woman I love.

"She needs undergarments, shoes... everything," I say as I start searching for my size in a pile of nicely folded jeans. I then steal a look at Christina, who is holding a dress up to Ember. "I think Ember will prefer flats too. My mother is trying to break her ankles in those heels she loaned her."

Rather than brushing me off or telling me that women must wear what's in style, Christina nods and says, "I have the cutest ballet flats that are going to look amazing on you. We have several colors, and I think Christopher's credit card demands to have one of each."

I laugh, watch Ember hold back laughter with mischief in her eyes that I love seeing, and call out, "Whatever Ember wants."

What feels like an eternity of watching Ember go into the changing room, out of the changing room in clothes that fit her perfectly, and then back into the changing room to repeat, and repeat, and repeat, we are finally done. I don't even look at the final total, nor do I care. I would buy the entire store for Ember if she wanted it. The woman deserves to be pampered, even though she doesn't even know what that is.

"Is there anything left in the store?" I tease, but I walk up to Ember, wrap my arms around her from behind, and kiss the side of her neck. "You looked beautiful in everything."

"Oh, I had a little mercy," Christina says. "A little."

"Are you sure?" Ember asks as she looks at me for approval. "We don't have to get everything if you feel it's too much."

"Let's bring the bags to the driver," I say, ignoring her concern. "He can bring them home while we're having dinner." I give Ember a kiss on her forehead. "It's the first of many shopping trips. You'll never do without or have to borrow clothing from anyone again."

I spin her around to get one more look at her, which has her blushing and laughing lightly. Ember remains in a dress from the shop that has flowers on it. It sort of reminds me of the floral dresses she wore in Hallelujah Junction, but it actually fits her, isn't faded, and is modern and from this decade.

I look down at her feet in a pair of beige flats and ask, "Do those feel all right?"

She follows my gaze to her feet and says, "They still feel... restrictive. But much better than those other awful shoes I was wearing. How do women wear those all day?"

"We're masochists, my friend. Masochists," Christina says with a sparkling laugh. "But no need to be like us. You look amazing today, and I love your style. I wish I could pull off the innocent, pure look you have. Work it to your favor."

"Thank you so much," Ember replies. "You have the most beautiful clothes in your store, and I can't thank you enough for helping me. I wouldn't have known where to start." She then walks over to where I stand putting my credit card away and wraps her arms around me tightly. "Thank you, Christopher. Thank you for arranging this and for getting me all these clothes and shoes. I needed to get out of the house. I appreciate everything, but—"

"I know," I interrupt. "It's a lot." I kiss her briefly on the lips. "And no need to thank me. We're married now. It's a husband's duty to spoil his wife."

"Oh, it's just the beginning," Christina says. "We're going to enjoy spoiling the hell out of you." She bags up the last of the purchases and looks at her watch. "We finished just in time to head to Luciano's. Michael will be waiting for us with a meal like no other. We need to fatten you both up a little."

I pause and take in the happiness I see on Ember's face. It's a look I've never truly seen before, and a look I plan to make happen every single day.

My captive bride is finally happy. A little taste of freedom is all it takes.

8

EMBER

I'VE NEVER BEEN TO A RESTAURANT BEFORE. LIKE EVERYTHING WITH my life, I've read about them, imagined them, but never thought I would actually be inside one, sitting at a table, and about to eat at one.

"Sit, sit, sit," Michael says with more excitement than I've ever seen.

He motions us to a table that has a white tablecloth, candles burning, and place settings waiting for us to eat on. I feel out of place, but his warm smile reminds me of his wife's, and I start to warm up to the situation the minute I realize it's just Christopher, Christina, Michael, and me.

Once we sit down, Michael places his hand on Christopher's shoulder, and his joyous expression morphs to one of seriousness. "It's good to have you back, buddy. It's so fucking good to actually see you here in front of me."

"You aren't going to get all mushy on me now, are ya, Mike?" Christopher teases.

"Asshole," Michael mumbles, but he playfully punches Christopher before announcing, "I have the best pasta dishes made up in the kitchen. I'll be right back."

When he turns to leave, Christina reaches for a bottle of open wine and pours it in all four glasses. Papa Rich didn't believe in drinking—well... he didn't believe in *me* drinking. He would drink hard liquor from time to time, but nothing for me. I'm not about to say anything, however, because I desperately want to fit in. For the first time since we left Hallelujah Junction, I feel somewhat normal in my new clothes and my pair of shoes. I like the way Christopher looks at me.

I like the way I looked at me when I saw my reflection in the mirror.

I no longer look like the ghost of Hallelujah Junction and the daughter of a serial killer.

Michael returns with a large tray full of bowls of different pastas and breads. Unlike how I felt this morning being served by Ms. Evans, this time feels different. This time feels like Michael is getting enjoyment out of cooking and serving the ones he cares about. I like being part of it. I like that I seem to be giving him joy simply by sitting and welcoming his food.

He sits down, picks up his full glass of wine, and raises his glass for a toast. We all lift ours as well, as he says, "To Christopher, for returning to us safe when we had all given up hope. To Ember, for joining our often crazy but very loyal clan of friends. And to friendship. May we never be parted again."

We all tap our glasses, and I sip from the wine as if it isn't the first time for me. I steal a glance at Christopher, who is smiling at me as he drinks. He knows I've never drank wine before, but he seems pleased I'm so willing to try to assimilate to the experience.

"Okay, now that we are seated and eating," Michael begins as we all start digging into the delicious food, "I have *got* to ask some questions. Christina filled me in on everything you told her over the phone, so I understand the back story, but there is so much. It seems so unreal."

Christopher lifts his eyes from his food to me with a look of concern. And though I appreciate it, I'm also comfortable with these people and don't have the feeling of wanting to flee. Even though I just met them, there is something about them that make me feel safe.

"Ask whatever you want," I say, giving a warm smile as reassurance that I mean every word. "I'm sure you are both happy to see your friend return and shocked to see him bring someone back with him."

"What happens now?" Michael asks, and Christina stops chewing to await the answer as well.

"Good question," Christopher says. "Ember and I don't really know. Obviously, I have to start working again, and luckily *Rolling Stone* is interested in having me back. I need to find us a place to live, since my mother sold my apartment, and all of us living under the same roof is something that can only last temporarily. If I don't kill my mother, Ember may," Christopher teases with a wink to me.

"What about you?" Christina asks me. "How is all this for you? It must be a lot to take in, since you've never experienced anything beyond that schoolhouse and town, right?"

"It feels like I'm in a thunderstorm. It's loud. It's windy. It's full of electricity, excitement, but also fear." I lift my wine glass and take another swallow before adding, "I'm happy to have Christopher by my side in all this. I'm also happy to have met the both of you. Your kindness has made a pretty bad day end on a good note."

"So, are you guys really married?" Michael asks.

Christina kicks him under the table not so subtly. "I told you they are."

Christopher nods, reaches over the table, and takes my hand in his. "We are. Far from normal circumstances, but Ember and I have a bond that no one can understand."

Michael chuckles, and he pours himself more wine. "I never thought I'd see you married, bro. Never thought the old ball-and-chain was your style." The minute he said the last sentence, his mouth opened wide, and Christina once again kicks him under the table. "Ah shit, man. Sorry. Poor choice of words."

Christopher laughs... and then continues to laugh so loud and for so long that tears form in the corners of his eyes. "That's fucking funny." He looks at me, and although I didn't catch the joke right at the beginning, I do now. I join in on the laughter until we are all hysterical.

Once the table settles and we're back to eating and drinking, Christina asks, "This might be a sensitive topic, but I'm going to ask anyway. What about Marissa? How is she handling all of it?"

Without even making eye contact with Christopher, I know the question has him tense. I know he's worried how I will respond, so I answer first to try to ease the tension. "She was waiting for us when we arrived yesterday. I know it was really hard for her to see me. To see that Christopher now has a wife. I feel bad for her and wish no one else has to feel pain over actions caused by my father."

"Yeah, it was awkward. Not exactly the homecoming I was expecting," Christopher chimes in. "But a lot has changed since I was last here—one being Marissa. She's a great woman and deserves someone just as great. But... I'm with Ember now. It's not like I planned this or asked for it, but it is the way it is. The past is the past, and we have to move on."

"And your mother?" Michael asks with a smirk. "I'm sure she's loving the attention just as much as she loves having her son back."

Christopher sighs as he takes a large swallow from his drink. "You know my mother well."

Christina pats my hand and says, "You don't let that woman intimidate you. I know she can come across as a cold-hearted bitch, but she's harmless. She can't hurt you."

I feel relief in knowing that others find Louisa Davenport... unlikeable.

"She's trying," Christopher defends. "But she is going insane with the idea of me staying married to Ember."

"What does she want you to do? Throw her out on the street?"

Michaels asks, shaking his head. "Wait, don't answer that. I already know the answer."

Christina looks at me and asks, "What about you, Ember? What dreams and hopes do you have? Christopher has his career, but what about you?"

For a minute, I wait for the thunderstorm to return. I wait for the rush of electricity and fear to come, but I'm still at ease and realize Christina isn't judging me or asking out of morbid curiosity. She genuinely seems to care.

I shrug and look around the room as if the answer is waiting for me here within these walls. "I don't know. I never really dreamed of anything before. It wasn't my life. And when Christopher came and we got married, my dream was to be a good wife. It's still my dream. But beyond that, I don't know."

"Do you have any passions? Hobbies?" Michael asks.

"I like to read," I answer. "I also liked to cook, but I could never cook as good as you." I point at the food on my plate. I pause for a moment and add, "But I never dreamed of being anything career wise. I never thought I'd leave Hallelujah Junction. I didn't give myself permission to have hope for anything more than what I already had."

"It's time you start dreaming," Christina says softly as she pats my hand with hers. "The world is yours now. You can have anything you want."

"I think it's going to take Ember awhile to believe that," Christopher says as he leans back in his chair with the wine glass in his hand. He's looking at me with love in his eyes, and heat prickles the back of my neck as his leg brushes mine, and I feel his security and connection flood through me. "Richard messed with her head. He sure as fuck messed with mine. It's going to take us both a bit to get going, but we will."

"Well, if you ever want a job, Ember," Christina chimes in, "the boutique will hire you in a second. I could use the extra help."

"The restaurant too," Michael adds. "If you want to work in the kitchen and around food, I'd love to have you."

"Hey!" Christina teasingly slaps Michael's arms. "Stop trying to steal my employee."

I've never seen this kind of playful banter before, but I like it. I like it a lot.

Friendship.

I know I missed out on a lot of things growing up. I know Papa Rich shielded me from all the world had to offer. I believe that part of him meant well. He was protecting me from all the evil and all the modern society he believed corrupt. But he also kept me from something so very important.

Friendship.

And though I may be wearing shoes for the first time in my life—and yes, I've never drank wine before tonight—the thing that is really standing out to me that I've missed out so much on is that I've never had others care about me simply *because*.

I sit at a table with three people who I don't fear. I don't worry about what they will say or do to me. I don't feel I have to act a certain way or be submissive in every act I do.

For the first time in my life, I feel excited about the future, excited about what's to come.

"I might take you up on the job offer," I say, looking at Christopher to see what he feels about it.

He nods in agreement. "It could be good for you. But first, we need to stop the circus by feeding the animals. We have an interview with *Rolling Stone* tomorrow. My mother's PR person feels it's best to get the story out there in hopes they will grow bored eventually and move on. As long as we keep the mysterious element, they won't go away."

"It's so messed up," Michael grumbles. "You both have enough to deal with right now without all those people hunting you down." He pours us all more wine from the third—maybe fourth—bottle he's opened since the meal began.

Christina lifts her glass to me with a twinkle in her eye. "Wear the blue dress. It will make your eyes pop and your hair shine. I think it will be perfect for the interview, and I know you both will do amazingly."

"Thank you," I say to her. I then look at Michael. "Thank you both. It means a lot to me that you have been so welcoming. I needed this. I didn't know I did, but I feel like I can breathe a little better now."

"We both do," Christopher agrees.

9

CHRISTOPHER

WE TIPTOE INTO THE HOUSE, WHICH I FIND A LITTLE counterproductive, since opening the door allows the noise of the reporters to roar in, but it's late, and I'm hoping my mother is asleep. By the dim lights and the silence inside, it seems that she is.

We make our way to our room and close the door behind us. I don't even have a second once the door clicks before Ember is turning on her heels and wrapping her arms around me.

Pressing her lips to mine, she whispers, "Thank you for tonight. I had the most amazing time."

I kiss her back, dancing my tongue with hers, feeling a little lightheaded from all the wine we drank as my body responds immediately to hers. "I liked seeing you truly smile," I confess. "If I can make that happen every single day, I will."

"My heart feels alive," she says, lowering her hands to my pants, freeing me from my restraints. "I didn't know I could feel this way. My body is buzzing."

She then lifts the dress she'd been wearing over her head, tossing it to the ground. I'm surprised to see her wearing a white lace bra with matching panties. Seeing her in something so normal and everyday fills me with a sense of pride that I can give her such basic things, but they mean the world to her.

"You're beautiful," I say, helping her in our now common goal by lowering my pants as I kick off my shoes and shed my shirt all at the same time.

I like her aggressive act and show of making the first move. Maybe she too is feeling the afterglow of the wine, but it's clear we don't want the night to end quite yet.

"You made me feel special," she says as she runs her finger over my lips, down my neck, over my chest, dipping past my stomach, and then runs a gentle circle over my hard cock. She then removes the last of her clothing.

Pure goddess perfection.

My breath hitches, and my cock aches for more as we're both fully naked and have nothing stopping us from doing more.

I remain standing in place, curious what she has in mind. The girl seems to be on a mission, and I have no intention of stopping her.

Looking up at me through thick lashes, she lowers herself to her knees in front of me. My cock stands at attention before her, and I groan as she takes hold of the base and guides it to her mouth.

"I want to thank you," she purrs as she licks the head of my dick, tasting me, savoring me with her hooded eyes looking up, glazed over in lust.

"I'll take you shopping and to dinner every day if this is the thanks I get," I say as I reach back and find the wall with my palm to help keep my balance.

Her mouth slides down my cock all the way to the base. A tiny gag comes from Ember, which only lights an inferno deeper within my core and with more intensity. I want to tear into the back of her throat with hard pushes but fight the urge and allow her to take control.

Pulling my cock out of her mouth, licking every inch as she does, she whispers, "I want you to do dirty things to me. I don't want to make love. I don't want gentle and loving. I want raw. I want my pussy to feel as alive and buzzing as the rest of my body." She circles her tongue around the tip of my cock again. "Dirty."

"Fuuuck," I barely say on a gasp.

I nearly come at her words. To see my sweet, angelic, naive, innocent Ember nearly growl out these filthy and hot-as-fuck words has me coming undone.

Not thinking, not planning, I take hold of her hair and pull her up to me so I can sink my tongue into her mouth. I want to claim her as mine in all ways. All.

"Get on all fours on the bed," I command.

We have crossed the point of no return. She will do what I say. She will take all the erotic abuse I'm about to give.

With wide eyes, she waits until I release her hair, turns, and obediently does as I ask, sticking her firm ass up on display. She looks over her shoulder at me with vixen blue eyes that make my primal need surge. I crawl up behind her and slap her right ass cheek hard, then the left.

"How dirty?" I hiss.

"Filthy," she answers as she lowers her front half down on her forearms, presenting her ass even more.

My cock twitches in need, but I resist the urge to slam it right inside her with no warning at all.

"Tell me," I order. "Tell me what you want."

"I want you everywhere. I want you to take me where you never have."

I place my finger on her anus and ask, "Where?"

"In my ass," she whispers. "Fuck me in the ass."

I know she's not ready, no matter how much she thinks she is. But that doesn't mean I can't *make* her ready.

"Play with your clit and make yourself nice and wet."

She does exactly as I ask as she balances on one arm and reaches beneath her to stroke her pleasure point with the other. I move my finger from her anus and begin collecting her juices, painting them all over her opening.

"I'm going to stretch you so you can take all of me. It's going to sting. It's going to bite."

"Yes," she moans with a nod, her pussy getting wetter and wetter by the minute. "Yes."

With my finger coated in her arousal, and her asshole nice and slick, I press a finger past the puckered flesh. She whimpers as I do so but doesn't try to wiggle free or break her sexual position even slightly. She simply rubs her clit over and over, her breathing becoming more ragged with each passing second.

In and out, I move my finger, feeling her hole squeeze tightly. It takes everything inside me to not just take her right now.

"Wetter," I say as I dip a second finger in her pussy, soaking the skin.

Not waiting, I push the second finger into her ass, joining the other.

She cries out but pushes back toward my hand. I can see she doesn't want me to stop even though I'm spreading her wider than she can handle and still remain quiet. I don't mind her cries; in fact, they make my dick harder with each mewl that passes her lips.

"Does it hurt?" I ask as I lean forward and kiss the taut skin of her ass.

"Yes," she cries. "But I like it. I want more. I want you."

Unable to control myself any longer, I quickly get off the bed and pull some lubrication out of the bedside table. This isn't going to be easy.

Slicking my dick, I retake my position behind her and position myself at her back entrance. "I'll try to take this as slowly as I can." Though I don't know if this is a promise I can keep.

The minute I breech the entrance, Ember squeals, tenses, but doesn't tell me to stop.

I push a little farther, pausing so she can adjust to the size of me and the stretch. The tightness around me nearly makes me come, but I'm determined to be buried balls-deep before I do.

"Keep playing with that clit," I coach. "Relax and take deep breaths."

Like a good student, she does exactly that, moaning and eventually pressing her ass against me, driving me even deeper inside.

"Fuck me," she coos. "Fuck my ass, Christopher. I don't want you to hold back."

Grasping her hips, I begin pushing and pulling her forward and back. I inch my way deeper each time, claiming her ass as she had so animalistically begged me to do.

Sweat glistens on her lower back, and her moans grow in intensity until a shudder works over every inch and every muscle of her body. The tightness in her ass convulses around my cock, and no matter how hard I try to fight it back, I explode in her ass with a roar of passion.

She collapses onto her stomach with me falling on top of her, my cock still firmly planted inside her ass. I give her tiny kisses on her neck, on her shoulder, on her upper back.

"You've got a hidden vixen inside this innocent body of yours," I pant as I regain composure.

"You bring it out in me." She giggles as goose bumps cover her skin caused by my kisses. "I liked the wine. It made me... hungry."

I chuckle as I finally pull out of her and roll onto my back, staring at the ceiling. "Clearly." I turn my head to look at her wild hair and satiated eyes. "I'm going to make sure the wine cellar stays fully stocked."

10

EMBER

WE SIT ACROSS FROM A REPORTER WITH *ROLLING STONE*. Christopher tried to prep me the best he could before today, but I know he doesn't think I'm ready. He never thinks I'm ready, and maybe he's right. But I can only speak my truth. He told me that the reporter will see right through me if I lie. He told me the reporter will eat me up and spit me out if he even for a second feels I'm not being genuine. He also told me that if I'm uncomfortable with a question, then to simply say I'm not comfortable answering, but if that were the case, I wouldn't answer a thing. I can't see how I'll be comfortable speaking about my father who everyone thinks is a villain, and who I think is either haunting or stalking me now.

"Hello, Ember, Christopher. Thank you for joining me today."

Rolling Stone doesn't usually do television interviews, but they decided to shoot the interview as well in case they want to sell the story to a network to air. They're covering all their bases. From what Jason told us, there's going to be a bidding war from the networks.

We're surrounded by large lights, big reflectors, and three different cameras placed in strategic areas to get all three of us as we speak. I'm happy Jason took hours prepping Christopher on what exactly to say and what not to say. I could tell it frustrated Christopher, but I know I needed it. This entire process scares me. I don't want to mess it up for us. I want to be able to move on, and Christopher believes this is the only way to do that.

"Do either of you have any questions before we start?" he asks.

"Let's just get this over with," Christopher says as a woman runs a makeup brush over my cheeks and the tip of my nose again.

When another man by the camera signals it's time to start, the reporter begins by introducing us and giving a brief description of our story. I try to tune out all the words he's saying the best that I can. I hate hearing how Papa Rich hit Christopher from behind with a mallet, kidnapped, and chained him up in the cellar. I also hate that they refer to him as a serial killer who murdered dozens by pushing them to their deaths in the acid pits of the mill. It sounds so awful and makes him worse than the devil. And though I know deep down he's all they say and did everything mentioned... I still hate hearing him spoken of in this way.

He tells the story of how we burned down Hallelujah Junction, and I'm ashamed we destroyed something so beautiful and so rich and full of history. That town was there long before us, and yet we ruined it all. I can't help but feel that it was the most selfish act we could have done. I know we were escaping, but I hate the fact that those ashes left behind are because of me.

"So, Ember. Let's start with you. Is it true you lived with Richard since you were five years old?"

"Yes," I say softly but then remember Christopher coaching me only minutes ago to speak loud and clear. To show confidence, even if I'm not feeling it. "I went to live with him when I was five. My memory is fuzzy around that time."

"Did he kidnap you?"

"I don't think so. I don't remember being afraid or feeling like

I was kept against my will. But like I said, it's all a bit fuzzy around that time. It's like another lifetime ago."

"Did he change your name from Amber to Ember? Isn't your real name Amber Jennings?"

"I guess so, maybe?" I say with a shrug. "Or maybe I told him Ember. I don't really remember, to be honest. I've always known my name to be Ember, and I never knew what my last name was."

The reporter pauses as if he's carefully watching my every move and analyzing my every word. I feel like he's waiting for me to mess up somehow so he can pounce and not have to be so polite with me. He finally continues with "When he kidnapped you, did he keep you chained in the basement like he did Christopher?"

Memories of the times he did lock me in the cellar—for my own sake—come flooding in. "Yes, sometimes. But mostly, I stayed in the schoolhouse during the days and walked underground in the tunnels to the main house. He wanted me to stay out of sight from everyone. He told me that my life was in danger, and he was keeping me safe from those who wanted to do me harm."

"Who wanted to do you harm?"

"He told me that my mother did. I believed him." The look the reporter gives me makes me uneasy. I can't tell if he thinks I'm stupid or is showing a look of pity.

"Did you ever think of escaping?"

I look at Christopher briefly, and he simply nods his encouragement for me to answer and keep the interview moving along. "No."

"Was it because you were afraid of him?" the reporter asks.

Honest.

Be honest.

But what if Papa Rich will read the interview or see me on television? What will he say? How will he react if I tell the reporter my truth?

Be honest.

"Yes, I guess I was. I was afraid of what he would do. I witnessed what happened when people broke his rules. I didn't want it to happen to me, so I followed his rules no matter what they were."

"Are you talking about the acid pits? How he brought innocent people to the mill and pushed them to their deaths while you watched?"

"She was a child," Christopher defends. "She was brainwashed to believe that Papa Rich knew best. And there was nothing she could do to stop it. I saw it in full action. The man was demented and frankly not someone you wanted to cross."

The reporter turns his attention to Christopher, which allows me to breathe out a sigh of relief. "And did you witness him killing people in the same way?"

"Sadly, yes," Christopher says. "Ember and I came close to escaping one other time, and a young man and woman were trying to help us. We came close but failed. Richard took the couple to the pits and made us watch as he pushed them to their deaths. He then threw Ember's cat into the pit to punish her even more."

I snapped my eyes toward Christopher, angry he's bringing up my dead cat, Pine Cone. There's no need to discuss my cat. It's a detail that doesn't need to be said, and it stabs my heart and rips out my soul, having to relive that awful memory.

"There are reports that you and Ember are married. That Richard had a pastor come to the property and marry you. Is that true?" the reporter continues. I wonder where he's getting all his information and am angry our personal business is so easy to come by.

"Yes, Ember and I are married. The entire reason I wasn't killed in the pit like the other victims was that Richard wanted me to marry Ember—who he considered his daughter. He treated it like an old-fashioned arranged marriage."

"So let me get this straight," the reporter says, shaking his head as if it will help him make sense of our twisted tale. "You were kidnapped, chained in a cellar, and then forced to marry the woman who this man kidnapped as a child. A woman who had been hidden away in a ghost town?"

Christopher reaches out and pats my knee as he nods in agreement. "I know it's hard to believe. I think one of the most difficult things about being held captive was trying to come to terms that the nightmare was real. That the man was truly serious and believed he was acting under God in his decisions. There was no reasoning with him. There was no way I could threaten, bribe, or even plead my way out of it."

"Why would Richard want you to marry his daughter? Why?"

"He loved me," I say flatly. "He wanted the best for me. Family, old-fashioned values, God, and... regardless of what he did, he did have a strong belief in those. And he loved me."

"Love?" The reporter raises an eyebrow and smirks. "You call locking you away from civilization for your entire life love?"

I nod, confident in my statement. "Yes, because in his mind, modern civilization is dangerous, corrupt, and sinful. He saw it as protecting me. When he killed all those people... he justified it as a show of love. Protection."

"I saw it with my own eyes," Christopher adds. "The man truly saw Ember as his daughter. But he was so sick and twisted. His level of control via fear is what made it so hard to escape."

"Ember," the reporter redirects his attention to me, "did you help him kill those people?"

I don't even have a chance to open my mouth before Christopher snaps, "She was as much a victim as them. She was a child who had to grow up as a prisoner for her entire life. She was forced to witness awful acts that will stay with her forever. Of course she didn't help kill those people. Richard was a madman. He was a killer, and Ember is lucky to finally be free of him. She is finally free."

The reporter seems satisfied with the answer, because he changes topic slightly. "Yes, let's talk about free," he says. "Ember, if you have been locked away for most of your life, what's it like to be *free*? How are you adjusting?"

"It's scary," I say softly but then clear my throat before speaking loudly again. "I've read about a lot of this stuff—life— but to actually see it, hear it... it's scary."

"Ember is adjusting well. It's going to be a slow process, and we're trying to introduce her to modern society in baby steps," Christopher adds. "My family, friends, and I plan to be with her every step of the way."

"And what about you?" the reporter asks. "You've been gone for months. I'm sure there were points in captivity that you feared you may never be free again. How are you adjusting to being back?"

"It's a process too," Christopher admits. "I'm starting to get back to work, trying to get my normal routine back. But that man, Richard, really messed with me." He looks at me and takes my hand in his. "My focus is primarily on Ember right now, however. I feel this need to protect her, even though mentally she's by far the strongest person I've ever met."

My heart feels as if it erupts in happiness. Strong? Christopher considers me strong?

He's complimented me many times, but nothing is so rewarding as hearing the word *strong*. I've never been one to think that is a word to describe me, and yet Christopher believes it does.

The reporter nods as if he too agrees I'm strong and then asks, "Is it true Richard could still be alive and on the run? Do you believe he's still out there?"

I think the reporter is asking me, but Christopher answers. "When Ember and I were leaving the burning town, we saw Richard run into the main house, which was engulfed in flames. We assumed he died but were later told they never found his body. So yes. He could still be alive, and he could still be out there."

"Are you afraid of your 'Papa Rich'?" the reporter asks me.

"Are you afraid he may find you again and take you back? He's a serial killer. Do you fear he may come to you and Christopher and finish the job?"

I notice that the reporter used the name Papa Rich rather than Richard, and I don't know why. But regardless, I answer, "He can be a very dangerous man."

Even admitting the words has me trembling. This is the most I've had to think of Richard and my past since arriving in New York, and I'm reaching my max. I hate hearing him be referred to as a serial killer, even though I suppose in definition he is.

He killed a lot of people.

Not once. Not twice. A lot.

So many screams and people begging for their lives. So many innocent lives gone forever.

I need air. I need a break. I need to stop being looked at like I'm a zoo animal.

"Ember, did Papa Rich ever abuse you?

"He was a very strict man."

"Did he ever sexually abuse you?"

My face heats at the thought. How could someone think such a thing, and yet... Papa Rich did bad, bad things. "No."

He looks at Christopher. "Richard forced you to marry Ember. Did he also force you to consummate the marriage?"

"I'm not comfortable answering this question," Christopher says calmly. "Intimate details about Ember and me are private."

The reporter is clearly not happy with the answer. "Were you expected to be married as a true husband and wife would be? Did Richard want children to come from the marriage?"

This isn't right. We shouldn't be talking about... sex. It's sinful. It's wrong.

"Can we take a moment?" Christopher asks, clearly picking up on my emotions and the tension in my body.

The reporter looks at the camera and says, "Cut." He then looks at me. "We'll take a little break. Let you get up and stretch your legs for a sec. You're both doing great. Only a few more questions."

The reporter is the first to stand, and I watch him take out a package of cigarettes and walk to a door with an exit sign shining in green light above it.

"You are doing great," Christopher praises as he kisses me softly on the cheek. "I'm proud of you."

"Do you really think the media will leave us alone after we do this interview?" I hate every part of this day, but if it means the people out front of the house will go away, I'll do anything.

"Maybe not at first, but the big scoop will be covered. Eventually, a new story will hit that will pull them away from us. Jason's right in pushing for us to do this. I hate having my business out on full display too, but if it means we can eventually get back to normal, then so be it."

Normal.

Will I ever know what *normal* is supposed to be?

It's not long before the reporter is back and ready to go. Christopher and I had a chance to use the restroom and get a drink of water, but nothing more. I'm happy that not a lot of time passed, because I want this over with as fast as possible.

Not wasting any time, the reporter dives back in the minute we are all sitting and the camera's red light is on. "There are a lot of families looking for answers right now about their loved ones who died in Hallelujah Junction. Have the authorities used you in identifying the victims, Ember?"

I nod. "I tried to help them the best that I could. But when it all happened—the acid pits—I tried not to look. I tried to close my eyes and block it all out. I don't remember the faces as much as the authorities hoped I would. It's awful what happened. I just hope the families can finally find some peace. Closure maybe?"

"Richard deserves to pay for what he did," Christopher says. "Ember and I will both cooperate with the FBI in any way we can. If he didn't die in that fire, then we hope he's caught, and justice can be served."

The reporter points to the camera. "Ember, if Richard is watching right now, what would you say to him?"

I look at the camera, at the reporter, and then back at the camera. I don't know what to say. Maybe I have nothing to say. Maybe words can't express my thoughts. But I know the reporter is waiting. The men behind and next to the camera are waiting. I have to say something. Swallowing hard, I say in the loudest and most confident voice I can somehow muster, "You were wrong. What you did, what you said, and what you believed... wrong. You were wrong."

The reporter then asks Christopher the exact same question. Christopher, however, doesn't take as long to answer as I did. "Richard... if you're out there and you're watching, just know one thing. I'll find you. You'll pay for what you did to me, to all the innocent people who died, and to Ember. I'm coming for you."

11

EMBER

I LOOK DOWN BELOW AND NOTICE THE CROWDS OF REPORTERS ARE getting smaller and smaller each day that passes. Jason was right when he said they would grow bored and we would be old news after the *Rolling Stone* interview. I know Christopher is happy about it; he seems more relaxed and able to go to work without having to fight through a wave of madness.

A knock on the door has broken my thoughts, and I turn as Ms. Evans pops her head in. "Ember? I'm sorry for just opening the door—I've been knocking."

"Oh sorry. I must have been lost in thought," I say, not sure how long I've been staring out the window.

"I've come to tell you that Christopher called and said he won't be home for dinner. But Mrs. Davenport is joining you tonight. It will be done soon, so you should come downstairs. Mrs. Davenport likes the meal and her guests prompt."

I'm surprised to hear I'll be having dinner with Louisa... alone. I haven't seen much of her since arriving. Christopher told me she's extremely busy with all her social engagements, but I also get the feeling she avoids me. Looking down at my bare feet, dreading putting shoes on, I wish she'd still avoid me—especially with Christopher not being here. I'm used to him working late, and have gotten accustomed to eating alone, but now... I'm not ready for dinner with Louisa.

Taking Ms. Evans's advice, I freshen up, put on the awful shoes that make my feet feel like they are being strangled, and make my way to the dining room. Louisa is already sitting at the head of the table, her palms resting on the polished wood. Candles are lit, fine china and silverware adorn the place settings, and crystal glasses are already poured with wine. It's been like this every night, as it's the rule of the Davenport household to have formal dinners, but for some reason, having Louisa present makes it even fancier.

"Glad you could make it on time," she says, but based on her glare at me, I feel like I'm tardy even though I came straight down.

"I didn't know I'd be having dinner with you," I say as I quickly sit down, grateful to have her not examining my outfit any longer, since I can hide beneath the expansive table. "But I'm happy that I am. I've been eating alone all week with Christopher being back at work now."

"Yes," she says as she sips her wine, her eyes focusing in on me over the glass. "At least he was able to get his job back. With all the negative attention he's getting, I'm so happy the magazine is willing to look past it. Of course, as you know, he doesn't *have* to work. Being a Davenport allows him comforts in life if he chose to take them. But he's a proud man."

We sit in awkward silence until Ms. Evans serves us roasted chicken and vegetables. I wish she'd sit down and join us, but I already learned it isn't the role she plays, and there are no exceptions.

"How are you adjusting?" She finally cuts the silence. "I'm sure living in such a large house compared to where you came from has to be... foreign."

"You have a lovely house. I've walked around and really love all the artwork you have."

"Yes, Christopher's father, my late husband, was a collector."

"Christopher told me that once I get a passport, we can travel to places with museums and galleries. I want to actually see all the art I've read about."

Louisa places her glass on the table and finally takes her first—very dainty—bite of chicken. "Do you really see that happening?"

Confused by the question, I ask, "What do you mean?"

"Travel. With Christopher. Do you really think you will ever be ready to do such a... normal task?"

I don't know if her question is meant to be an insult, but it certainly feels as if it's one.

"I hope so," I say, deciding to not make an issue of the question. "I know Christopher is busy with work right now, so I know it's still a ways out. Plus, we need to start looking for a place to live. He told me last night that he'd arrange for us to meet with a real estate agent soon."

"Do you think that's a good idea? Who will take care of you when he's at work? Ms. Evans and I won't be present."

"I don't feel I need to be taken care of." I look to the door leading to the kitchen. "The only reason I don't cook for myself, and even for the entire household, is because Christopher told me it's Ms. Evans's domain, and I could upset her if I do." Lowering my eyes to the dinner presentation, guilt attacks. Had I made a mistake in listening to Christopher? "I'd be more than happy to do more around the house if you'd like."

"That won't be necessary. It's not about the housework. I'm referring to your mental state."

"Excuse me?" I'm fighting back the urge to stand up and storm out of the room. Not only is the conversation attacking in nature, but it's awkward and uncomfortable. I don't know how to respond properly, nor am I sure if I'm just being overly sensitive and reading her questions the wrong way.

"Come now, Amber," she says as she dabs the corner of her mouth with a linen napkin. "You are essentially a caged animal that has been released. It's not natural or even expected for you to behave in normal society after the upbringing you've had."

"Ember," I correct, trying to ignore her calling me a caged animal.

"In my house, we go by our proper birth-given names." Her face is emotionless, cold, and full of disgust. This woman doesn't like me, and even a *caged animal* can see that.

I poke my fork into a carrot and try not to respond while anger bubbles from my stomach to the back of my throat.

"Let me ask you something," she says after a few moments of silence.

"Yes?" I look at her, readying myself for a bullet to the heart. I can feel she's going in for the kill.

"How was your wedding? I ask because it's a mother's dream to be part of her son's wedding. To dance with him on his special night. To be part of the planning. To witness the vows to the new woman in his life. I had none of that. You stole that from me. So, tell me... how was your wedding?"

"I... I'm sorry."

"Tell me. I'd like to know."

"It was just Christopher, Papa Rich, me, and Scarecrow. It wasn't really a wedding. No cake or anything."

She gives a sickly smile. "No cake? Oh, what a shame."

"Louisa—"

"Mrs. Davenport," she snaps. "You have not earned the position to call me by my first name."

Again, I'm only doing what Christopher said, but I decide it best to not argue or point out that her son disagrees.

"Mrs. Davenport," I say evenly. "I'm sorry that my marriage to your son is upsetting. I completely understand why it would be. I wish things were different and that it didn't happen the way it did."

"Then end it," she blurts. "It's quite simple. It's not legal, and my attorney doesn't even have to draw up any papers to divorce. You simply have to walk away." She raises her hand when I open my mouth to object. "I'm not expecting you to just walk out of my house with nothing. In fact, I can be very generous and will be if you choose to go. I can set you up in an apartment and give you a nice little bank account that allows you to live comfortably. All I will ask in return is that you stay away from Christopher. You don't have any contact with him from this point on. I can have assistants here within the hour to take you away. I can make it very easy for you and have them handle it all."

"He's my husband."

"No, Amber, he isn't."

"I'm not going to leave Christopher. I'm sorry. I'm not."

"Then you're just as bad as Richard. He may have forced you both to get married, but *you* are forcing it to continue. My son was a victim of your father. But you, Amber, are torturing him more than Richard ever did."

I shake my head, tears escaping my eyes no matter how hard I try to fight them off. "That's not true. I live every single day to make Christopher happy. I love him. He loves me."

She laughs. A laugh so evil it sends a shiver down my spine. "He doesn't love you. He feels obligated. You are his responsibility. He brought home a stray and now has to feed and house it. It's not love. Understand that. It's far from love. You can't force love, and that is exactly what you and Richard did to him."

I push away from the table and drop my napkin on the plate. "I'm sorry. I've lost my appetite."

Without waiting to be excused or allowing the conversation to continue, I spin on my heels and march up the stairs. I'm careful not to run. I take each step evenly and slowly. I don't want to seem hysterical and out of control. I want to scream and yell. Actually, I really wanted to throw my wine glass at the woman's head but restrained myself.

Her words sting so badly it feels like a nest full of hornets is attacking my heart, shredding my soul.

Is she right?

Does Christopher not really love me?

Am I nothing but a stray dog that has just been let out of her cage?

12

CHRISTOPHER

"You missed dinner," I hear to my left when I walk into the house.

I enter the dining room and see my mother sitting at the head of the table, sipping her wine. Her half-eaten plate still sits in front of her as well as another barely touched plate, which I assume was Ember's. She hadn't had much of an appetite since arriving, and I make a mental note to keep an eye on how little she is eating. She's tiny enough to begin with, and I need to make sure she keeps up her strength.

I pick up a potato and pop it into my mouth as I lean against the back of Ember's chair. "Shoot ran long," I say. "Sorry."

"Sit," she says as she motions for me to sit. "I'll have Ms. Evans bring you out your dinner."

"I'm fine," I say. "I ate at the shoot."

"Still... sit."

I can see she's serious, and I decide to humor and give her some time. I hadn't had any real alone time with her since arriving and figured she'd like some with me without all the crazy media, and even without Ember.

As soon as I sit, she begins. "I'd like to talk about your future."

I nod. "I know. I'm working on it. Ember and I will be out of your hair as soon as we find a place. I've been so busy, and with everything going on, I didn't feel it was right to just dive right in. I don't want to move Ember from one rental to another, so I'm looking at buying a place. I want it to be just right and not settle."

"When will you stop with the dutiful husband act?" Her words come out like sharp glass, slicing at my calm and relaxed mood I had been in when entering the house.

I sigh loudly and reach for the bottle of wine, pouring Ember's glass full so I can have a little liquid courage for what I know will be a conversation that won't end well.

"Go ahead," I say. "Tell me how I'm making a mistake. How I'm ruining my life. How I need to kick Ember out on her ass. Get it out of your system so I don't ever have to hear you say this shit again."

"It's all true. You just said it, because you know deep down it's true."

"Wonderful. Are we done?" My jaw locks as I take deep breaths to try to keep my cool.

"No, far from it. Have you even tried calling Marissa? That poor girl deserves a phone call. I know she's trying to be understating and give you space, but you should be putting her feelings into consideration. Have you even tried reaching out?"

Clearly, my mother already knows the answer to that question, or she wouldn't be asking. "No. I need time. I will when I'm ready."

"She was your girlfriend. You loved her. Is this how she deserves to be treated?"

"Of course not," I snap. "I know I need to face her and deal with this, but it's not exactly easy. And it's not as if I haven't had my hands full. Call it selfish, but my bandwidth can only handle so much right now. But yes, I plan on talking to Marissa. She deserves closure."

"Why closure? Why can't you be with her? Just because you went through an ordeal doesn't mean you have to stop loving her.

She was marriage material. You and she both had something great, and I knew she'd be the perfect wife. Her social standing matches yours, and together, you can really be a power couple. She'd be good for your reputation and career. She's worthy of the Davenport name."

"We were not going to get married, Mother. Not even close. I was so far from thinking about marriage—"

"And yet you marry *her*!" my mother cuts in.

"I told you. I didn't have a choice. I had to do what I had to do and say what I had to say to survive. I had to plan my escape and outsmart Richard. I told you all this."

"And yet, you are still with her. You don't have to be."

I pinch the bridge of my nose and close my eyes. "She's my wife. I've chosen to stay with her. I want this. I want to be married to her. I know it's hard for you to understand—"

"It's insanity! I don't think you're thinking clearly."

I put down the glass of wine I consider downing in one gulp before I reach for the bottle and finish it off in seconds, but I don't. "That's just it. I'm finally thinking clearly for the first time in a very, very long time. Before I was kidnapped, a single day didn't go by that I didn't drink or pop pills. My camera bag was a traveling pharmacy. I was under one form of influence or another since I can remember."

Her lips twitch, but her eyes remain steadfast on me. She's prepared for battle, and nothing I say is going to rattle her, but I'm going to be brutally honest.

"I know you think that me being chained in a cellar was my darkest moment in life. In all actuality, the life I was living before it was far darker. In many ways, Ember saved me. She didn't just help me escape Richard, but she helped me escape the spiral of booze and pills I was in."

"You weren't that bad," she counters.

"You saw what you wanted to see." I push the wine away just to prove to myself that I can. "I'm a different man now. And yes, I know I'm fucked up from everything that happened and have a lot to deal with in regards to that. But there is a bright light that came from it all, and it's Ember. It's also that I walked away with a new outlook on life. I want to be a better man. I want to provide and protect that woman upstairs. I want to take care of her and put her needs before my own. Which frankly, Mother, makes me a new man. The old Christopher only thought of himself and no one else. I came first. Me and only me."

"She's trapped you," my mother says simply as she takes a sip of her wine, leans back in her chair, and crosses her legs. She is still poised for the battle to continue. "Richard did it first, and she followed. She's no better than him."

"No," I say softly as I shake my head. "She's given me hope. I'm looking forward to our future. And if you want to know the painful truth, it's that I'm finally happy. I don't know how long it's been since I've felt that. Yes, my life is in chaos, but she's my lifeboat. I need you to try to understand that. I need you to give that woman upstairs some understanding. I get it. I know she doesn't have the social graces and status you're used to me bringing home—"

"You've brought home a mangey mutt!"

I scoot my chair back and glare at her as I do. "I'm not going to sit here any longer and allow you to attack my *wife*. My wife!"

She swallows hard to simmer the rage she just released. "I'm trying to make you see reason, Christopher. You have a woman who, though is very sweet and innocent, is also sick. She needs mental help that we are unable to give. I have a list of some very well-respected hospitals that are willing to accept her. Of course they will give her her own room, and I'll make all the arrangements. We can keep this extremely discreet."

"Are you kidding me?" I hiss. "Are you suggesting we commit Ember to a mental institute? Please tell me you aren't saying this."

"I've heard her crying out at night with the bad dreams. I see the way she stares off and is lost in thought. With what she's been through, this could be very good for her. She needs to be in a safe environment where she can learn how to survive in the real world. She has demons and ghosts haunting her, and she always will. You're strong, Christopher, but not strong enough to handle this. To handle her. You would be doing her a favor."

"Do you hear yourself? How is committing my wife to a loony bin doing her a favor?"

"Because she needs the help. She may never be able to heal unless we give her the assistance to do so. She needs someone who specializes in abductions like this. I've been doing some research. We can have them come to her here to take her away. They can do it all without hysterics and drama. They can convince her it's for her own good, because it is! It's for her own good!"

"This conversation is over." I turn to leave before I say something I'll regret.

"Christopher," she calls before I can get away. "I'm asking you to consider this. Think on it. If she goes away to get some help, and you both have some time apart... well... if you still think being with her afterward is a good idea, then I will give my full blessing in the union."

"Good thing I'm not asking for your blessing. Now, if you'll excuse me, I'm going to see my wife."

13

EMBER

"Ms. Evans?" I call out as I peek my head into the kitchen. "Are you in here?" I'm afraid to fully enter her domain without asking permission.

"Ember?" She walks into my view with a look of confusion on her face. She's wiping her hands with a dishtowel as she approaches. "Is everything all right? Are you hungry? I noticed you didn't eat much for lunch. Would you like me to fix you a snack?"

I push the door open wider and enter. "Is it okay if I come in?"

Ms. Evans seems surprised by my question. "Of course." She takes a few steps backward to the massive kitchen island.

I see a large pot on the stove, which is at least three times the size of the stove I had in my kitchen, and I wonder what wonderful meal she's preparing.

"I was wondering if I could help you with dinner," I say, nervous to do something that could upset the woman if what Christopher said was true. "It's just that... I'm used to cooking."

Ms. Evans smiles and points to the carrots lying on the chopping block. "I don't have much left, but you can help me by chopping the carrots."

Relief washes over me. I quickly pick up the knife and begin before the woman can change her mind.

She returns her attention to the pot on the stove and begins adding different seasonings in the bubbling liquid.

"Thank you," I say, focusing on my task. "With Christopher at work all the time now, I'm starting to get a little stir crazy. The walls are closing in on me."

"You should get out and go for a walk. Take in the sights," she suggests.

"I've thought of doing that. Especially since the media outside doesn't seem as crazy anymore. But all I see is concrete. Buildings. People. It makes me miss Hallelujah Junction. Which I know must sound crazy. But I miss the sounds of nature." I'm not sure why I'm confessing all my feelings. Maybe it's being in a kitchen doing familiar tasks, but the honesty floods out of me. "I wouldn't know where to go."

"Hmm," Ms. Evans says as she walks over to where I stand and leans against the island. "You should go to Central Park. I think you'd love it there. It's a little piece of nature in all this city. It's beautiful and could be just the fresh setting you need right now."

"Sounds lovely, but Christopher wants me to stay close to home, and we have supper to cook, and—"

"Forget about dinner. It's on autopilot now, and besides, I get paid to worry about it. Not you. And don't you dare tell Christopher this, but I think he's hovering over you a little. I think you can handle yourself just fine to go for a little walk. An adventure will do you good." She taps her finger on her chin. "You like books, right?"

I nod, unsure why I'm getting excited at the idea of leaving when I know Christopher wouldn't like it one bit.

"There's an *Alice in Wonderland* statue at the park. Just like the book. I think you'll love it. I always do. And if I weren't on shift right now, I'd take you." She pauses and studies me. "But I also think this little bit of independence can do you good. Because you're right. You've been holed up in this house for days. It's not healthy. You need to stretch your legs and soul a bit."

She's right. I have been locked away. Just like I was locked away in the schoolhouse.

No.

Things will be different this time.

I won't be locked away.

And I want desperately to prove to Christopher that he doesn't have to watch over me every second. That I'm capable of doing things on my own and becoming a functioning adult in this new world.

"I love *Alice in Wonderland*. It's one of my favorites."

"Then it's decided," Ms. Evans says as she walks over to a counter that is holding a phone. "You go get ready, and I'll call a car for you."

Before I change my mind, I do exactly that and rush out of the kitchen, prepared to show everyone who worries if I can ever be independent that they are wrong. I can do this. I can.

The eyes of Alice stare back at me. The statue is bigger and more magnificent than I could have imagined. The Mad Hatter and the hare... I want to touch it, but I'm not sure if I should. A bronze Alice perched high on a giant mushroom, surrounded by the Mad Hatter and the White Rabbit as he checks his pocket watch. Engraved around the base of the statue, there are parts of a poem that stand out to me most:

He took his vorpal sword in hand;
Long time the manxome foe he sought—
So rested he by the Tumtum tree
And stood awhile in thought.

And, as in uffish thought he stood,

The Jabberwock, with eyes of flame,
Came whiffling through the tulgey wood,
And burbled as it came!

One, two! One, two! And through and through
The vorpal blade went snicker-snack!
He left it dead, and with its head
He went galumphing back.

"And hast thou slain the Jabberwock?
Come to my arms, my beamish boy!
O frabjous day! Callooh! Callay!"
He chortled in his joy.

Ms. Evans was right about the park giving me a piece of nature I so desperately missed. I needed fresh air. I needed to see and hear birds. I needed to see trees and grass and not just buildings and roads. But my heart also beats so fast and furious that I struggle to breathe normally. The driver of the car promised to wait for me, so at least I know there is a way to return home, but being so far away nearly makes my knees buckle. What if something happens? What if I can't reach Christopher?

I clutch my cell phone in my pocket as a reminder that I'm only a phone call away.

There are people here. Lots of people, but they aren't looking at me. They're busy. They are preoccupied with themselves. So in many ways, I'm alone, even though I'm within arm's reach of strangers.

I take a few steps to the right of the statue so I can see it from another angle. I relate to Alice. I too have gone down my own rabbit hole. I'm in a Wonderland of my own. A mad, mad world where everything is foreign and different. But I'm coming out of it stronger. I have to believe that.

Each day that passes feels better. I'm starting to feel as if I'm no longer the scared little girl in the schoolhouse. I know I have a long ways to go, but coming here by myself, in an expansive park I've never been in, I'm proving this to myself.

I love Christopher, but I don't want to need him.

I want him to love me but not feel he has to shield me from everything.

Alice found her own way in Wonderland by herself. She was strong... and so am I. I can do this. I can find my own way. I have to. I want to.

"One of my favorite parts of Central Park," a man's voice says beside me. "It's nice to see someone else take the time to appreciate it like I do."

I turn to find an elderly man standing next to me, staring at the statue like I was.

"I didn't expect it to be so big," I say.

"First time?" he asks. "Where are you traveling from?"

"I live here now. I'm trying to learn the city and was told to start here."

"Wise choice, and welcome. I've lived here most of my life. New York is the best place to live in the world, but I'm biased." He chuckles. "Where are you from?"

I don't know what to say. I don't want to lie, but I can't exactly be honest either. Then it dawns on me. I'll never be able to truly talk about my past with anyone. That part of my life died, and I have no choice but to try to push it out of my mind. I can't talk about my childhood. I can't share memories neither good nor bad. I have to start over.

Unlike Alice, I have no home to return to. I can't leave the rabbit hole. I'm in it now. I'm always in it. This isn't a dream I can wake up from.

"You know," the man continues when I never answer his question, "Alice is considered to have paranoid schizophrenia, and the Mad Hatter being bipolar. There are even mental illness syndromes named after them. I don't know if everyone knows that, but it's true."

I tilt my head and look at the statue through different eyes with the little-known fact. "I can relate with Alice. Everything in her life was so... big. Or small. I feel that way sometimes. Nothing is the right size around me."

"I know who you are," the man says. "I feel I should be forthcoming and tell you that. I don't know why I acted like I didn't."

"I'm sure I stand out," I say, not feeling uncomfortable by his confession. Maybe I should, but I don't. "And I understand why you wouldn't want to act like you know who I am. I get it."

"You know, I can relate with you in some ways," he replies.

I turn my head and look at him. "How?"

"I was a prisoner of war for years. I served in the Korean War. Held captive for so long that I lost time. And when I was eventually rescued and returned to the land of the living... well, I felt like everything was either too big or too small as well. I felt more captive than I ever did before. Sometimes I missed my prison. At least in my prison, I knew what to expect. I had learned my prison. It was part of me. Being free didn't always feel free."

I don't say anything but stare at the statue again, examining the parts of the artwork that have been polished to a smoothness that nearly erases the texture of the surface. The man seems to say exactly what I'm feeling. I don't think anyone would understand me if I told them I miss not being able to leave the schoolhouse.

I miss my cat.

I miss what I considered my home.

I miss Papa Rich and knowing his schedule.

I miss watching the tourists from afar.

I liked knowing I was safe behind the **No Trespassing** signs. Now, there are no signs to keep me safe.

"How did you deal with it?" I ask. "How did you find your place again?"

"I didn't for a really long time. And if I'm being honest, I'm always a little off the normal path others walk. I tried to fit in the perfect bubble, but it suffocated me. Therapy helped, and I sometimes still go. I think it will always be there to haunt me. But I can tell you it does get easier with time. It's also okay to accept yourself for the way you are. You're different. You experienced a different life. There's no way anyone can truly understand you except you. So, love yourself. Be patient with yourself. Give yourself the grace you need to heal. Now that you are away from the enemy, you're going to realize the real enemy is you."

"I want to be normal. I don't want to be different," I confess. "And it's hard to love myself. I wish I could just be like everyone else. I wish the nightmares would disappear. But they don't. No matter what I do, they are here. And not just when I'm asleep. I have waking nightmares."

"That's okay. I had them too. I sometimes still do, but they ease too."

"I hope so. I really do."

"Embrace who you are. It's taken me a long time to be able to do that myself. You're young and will eventually find your way."

We stand in silence for several minutes, both staring at the bronze sculpture.

"I really should be going," I say, feeling as if others are starting to recognize who I am, and it's just a matter of time until pictures are taken and the media arrives.

The elderly man nods. "Thank you for taking the time to listen to the ramblings of an old man. You have a nice evening. And enjoy New York. I think you'll like it here."

"Thank you for your kind words and advice," I say as I scurry away and head back to the car.

Christopher

. . .

"What do you mean she's gone?" I demand when Ms. Evans tells me Ember isn't home.

"She was getting a little cabin fever," the woman explains calmly, when I'm feeling anything but. "She went to Central Park."

"Central Park? Alone? Are you fucking kidding me? How did she get there? Whose idea was this? Ms. Evans! You were supposed to keep an eye on her!"

She reaches out and places her hand on my upper arm. "Calm down. She'll be fine. She has a driver with her and will be home soon."

"Ms. Evans! Ember can't just leave the house and walk around. It's New York! Are you crazy?"

"You can't keep her locked in a gilded cage, Christopher. She needs to explore and learn to grow. I understand your need to protect her, but you're hurting her by keeping her locked away in this house with no one but me as her company. I'm watching the poor girl fall into depression. It's not healthy, and you know it. She needs to get out, meet people, and be active in day-to-day life. She also doesn't want to disappoint you, Christopher. So I think she's not being completely open and honest with you. And she's trying hard with your mother. I can see she wants her approval so badly."

"No one gets my mother's approval," I snap. "I'll inform Ember on this. But still... Ms. Evans... she can't leave the house! It's not safe."

"She needs to be let out of the cage." The woman refuses to back down, and it infuriates me.

"I trusted you to watch over her!" I boom, turning to storm out of the house and hunt her down.

"I don't need a babysitter," I hear Ember's voice say as she enters the living room. "I was perfectly fine and am now home safe." She motions to her body to indicate she's all intact and smiles. "As you can see. I'm here in one piece."

I rush to her side and take her into my arms, grateful to see her back. "Jesus. Why did you leave? If you wanted to go there, all you had to do was ask, and I would have taken you."

"It was fine. I had a really nice time, actually. I went to see the *Alice in Wonderland* statue, spoke to a nice gentleman—"

"Who?" I interrupt, breaking my hold of her to stare at her eyes. "You can't just go talking to strangers. It could be a reporter or... you can't just talk to complete strangers." I turn to glare at Ms. Evans. "See? This is why she needs to be with me. She doesn't understand the way people act yet. She could get chewed up and spit out."

Ember takes the step that separates us and goes on tiptoe so she can kiss my forehead. "You'll get permanent wrinkles if you keep furrowing your brow like this. Stop being angry at Ms. Evans. She was right in helping me. I needed to get out and explore a little, and no harm came of it. And you can't always be with me, Christopher. I needed to get out, and nothing bad came of it. So calm down." She briefly pecks my lips and winks at Ms. Evans. "Thank you for the suggestion. It was fun. I want to go back when I have more time to really explore the entire park. I only had time to take a short walk."

"With me next time," I say, glaring at Ms. Evans and then at Ember. I can tell I've lost this battle and being angry isn't going to get me anywhere, but I still want my wishes known.

Ember giggles and nods. "Whatever you say, husband. Whatever you say."

I can tell she's mocking me, but I have to admit I like it. She does seem refreshed and happy. Yes, I want her safe... but more than anything, I want her happy.

14

EMBER

I'm happy to see Christopher getting back to work, but a selfish part of me doesn't like it when he leaves, especially after the awful dinner I had with Louisa the other night. Luckily, I hadn't seen her since, so I'm doing my best to act as if nothing happened. I don't want to tell Christopher about the dinner, because I don't want to upset him. I believe it's best to just ignore and move on. The woman needs time to adjust.

Papa Rich used to tell me that an injured animal is dangerous. Pain can make even the nicest creature vicious. And that is exactly what Louisa Davenport is. Hurt. I can understand that. She missed a milestone of her son's life. Hurt has made her mean to me. I have to rise above that. I have to.

But I do miss Christopher. There have been long days where he's gone from the time we wake up until after I've already fallen asleep. He's in demand now since the interview. His "fame" has helped his career even more, and he's getting freelance offers that he's struggling to turn down. People want him to travel all over the world, and when I tell him to take the opportunity, he brushes off the idea. He tells me that he doesn't want to leave me for so long and doesn't feel I'm ready for international travel.

He's probably right.

I'm adjusting, but not well. The sounds of the city are loud, and the constant movement has me jittery. Taking a simple walk gives me anxiety, and though I try to hide the feelings from Christopher, I know he sees it. He feels it.

And then there's Papa Rich.

I know he's alive. I can feel it in my bones.

Christopher tells me over and over again that even if he's alive, he can't hurt us again. He can't reach us.

I don't believe him.

He doesn't know Papa Rich like I do, and even though I'm practically locked away in Louisa's tower like Rapunzel, Papa Rich will find a way to reach me. It's just a matter of time.

"It's one night," Christopher says as he throws some clothes in a small black suitcase. "The shoot is in LA, and I can't make it a turnaround trip like I want to. One night, and I'll be home."

I don't know if he's telling me this to make me feel better, or for him to feel better about leaving me.

"And my mother is here. And she's having the party tonight that will be fun for you to attend and keep you busy. Louisa Davenport is known for her social gatherings with all the glitz, fantastic food, and expensive wines."

"Are Christina and Michael coming?" I ask, hating the idea of attending a party without Christopher. I sit cross-legged on the bed, watching his every move.

He chuckles as he folds a shirt. "They aren't exactly in her social circle."

"Maybe I should just stay upstairs and read," I offer.

He pauses, looks at me, and then smiles. "Make an appearance, let everyone see how beautiful Louisa Davenport's daughter-in-law is, and enjoy a bite to eat. If you're having an awful time after that, then feel free to excuse yourself. But I think it will be good for you to interact with some new people and keep your mind off me being gone."

"I suppose you're right," I agree as I fiddle with the hem of my skirt between my fingers. "But with all the people coming, will we all be... safe?"

"The media won't be allowed inside. Don't worry; my mother still has security outside the house. If anything, it will add to the elite and exclusive element of her party. I'm sure she simply loves it."

I'm not referring to the media, but I don't tell him that I actually meant if we'll be safe from Papa Rich. He could walk into the party undetected if there's a constant flow of people entering and exiting the house. The FBI team assigned to the case officially announced Richard as a wanted man. They are also searching for Scarecrow, as they haven't been able to locate him either. They found Scarecrow's old mining camp they believe he was living in, but it had been vacated. Their assumption is that Richard and Scarecrow are on the run together. They've ruled me out as an accomplice, or at least that's what Christopher's team of lawyers have told us.

Every time I bring up Papa Rich to Christopher, I can see it annoys him. Each time, he is getting a little more short with me and a little more impatient. I hate keeping things from my husband, but at the same time, maybe he's right. Maybe I'm being paranoid over nothing. Maybe I need to set that ghost haunting me free.

Maybe Papa Rich died in that fire.

Or at the very least, maybe that fire and our escape really will be the last I'll see of him regardless of if he escaped or not. I know I can't heal until I stop thinking about him. I know that.

Christopher is trying to convince me to see a therapist to help me work through my feelings, but I don't want to speak to a stranger. At least not yet. I know it's not good that I really don't want to leave our bedroom. I feel safe in it. I feel secure. Every strange face that looks at me reminds me of a bee sting.

It was bad enough that I had to go to a doctor to be examined and to get vaccinations that I never had growing up. Christopher also convinced me it would be best to be put on birth control. I want a baby but have to agree that I don't want one quite yet. I didn't realize that it was so easy to prevent one from coming. But the experience at the doctor's office was awful. They asked so many personal questions, and I felt like I was a science project to them. I hated it, and I vowed to stay healthy so I never have to return... or at least until my next round of awful vaccines.

"I'm going to miss you," I confess as I watch him zip up his suitcase.

He leans forward and kisses me on the lips. "I'm going to miss you, too." He pulls away, runs his fingers through my hair, and adds, "I'll be back tomorrow night. Try to have some fun while I'm gone. I'm also just a phone call away."

Christopher gave me a cell phone when he started work again. I hate using it and keeping it on me at all times as he asked me to do. I feel so incompetent and inept in using it. I also don't like talking into something to hear my husband's voice. It feels unnatural and actually only makes me miss him more.

We walk down the stairs to the foyer hand in hand, something Louisa clearly hates when she sees us. Her eyes dart to our intertwined fingers, and if the daggers shooting from her heavy-lashed eyes could slice each finger off my hand, she would have.

"Are you sure you have to go?" she asks Christopher. "I was so hoping for you to be at tonight's party. So many people want to see you and talk to you. Everyone had been absolutely devastated at your funeral."

"I'm sure there will be many more parties," Christopher says as he puts down his suitcase and gives his mother a hug. "Ember will be there for the both of us."

"Alone? Do you feel that Amber should be alone?"

"Ember," I correct. I hate when she calls me Amber, which she now does every single time.

"Your name is Amber, dear. Amber Jennings. Remember?"

She's talking to me like I'm a child. She almost has a singsong tone to each syllable, and I want to scream at her. *My name is Ember. Ember!*

"Mom, we discussed this. Ember prefers the name she's always known."

"But her legal name is Amber."

"Mom," Cristopher warns. "As I was saying, Ember will love meeting your friends in my spot."

Louisa shoots another glare my way. "Are you sure that's a good idea? There will be a lot of people there and—"

"She'll be fine," he says as he walks over to me and quickly pecks my lips, and then adds, "I'll see you tomorrow night." He picks up his suitcase and walks out the door before calling out, "You ladies have fun tonight. But don't have too much without me."

When the door closes, Louisa turns her attention on me. "It's semi-formal tonight. If you plan on attending, make sure you are dressed accordingly." She points at my ballet shoes I've slowly gotten used to wearing. "*Those* will not do. You really should get some heels like a proper lady."

I usually feel a sense of shame every time Louisa points out something she finds wrong about me, but not in regards to the shoes. They were from a friend's store, and I'm proud of them. "Christina told me these shoes are very in style." I notice my voice is haughty, and although foreign, I feel it's appropriate to have toward this woman.

"Who? Christina? She has that boho shop I wouldn't be caught dead in." Louisa looks as if she's smelling something foul, but then she notices the catering department is not setting up a table to her specifications and runs toward them, barking orders before I can defend my friend.

I want Christopher's mother to like me, but it may be an impossible task.

Glad I have several dresses that are far fancier than the ones I've been wearing daily, I go upstairs to start getting ready for the party. I know it's important to Christopher that I go, and although

I'd much prefer not to ... I do have something to prove to Louisa. I'm not the poor girl who haunted the schoolhouse anymore. I'm not the victim of a madman.

I'm not Amber Jennings.

I'm Ember. Ember *Davenport*.

A Davenport. Mrs. Christopher Davenport.

15

EMBER

ALL DAY, I MENTALLY PREPARED. I TOOK A LONG BATH. I READ A NEW book. I focused on what I want out of the future—but more specifically, tonight. I thought of Christopher and how he clearly had faith in me before he left. And I spent some time thinking of Papa Rich. Not in a fond way, or a scared way, but in a way I believe is helping me heal. I realize I have to accept the fact that he truly is a bad man. What he did to me was bad. His acts were not out of love but rather from sickness.

I spent today trying to heal and become strong. And for the first time since arriving in this house, I started to feel like I was getting used to things.

Accepting.

I'm proud of myself and actually excited for the party. Standing in front of the full-length mirror, I know I've managed to pull off the semi-formal that Louisa wants for her event. Thanks to Christina thinking ahead and making me get a rose-colored satin dress with a dipping neckline I first thought too sexy, I'm happy I listened to her. I've also managed to pull my hair up into a twist, showing off my neck and shoulders, which is also something I'm not used to. I think Christopher would love seeing me like this.

I'm different.

I'm no longer the scared woman locked in a cellar, jumping at the slightest sound.

Right now, this very second, I see a reflection of confidence. I can be the brave woman society demands. I can be the woman Christopher deserves by his side. I can be her. I can.

The sound of guests already arriving downstairs doesn't scare me. It should... or at least it would... but not right now. Instead, I'm beautiful, and I know I can go down there and be charming. I can meet people as Mrs. Davenport. The younger and prettier Mrs. Davenport.

I laugh out loud at my thoughts and imagine what Louisa would think if she could hear them.

Still wearing flats—because it's all I own—I walk to the bedroom door. I don't care what Louisa says. I think they're pretty, and I'm going to believe what Christina says—that I'm in style. When I go to open the door, I can't.

It's stuck.

I jiggle the handle, trying to force the door open, but nothing I do is working.

Is it stuck? Or is it locked?

Who would lock the door?

I was in the bath for a long time and wouldn't hear the click....

No.

Who would purposely lock my door?

I knock on the door and call out, "Hello? Can anyone hear me? Hello?"

There's laughter and music downstairs, and I know no one can hear me from there, but maybe Louisa is upstairs, or Ms. Evans. I jiggle the handle harder this time, feeling a sense of panic. I don't like feeling... trapped. Locked away. Helpless and unable to flee.

It's just like the cellar.

It's just like the cellar!

I can scream; maybe I will be heard then. But I don't want to make a scene. I don't want to embarrass Christopher. What if it's just as simple as the door being stuck, and I overreact over nothing? They all already see me as fragile. I want to be strong and brave. I'm in the rose dress that gives me courage.

"Hello? Can anyone help? The door is stuck."

Nothing.

I walk over to the window and look down at the people below. I see guests dressed in gowns, furs, and suits entering the house. It's a blur of faces, and I blink away the building fear that something is wrong. Why am I locked in the room? Is someone coming?

Is Papa Rich coming for me?

Does he know Christopher's gone for the night, Louisa is preoccupied, and the security is distracted by all the people? He's smart. He could be watching. Planning. He could have known about this party days ago when the invitations went out. Maybe he's been watching Christopher's every move and has learned his schedule, even as chaotic and unreliable as it is.

Maybe I can bang on the window and the people down below will see me.

But as I get ready to pound on the glass, I pause. If they see me looking out the window, wide-eyed and in need... I will forever be the ghost looking out the window of the schoolhouse. I will never be free. That's how they will see me. That's who I will be.

Deciding to try one more time, I go back to the door and shake harder than before. I even throw my weight against the wood, hoping I can free it. The laughter and blending of voices on the other side taunt me with where I should be.

Maybe Louisa will notice I'm missing and come up looking for me.

I smirk and walk to my bed. Who am I kidding? The woman is grateful I'm not down there. She's probably pleased thinking I got too scared or worked up to attend. Instead, I'm holed up in my room, hiding out. Yeah... she won't come looking for me at all.

Looking at the cell phone on the side table, I consider calling Christopher. I don't know his mother's number or Ms. Evans's. Maybe he does and can call them to have them let me out of the room. But I know he's on a shoot, and I don't want to bother him with something as embarrassing as being locked in my room somehow. I definitely don't want to tell him I'm afraid Papa Rich could be part of it, as I'm pushing my luck already with my "irrational" fear. I don't want to be that wife. The crazy wife who calls in a panic.

Whatever. I didn't even want to go to the party to begin with.

But then, I did.

I do.

I've always had to watch from afar all my life. Families smiling. People laughing while having a fun day out. I was a spy on their time, and as I sit in the room on the edge of my bed, hearing the excited energy below, I'm still the same freak from Hallelujah Junction. I can hear them having a good time without me. I can listen on and do nothing, just as I had to watch from the schoolhouse without being able to be part of the crowds.

Feeling sorry for myself, I pull back the comforter of the bed to crawl in and try to forget this night all together. And then I see it.

I blink away the madness, but it remains rooted in place.

Straw.

There's straw in my bed.

They were here. Scarecrow. Papa Rich.

I know they were here.

It's their way of saying hello.

My eyes dart around the room as if I'm going to find them standing right before me. Oh my God. They've come for me. I knew they would. I knew it.

I bolt off the bed and run to the bathroom, needing to confirm they aren't inside waiting for me. Seeing the empty room doesn't make me feel better. It just means they are toying with me as my cat Pine Cone would toy with a field mouse that snuck in the house. I inhale deeply to see if I can smell onion and body odor but smell nothing. Yet...

Yet...

Yet...

They're here. They. Are. Here.

I run to the door and begin banging hard against it. I don't care if the guests hear me now. I don't care if I embarrass myself and Louisa. I need the safety in numbers. I can't just sit in this room and wait for them to come. I know they are waiting. They are waiting until the perfect time to kidnap me and take me with them. I know it! I feel it!

"Help! I'm stuck in here! Get me out! Help!" I start throwing my shoulder and full body weight at the door but only feel the hard and unforgiving door slapping me back.

No one is coming. The party is loud. The fun is overpowering. No one has time for a scared, crazy woman upstairs.

I sprint to the large walk-in closet and slam the door behind me. I see a lock and make sure I'm in control on this one. I'm locking myself inside. Sitting in the farthest corner, I pull my knees up to my chest and close my eyes. I try not to picture Hallelujah Junction. I try to force the visions of Scarecrow in my bedroom out of my mind. I try not to hear Papa Rich telling me I've been a bad, bad girl and must be punished. I can hear the sound of the leather lash against my bare ass. I can feel the sting on memory alone. I'm going to pay for burning our home. He's going to make sure of it. I know he will.

I notice that near one of Christopher's shoes is another piece of straw.

Scarecrow was in our closet. Was he hiding in here? For how long? Watching?

I cry out but cover my mouth instantly as I do. I don't want them to find me. If they walk into the bedroom, I want them to think I'm at the party.

Don't find me.

Don't find me.

Don't find me.

Looking at the locked door, I realize I left the cell phone by the bed. Should I go get it? And then what?

I can't call Christopher. What can he do? He's in LA and hours and hours away from me even if he did rush back.

I can't call the police. What will I say? Tell them I found straw in my bed and closet? They'd all think I finally lost my mind. The poor kidnapped girl finally broke.

Stretching out my hand, I take hold of the straw. I need to feel it between my fingers to make sure this isn't all in my head. I smell it but only smell straw. It doesn't reek, but did Scarecrow's straw ever smell?

This is all wrong. I should have never let Christopher convince me to escape. We were happy. We were. I could have been a good wife there. I would have worked every single day to please him. Chained or not, at least we would have been safe.

But now...

We've angered Papa Rich.

I've seen over and over what happens when you anger Papa Rich. There may not be the Old Mill anymore with the acid pits, but he'll find a new way to make us suffer. He won't let Christopher get away with what he did. Christopher stole his daughter, and there will be a brutal and agonizing price for that. He'll make me watch as he tortures the man I love. Just like he made me watch as he killed all those trespassers.

So many screams.

So many howls of misery.

And just like all those times before, there is nothing I can do to stop it. There's not Hallelujah Junction to return to and beg for forgiveness. Everything is gone. Nothing but ash. Nothing but the ghosts of all the dead. Nothing.

"Ember?" I hear called out from the other side of the door.

I freeze and look around for a weapon to use, but there's nothing but shoes and clothes.

"Ember? Are you in here?"

I recognize the voice. It's Louisa. She's here.

"In here," I cry out, wondering if it's all in my head. "In here."

My heart stops in anticipation. I'm frozen in place to see if what I hear is real or just wishful delusion.

The door to the closet tries to open, but the lock I used keeps it closed. I lunge for the door to unlock it but pause before I do. "Louisa? Is that you?"

"Yes."

Unlocking the door, I open it wide, anxious to be free of my prison. When I do, I see Louisa and three other women standing behind her. Each woman has her mouth open and eyes wide. One of them even gasps when she sees me.

Louisa puts her hand to her heart and takes a stunned step backward. "What in the world are you doing locked in the closet?"

"I..." I can see everyone is afraid of me. They aren't moving enough for me to exit the closet, so I stay in place. "I was locked in the bedroom. I couldn't get out no matter how hard I tried. I think Papa Rich did it. I think he's here. So I was hiding. He's here." My body starts to shake as I say the words. "He's here."

"What are you talking about?" Louisa asks, her eyes changing from a look of shock to a look of detest. "The door wasn't locked. We just walked in here perfectly fine."

"No. It was locked. I even called out for help, but—"

Louisa turns her head to look at her friends who have yet to stop staring at me as if I'm some sort of two-headed circus freak. "I'm sorry you ladies have to witness this. Ember has... been through a lot."

Their looks of shock morph to looks of pity. I hate these looks even more.

"You poor thing," one woman says.

"You're safe now," another adds.

"You don't understand," I say as I reach for Louisa's hand. She pulls away as if touching me would cause a chemical reaction to her creamy white skin. I pause when I realize these women—including Louisa—think I've gone mad.

"You need help, Ember," Louisa says, glancing at her friends for their agreement. The other three women nod as if they know who I am and are in a place to know what's best for me. "I've been telling Christopher this over and over again." She pulls out her phone from a small clutch she has around her wrist and begins dialing.

"Louisa, I'm not making this up. This isn't in my head. If you will just sit down and listen to me, you'll see we are all in danger. Papa Rich is a vengeful man, and he's going to punish us all for our misdeeds." I hand her the piece of straw. "This is proof that Scarecrow is here with him. He left it behind to mess with me, to mess with us all."

The other women all step away at this time. The movement allows me to leave the closet and enter the room, which only makes them cower farther away. They're all acting like I'm going to hurt them. Realizing these women are terrified of me, I retreat back into the closet to give them all some space.

To give me some space.

I can't breathe. I can't think. I can't process.

All I know is no one is listening, and we're all in danger.

"Come home now," Louisa says into the phone as she shoots daggers from her eyes at me. "It's Ember. She's lost her mind completely. You need to come home and deal with this immediately."

I open my mouth to tell her she's wrong. I'm saner and more levelheaded than I've been since arriving. I'm finally seeing what's going to happen. I'm no longer hiding from truth. He's coming. He's coming.

"Christopher! I'm telling you to come home."

16

CHRISTOPHER

It was time to face the demon head-on.

Maybe not the smartest choice, considering that my mind wasn't in the game for this photo shoot, but still, something had to be done. I took the opportunity of being alone—without Ember—on the plane to finally read all the information that had been gathered on Richard by my attorneys and Jason. I spent the last few weeks trying to get the thought of Richard out of Ember's mind, which meant not discussing him, not bringing up the investigation, and trying to forget this awful experience ever occurred. Ember needs to move on, and the only way I feel she can do so is by trying to erase Papa Rich from her memories and future thoughts.

But now that I'm alone for a longer stretch of time, it's time I see what the current status is.

Snapping picture after picture of the latest starlet, I try to focus on her, but all I can see are the beady and evil eyes of Richard. Reading the file fucked me up. What little healing I had done had just been ripped wide open and is now an oozing, festering wound again.

Richard is now referred as The Ghost Town Killer and

officially considered a serial killer. Twenty-two victims turned up missing in Hallelujah Junction and are now presumed dead per the accounts Ember was able to give the authorities. They believe The Ghost Town Killer is now responsible for all of their deaths. The information in my files reveals that not a single body was able to be exhumed from the acid pits due to the conditions. It truly was a genius move for a serial killer to use the acid pits as his mode for murder. No evidence left behind. Only two witnesses.

Me and Ember.

I saw a picture of the couple who tried to help Ember and me, which cost them their lives. It was like a punch to the gut repeatedly, and I can't help but feel like blood is on my hands. They died because of me. I put them in the situation, and I was helpless in saving them. But they were only two of the twenty-two victims. Which means poor Ember has twenty more deaths to feel guilty over than I do.

I can't imagine what that must do to her.

I know what two gruesome deaths is doing to me.

I have nightmares with their faces in them. I hear their screams still. I still remember the look in their eyes right before they were pushed to their deaths. I'm not sure I'll ever be able to forget.

The media is loving the story of The Schoolhouse Ghost and The *Rolling Stone* Photographer. Articles calling us a twisted and perverse love story.

A demented love affair.

In the file, Jason included official offers for book and movie deals I just briefly skimmed over. The last thing I want is to see our ordeal on the big screen. Who the fuck would they get to play me? I actually chuckled on the plane at the very thought.

Reading it on the plane had been surreal. It's hard to believe I not only lived it but survived it. But the hardest part isn't what happened—it's dealing with it all now. Yes, I got my career back, and yes, I'm a free man, but I often feel trapped. My breathing restricts often as my soul feels shredded with what occurred. I try to be strong for Ember, and yet, I sometimes wonder if she's far stronger than I am.

Or maybe we're both just fucked.

Fortunately for me and my model, my years of experience allow me to operate on autopilot, and I'm somehow able to finish the shoot and get some excellent photos that will work for what I need. I'm also happy the crew mostly leaves me alone during the shoot. I think word has spread that I'm not open to discussing the kidnapping and it's best to check your curiosity at the door if you want to work with me currently and for any future gigs. I've never been one to be a diva, but if that's the rumor, then good. They are correct.

I don't want to talk about shit.

Leave me the fuck alone if you just want to be a rubbernecker and be around the *Rolling Stone* Photographer married to The Schoolhouse Ghost. Move the fuck along.

As I'm packing up the last of my gear, I hear a familiar voice from behind me. "Hi, Christopher."

Looking over my shoulder, I see Marissa standing a few feet away with a warm smile but nervous hands fiddling in front of her stomach.

"Marissa?" I stand up from the crouching position I'm in. "What are you doing here?"

"I still have friends at *Rolling Stone*. I found out you were coming to LA on business, and well—" She repositions her weight from one foot to the other. "—I wanted a chance to speak to you alone. We need to talk."

I haven't seen or spoken to Marissa since the first day I returned home, and although I was hoping to avoid this conversation all together, I also know she deserves closure. I should have called her and explained long ago. It was selfish of me not to.

"Can we go get a drink?" she asks. "If you're all done."

"I'd like that," I say, glancing down at my phone to make sure

I didn't get any calls while I was doing the shoot. "Does Mickey's sound good?"

"I was hoping you'd say that." Her face lights up. "It's our favorite whenever we come to LA."

She's not talking in past tense, and I wish she would. It *was* our favorite. *Was.*

We both don't say much until we're sitting in our usual booth and have ordered our usual drinks and our favorite potato skins as a snack. Guilt runs through my veins at how routine and natural it feels, and a big part of me misses the normal of it all. There was a day that I never thought I'd be back to doing these kinds of things again.

I decide to be the first to speak. "I'm sorry I haven't reached out to you."

Her eyes lower to her drink, and she nods slowly. "I was hoping you would. I kept waiting. I wanted to give you space and time, but... I kept waiting."

"I don't know if I'll ever have enough time, to be honest." I take a drink of my beer and reach for a skin. "I don't ever think I'll be the man I once was."

"I watched you and Ember in that interview. It was hard hearing what happened to you. Even harder seeing you with her."

"I'm sorry."

"What about me, Christopher? Was I not your girlfriend before all this?"

"You were. Yes. But everything changed the minute that chain was forced around my ankle."

"Why? Why do your feelings for me have to change? You and I had something really special. We still do."

"Everything changed. I changed," I admit. "I tried to fight it every step of the way. I tried to resist. But sadly, your and my relationship was collateral damage."

"Did you resist *her*? Why did you marry her?"

"I was forced to. It was the reason I wasn't killed by Richard to begin with. He wanted me to marry his daughter, and that was the only way to survive. I was living one day at a time and trying to figure out a way to get out of there."

"Okay... I get that. But then why stay with her now? You aren't *forced* to be with her now to survive."

I sit back and release a rush of air from my lungs. I don't know how honest to be with her. I don't want to hurt her any more than I have to, but I also know if I'm truly honest, the words will sting like a son of a bitch.

"You're home," she adds. "I'm here, and I can be here for you while you recover."

"I'm married, Marissa," I state firmly. "I know you and others don't think I'm really married, considering how it was done and the legalities of it, but I made more than one vow to Ember. Something happened while we were locked up together. A bond and connection I've never had with anyone else. I'm sorry, as I know this has to be tough to hear. We both lived through something I can never explain, because there are no real words. I see her as my wife, just as she sees me as her husband."

"But do you love her?"

I reach for my beer as I consider the question. "I do." I look up at her and see tears wetting her eyes. "I know it's hard to believe. But I do. Trust me, I didn't think it was possible, and at the beginning, I was playing along so I could try to escape. But things changed. We changed while there. And yes, I do love Ember." I pause, taking a drink so I can wash away the words I know just destroyed the woman in front of me. "I'm sorry, Marissa. I truly am."

"I don't believe you. Or maybe you *think* you love her. But I think you feel a sense of responsibility for her. I think you know she has no one but you, so you feel guilty. I think you may be suffering from survivor's guilt or PTSD or something. But I don't think you truly love her."

I nodded. "I'm sure you're right in the fact that I'm suffering from all that. And yes, I do feel a sense of responsibility for her. I have an almost primal need to protect her. But that doesn't change the fact that I do love her, and I have no intention of ending the marriage with her."

She wipes at a falling tear. "Did you ever love me?"

"I did. But I'm not the same man anymore. Maybe I'm worse off, maybe better in some ways. Regardless, I'm not the same man."

"Your mother told me that Ember is crazy. Certifiably insane. She told me that you feel like you have to protect her. That you feel responsible. Could you be mistaking that as love?"

"She's not crazy," I snap. "Maybe broken, but then so am I. My mother has no idea. No one does. Until you face death head-on and worry if you're going to live another day, no one can judge us."

"It's not just your mother talking. Christopher, you look crazy too. You brought home this waif of a woman who is batshit crazy, and you're calling her your wife. And then you go on national television announcing it to all. I think you're fucked in the head." She pauses and swallows hard. "Which I understand after what you went through. But I'm here to try to talk some reason into you."

"She's my wife. She is. I'm sorry, but nothing you, my mother, or anyone else can say will change that."

"You always told me that what you liked about me was my independence. You liked that I didn't have to be rescued or taken care of. And yet, now you brought home a stray who needs you. *Needs* you." Her voice is rising, and I can see the pain on her face is quickly being replaced by anger.

I reach across the table to pat her hand, which she pulls away from as if I just burned her. "I know I hurt you. I know this isn't what you wanted to hear when you flew across the country. But it's the truth."

Marissa reaches for a napkin and starts dabbing at her eyes, careful not to smear her makeup. "I feel like you're self-destructing, and I'm watching you die right in front of me. This isn't you, Christopher. This isn't you."

"I agree with you that the Christopher who was your boyfriend months ago is not me. I agree."

"Let me stay with you tonight." When I open my mouth to object, she quickly adds, "One night. Just for you to see what it's like to be with me again. To remind you of what we had. Maybe so we can find that man you lost again. I think he's still in there. I believe you still love me. Let me show you. Can you at least give me that? One night?"

"Marissa—"

"One night. It's all I ask. You owe me that. At the very least to give me closure. I'm a victim in this too. Help me just like you help Ember." The tears are flowing down her face now, and no amount of dabbing is preventing the running of mascara. "If after tonight you still want to be with Ember, then I'll walk away gracefully."

My phone rings just as I get ready to respond. I glance down and see it's my mother calling. "I need to get this," I say, answering the phone before Marissa can object. "Mom? Everything okay? How's the party?"

"Come home now," she says firmly.

"What? Why?"

"It's Ember. She's lost her mind completely. You need to come home and deal with this immediately."

"Is she okay? Is she there with you? Let me talk to her."

"Christopher! I'm telling you to come home."

17

CHRISTOPHER

"WHERE IS SHE?" I DEMAND AS I STORM INTO THE HOUSE.

The flight across the country I managed to book the minute my mother called demanding I return home had me nearly exploding. Hours of feeling helpless, knowing Ember needed me and there was absolutely nothing I could do until I got back to New York. But now I'm home, and I need to find Ember and be with her immediately.

Ms. Evans is standing on the bottom stair with a tray in her hand. "I was just going to bring her up some food and drink."

My mother walks in from the living room, which still has signs of her party hours ago that the catering company hasn't collected. "She's hiding in the closet upstairs. She's completely lost her mind. I've never been so embarrassed in all my life. Veronica, Michelle, and Diana all witnessed it and left here simply mortified. It was awful, Christopher. Awful!"

"Why the fuck is she in the closet?"

My words appear to slap my mother, because she gasps before screeching, "How would I know? When she didn't come down for the party, my friends and I went upstairs to check on her. We entered her room to find Ember locked in her closet.

After calling out several times, she finally opened the door with her hair wild, her eyes bulging— Frankly, she looked as if she were on drugs. Then she started rambling about how Papa Rich was in the house and going to get her. She locked herself inside to hide from him. She told my friends they were in danger. I swear, Christopher, I may never live this down. I can't imagine what those women are saying about me now. Ember purposely scared them."

"Why would she think that Richard was in the house? Did something happen to spook her?"

"I went to check on her and if she needed anything," Ms. Evans chimes in. "And she spoke about there being straw in her bed and closet. But I didn't see any straw. I searched everywhere, but there wasn't any."

"Of course there was no straw!" Louisa snapped. "Ramblings of a madwoman. I can't have this going on in my house. She's unstable!"

"Mom, calm down. Ember's just going through a lot right now. Assimilating into this world, with the media, all the attention, and just.... Cut the girl some slack, will ya? She's not doing anything intentionally to upset you or your friends. She's scared."

"She needs help! Serious, professional help."

I nod in agreement. "And I'll get her some. You're right. Getting an expert to try to help her make sense of all this could be a good thing." I pause and then ask, "What about security? Did they see anything out of the ordinary?"

"Of course they didn't," my mother snaps. "There was nothing to see. You don't honestly think a one-legged man hobbled into my house, followed by one of the most wanted men on the FBI list right now, undetected? The girl has lost her mind. She's mental. I don't blame her for being mental, but the fact is that we are not equipped to deal with her. You can't make this woman your problem anymore. You deserve better."

"Mother," I warn, trying to be patient, considering Ember did frazzle the hell out of her. "I know you're upset. I'm sorry, and I'll handle it."

Ms. Evans holds up the tray. "She hasn't eaten or had anything to drink, and I was going to see if I could get something in her."

I take hold of the tray and start walking upstairs. "I'll do it, thank you."

I don't know what to think about everything. I shouldn't have left her. It was too soon. She snapped, because she wasn't ready for me to be away. I should have known better than to suggest she attend a party and then leave as if she's ready to deal with normal life so casually. This is my fault.

"Ember?" I call out as I enter the room, placing the tray on the desk. "It's Christopher."

I walk to the closet, and my heart breaks when I open it. She's sitting in a ball in the farthest corner with bloodshot eyes.

"I'm so sorry, Christopher," she begins on a sob. "I'm so sorry. I don't know what's going on anymore. I feel so.... I don't know what I feel."

I rush to her side and take her into my arms. "What happened? Why are you in the closet?"

"I was so afraid, and... I scared those women. I scared your mother. I made a fool of myself."

"Why are you afraid? Did something happen?" I begin stroking her hair and placing small kisses on her forehead as I hold her firmly against my body.

"It doesn't matter anymore," she mumbles into my chest and then begins crying harder.

"It matters to me."

She raises her eyes to me, and her lip quivers. "I'm always going to be the freak. I'm always going to be the girl who people stare at and talk about behind her back. And it's my fault. Mine. Those women saw me tonight and are going to walk away telling everyone they witnessed the crazy ghost girl they saw on the news. I'm living up to all the rumors. I had a chance to be normal tonight, and instead... this happens." She sobs harder than I've ever seen. Her fists dig into her eyes as she tries to wipe away the tears.

"It's all right. I'm here." I scoop my arm under her legs and pick her up. I carry her to the bed and place her gently on it, repositioning us so I can hold her in my arms again. I may never let her go.

"I saw straw—Scarecrow's straw—but then Ms. Evans said there was no straw. And... I thought they were here. I really thought they were here. I really thought I saw straw."

"You're safe," I soothe. "There's no one here."

Ember pulls away, wipes at her eyes, and stares up at me. "I don't think we are. I think Papa Rich is never going to give up on me. On us. We wronged him, and he's a man with conviction to right any wrong."

Frustration bubbles inside me, and though a part of me wants to shout and scream at Ember for once again letting that man control our thoughts, I know she's in a fragile state and I need to be calm. I also agree with my mother. Ember does need help. We both do. We need someone to help us navigate these fears and emotions of hers. She's afraid, and I'm pissed. I can't be sympathetic like she needs, and she can't handle the rage inside me.

"You need to stop calling him Papa Rich," I say as calmly as I can, but I know the words come out harsh. "He's not your father. He's not in our lives anymore and never will be again. I told you I'd protect you, and I mean it. He can't kidnap you again. It will never happen."

"I tried," she says softly as she rests her cheek on my chest again. "I really tried. I got all dressed up, did my hair, and was actually really excited to go to the party. But then I got locked inside, I swear I saw straw, and... I freaked out. Maybe I'm going crazy. Maybe I've always been that way."

"Anxiety can do that," I say. "Maybe you had a panic attack or something to cause this. I'm sorry. I left you too soon and pushed you too hard to live life like nothing happened to us. I think this was just your mind and body telling you that you aren't ready yet. And that's okay. We don't have to rush things. There's no timetable. We go at our own speed."

"I'm not sure I'll ever get used to this. I feel like I'm in a storm and, no matter what I do, I can't find shelter," she confesses.

"I know. I'm in that storm with you as well, but we will find shelter. I'm going to find us a therapist to help guide us in all this. Will that be okay?"

She tenses but then eventually nods. "Okay."

"I love you, Ember. Just hold on to that one fact when you feel lost. I love you."

There's a long moment of silence, and then she says, "Your mother hates me. I don't blame her." She sniffles, but it sounds as if she's at least done sobbing.

"She'll get over what happened. She's embarrassed. That's all, and you aren't the first person to have a scene at one of her parties. Trust me, she's witnessed far worse."

"I'm sorry. I really am. I'm also sorry you had to fly back so soon. I hope I didn't hurt anything with your work."

I sigh and pull her off me. "Work's fine. It's been a really long day for the both of us. It's late, and we could both use some rest. Let's get undressed and go to bed."

I'm pretty sure the minute my head hits the pillow, I will be out in seconds. The adrenaline is wearing off now that I know Ember is safe and by my side.

When we both crawl into bed to sleep, Ember curls her body up next to mine. I have a flashback of when we first slept together in the dank cellar with nothing but a couple of blankets to keep us warm.

"I'll try to do better," she murmurs as sleep is setting in for both of us.

"You're trying your best. I know you are." I close my eyes, no longer able to keep them open. "We'll figure it out," I say with a yawn. "We always have up until this point and will continue to do so."

I hear her breathing deepen, and I know she's off to sleep. I just hope she doesn't have any more nightmares. I hope the same for me.

Fuck you, Richard.

Fuck you straight to hell.

Part of me hopes he dares show his face here. I'd make him pay for everything he did to this woman. He's broken her, but I will make sure I pick up all the pieces and help her figure out how to heal.

Come, motherfucker.

Come to my *house.*

I'm ready for you.

18

CHRISTOPHER

Frustration is not something I handle well. Patience is not a quality I possess. Hanging up the phone with my real estate agent has me wanting to throw something at my editor's door. The only thing keeping me from doing so is that I'm borrowing his office after a shoot to have a little alone time, and trashing his office won't go over well.

"The market is crazy right now," he said.

"I'm working as hard as I can," he assured.

"I found a fixer upper, but it's not ready to move in to," he offered.

"Maybe in a few months, more inventory will open up," he ended the conversation with.

Ember and I need to get out of my mother's house before she truly drives both of us crazy. I can feel Ember is growing frustrated herself. She doesn't understand why we're in this holding pattern, and I know she's as anxious as I am to get in our own house that she can finally make her home. Transition into normal society isn't being helped by her walking the halls of my mother's elegant and stuffy estate, unable to call anything hers.

There's a knock on the door, and I figure it's Max wanting his office back. "Come in, I'm done," I call out, trying to shake off my annoyance at not having the call with my agent that I wanted.

"Max said I could find you here," Marissa says as she enters the office and closes the door behind her.

Fuck. She's not going to just let this be.

"I know I may not be the person you want to see," she begins as she walks fully into the room. "But you left so abruptly in LA that we weren't able to finish our conversation."

"I felt we did," I state, not wanting to be mean but still having to be honest.

"I spoke to your mother last night, and she told me that Ember is having a really hard time. That you both are considering having her get professional help. At an institute. I'm here to offer my support in any way. I know how hard this must be, and I want to be here for you."

I let out a breath at the same level and intensity a dragon would release a flame. "No. I'm not having my wife committed. It's never been an option, nor will it. This is nothing more than the ramblings of a hopeful but delusional old bat."

"She told me you're struggling with the guilt."

"Marissa... I don't know why you're talking to my mother in the first place. But I can assure you that Ember is doing just fine. She's getting stronger each day. And yes, I've gotten her a therapist to help navigate the waters, but we are far from talking mental hospital."

She looks down at their manicured nails in what I can only assume is disappointment.

"I'm sorry if you thought that opened a door for you," I say much harsher than intended.

She looks up at me with tears in her eyes. "I'm struggling here too, you know. Do you even care about that?"

"Of course I do," I say, softening my voice. "But I've been honest and straightforward with you, Marissa. I'm sorry. We are over... and will *always* be over. Maybe I should have said the last sentence to you earlier. I'm sorry."

"There's going to be a day Ember won't be with you. She's unstable. It doesn't take a therapist to see that. We all see it. Everyone around you sees it. And we all see you are still held captive. You haven't truly escaped yet. I want to be there for you, but I can't just stand here and watch this." She takes a step toward the door and then looks over her shoulder at me. "I wish you luck, Christopher. Based on what your mother has told me... you're going to need it."

She leaves, but the door is still left open. Before I can get up to close it, Max enters his office. "You okay, man? Marissa looked pretty pissed."

"Yeah," I say, walking from behind his desk and sitting on the nearby couch. I run my fingers through my hair and sigh. "How did my life get so damn complicated? What did I do to deserve this? My karma is fucked."

Max goes and sits down at his desk, shaking his head. "I wouldn't want to walk a day in your shoes; that's for sure." He leans back in his chair and begins rocking casually. "You sure you're up to getting back to work so soon?"

"Yeah, I need to. I have another person to be responsible for."

Max rolls his eyes. "Whatever, Christopher *Davenport*. I don't think you're exactly hurting for money."

"You know I don't touch that money," I say as I sigh. "But I'm getting tempted to. I'm struggling to find a place for Ember and me to buy. At least a place that doesn't require me to touch the trust."

"If you need some time off, just let me know. I think the fact that you were held captive in a basement by a serial killer earns you some personal days."

I chuckle, trying to shake off my bad mood.

"Marissa isn't handling Ember well, is she?" he asks.

"I don't blame her for feeling the way she does," I say. "But I can't change what happened."

"Do you want to? Change it?"

I pause to consider the question. "Actually, no. I mean, it's not like I wanted to be married. I may have never gotten married. But now that I have Ember, I don't want to change it. I know that might seem crazy, but it feels like we belong. Like we were meant to be."

"I get it," Max says with a nod. "When do I get to meet this girl?"

"Soon," I reply. "I've been really careful not to throw too much at her. The media insanity really made things tougher to get acclimated than I wanted. I mean, the girl hasn't ever lived. She's been locked up in a ghost town her entire life. So many things that you and I take for granted is all new for her. I forget that sometimes and am reminded when I see her wide eyes take something in for the first time."

"I can't imagine what's that like. What about you? Did all of that fuck with your head? PTSD and stuff? Nightmares?"

I pause before answering. Part of me wants to lie and tell him all is fine, but I've always been straightforward with Max. "I have nightmares. Not as many as Ember does, but I still dream about Richard, the cellar, and the acid pits. The couple I watched die still haunts me. I've gotten a therapist to help Ember and me work through it. He says it will take some time, and I know that. It fucking sucks sometimes, though. I wish I could speed up time so the healing could be done with."

"I'm not worried about you. You're one of the strongest motherfuckers I know. But do you ever worry about Ember? I mean... I can't imagine how someone can bounce back after what she's been through."

"She's getting stronger day by day. I worry about her... maybe too much. But she has a fighting spirit."

"Did that Richard fucker... rape her?" He cringes the minute he asks the question. "Sorry... that may be too personal."

"He's a sick fucker, but no, he didn't rape her. When we had sex on our wedding night, she was a virgin. Although the asshole forced all that to happen, so yes, rape in its own way."

"Sorry, man. Jesus, it's really unbelievable."

"And yet Ember is the most loving and open woman I've ever met. She's broken in many ways, which is understandable, but she doesn't hold back on her feelings. She's free with them. It's refreshing to have someone who doesn't play all the mind games or manipulate. It's not in her makeup. She's genuine and true. I'm in awe every day with how she looks at things. She doesn't see herself as a victim, which I find admirable."

"You look healthier," Max says. "I expected you to be a waif of a man, beaten, and scarred."

"I am healthier. My life is back on track. I have focus now. That, and I'm done drinking and popping pills nonstop. I like being sober. Fucked up that something like being hit upside the head by a killer had to do it for me, but regardless, it's one of the good things that came from this nightmare."

Max looks at his computer and types on his keyboard. "Okay, well, I emailed you your schedule for the next month. It's full. So if you ever feel it's too much, you just tell me. Don't feel you have to stress you or Ember out over it. I can find substitutes."

"I can handle it," I say. "I want to work. I need to work. It's the one area I feel I have complete control of right now." I smirk. "That, and I'm homeless."

Max laughs. "A Davenport homeless. That's a good one."

19

EMBER

DR. STEVENS THINKS I'M IMPROVING, AND I HAVE TO AGREE.

He's helping me realize that Papa Rich— Richard is not and has never been my father. Hallelujah Junction is not my home, and therefore, I can stop missing it, or at least can start the process in saying goodbye to that part of my life. But he also allows me to grieve everything without feeling ashamed for it. He tells me the feelings and thoughts I'm having are normal. He makes me feel... sane.

Walking out of the bathroom, drying off my hair with a towel, I'm excited for the evening. Christopher has promised to take me to Luciano's for dinner, and I'm looking forward to seeing our friends again. Getting dressed in one of my favorite dresses from Christina's, I decide I want to ask Louisa if she has any makeup I can borrow. Maybe she'll offer me some tips. I haven't really put makeup on yet, unless you count lip gloss, and I think tonight will be as good as any night to start.

I walk toward Louisa's room and stop. I hear something. Whispers.

Whispers from downstairs.

I know Ms. Evans is still here, and I know Louisa is in her

room getting ready for her own social engagement. But the murmurings are male. Though I can't hear what's being said, it's masculine. And it's clearly whispers. Whoever is downstairs is purposely trying to keep their voices concealed.

My heart stops, and I don't know why. I shouldn't be concerned. I shouldn't be worried.

Tiptoeing to Louisa's double doors, I try to turn the handle. I don't want to knock in case the people below hear me. Why I care if they hear me or not, I'm not sure, but something in my gut tells me to be quiet.

Louisa's door is locked.

I glance down the hallway at my door and consider running back to my room and locking myself inside. But I feel silly. Why am I afraid? Why am I assuming the worst?

The whispers stop, and I freeze, listening.

Darting my eyes to the top of the stairs, I see a piece of straw, and then another. In fact, there is straw in several places along the landing and near a table that has a collection of glass vases on display. I run over to the table to see the straw closely.

Dr. Stevens would tell me that I'm creating the straw in my mind due to the trauma, but as I pick up the dry fiber and run it in between my fingers, I know I'm not making it up.

The whispers...

The straw...

They're here.

I pick up a vase and hold it as a weapon. If they're going to try to kidnap me, I'm going to put up a fight. I won't go willingly. I won't leave Christopher. I won't let them hurt him, or Louisa, or Ms. Evans. I look over the railing to see if I can tell who is down there. I now know there are men down there. I know. I know!

I need to be strong. I need them to know I'm not weak; I'm not someone they can mess with.

Not thinking but acting on the need to rid them from my life, I toss the glass vase over the stair railing to the foyer down below.

"Get out of this house now!" I scream as the shards of glass shoot in all directions as it crashes down below.

When I don't hear footsteps running away, or even see bodies running out the door, I reach for another vase and throw it down below.

"I said get out! Get out!"

"What are you doing?" Louisa screams. "My vases! Stop! Ember, what in the world are you doing?"

I see Ms. Evans run to the bottom of the stairs, terror in her eyes as she looks at Louisa and me. She pauses for a moment but then charges up the stairs.

"What are you doing?" Louisa asks as she approaches cautiously.

"They're downstairs!"

Louisa looks at Ms. Evans, who is just now at the top of the stairs. "Do we have guests?"

Ms. Evans shakes her head. "No one is here, Ember. It's just the three of us."

"I heard men speaking downstairs. I heard them."

"There are no men in this house, for Christ's sake. You've lost your mind," Louisa says, clearly upset about her priceless vases.

But she should care about her life! Not the vases.

"You both aren't listening to me. No one is listening to me! I heard them. I can feel them!"

"No one is here, Ember," Ms. Evans says calmly with her hands out to try to placate me.

"I'm not making this up!" I scream. "It's not in my head!"

But maybe it is.

Maybe I am crazy.

Maybe Dr. Stevens hasn't been helping me at all.

Maybe....

Ms. Evans runs past Louisa and tries to reach for my hand as I grab another vase and throw it against the wall as I scream to the world. Rage fills me. A pure, uncontrollable rage. Why? Why did this happen to me? Why did Papa Rich do this to me? Why do I have to live in New York hating every day that passes because I feel like a stranger in my own body and in my own existence?

I don't belong here!

I don't belong!

"She's lost her goddamn mind," Louisa shouts as she reaches in her pocket for her phone. I know she's going to call Christopher.

"Stop!" I scream as I lunge for the woman's hand. "Don't you call him! Don't you dare!"

The ringing in my ears won't stop. The voices are getting louder. They're screaming at me to leave. To run far away and never look back. The straw is here. *They* are here.

But maybe I want them to be.

Maybe I want to run *to* them instead of away.

Maybe I want to beg for forgiveness and hope Papa Rich will take me back.

Is that crazy?

Yes, that's fucking crazy!

"Ember," Ms. Evans says with an even voice as she takes a cautious step toward me. "Calm down. It's just us. Calm down. Everything's going to be okay."

I can see Ms. Evans is scared. So is Louisa. I don't blame them. I'd be scared of me too. But they should be so much more terrified of who is lurking in the shadows of this house. Papa Rich will kill them both for keeping me in this house. In his eyes, he'll see it as the ultimate sin. They will pay.

"You better run," I warn. "He's here." I pick up another glass vase and hold it like a weapon, ready to attack. "If he finds you, if he finds you both, you're dead."

"No one's here," Ms. Evans says calmly. "It's just the three of us." She tries to reach for the vase, but I only lift it higher and angle my body so she can't. "You don't need that vase. You're safe."

Louisa takes this opportunity to dial her phone. She takes several steps away from me and calls Christopher. I know she is.

And good. He needs to be here. Not to protect me, but to protect *them*.

"Look," I say, bending down to my knees and pulling the pieces of straw from the broken glass. "Straw!" My finger is bleeding from cutting it on the glass, which drips off the straw. "You see it now, don't you? Straw!"

Louisa screams into the phone. "She's holding a vase, ready to hit us. She told us to run and that we're in danger. She's breaking all the vases and screaming. Christopher, she's out of control. Hurry! Hurry! She's going to hurt us."

I'm not going to hurt them. Not me. But yes, they are in danger!

20

EMBER

"GO TO OUR ROOM NOW!" CHRISTOPHER SHOUTS AS HE POINTS TO the stairs.

"You don't understand! They're here! They're here!"

"You're out of control!"

"Listen to me. He's here! Or at least he was!"

Christopher marches toward me and places his hands firmly on my shoulders. "Ember, listen to me. I just searched this house from top to bottom. There is no one here! No one has ever been here. This is all in your head. Do you hear me?" He's screaming now. He's shaking me as tears run down my face and my heart beats out of my chest. "You are losing your mind and bringing me to the loony bin with you!"

"You have to listen to me—"

"I warned you, Christopher," Louisa interrupts. "I told you that the girl needs help. Serious mental help that we aren't equipped to handle here. She's needs to be committed. She needs to be put away, so she doesn't hurt herself or someone else."

I spin on my heels, breaking free from Christopher's hold. "Shut up! Shut up!" I hate her words. I hate that she is telling my husband I need to be away from him. "Shut up!" My screech is so loud and high-pitched that I wonder if it will shatter the vases I haven't managed to ruin.

Christopher takes hold of my upper arm and shakes me. "Our room, now! Ember, I swear to God, go to our room!"

Louisa has her hand on her chest and acts like I punched her. I want to punch her. I do. How dare she tell my husband I need to leave him and that he needs to leave me? How dare she?

"I have a very important party to be at tonight," Louisa says as she fans her face. "How am I expected to function when I have a madwoman living under my roof?"

I look up to Christopher's dark eyes and consider engaging further but decide we need to talk in private. So rather than saying another word, I charge to our room and throw myself on the bed, crying in rage, fear, and frustration.

There's no way I'm imagining this. I saw the straw. Why would there be straw in the house? But I also know how this looks to Christopher.

"Why can't you at least try?" Christopher booms as he charges into the room, wild eyes, fury etched in every feature.

I scurry back against the headboard, hating that he's so angry.

"I can't be here all the time, Ember! You have to understand that. I have a career. I have to earn for our futures. I need you to be able to stand on your own two feet while I'm gone. I can't deal with the insanity. Why can't you give me that?"

"He was here!" I shout, the sound foreign to my own ears. "I saw the straw. He has Scarecrow either with him or doing his bidding. I saw the straw! I'm not making this up. I'm not losing my mind. I told you from the beginning that he would never let me go. You think I'm safe here, but I'm not. Not from him. Not ever."

Christopher crosses the room to me, hands fisted and rage in his eyes. "Do you hear yourself? I need you to be strong, Ember. I'm trying to be patient. I'm trying to understand what you went through."

"What I'm going through now is far worse than anything I

endured in Hallelujah Junction." I instantly regret my words and wish I could take them back, but they're out, and I might as well be honest now. "I feel like I'm in a prison. Like I'm in shackles on display for all to judge me. I'm the freak from the ghost town, who poor Christopher feels he has to take care of. You think I don't hear? You think I don't see? I know what I am to your mother and your friends."

"Then stop acting like a freak!" he screams.

His words feel like a punch to the gut or a blow to the face. I know his mother thinks I'm a freak, but Christopher? Does he?

He begins to pace the room back and forth like a caged animal. And a caged animal is clearly what he is, and I'm the keeper of the key.

"My mother said you started screaming hysterically and throwing her priceless vases. Explain to me why you did that." His voice is calmer, but he hasn't stopped pacing, and his face is growing redder by the minute.

Of course his mother painted my actions in the worst light.

"I screamed when I saw the straw. I thought I heard Scarecrow and Papa Rich whispering down below. I felt he was near... maybe with Papa Rich. I picked up a vase for protection, and I... I didn't just purposely throw the vases around. I would never do that."

"My mother said both she and Ms. Evans saw no sign of straw anywhere. No sign that anyone had entered the house. You have them both in a near panic now, thinking some one-legged man has broken into the house. My mother had to take medication to calm herself down."

"I didn't mean to scare them," I say as I look down to my hands trembling in my lap. "But he was in the house, Christopher. I know he was."

He takes a deep breath and then exhales. He does this a couple of times with his back to me before turning around and slowly walking to the bed. He sits down, and I flinch as he does, preparing for a punishment of some sort.

He notices my cowering. "Why did you just flinch? Do you really think I'd hit you?"

"You're angry with me," I say softly.

"Yes. But that doesn't mean I'd hit you. I'm not Richard."

"I know you aren't him, but I've also never seen you so mad at me."

I know deep down Christopher would never really hurt me on purpose, but then at the same time, there have been times I don't recognize the man in front of me. It's like there is a passing sun over him. Sometimes, he's in the shade, and other times, the sun is beaming on his handsome face. Sometimes dark and sometimes light.

He reaches for my hand and closes his eyes for several moments before looking at me with such sadness. "I'm frustrated. Extremely frustrated. But not just at you. I know this hasn't been easy on you, and it sure as fuck hasn't been easy on me. I'm trying to do the best that I can. I understand you're afraid. I'm trying to be sensitive to that fact, but you have to stop with the Scarecrow and Papa Rich talk. If not for your own sanity, then for everyone's around you."

I want to argue. I want to shake some sense into him and make him see the truth. Scarecrow is out there. Papa Rich is out there. They are waiting and watching, and Christopher is too blind to prepare for the attack. And an attack is most definitely coming. But Christopher has just started to calm down, and I don't feel like continuing down the path of fury any longer.

"I'm having a hard time letting go of my past. I'm having a hard time accepting my future," I confess. "And I know you say you love me, but I feel like I'm a burden or an obligation. I can't help it."

"You aren't either of those to me," Christopher states firmly. His jaw is locked again, and his brow furrows. "Have I not shown my devotion to you? My commitment? I don't take either of those lightly. And I've been working my ass off to try to get our lives started. I wish it could all happen overnight, but it can't."

"I don't want to be left alone anymore. The walls are closing in on me here. You go off to work and to work events in the evenings, and I'm here, alone." I'm changing the subject from Papa Rich, but this is another issue I feel I need to address. "I stare out our bedroom window just like I stared out the window of the schoolhouse. Nothing has changed. I'm still a ghost just haunting a different place."

"I have to for my work, and the only reason I haven't taken you to the evening dinners and parties is that I'm worried you aren't ready. It's a lot of people. A lot of questions."

"But I want to. I'm your wife. I want to be by your side. I have to start figuring out this new way of living. I need to stop being the 'freak' everyone thinks I am."

He circles his fingertip on my hand again, which I'm realizing is something that gives me comfort. "Fair enough," he says. "I can't keep you locked up in a gilded cage safe and protected forever."

I almost want to scream out that I'm not safe. Far from it. Scarecrow and Papa Rich are here! But I stay quiet. I need more proof. I need to wrap my head around the hows and the whys before I try to make people believe me. I can't keep saying my *gut* or because I *feel* they are.

"Tomorrow night, there's a party at a politician's penthouse. He's trying to get donations for his campaign and to earn goodwill. I normally wouldn't go to something like this, as it's pretentious, arrogant, and everything I'm against. But I promised my editor I would, and I'm trying to prove in my own way that I'm also not the 'freak' some people think I am now." He moves a little closer to me and pulls me into his arms, holding me close. "Let's go tomorrow as husband and wife."

I snuggle in close to him, pressing my face to his chest and inhaling his essence.

"I'm sorry I lost my cool," he says as he begins petting my hair softly.

"I'm sorry I angered you. I'm also sorry I broke all those vases.

I'm sure they were really expensive. I owe your mother an apology at the least."

"My mother will be just fine. It's not like she hasn't had her bout with hysterics a time or two."

"I still shouldn't have broken what isn't mine. I was scared. I know you feel I shouldn't be. But I was. I just don't want you to think... less of me. I don't want you to think I'm a freak."

"I love you, Ember. I truly do. I've never been good at knowing or showing what that exactly means... love. But I know it's something I feel for you."

As if he just released a flood gate, I cry. I can't help it. "I love you too. I don't know what that looks like either or how it's supposed to feel. I've been told all my life how it should be and how it should feel. Love confuses me. I thought I loved Papa Rich. I still sometimes think I do. But then I met you. And I'm with you now, and... this is what love is supposed to feel like. How I feel right now in your arms."

He presses his lips to mine and kisses me with more passion than ever before. It's like the kiss is needed to repair what we may have broken. It's a kiss to bandage the wounds inside.

"You're my wife," he mumbles into my hair.

"You're my husband."

"I want to fuck you," he states so simply.

"I want you to fuck me."

How we can go from yelling to tears to wanting to fuck, I have no idea. But I want Christopher inside me, tearing and clawing his way in as he does it.

"Hard," he whispers. "I want the tears staining your face right now to be from how hard and deep I'm going to fuck you. No longer out of sadness or fear."

"Yes," I breathe out, wanting something more raw and primal. "Punish me. You may not hit me. You may not beat me. But I want my husband to punish me *his* way. I want there to be consequences for what I did... bad, bad consequences." I playfully wink as I lean forward and kiss him again. "Your wife has been a bad girl."

"Ember," he moans as he begins yanking and pulling at my clothes.

He doesn't take his time. He doesn't let me help. He just strips me of my clothes like a beast would devour his prey. He stands up just long enough to unfasten his belt and to pull it from the loops. The swishing sound sends a shiver down my spine, and I fear he's going to belt me and truly discipline me, but before I can allow any sense of panic to set in, he's reaching for my wrists, pulling them together, and fastening them tightly with the leather belt. Once he is standing naked in front of me, he pushes me back against the mattress, my bound wrists up above my head.

"I'm going to fuck you like I've always wanted to. Not easy. Not gentle. I'm not going to hold back. I'm going to make you cry. I'm going to make you scream. I'm going to make you forget everything except me. You will only be able to focus on my cock as I spread you wide. There's no one here tonight to hear you. There's nothing to hold me back. You're going to scream my name over and over again. It's time you're punished, Ember. It's high time I show you what happens when you piss off your husband."

He doesn't pause but mounts me like an animal out of control. His cock penetrates me without warning, and he's deep inside, pounding away with fervor. My body rocks beneath him, hands still bound above my head. He squeezes my breast and then lowers his head and nibbles the other. I'm already reaching climax, and he's only begun.

The force of his cock pumping in and out is bruising but so damn hot that I cry out as the first of what I know will be many orgasms washes over me.

"Christopher," I cry out, wanting so badly to cling to his back with my hands. I want to claw him. I want to mark his flesh with the signs of my pleasure, but I'm bound and at his mercy.

"That's right, baby. Come around my cock."

He continues to drive into me with aggression and primal

need. He groans as he does so, and all I can do is lie there and allow him to do as he pleases to me. My legs are spread wide, my pussy even wider with his large shaft mastering my entrance, and my arms are cast above my head. I have no control, but I love that he's got it all. My Christopher. My husband. Mine.

I cry out loudly as another jolt of electricity sizzles through me. My body has no time to recover before Christopher continues with his relentless fucking. He was right when he said he would fuck me to tears of pleasure, because that is exactly what's happening. My body is alive. Fear is gone. Any insanity I experienced while shattering precious glass has been replaced with a new level of insanity.

A primal insanity.

An erotic insanity.

An insanity that I never want to be cured of.

When it comes to Christopher, I never want to be sane again.

"Come with me," he rasps as he lowers his hand to my clit and circles the sensitive area to where I have no choice but to oblige him in his request.

His deep moan of pleasure blends with my screams of completion, and any argument, any signs of displeasure from before, are vanquished. Just like that, we have healed the wounds... at least for now.

21

EMBER

CINDERELLA.

I remember reading that story repeatedly, but never once did I ever think I would get to live the fairy tale myself. I now have my Prince Charming, and I also have my happily ever after... or at least we are working toward that.

But as I stand in my new dress that Christina found for me, wearing makeup she also taught me how to apply, I know I look like a princess.

"Gorgeous," Christopher says from behind me. He approaches and places his lips on my bare shoulder. "I may want to stay home tonight and keep you all to myself."

"Are you sure my dress isn't too black?" I ask, loving how the fabric and cut accentuates every curve of my body. *Seductive* was the word Christina used to describe it. But I wasn't used to wearing black.

"I may have to remove the dress just to show you how beautiful you are." He sighs. "But the car is waiting outside for us."

I giggle, and my face heats. Turning to face him, I kiss him on the lips before saying, "I'm ready."

He leads me downstairs and adds, "Remind me to thank Christina for all her help with getting you ready. You're stunning."

"She seemed different today," I say, remembering how she seemed to space out, not always hearing what I said. "Sort of sad."

"Michael is having some financial issues with Luciano's. I think they are both just going through a hard time. I know them, though; they'll get through it." He spins me around in a little dance when we reach the front door. "But tonight is all about you and me. I will have the most beautiful woman in the room by my side. I can't wait to show off my wife."

Not allowing myself to overthink or get myself worked up, I think of nothing else but what a fun time Christopher and I will have. Dr. Stevens told me in our session today to not always plan for the worst. To not think something bad will happen. If I focus on the good and the light, then I'll be able to fight off the bad and the darkness.

I am determined to listen.

My very first party, and although the number of people attending is more than Christopher is comfortable with for both of us, he's been nothing but supportive and encouraging of me attending. I feel welcomed and not a burden. I actually feel Christopher is proud to have me by his side.

When we walk into the building in what he tells me is in Manhattan, I'm surprised to see how large it is and even more shocked to find out the owner has converted several floors into his home. The party is on the main penthouse level, but we start on the first level and leave our coats in a room bigger than the schoolhouse of Hallelujah Junction. I thought Louisa's house was large, but it's nothing in comparison to where we are now.

"If you ever feel uncomfortable or want to leave, you just tell me. We'll leave whenever you want to," Christopher says as we choose to take the stairs to the penthouse rather than waiting for the elevator with some other guests.

"I don't want you to worry about me," I say. "I'll be fine. I want you to be able to network and do what you need to do for your career." I reach for his hand and squeeze it. "I'm a big girl. I can handle myself. I need to start sometime if I want to be married to the famous *Rolling Stone* photographer who is in such demand."

Christopher rolls his eyes as he opens the door to the party. The sound is intense at first, but I quickly shake off any nerves it causes.

"Let's get a drink," he says, leading me hand in hand to a bar near a huge floor-to-ceiling window that overlooks the entire city. The lights of the skyline and all the buildings are absolutely stunning and nearly take my breath away. "Yeah, this place has one of the best views in New York."

"I've never seen anything like it. It's gorgeous." I look around the penthouse as Christopher orders our drinks and soak in the opulence.

All the furniture is white, and the only color is in the bright artwork hanging on the walls. Huge chandeliers hang from above that sparkle right along with the city views that master the room, since huge windows surround the entire penthouse. Music is playing faintly, but the constant hum of the people milling around really creates the melody of the room. There are so many faces I don't recognize, and yet no one seems to pay any attention to Christopher and me. We're blending in with everyone else, which is odd but refreshing. I'm so used to having all eyes on me, but right now, at this party, they're anything but.

"No one is staring," I tell Christopher as he hands me a glass of white wine.

"Yeah, the one nice thing about attending parties of this caliber is the people in the room are celebrities, power players, socialites, criminals, or politicians. Everyone has their own story and their own spotlight. We are just another star shimmering in the sky here."

"I like it."

We spend the next couple of hours moving from one grouping of people to the next. I never realized just how charming and personable Christopher is, but he truly impresses me with his ability to work a room, never once leaving my side or making me feel like I didn't belong. And he was right in saying we were just another star in a sky full of them. Aside from an occasional question or mention of how they heard of me, the topic of conversation seemed to stay away from my former life and my serial killer father.

I'm pleasantly surprised when I see Christina at the party. Last I spoke to her, she wasn't sure if she and Michael would be attending. She didn't want to come without him, and she wasn't sure if he'd be able to break free from the restaurant.

Christopher is still in heavy conversation with a man about stocks or something of that nature, so I politely excuse myself for a minute and walk over to my friend.

"You came," I say as I approach.

She smiles but doesn't seem her usual self as she does. "Michael and I decided to come after all."

I look around for her husband but don't see him anywhere. "Where is he? I want to say hello."

Christina shrugs and reaches for a flute of champagne being carried on a tray by a waiter. "Who knows. Drinking with friends or something."

It's not hard to see she isn't exactly pleased with her husband. I decide to try to cheer her up by saying, "You look pretty. I love your dress."

She glances down and then chuckles. "Glad someone noticed." She takes a deep breath, a large drink from her champagne, and then adds, "Okay, I'm shaking off my bad mood. No need to ruin a party." I watch her paint on a new smile—a fake one—but regardless, she does appear to be shaking off her mood. "Where's Christopher?"

I point in his direction. "I've met some really interesting people since being here. The party's fancier than I'm used to, but I don't feel nearly as out of place as I was expecting."

"I'm glad you're having a good time," she says.

"I am, but if you'll excuse me, I'm going to go use the restroom."

I find where one is and see a small line waiting outside to use it. I take my place, feeling a little uneasy as all the other women seem to know each other and are talking. They clearly came to the bathroom as pairs or threesomes. I wish I had convinced Christina to come with me now, but I didn't realize going to the bathroom was a group effort.

Standing by myself, trying not to stare at anyone, and hoping I look casual and confident, I see Marissa approach me. I haven't noticed her before at the party, nor did I know she'd be attending, but then again, there are so many people that I can see how that's possible.

"Hello, Ember," she says with a smile.

The friendly greeting doesn't seem genuine, but I reply just as sweetly with "Hi, Marissa. Nice to see you." I hate lying. It's not nice to see her. My stomach dropping and my palms sweating prove that fact.

"I've been worried about you. How have you been since your *incident*?" she asks, not quietly, so anyone around can hear if they want to.

"What incident?" I have no idea what she's talking about.

"I was with Christopher in LA when his mother called us about you having your... incident."

"Wait... what?" A ringing begins in my ears, and bile forms in the back of my throat. "You were in LA with Christopher?"

I can't breathe.

I can't breathe.

She nods and replies as if it's only natural she'd be with Christopher. "We were at our favorite pub when the call came in. We were both so worried about you. With everything you've been going through, it's so kind of Christopher to be there helping you work it out." She reaches out and pats my arm. "Christopher and I are *both* here for you. You can count on me too."

I inhale deeply, but air doesn't seem to enter my lungs. I scan the room for my husband but don't see him. I want to puke, but the line for the bathroom isn't moving. All I know is I can't stand here any longer. Not with her.

Not with Marissa.

They were in California together. He was going to spend the night....

They were at their favorite place.

He's helping me out... so kind of him....

"Excuse me," I say as I push my way by her and storm out of the penthouse.

I need air.

I need to leave.

I need.... What the fuck do I need?

Running down the stairs to the coat room, I close the door behind me so I can have a minute to myself and gather my senses. I can't just go home. Home...? Where is my home?

Has Christopher been seeing Marissa the entire time? Is he just being nice to me and pretending to be my husband until I get mentally stronger? Is that why he's helping me learn how to be independent? Is his plan to leave me and be with Marissa the minute he feels I'm ready to be alone?

The door to the coat room opens, and Michael enters. "Ember? Are you okay? I saw you running in here. What's going on?"

He approaches me, and though I'm happy to see a familiar face, I can see his eyes are glossy, and he stumbles a bit as he walks to me. I smell heavy booze on his breath as he takes me into his arms in an embrace.

"I'm here," he adds. "Tell me what's wrong."

I try to wiggle free from his hug, but he holds me tightly against his chest. "I'm fine. I just want to go home."

"You don't seem okay," he murmurs into my hair.

I push my hands against his chest and am able to break the connection by taking two steps back toward the wall. "I need some space. It's a lot of people and activity upstairs, and—"

"Where's Christopher?" he interrupts, and he closes the distance between us, pushing me up against the wall of the room. Coats are now all around us, and even if someone came into the room, I doubt they would be able to see us behind all the furs and leathers.

"Can you please go upstairs and tell him I'd like to go home?" I ask, panic setting in as Michael is not backing away but pinning me against the wall instead with his hands on each side of me.

"Ah, you don't need to leave now." His breath is on my face. "Not when you are upset. Let me make you feel better."

Michael places his lips on my neck and begins assaulting my skin with wet kisses all over.

I try to push him away, but he's not budging. "Michael, stop. Stop!"

"Shh," he says as he moves his lips to my mouth and kisses. "You don't want someone to hear us. If Christina comes in and catches us, she'll be devastated. You don't want to do that to her, now do you? Not to your friend. And Christopher... what will he think if he catches us being intimate?"

"I don't want this," I say in a low voice, trying to turn my face away from his kiss, but he only pushes harder and with more force.

His hand lowers and finds the bottom of my dress. He lifts it out of the way and fingers the edge of my panties before I'm able to do anything. I try to take hold of his wrist, but nothing I do stops his advance.

"Michael, I think you've had too much to drink," I say as I do whatever I can to break free from his hold but can't fight off his strength. "Please don't do this. Christina and Christopher—"

"Will never know," he cuts in as he somehow lowers my panties to my thigh. "It will be our little secret."

His finger pushes past my folds and enters inside me. I gasp at the intrusion. Shame and fear make my knees weak, but I'm too paralyzed with indecision to fight him off. I want to scream for help, but I don't want Christina to know what her husband is doing. Michael's right in the fact that she'd be devastated. And what will Christopher do if he finds out his wife has another man's finger inside her pussy? He may never forgive me.

I can claw and punch, but then that can draw attention to the coat room as well. No, I have to handle this discretely. This has to be *our little secret*, like Michael said.

"Don't do this," I plead. "Michael, I'm asking you to stop. No one will have to know this happened. I won't tell anyone."

"Exactly," he says, pushing his lips hard against mine and pulling us to the ground. "No one has to know."

Within seconds, he's on top of me, lowering his pants. My dress is pulled up to my stomach, my panties down to my ankles now, and I know what's coming.

I push against his chest hard, considering gouging out his eyes, but before I can decide if I possess the internal fortitude to do so, he reaches for my hands and confines them up above my head. With his weight and strength, there is nothing I can do.

His penis is rubbing against my pussy, and he's trying to find the hole to enter. His dick isn't hard, so he's having a hard time at finding his way inside.

"Michael, think of Christina," I say as tears run down my face, soaking my hair. "Your wife. Think what your wife would think. And Christopher. He's your friend. Don't do this. It's not you. Please don't do this. Christina, Christina, Christina," I begin chanting.

He freezes, his limp cock resting against my violated sex. He lowers his face to my hair and begins to cry.

"Don't say her name. Don't."

"Christina," I say again. "Think of what this will do to Christina."

"I'm so fucked up," he murmurs. "I'm so fucked up."

I take this opportunity of his weakness and use it to my advantage. I'm able to push him off me, springing to my feet as I pull up my panties and lower my dress. I look down at him, still lying on the ground with his pants lowered, sobbing. I consider kicking his ribs. I think about beating him over and over again. But rage doesn't exist inside me. Only sadness. I'm sad for him, I'm sad for me, I'm sad for all. I should hate him, but I don't. I should want vengeance, but I don't possess it.

We all sin.

We all fail.

He's no different.

Evil is everywhere.

I leave him where he's at and grab my coat as well as Christopher's.

I bolt out of the coat room without saying a single word and see Christopher exiting the elevator.

"Hey, where did you go? I've been looking all over for you," he says with a look of concern—or maybe annoyance. I can't tell.

"I'm ready to go home," I say, lifting the coats I'm carrying to show him. "I was just going get you."

"Is everything all right?" He approaches and takes his coat, puts it on, and then assists me in putting on mine as a true gentleman would.

A true gentleman who is taking secret trips with Marissa.

He leans in and kisses me on the cheek. His breath smells like Michael's, and I cringe.

Christopher notices and worry darkens his eyes. "Did something happen? You're acting differently than earlier."

I can't tell him about Marissa. I don't want to tell him what Michael just did. What good would come out of either? I don't want to face my demons anymore. I want to slink back into the shadows where it's safe.

"I'm just ready to go home."

22

EMBER

"What's going on with you?" Christopher asks as we sit in the back of the town car taking us home. "Did something happen at the party?"

I shrug as I watch the passing scenery whirl by faster than my eyes can adjust and take it all in.

"You went to the bathroom and never came back. Did something happen?"

I don't know how to tell Christopher the truth. Do I just blurt out that I found out he cheated on me with Marissa and then was nearly raped by one of his best friends? Would he even believe me if I told him? And if I tell him what I know about Marissa, will he finally confess and tell me he's been waiting for the right time to leave me? Will it be over?

I'm not ready for it to be over.

"I had a really good time." Which isn't a lie. I did at first. "I just got a little overwhelmed by it all at one point. That's it. I'm not used to so much so fast."

Christopher remains quiet for several minutes. I wonder if he's believing a word I say.

"I have a surprise for you," he finally says as we pull up to the house. "If you aren't too tired, I'd like to show you."

I want to crawl in bed and try to forget this awful night, but I can also see the excitement in Christopher's eyes, and I don't want to disappoint him.

"Surprise?" I ask, working harder than ever to paint a fake smile on my face.

He helps me out of the car and into the house. "Shh," he says. "I don't want anyone to wake up and be part of this surprise. It's going to just be our secret for as long as we can keep it that way."

Michael's words flood in, and I feel as if I'm going to vomit. *Our secret.*

"Ember," Christopher says, snapping me back into reality. "You okay. You seem... off."

I give the fake smile again and hold his hand as reassurance for him as well as for me. I need his strength to get me to put one foot in front of the other.

Is this what it feels like when your life is crashing all around you?

Christopher leads us up the stairs and then down to the end of the hallways. He then pulls a string to a hatch in the ceiling, opening it to a staircase.

"An attic?" I say.

"Yes, but more." He climbs the ladder and then turns around to extend his hand to me.

We enter the attic full of dust and boxes. We don't stay long, however, as he leads me to double doors made of glass. When he opens the doors, we step out onto a rooftop terrace. Strings of lights are hanging above us from the tip of the roof to the railing. It's like a curtain of stars.

"I know you've mentioned how you feel the walls are closing in on you a few times," Christopher begins. "And I know we have this terrace that's never been used, or at least in my adult life. So, I've been working on having it fixed up for you."

He leads us farther out, and I can see patio furniture

displayed around a fire pit, pots of flowers, and plants all around. Trellises of ivy cover the walls, and little animal and gnome statues are tucked away in the corners. There's even a water fountain to help drown out the sounds of the city.

"I wanted you to have an outdoor spot that is just yours. A place for you to get out of the house. At least until I find us a place of our own. And I promise I'll give you an outside environment just like this, if not better, when we do move."

I turn to face him, tears rushing from my eyes, and I burrow my face into his chest and cry. I sob so loudly that I can hear myself over the fountain and the bustling soundtrack of New York.

"Hey," he soothes as he rubs my back and kisses the side of my head. "Why is this making you cry?"

I keep crying until my sobs turn to hiccups and my hiccups turn to ragged breaths as I try to regain my composure. Christopher allows me to cry, holding me closely, kissing me, rubbing circles on my back, and simply being there for me. When I finally calm down, he brings me to a two-man chaise lounge and lowers me onto it, then sits beside me. We are overlooking the city now, and the view distracts me from my anguish.

"Okay," he says softly. "Are you ready to tell me what has you so upset?"

I nod as I wipe at my nose. "I saw Marissa at the party," I begin.

I feel Christopher's body tense. "I didn't know she'd be there. I'm sorry. Did something happen?"

I like that we are sitting side by side. I don't have to look him in the eyes as I say, "She told me she was with you in LA. That you guys were together at your favorite place when Louisa called, asking you to come home because of me."

Christopher sits up straight and twists his body so he's facing me. "Whoa, this is not what it sounds like. I did not go to LA with Marissa."

My lip quivers as I say, "Please don't lie to me, Christopher. That's all I ask. Don't lie."

"I'm not lying," he says with more passion and conviction than I'm used to seeing. "I swear to you. I was in LA, and Marissa showed up. I had no idea she was going to come. It was a complete surprise. I swear." When I don't respond but rather narrow my eyes instead, he adds, "I know how this looks. Hell, I'm sure it's how Marissa wants it to look, but I did not have a getaway with her. That was the first time I had seen her since we first got back, and it was a complete surprise."

"You didn't go have drinks with her at your favorite place?" I ask, unsure if I believe Christopher or not. I've never known him to lie to me, but it doesn't make sense how this all could just be a misunderstanding.

He lets out a deep breath. "We had drinks at *my* favorite bar. I always go there when I'm in LA. And we only went to talk. I felt I owed her that. She deserved to have closure, since I had been avoiding her. That's all it was."

"She made it sound like you guys went together and that you were sitting there trying to figure out a way to help me. As a couple. You and her... a couple." I begin to cry again. I can't help it, and I'm surprised I even have tears left.

Christopher takes my chin between his fingers and pulls it up so I have to look into his eyes, which do appear to be sincere. "Never, Ember. Never. I told her I love you, and I do. I told her I want you as my wife, and I do. I made it very clear my intentions are to be with you and always you. I need you to believe that. I need you to have faith in that."

I break free from his hold and look away. "Why would she lie? Why would she tell me the things she did if they weren't true?"

"Because sometimes hurt people do mean things. And that's all this is. She's hurt, and she wants you to hurt too. She doesn't want us to be together and was trying to cause trouble. I'm sorry, Ember. I'm sorry you had to believe I would do that to you for even a second." He leans forward and kisses me softly. "Please tell me you believe me."

"I want to. But a part of me wonders if you're just saying what I want to hear. If you're too scared to tell me your true feelings."

"I'm not going to lie to you, Ember. I'm not. Yes, I'm guilty of not telling you things in order to protect your feelings, and I know it's wrong. I don't give you credit for being as strong as you are. I have to remind myself that you're the woman who helped me burn down a town and escape. There isn't a weak bone in your body. I'm sorry. I should have told you about Marissa earlier. Do you forgive me?"

I kiss him back as my answer.

I press my tongue into his mouth and swirl it around. I need the familiar taste, his touch, his smell. I consider telling him about Michael, but what will come of that? Christopher will rage and go after him. Christina will find out. And secretly, each person involved will blame me. No, it's not my fault, but they will. How could they not?

Michael and Christina could be over because of it. And maybe Michael deserves it to be over. But does Christina deserve to have her entire life destroyed?

And though I don't think Christopher would blame me or think I truly wanted any part of it, I wonder if it will just be one more thing that makes me a victim in his eyes.

Again.

I don't want to be a victim over and over again.

I'm fucking tired of being weak.

I'm tired of the damn tears.

I don't want to be afraid and in need of a Prince Charming to save me.

Life is fucking tough. The real world isn't a fairy tale. And I need to learn that. I need to deal with it. I need to survive it. *I* need to. Me. Not anyone else.

So, no. I won't tell anyone about Michael. How I choose to handle that situation will be up to me. Me.

"Thank you," I finally say, breaking from the kiss. "It's beautiful up here. It's like a storybook, magical area. I love the fairy lights and the fountain. I love it all."

He smiles and looks around. "My mother is a damn vampire, so I'm not worried about her coming up here. It's all yours. I'll work on getting the attic cleaned up too so it's not so dusty for you when you do come."

"I needed this," I confess. "The room is getting to me, and the house... well, the house is your mother's. I needed this." I lean in to kiss him again. "You always seem to know the exact right thing to do for me."

Needing to end the night with the last touch on my body to be from my husband rather than Michael's drunken molestation, I swing my leg over his lap and mount him, lowering my lips to his again. I bring my hand to his zipper and free his cock from the restraints with a skill I'm happy to be gaining as my sexual experience increases. I like the power I have when it comes to sex. As I grip his dick, hear his gasp, and watch his eyes close, I savor the control I'm in.

"I love you," he growls as I begin rubbing my palm up and down the shaft. I'm watching his face as I do so.

"I know you do," I say, applying more pressure as I stroke. "And I love you."

And for a splitting moment, I wonder if love is enough. When the world is determined to keep you apart, can you fight off all the enemies? Papa Rich, Scarecrow, Louisa, Marissa, Michael... ghosts who haunt us to the brink of madness. Can we fight them off? Is it possible?

Christopher takes hold of my hips and gets ready to flip me over, but I stop him.

"No. I want to make you come." I tighten my grip on his cock. "Like this. I want to watch your face as you come in my hand." I lift his shirt up so I can see his bare chest and the ripple of his abs. "I want to see your cum spill all over your smooth skin."

His breath hitches, his head falls back, and with an open

mouth, he moans. He's getting pleasure from me and no one else. It's just the two of us. No one else.

"God, that feels so good," he praises as his cock grows even harder and bigger in my ministrations.

I jack him off, watching every facial expression, listening to every sound of pleasure. I tighten, I loosen, I speed up, and I slow down. He's close, and I know it. I love it. He's going to do exactly what I want him to do.

I'm in control.

My choice.

My decisions.

I'm in control.

23

EMBER

IF I DON'T CHANGE, I'M GOING TO BE STUCK IN TIME.

I know this, and although I feel like I'm taking steps forward, there's always something that happens that pulls me back.

I see shadows.

I hear whispers.

I try to pretend they aren't there, but they are.

The ghosts of Hallelujah Junction still haunt me.

The Feds notified Christopher yesterday that there had been several sightings of Richard. In Nevada, in California, Wyoming, and now Virginia. He's getting closer and closer to New York, and I know why.

He's coming for me. And no matter how much Christopher reassures me that he isn't and that I'm perfectly safe, I know the opposite. Christopher's wrong in this case. So very wrong.

And then there is Louisa Davenport.

She hates me. I see it. She wants me to go crazy. I see her smile every time I get spooked or am uneasy. She takes pleasure in my fear, but I can't tell Christopher this. It's his mother. He loves her. He won't believe me on this either. But I know she's waiting for me to snap so she can send me away to a mental institute. I'm not blind. I see her waiting. Waiting.

And then there is Christina and Michael, who we haven't seen since the party, and I seriously doubt we will. How? How can I face either of them again?

I often think Louisa is right; I should move away and start over. Sometimes it seems as if it's the only option. Go and hide. Hide from everyone.

"We'll get your passport soon," Christopher says as he brings the last of his bags down the stairs. "I really wish you could go to London with me. But I'm swooping in and swooping out as soon as I'm done with the shoot. I didn't even book a hotel."

"You didn't have to do that," I say. "You can stay. I'll be fine."

"We'll go back there together and travel the entire area once we get the passport. I promise." He gives his bags a onceover to make sure he has all he needs. "I'll be back as soon as I can." He presses his forehead to mine, our lips so close. "Are you sure you're all right with me going?"

I pat his chest and smile. "Yes. Go take wonderful pictures, and don't worry about me."

I glance up the stairs and see Louisa looking down on us. Her face is solemn and eyes dark.

Christopher reaches for the back of my head and pulls me into a kiss. A tingle runs up my spine from the intensity, and I wish we didn't have an audience, or I'd let my hands explore as we kiss goodbye.

"I love you, Ember," he whispers as he breaks the kiss. "Don't ever forget that."

"Goodbye, Christopher. I love you."

He picks up his bags and leaves the house to meet the driver waiting on the stoop.

I don't wait to see him drive away but decide to head to my room instead. I don't want to be around Louisa and her judging eyes. I definitely don't want to speak with her unless I have to. I hope she doesn't take this opportunity to have any more of her heart-to-heart talks with me.

No thank you. Hard pass.

No need to keep pretending. We both don't care for each other, and there is no point in continuing the façade. I hate lies, and I don't want to keep one up if I don't have to. And I no longer have to. I'm at peace with how the woman feels about me. I'm at peace.

I enter the room and freeze.

The skin on the back of my neck prickles. A whoosh of eerie silence surrounds me as I close my bedroom door.

Straw.

A lot of straw.

In the middle of the room is a cross made from nothing but straw. A Godly and haunting greeting from my past. There is no mistake. There is no way this is coincidence. And there is no way this is in my head.

I can run. I can scream. I can spin on my heels, lock myself in my room, and call the police.

I have so many options.

But truly, deep down, I know there is only one choice. I have to face my insanity head-on.

I notice a familiar object on the desk as well. An old hardback book of *The Secret Garden*.

I lift the book from the table and feel the weight in my hands. It's a story that has followed me here—from the schoolhouse.

I read the book over and over again growing up. So much so that the pages were worn thin in places and even tearing. So much so that I had to tape the book together in some places.

I flip through the book from the desk and stop on page 49. Page 49, which is held together with scotch tape. Just like I had taped page 49 of my book back in Hallelujah Junction.

It's the same book.

"Do you like the book?" I hear Louisa ask from behind me. I

hadn't noticed her entering the room, but my nearing nervous breakdown can be blamed for that.

I turn to face her and run my finger over the tape. "This is mine from the schoolhouse." I look up at her, already fearing the answer to my question before I ask, "How did you get this?"

I had been trying to get out of the storm since leaving the only home I knew. Walking through the dark, I hoped so badly that I'd find the light. But as I stare at the woman before me and face the raging hurricane around me, I know there's no hope on weathering the storm.

"The straw," I say, pointing at the cross, seeing the truth for the first time. "You've always been the one behind the straw, right?"

She says nothing but simply smiles.

"Why? Did you want me to lose my mind? Did you want to scare me to the point of insanity? This was your plan all along, wasn't it?"

Her smile doesn't waver.

"Are Papa Rich and Scarecrow here? Do you know where they are?"

I need to know the answer. I need to know I hadn't been losing my mind the entire time. They had been lurking in the shadows, watching, tormenting, stalking me to the point of insanity. And Louisa... she played the cat-and-mouse game with them. Hadn't she?

Or does she want me to believe they are here simply by planting the straw herself?

"Tell me," I demand. "Do you know where they are? Or is this all a sick game? How did you get my book? Who left this cross of straw?"

Her sickly smile only grows bigger as she takes a step toward me. Not answering my questions I so desperately need answers to, she finally says, "You know what you have to do," she says. "If you love my son like you claim, then you know you have to leave him. He can't take care of you forever. He can't watch your every move. You'll suffocate him, drown him in the broken shards that will forever be your history. Have mercy on my son. I'm asking you to do that, even though I shouldn't have to. *You* know what's right."

"Did you do this?" I scream, feeling the room begin to spin. "Tell me what's going on! Tell me!"

"I need you to come with me downstairs," she says, hooking her finger at me to follow.

I'm paralyzed for a moment, but as if under a trance, I eventually follow.

As we reach the top of the stairs, my knees nearly buckle as I look down below. As insanity nears, I hear her say, "They're waiting for you."

THE END

Is there really such a thing as a Happily Ever After for two broken people? I guess we'll find out.

Be sure to see what's next for Christopher and Ember in **TAKEN BRIDE.**

TAKEN BRIDE

THE SECRET BRIDE SERIES - BOOK
THREE

DEDICATION

*To the victims of the Dixie Fire in Northern California. I wrote this
book as an evacuee, and will always remember the raging fire around
me as I wrote.*

1

EMBER

DESERT THUNDERSTORMS POSSESS AN ENERGY THAT CAN'T FULLY BE described. You must live it. See it. Breathe it. Be it.

Powerful, majestic, beautiful, and even eerie.

You can feel the intensity in the air right before they begin. Your senses come alive; your skin tingles as you anxiously wait for the storm to come.

You can also smell it. The sagebrush releases a scent as if to welcome the dark clouds. Almost like an aphrodisiac seducing the storm to come. The dust settles, and for a brief moment, the desert has a certain freshness to it. That is, until the rain comes. The rain replaces the fresh with an earthy musk as the droplets bounce off the hard and dry ground below.

I always loved thunderstorms in the Nevada desert. Summer nights were riddled with them, and I welcomed each one with excitement and appreciation for how the lightning daggered across the gray sky. They were loud, scary, even dangerous, but I gladly watched each one with awe. I loved how they rolled in unexpectedly at times, and other times, you saw them coming from miles away.

But the thunderstorm around me right now is threatening to

strike me down. The lightning going off in my heart and soul is tearing me to shreds. The storm brewing is so intense that I may not walk away from the wreckage it's causing.

"I need you to come with me downstairs," Louisa says, hooking her finger at me to come along.

I'm paralyzed for a moment, but as if under a trance, I eventually follow.

As we reach the top of the stairs, my knees nearly buckle as I look down below. As insanity nears, I hear her say, "They're waiting for you."

She's led me into the eye of the storm, and the hurricane of emotions steals what little bit of sanity I have left.

Papa Rich.

Scarecrow.

They're here.

Oh my God, they are here.

I try to blink away the madness, but it's determined to stay.

"You knew where they were all along, didn't you?" I prompt Louisa without looking at her. My eyes are pinned on Papa Rich and Scarecrow down below in the foyer.

"No, but I have the resources to hire the best in the world to hunt them down. I had no intentions of resting until they were found."

"Why?" I barely squeak out. "Why do this to us? You knew Christopher and I were trying to stay hidden. We wanted to keep the darkness away. You knew this. So why?"

"Because I'm a mother. I understand your father in many ways. There's nothing a parent wouldn't do for their children. Nothing." Her voice—calm and collected—sends a shiver down my spine.

"Ember," Papa Rich says as he reaches his hand up to me. "It's time to leave."

This can't be real.

This can't be happening... and yet it is.

I look over my shoulder at Louisa, not sure what to do next.

Alarm bells are banging against my bones, feeling as if they're splintering beneath my flesh. Internal screams are demanding I run away from everyone in the house as fast as I can.

I need to find my husband... *now*. Christopher will fix this. Christopher will make it safe again. He'll save me. He'll save us.

But my feet are planted, and no matter what I do, I can't move.

Insanity is a sticky motherfucker.

"Christopher—"

"Deserves to be set free," Louisa interrupts. "He didn't choose you. He was forced to take you as his wife, and then his morals and overall good-natured personality made him feel responsible for you. This is not love, Ember. Maybe it's devotion at most, but not love. You are just as bad as Richard. You are stealing his freedom. You are shackling him to your broken self. *You* are his captor now, and I'm doing everything within my power to save my son. Nothing more than that. He deserves to be rescued."

You are his captor now.

You are his captor now.

You are his captor now.

Maybe I always have been....

"We need to get moving, girl," Scarecrow chimes in from below. "The pilot said he'll only wait one hour."

If my eyes were lasers, they would sear Louisa's Botoxed skin from her old lady bones. "You brought them here. You didn't just find them, but you also helped them come to New York to take me back with them, didn't you?" I ask Louisa, not glancing down at Scarecrow as he spoke.

Maybe if I don't look at them at the bottom of the stairs, they will disappear like ghosts. Maybe this is a nightmare. It's not real. If I just don't look and see them....

Louisa still hasn't moved an inch. She's near, but not close enough for me to strike out and hurt her, which I'm considering doing—if only I could move.

"I have the power to help people, and I have the power to hurt people. In this case, I've chosen to help your papa Rich."

She says his name as if it burns her tongue. The sneer on her face is not pleasant, and I'm sure she'll need more Botox after this conversation, for she's surely breaking the plastic shell with her looks of disgust.

"But I want you to remember something, Amber. I can *hurt* far more easily than I can help. So, leave here, and never look back again. Leave my son alone. Forget he was ever in your life. Your father kidnapped him once. You chose not to help him then, but I'm asking you to help him now. This is the last time I'm asking. Consider it your last warning." She doesn't yell or raise her voice even slightly, but the threat in her tone is obvious.

I don't want to go to battle with this woman. I'm too tired to battle anyone.

And she's right.

I didn't save Christopher. And even now, I'm keeping him captive and chained to me until death do us part.

I know this.

Louisa is speaking the truth.

I turn my attention back on Papa Rich and study his face. He's not angry or full of rage. Dark circles are under his eyes, and he appears as if he's aged in the short time we've been apart. I hurt him. I can see just how deeply I did.

He's been out there the entire time, hiding in the smoke from the flames of Hallelujah Junction. He didn't give up on me. He never would. Never.

When our eyes lock, he calls up, "It's time, Ember."

"But I'm married, Papa. *You* married us. *You* chose Christopher for my husband. I can't just leave him. I've tried to be a good wife. I have."

My voice sounds weak. I'm weak.

I hate it.

I thought I'd grown stronger, and yet, with just his presence in the room, I'm a coward once again.

"I allowed the devil to enter me," Papa Rich says as Scarecrow nods beside him. "The decision was a poor one. I misjudged. I wanted a strong man for you, Ember. I wanted one who wouldn't cower to me or anyone and would protect you at all costs, but—" He looks down at his boots and then back at me. "—when Christopher arrived that day in Hallelujah Junction, I thought it was a sign from God. I now know it was a temptation from the devil. I'm merely man, however, but have repented for my sins for allowing the evil within the walls of my home. Fire burned down that evil." He takes a deep breath, his broad shoulders rising and falling in what appears to be defeat. "I chose the wrong husband for you. I will rectify that decision now." He extends his hand again. "You don't belong here, Ember. I'm here to save you from the grips of the devil's work."

"Go pack your bags," Louisa instructs loud enough so that Papa Rich and Scarecrow can hear. I can tell her patience is thin, and she's not going to allow anything negative to be said about her son any longer. "That man—Scarecrow—is right. The pilot I hired won't wait for long. He's risking a lot by flying you all back to Nevada." When I don't move right away, she adds with more force, "Go. Hurry up."

"I can't leave without speaking to Christopher." I swallow against the lump forming in the back of my throat and blink against the burning of tears threatening to fall. "I need to at least say goodbye. I don't want to hurt him."

"You hurt him by staying," Louisa snaps. "And if you don't leave while he's at work, he'll never let you go. You'll be trapped, and so will he. Is that what you really want? You're going to drown him, Amber. You know this. I can see that you know this."

I glance at Papa Rich and Scarecrow and consider her words, even though they shatter me from my very depths.

I don't want to leave.

But I don't want to stay.

"Go pack, Amber. Hurry. We only have a small window," she repeats with more force.

As if her words are the key to curing my paralysis, I do exactly as commanded.

She's right. I know this is not the place for me. I don't belong, and I seriously doubt I ever will, no matter how hard I try. And Christopher has his life here. His work, his friends, his social stature, and his family. He has slid so easily back into who he was before me, and frankly... deep down, I know there is no room for me in that life.

But I love him.

I love him so much.

But love is not always enough. I can't live in the fairy tales I read back in the schoolroom. This is reality—as cruel as it may be.

I enter our room and try my best to not look at the bed we shared together. I don't want to remember his touch, his kisses, his promises that all would work out in the end.

No, Christopher. It won't all work out in the end.

There's only one thing left to do.

Dear Christopher,

I'm going home.

What that means, or what that looks like, I don't know. But it's time I find out.

Papa Rich and Scarecrow came to get me. I knew they would, and to be honest... I think the reason I was so afraid they'd find me is that I knew deep down I would want to go with them willingly. This is not a kidnapping. This is not a choice forced upon me.

I'm leaving because I want to.

You and I both know that I never fit in. Yes, I was trying... God, how I was trying. But this is not my home, just like Hallelujah Junction wasn't yours. You were held captive against your will, and in many ways, that is how I feel now. I've had a chain around my ankle, and I finally found the key.

It's Papa Rich... my family.

I know this doesn't make sense to you. I know he's a bad man in many ways, but fate brought us together when I was five, and fate has brought us together again. This is how it's meant to be. And you living your life free of any obligations is how you are meant to be.

I know you love me, and I love you. I love you so very much, but love isn't enough to blend our two lives together. I've always wanted to be a good wife. But I can't in New York, no matter how hard I try. And I want to walk away knowing you love me before the love turns to resentment and even hate.

I've seen all the articles about you and me.

"A Demented Love Story" is the one that stays with me the most. Because it's true. But in this love story, our happily ever after is not the traditional.

Do we still get a happily ever after? Yes, I believe so. It's just that our story must have two different endings—one for you, and one for me. What's happy for you is not going to be what's happy for me.

It's how our demented love story ends.

I should have freed you the minute you were taken captive. I should have removed that chain around your ankle on day one. Well... I am now. You're free, Christopher.

I'm removing the chain.

You're free.

~Ember

It's time our demented love story comes to an end.

2

CHRISTOPHER

"What do you mean she's gone? Where did she go?" I ask, looking at my mother and then at Ms. Evans, who diverts her eyes from my glare. "To the park again?"

I don't like the idea of her being alone, but I also understand I can't be with her at all times either. I can't expect her to stay locked away in her room all day.

"No, son. She left for good. She packed her bags and left."

My mother's words don't make any sense. "What are you talking about? Where would she go? With what means? To whom? What the hell are you talking about?"

"Go see for yourself," my mother says as I'm already halfway up the stairs, heading to our room.

It feels as if someone is gripping my heart and squeezing tight as I storm into the room and see a letter resting on the foot of the bed. I don't need to check the closet to know Ember's gone. I can already feel she's not here.

Picking it up with shaky hands, I read the Dear John letter from hell. The words swim on the paper, and no matter how hard I struggle to focus on Ember's delicate penmanship, I'm unable to let the words sink in. What is she saying? How can this be true?

She left.

She left with Richard!

She willingly left with a madman.

I sit on the bed, because I have to or fall to the ground instead. I keep rereading the words over and over in hopes that they will make sense to me. In hopes that there is some explanation or cure for the shattered heart that's somehow beating a mile a minute in my chest.

A demented love story.

I'm removing the chain.

You're free.

It's how our demented love story ends.

"It's for the best," I hear from the doorway of the room.

"What the hell happened?" I ask, looking down at the letter. How could Ember write these words to me? I then shoot my eyes at my mother, feeling rage replace the sinking hole of despair in my heart. "You let those crazy men take her? Did they threaten you? Please tell me they held you at gunpoint, because that is the only defense for allowing Ember to leave with them." I drop the letter as if it's burning my fingertips and run my hands through my hair. "Jesus Christ. We need to call the police."

"She chose this," my mother says as she enters the room. "I wasn't going to stand in her way. I'm not going to hold her captive like they did to you. Hate me for it, son, but I believe she made the right choice."

"The right choice! Are you fucking kidding me?"

My mother nods, unfazed by my shouting. "She didn't want to be here. You may not have seen it, because you're in denial, but she didn't want this life. It's *your* life, Christopher. Not hers."

"I can't believe what I'm hearing. Richard is a killer. You allowed a serial killer to enter our house and take Ember, all because she was struggling with getting acclimated to modern society? Not to mention this is the man who kidnapped your son! He chained me up in a cellar! You let my kidnapper into this house! Is that what you're telling me? Please tell me that I have this all wrong, and this is a huge mistake. Because a mistake is the only way I'm going to forgive this. Tell me this was an awful fuck-up, and you want to beg for my forgiveness. Tell me!"

"I'm telling you that I wasn't going to stand in her way of what she wanted to do."

I reach for my phone to call the police.

"Calling the police isn't going to help. She's gone. She's been gone for a while. She didn't put up a fight. She walked out the door with bags in hand and left of her own free will."

"Fuck!" I scream as I throw the phone across the room. "Fuck!"

Anger? Intense sadness? A suffocating fury? Devastation? Relief?

No, not relief. Ember should be here. She should fucking be here!

"Fuck!"

I have no idea what I'm feeling. A mixture of grief and rage is a potent combination, and it makes me feel as if I'm losing complete control of everything.

Why the fuck would she leave with them?

"She's on the run with them now," Mother adds. "Which tells me that she was part of their sick acts all along. You know the police will see it that way. She's a criminal on the run."

"That man has brainwashed her. Nothing more," I defend. "You have no idea just how sick in the fucking head he is."

I can't allow myself to believe that Ember would ever condone or be a part of killing. She's merely a puppet and he the master.

I glance back at the letter.

"She knew deep down that they'd find her. How they did, I don't know. But I bet she was scared for me. For us. I bet she left as a way to sacrifice herself. That's the only explanation," I say, my voice coming out gruff and muffled.

My mother simply shakes her head.

I point at her. "You never liked her. You never made her feel welcomed. She sensed that. She knew!"

"You can blame me if that makes you feel better," she says calmly, which only infuriates me more. "But the person to blame is you. You should never have brought her home. And you should never have left her to figure things out on her own. That poor girl was thrown to the wolves by *you*."

"Yes!" I shout. "And you were the leader of the pack. Why couldn't you have been nice to her? Why couldn't you have acted like a mother figure she so desperately needed?"

"It wasn't my job to love her. It was yours."

Her words were like a punch to the gut. It was my job to love her, and clearly I didn't make her feel loved enough, or she would have never left me. If she truly knew how deeply I did....

"You truly are a despicable woman," I snap. "I've lived my whole life trying to be better than you. Trying not to let money change me like it clearly changed you. You have been the perfect example to me as to what *not* to be."

"I know you're angry and acting out," she says, proceeding as if she doesn't hear a word I say.

"No," I reply, shaking my head in disbelief that this woman is actually my flesh and blood. "This is no act. I've reached my max, Mother. I can't ignore who you are or the things you do any longer. I've spent my whole life making excuses for your behavior. I used to write it off as it just being part of you being a rich socialite. But I was just putting my head in the sand. You simply are a bad person. Period."

"Listen to me," she says, walking over and placing her freshly manicured hand on my shoulder. "You refused to see just how unhappy Amber was here. You also didn't want to face how broken she was. She needed help, and you were too busy with your job and trying to get your life back on track to see it. But at the same time, you can't fix her. She's lived that life for far too many years to just step into our world and survive. I knew this the minute you brought her home. You can't tame a feral, son. It's against nature."

I snapped my shoulder away from her touch, stormed over to my phone, and picked it up off the ground. "She's not a fucking stray! She's my goddamn wife, and you allowed her to leave with monsters!" I pointed to my door and then dialed the detective in charge of the case. "Get out while I deal with this. Get out before I say something I'll regret."

"Christopher—"

"Get out!" I shout. "Now."

"You'll see soon enough why I made the decision I did. Someday, you'll understand."

"Get. The. Fuck. Out."

3

CHRISTOPHER

AGENT MARTINEZ LOOKS AS ANNOYED AS I FEEL. "SO, LET ME GET this straight," he begins. "A serial killer and his possible accomplice enters your house, and you don't call the police?"

"What do you think we're doing right now?" My mother counters his question with the cool demeanor only she can pull off.

"And you allowed Ember to walk out the door with him?"

"She chose to go with him," my mother says, darting her eyes at me. "I've always felt from the beginning that Amber wasn't completely innocent in all this. She showed me today that she isn't afraid of Richard one bit."

"Because she's brainwashed," I cut in. "She grew up believing he was her father. She loves him, no matter what he did. She can't help it. Just because she left with him, doesn't mean she's guilty of any crime."

"I think that's left to be decided," Agent Martinez says as he nods to another man standing next to him, who is taking down all the notes in a black leather pad. "Christopher, did Ember have any phone calls or contact with Richard since returning?"

"Absolutely not," I snap. "She was terrified that he was going to be able to find her. All the media and attention really scared her for that reason. She believed he was coming for her, and that is exactly what he did. He came and took her."

Agent Martinez looks at my mother. "But your mother just said she went with him willingly."

"She's wrong," I say. "It might have appeared that way on the surface. But I know Ember. She wouldn't want to go back to a life with that man. There's some other reason why that we don't know."

"Mrs. Davenport," Agent Martinez says, acting as if my words aren't even heard, "do you have any idea where they were headed? Did they give any clue or say anything?"

My mother shakes her head and gives a slight shrug. "No. Richard simply told Ember to hurry up and that they had to get out of here quickly. Ember rushed upstairs, packed a bag, and was out the door before I could do anything. I wasn't exactly going to try to fight with a serial killer. Frankly"—she looks at me —"I was scared. But this wasn't the first time I've been scared in my own home since that woman entered our lives."

"Why did you wait to call us until after Christopher got home? Why didn't you call 911 the minute they left?" Agent Martinez asks.

Yes, Mother, why?

"For Ember," she answers with a deep sigh. "I knew how this would look for her. And regardless if she's innocent or guilty, I wanted my son to hear it from me first. I wanted him to handle this and make the decision. She's his... wife. And, well... maybe I should have called right away, but like I just said, I was scared."

My mother's lying. I know why she didn't call right away. She wanted to give them a head start. She wanted Ember gone, and here was her chance to have her desires granted. If she called right away, they could have been caught. She's hoping that Ember, Richard, and Scarecrow get as far away as possible. She doesn't ever want to see Ember found. I know this.

My own fucking mother....

Ultimate betrayal.

I can't stand to be in this living room another second. I stand up and say, "Unless you have any more questions for me, I'm leaving."

Ms. Evans finally steps from the farthest corner of the room, where she's been the entire time, standing quietly. "Is there anything I can get you for dinner?" she asks. I can tell she's distraught, and out of everyone in this house, the housekeeper treated Ember the nicest.

"No thank you. I just need to be alone."

Not waiting for Agent Martinez or my mother to speak, I charge upstairs as a million thoughts swirl in my head.

I enter my room... *our* room... and feel my knees weaken.

She's gone. My wife's gone.

Something inside me tells me she's never coming back here.

I sit on the edge of the bed and inhale deeply. I close my eyes and try to focus on her smell that still lingers in the room. Strawberries and flowers—her delicate fragrance since the first day I met her.

I have no idea what to do now. If the police haven't found Richard up until now, what'll make that change now? Is Ember truly gone forever? Would she leave me like this?

Her letter said goodbye, but... how can she simply walk away from us? We have love. We truly do love each other. This I know.

But the biggest question of all, and one that makes me ill just thinking of it, is—is Ember in danger? Will Richard hurt her?

He has to be angry for how we escaped. We burned down everything and left his body to go into flames with it. Would he punish Ember for it? Would he kill her in order to never let her truly be free? Would he chain her up someplace far worse than the cellar I was chained in? Is she suffering?

Is my poor wife suffering right now?

A knock on the door interrupts my morbid thoughts that are growing darker by the second.

"I want to be left alone," I shout, hating that they can't give me a moment to fucking grieve my wife leaving. "Give me a goddamn second please!"

"Christopher?" I hear Ms. Evans's voice call from the other side of the door. "May I have just a moment of your time? Please? It's important."

I get up and open the door. It's unlike Ms. Evans to be pushy and not give me privacy when asked. "What is it?" I ask, softening my voice as I allow her inside the room.

"There's something I need to tell you," Ms. Evans says, her hands fiddling with each other in front of her. She avoids eye contact but eventually takes a deep breath and looks me directly in the eye. I see pain, fear, and even anger. So many emotions are dancing in the eyes of a woman I've come to love like family.

"What going on?"

"I've worked for your family for a very long time," she begins. "I've seen you grow from a rambunctious little boy to a respectable man."

I study her face, looking for signs of what she is clearly struggling and even procrastinating to tell me.

"What I'm about to tell you will most likely cost me my job. But I can't in good faith stand by and allow what I know to remain a secret anymore. I've always been loyal. I would do anything for your mother... at least until now. I can't be part of it. It's wrong, and you have the right to know."

"What's wrong? What do I have the right to know?"

I know she's talking about Ember without her saying so. I also know my mother never liked her and feels her leaving is good riddance. But seeing the turmoil blanketing every feature of Ms. Evans, makes me realize there could be more.

Much more.

"It all started with the straw," she begins with shaky breath. "I caught her in the act. Your mother. She was placing straw in places that Ember would see. She was trying to convince Ember that Scarecrow and Papa Rich had been in the house. They never were; it was your mother doing it."

"What?" Her words are like a slap to the face. "Why would she do something like that?" My mother could be a ruthless bitch at times, but never devious. Never evil. And her claws only came out for her enemies who, in many cases, deserved her wrath. There has to be some sort of miscommunication.

"I think she wanted to make Ember feel like she was losing her mind. She wanted you to think she needed mental help. Maybe you'd send her away to a mental institute. I know Louisa was researching many facilities and trying to find one that would be a good fit. Her goal all along was to get Ember out of your life."

Sighing, I say, "I know she thought Ember needed psychological help, but... placing straw around the house seems farfetched. Are you sure? Did you actually see her do it?"

Ms. Evans nods. "She did it. I saw it with my own eyes. And Ember was such a sweet girl. She didn't deserve to be treated the way she was. Your mother... she didn't make her stay here easy."

I know she didn't welcome Ember, but—

"There's more," Ms. Evans blurts as if she had to or risk never telling me the truth.

I can't process the idea of my mother tormenting Ember by trying to scare her with the straw, so I welcome hearing something else. Anything else.

"Louisa hired a private investigator to find Richard. Actually, she hired a few."

I nod, not really surprised by the news. My mother has always been the type of woman to take matters into her own hands. In her eyes, if she wanted something done correctly, she'd do it herself... or *hire* someone to do it for her.

"She found Richard. Her hired investigators tracked him down, hiding with Scarecrow."

"So, she knew where they were hiding all along and didn't say anything? She didn't let the authorities know?" I ask, stunned by the news. Why wouldn't she help in having the man arrested? It makes zero sense as to why she'd keep his whereabouts a secret.

Ms. Evans took a deep breath and looked out the window

before saying, "She hired a pilot to fly them from Nevada to New York. She was the one who brought them to the house. She helped them come for Ember. She also helped them go off into hiding again."

Each word that comes from Ms. Evans's mouth feels like a bullet piercing my gut. I knew something was off with the way Ember left, but no way could I have imagined this.

Betrayal.

Sick, twisted, evil acts.

Criminal.

I shake my head in hopes that blinding rage won't take over. "My mother is guilty of many things. She has her own moral code at times, but no way could she do something so awful. You have to be wrong on this. Maybe you misunderstood something or just don't have all your facts right."

I'm lying to myself.

I know Ms. Evans is only telling me the truth, but I need a moment to lie to myself to simmer down the madness that is threatening to engulf me.

My mother couldn't have done this to me.

To me. Her only son. To a man she loves. To *me*!

She couldn't have. No way.

But she did.

She fucking did.

"I didn't help your mother, Christopher. But at the same time, I didn't stop her. I started figuring out what she was doing, and I should have told you sooner. But you have to understand just how deep my loyalty is to that woman. I would do anything for her. But this... I can't stand by and let this happen. I can't watch you and allow you to believe Ember left of her own free will."

"Did they force her?" Rage begins to fully set in no matter how many calming breaths I take. "Did my mother lie about that? Did she not walk out the door with them?"

"Ember left with them. But she was driven to do it. I can see why she did. That poor girl never had a chance under this roof.

She was miserable and scared, and Louisa made sure to keep it that way."

And I didn't fucking see it. I chose to put my head in a damn hole and avoid the feelings of my wife. I should have been here. I should have watched, listened, and felt that something was off. But I was too damn focused on making life return to normal.

Normal.

Nothing would be normal again.

And what the fuck is normal anyway?

All I know is I want my goddamn wife back. They took her from me, and I want her back.

"Do you know where they took Ember?" I ask.

Ms. Evans shakes her head. "I overheard them saying they were going back to Nevada for a short time. I know your mother allowed them to use her pilot to get there. But that's it." For the first time, she approaches me and tentatively touches my arm. "I'm sorry, Christopher. I should have told you sooner. I have always tried to mind my own business when it comes to your family. I hear things but try not to react. It has served me well up until now. I even tried to be a friend to Ember, because God knows the woman needed a good friend. But I couldn't be enough. She deserves happiness. You both do. And I sincerely believe you love her as she loves you. I hope you can find her. I hope you can take her back."

I nod as a million thoughts on how exactly I am going to try to do it run through my head.

"But, Christopher," Ms. Evans adds, "if you do find her... don't bring her back here. Start a new life with her. A life that you both create. *Your* life is not for her. So, create one that belongs to the both of you."

Without saying the words, Ms. Evans makes it very clear to me... I had a part in all this too. I tried to force Ember into a world she didn't want to be in. I was selfish. I was focused on the past, rather than the future with my new wife. I did this. I fucking did this.

"Do you know where my mother is?" I ask between clenched teeth. I can't even breathe through the fury attacking my body.

"She's downstairs."

My mother... how do I forgive what she's done?

I may never be able to, but for now, I need to focus on finding Ember. My mother will at least know where the plane went, and I can start from there. I'll find Ember, and I'll make my mother help me in doing so. She'll pay for what she did to my wife. For what she did to us.

4

CHRISTOPHER

"I'M TRYING REALLY HARD NOT TO SCREAM AND STRANGLE YOU right now," I say, clenching my fist to try to contain the rage that wants to erupt from inside. If she weren't my mother....

Lucky for her, she is.

"You can be mad at me all you want," she calmly says, not showing the slightest remorse. "But I did it for Ember. The girl didn't belong here and never would. You were bringing home a broken person. I told you this, but you were being too selfish and wrapped up in your own world to see it for yourself."

Her words are like a blow to the face. Maybe because they're true. I was selfish. I did want my life back, and that meant forcing Ember to live it. Was she miserable? Was she lonely? Clearly, she had to be if she left on her own. She saw Richard and Scarecrow as a way out... a way out of the prison I put her in.

"So let her go," my mother adds. "I know you want to go find her. I know you want to save her. But you can't, Christopher. You need to allow that awful part of your past to remain just where it is now. Behind you. You deserve better, but so does that woman."

"You're right," I say, clenching my fists and then focusing on releasing the tension as I let out a deep breath. "Ember does deserve better. She deserves to be happy, but she also shouldn't be with those crazy men. I might have failed her, but I sure as fuck am not going to allow her to be with those two. She doesn't deserve them either. I need to give her the option of an out. I have to at least try."

"She wanted to go with them! Why can't you listen to me? It was her choice!" I'm not used to seeing my mother get so frazzled, but then again, she's not used to people not listening and not complying to her every whim either.

"She left because she felt there was nothing else to do. You mentally tortured her, Mother! You made her think she was losing her mind. And all but ignored her." Sickness rolls around in my belly as I run my hand through my hair, trying to control the fury and the deep guilt inside me. "I thought I was protecting her, and all I did was…. Fuck. She deserved so much better."

"You can be angry at me," Mother says, calmer this time. "But I did what I did to try to fix a mistake that should have never happened. You brought your nightmare home with you."

"No, Mother!" I shout. "I brought home my wife. I brought home a woman who doesn't have a mean bone in her body. She's genuine, true, loving, and, frankly… the kindest woman I've ever met in my life. And she loved me. She truly loved me for who I am, rather than *what* I am. Money didn't mean anything to her. The Davenport name held zero value to her. She loved me for me, and I'm standing here watching her slip between my fingers. Because of you, and because of me… I could lose it all."

"She's gone, Christopher. There's no finding her. So be mad, grieve, or do whatever you need to, but she's gone. Accept it and move on." She takes a step toward the door to leave, then pauses and adds, "I'm not going to apologize for what I did. You're my son. There's nothing a mother won't do for her son. My job is to protect you, and that is exactly what I did."

"No. What you did was awful. It was cruel. Frankly… it was downright evil."

She makes eye contact with me but shows zero emotion. It's as if my words aren't even being heard.

"And you're going to help me make it right."

"I won't," she says, stiffening her spine. "Good riddance."

"You are going to help me," I say with conviction. "Either you help me find her, or I call Agent Martinez right now and tell him that you assisted Richard in kidnapping Ember. You broke the law, Mother. You'll go to jail for this."

Her lips purse, and for the first time in this entire conversation, I see a mixture of fear and defeat flicker in her eyes. It's brief, but I can see my words have finally sunk in a little.

"I don't know where they are," she snaps. "All I know is where the pilot flew them to. I can give you that information, but that's it."

Renewed hope surges inside me. "Good. At least we can start there."

"You're making a mistake, Christopher."

"I'm fixing a mistake. I'm going to offer her options. I'm going to save her from her hell but will never bring her into another version of one again. Don't worry, Mother," I say with a sneer. "You won't see her again. I'll make damn sure of it."

"Christopher—"

"Get me the location, now!" I interrupt with enough anger in my voice that she flinches. "I don't want to discuss this any further. I have my wife to find. I have to make it right."

Not saying another word, she leaves in a huff, but I know she's going to do exactly what I demand.

I quickly begin sending texts off and emails to make arrangements to take some time off. It's no easy task canceling all my upcoming photo shoots, and that alone should tell me something. I was practically burying myself with work when I had a wife at home who truly needed me. I should have been here with her. Had I been, my mother wouldn't have had the power to play her twisted mind games on her.

Am I pissed at my mother? Yes. But I'm angrier at myself. I

fucking know better. I know exactly how my mother operates, and I knew all along that she didn't care for Ember. Did I really think she would treat her with any compassion or respect?

I can stand here all I want and rage at her, but Louisa Davenport is never going to change her stripes, and I didn't want to face the truth and deal with it. I should have moved us into our own place right away, but if I'm being honest with myself, I was too busy with... me. And I didn't want all the responsibility of Ember on my shoulders.

Yeah, I had been a bastard.

No wonder she left me.

The saddest thing of all is she chose that sick killer over me... which truly shows just how much I failed her.

A knock on the door pulls me away from my self-loathing.

"Christopher?" Marissa opens the bedroom door and peeks inside.

"I don't have time for this," I snap, seeing straight through this woman too. My guess is that my mother used her to fuck with Ember as well. "Convenient that you come up here right after I tell my mother to basically go fuck herself. Don't make me do the same to you."

She takes a step inside and lifts her hands up as if she means no harm. "Yes, Louisa asked me to come up here to try to talk some sense into you."

"Don't bother." I give her a dirty look as I reach for a bag and start throwing clothes into it. "I expected better from you, Marissa. I don't know why I did, but I did."

"I didn't come up here to do her bidding," she says as she walks fully into the room and closes the door behind herself. "But I do think you should pause and think this through. You've always been impulsive—"

"Don't stand there and act like you know me," I cut in without even bothering to look up at her. "I tried to be nice to you. I tried to be... sensitive, considering you were an innocent victim in all this too. But I'm not blind. I know you want Ember out of the picture just as much as my mother does."

"Do you blame me?"

"You act as if you and I were engaged or something. We were dating. It was far more casual than you're making it seem."

"You're just being mean now," she says as she walks around me so she's in my line of sight. "And I don't deserve that."

"No?" I ask, looking up at her with a raised eyebrow. "Really? You and my mother have been in cahoots from the beginning. Perfect example is right now. Why is it you're here? Let me guess. My mother called you and told you to rush right on over here to be by my side. To try to console me and also tell me I'm better off without that 'loon.' And let me also guess, that when my mother tells you to jump, you always reply with 'how high'."

She takes a deep breath, her shoulders rising and falling. "Yes. You're right. But—"

"I don't want to hear any more," I say as calmly as I can, but there isn't much more restraint in me, so I know I sound short and pissed.

And who the fuck cares how I sound?

I am pissed.

"Fine, I get it. You and I are over, and whatever we had is done." She glances down at her feet. "But I did want to come up here and tell you I had no part in helping bring that Richard man here. I didn't know your mother was doing that. The first I heard of it is right now when she filled me in on what happened and why she did it." She takes another deep breath. "I know you're angry with her, but do know she did all this because she loves you. She only wants the best for you."

"She doesn't know what love is, and I'm not going to have this conversation with you. So, if you don't mind, get out."

"Christopher, I just don't want to leave here with you thinking I helped Ember leave. I may have been on your mother's side, and I did want her.... Well, I didn't do this."

I still look at her skeptical, not sure I believe a word she's saying. I was too nice in handling her. My own guilt and people-pleasing personality got in the way of thinking about Ember. I shouldn't have had a drink with Marissa in LA, no matter how innocent—in my mind—it was.

And really, that is exactly why I'm here right now, wondering where the fuck my wife is.

I didn't put Ember first.

Her feelings, her healing, her coping with a new way of life should have been my number-one priority, and it simply wasn't. And now I'm facing the consequences of that.

"I mean it," she says. "I didn't like Ember. I wanted her gone. But not *really* gone. Not like this."

It really doesn't matter if I believe her or not at this point. I need to leave. I need to go hunt down my wife. And I need to walk away from this toxic life for my own well-being. I just hope to God I can find Ember and, when I do, that she won't send me away.

I focus my attention on folding a T-shirt to pack. "I wish you luck in the future."

"So, you're really going? Do you actually think you can find them? If the police can't, what makes you think you can?"

"I'm going to try," I say. "I owe Ember that, and I won't be able to live with myself if I don't. She deserves someone to fight for her, which is something I should have been doing all along."

5

EMBER

THE HIKE TO AN UNKNOWN DESTINATION FROM WHERE THE PLANE left us was brutal. The brush was thick, the trails nonexistent, and the incline so steep I had to use my hands at times to climb. For the first time since wearing shoes, I was really happy I had them on during the trek.

I had no idea where Papa Rich and Scarecrow were taking me, but I wasn't going to ask. I knew we were back in Nevada or maybe California, simply because I recognized the terrain—the trees, the plants—and based on how long the flight was. It made sense that we would return to Papa Rich and Scarecrow's stomping ground, but this time, it wasn't the desert. We were in the mountains, and based on the ridges and cliffs around, the elevation was high.

The plane ride had been quiet. Neither one of them spoke to me but kept their conversation to themselves. I could tell Papa Rich was disappointed in me by how he avoided eye contact, and Scarecrow was smug, as if he knew he'd been right all along, and now he was helping clean up the mess.

The silence was far greater a punishment than if he would have just yelled. I burned down his town, and for that, I feel guilty. I know *why* Christopher and I did it, but that doesn't take away the fact that it was our home. And now, because of me, Papa Rich is homeless.

"I have to hand it to you," Papa Rich says, winded. "You picked a location that is secure. No sane man would make this climb to find us."

Scarecrow huffs, somehow seeming to make his way up the mountain easier than both Papa Rich and me, and considering he only has one leg and crutches, the feat is definitely impressive.

As we reach the top of the mountain, Scarecrow uses his crutch to point at a dilapidated—but still standing—church on the edge of a cliff. "There it is, Ember," he says. "Your new home."

I brush off my hands and pick out the thorns that are embedded in my palms. "It's so high up here," I say more to myself than anyone else. The lower clouds surround us, filling my taxed lungs with moisture.

"They were smart back in the day. The folks built this church on this here ridge to keep a look out for Indians. You can look below and see for miles, and as you just saw from our hike, it's not easy getting here. Gave them the upper hand against invaders, just like it will do the same for us."

"People lived here?" I see an old church, an outhouse, and there do seem to be signs of houses from a long time ago, though the structures are not standing and are nothing but a pile of debris.

It reminds me of Hallelujah Junction simply in the fact that there are signs of the past, of a civilization once here, and whispers of the ghosts of settlers. But unlike Hallelujah Junction, there is not a full town remaining. If there ever was one, Mother Nature destroyed it.

"They built a mighty fine church," Scarecrow says, wiping the sweat off his brow. "And it makes a good homestead for me and my wives."

Wives? Scarecrow wasn't married when I lived in Hallelujah Junction. And he said *wives,* as in plural. I still remember how he wanted to marry me. He wanted Papa Rich to find him a wife as well. Had he actually found two?

"Come on, let's get settled in before nightfall," Papa Rich finally says, his breathing getting back to normal quickly.

We follow Scarecrow as he hobbles his way to the white chapel that reminds me of the schoolhouse I spent most of my life in with my cat in Hallelujah Junction. It feels like a lifetime ago, and yet, at the same time, it seems as if time has stood still. I'm back to where I started. I'm in an old settlers' town. I'm with Papa Rich and Scarecrow. And I am hiding from the rest of the world once again.

"It ain't much," Scarecrow says as we approach the door of the chapel, "but my wives are fixing it up mighty nice."

He opens the chipped white door, and two wide-eyed women turn to face us. They cower, and I can't tell if it's because they think we're invaders, or if that's simply how they respond to seeing Scarecrow return home.

I can't say I'd blame them for either.

I scan the room as we enter. So much of this chapel reminds me of the old schoolhouse I once loved. The musky smell, the chill in the air, and the feeling of *old*. I can almost hear the whispers of the ghosts that still lurk in the shadows, and it brings me to a place I didn't realize I actually missed.

The old pews are missing, and in their place is an old wooden table, four hardy chairs to go with it, and a rocking chair nearby. In the far corner of the room, where the altar would have been, is a camp cooktop hooked up to a small propane tank. There is also a hole that has been created in the ceiling; beneath it is a fire pit that has a cast iron pot hanging over it. A green tarp is being used to try to shield some of the wind coming in through the hole, but not too much, as the hole was clearly created for ventilation for the fire.

There are parts of the open church that are sectioned off by hanging, tattered curtains. I'm assuming they're the wives' rooms. Maybe Scarecrow has a private space? I have no idea how the sleeping arrangements work with having multiple wives, and I can't see behind the curtains to know how many beds there are—if there are any.

There is also a clothing line running from one end of the room to a post where other dresses, some undergarments, and some blue jeans for Scarecrow hang. The women have obviously tried their hardest to keep the place organized and as homey as possible, considering. It even appears as if the beginnings of a chimney of sorts is being worked on. I see a pile of stone and a bucket of mud near the hole. It's a wise move, considering winter is coming, and having a fairly large hole in the chapel will make for a chilly living space.

"This here is Wife Number One, and Wife Number Two," Scarecrow says to me.

I notice Papa Rich is taking off his jacket, putting down his bags, and paying no attention to the introductions. He obviously already knows who these women are, or he doesn't care.

"Wives, this here is Ember. She's going to become Wife Number Three."

My heart stops, and I make eye contact with Papa Rich, who looks up at me when he hears Scarecrow's statement. His eyes say it all. He agrees with me marrying him. He gave me the opportunity to marry someone else, and we know how that ended.

But I don't want to marry Scarecrow.

I'm married to Christopher!

Even though I'm not physically with Christopher, surely our wedding vows mean something. How can Papa Rich want me to go against my vows said under God? If that's not a sin, then I don't know what is. And even if he wants to deny that Christopher and I are truly married—just as Louisa did—how can he possibly think Scarecrow is a good match for me? Especially since he already has two wives!

But I also know this is not the time to argue. I'm not sure if I can ever truly speak freely to Papa Rich again, but I know now is too soon. I can't read his anger yet. All I see is disappointment and even sadness in his features, but something tells me he is on the very edge of what could turn into pure rage if pushed the right way.

I redirect my attention to the two women who Scarecrow hasn't called by name yet. Both women have stringy brown hair that is braided loosely down their backs. They are dressed in worn and faded flower dresses that go to their ankles and remind me of dresses I once wore back in Hallelujah Junction. They are also both barefoot, and suddenly my shoes feel very foreign, out of place, and extremely restricting on my feet.

"Where's supper?" Scarecrow asks.

Wife Number One looks at Wife Number Two, and this time there is no denying the fear in their eyes.

"We didn't know you were coming back today," Wife Number One says softly.

"We would have had supper ready, but we were trying to ration out the food until your return," Wife Number Two adds, wringing her hands in front of her as she refuses to look Scarecrow in the eye.

The wives look close in age and appearance. Sisters maybe? Regardless of their relation, they both respond to Scarecrow the same way. It makes me want to step in and offer assistance somehow. Maybe I can suggest that I make supper and deflect some of the tension in the room. But before I can say or do anything, Scarecrow grabs Wife Number Two by the arm and leads her to the table and chairs.

"Bend over, dress up, drawers down," he says as he begins to unfasten his belt.

I see her lips tremble, but she quickly complies with his order as only an experienced punished wife would do. I can't help but glance at Papa Rich and wonder if I'm next. Is he saving my punishment for when he's more settled? It's been a long time since I've felt the strike of leather on my bare skin, but not so long that my heart doesn't skip, and my knees weaken in anticipation.

"You know I like to come home to a cooked meal and a clean house," Scarecrow begins to lecture as he doubles over the leather in his hand.

Wife Number Two is bent over the table, and her bare bottom is on full display for all of us to see. Scarecrow clearly doesn't care about discretion or who sees his wife's nudity, nor does he care that we are about to watch him whip her.

"If you don't meet my expectations, there will be consequences," he says as he brings down the belt onto her creamy flesh.

She yelps but holds her position, clenching the table on both sides with her tiny fists. Her sisterwife stands stoically near with no emotion on her face other than a slight flicker of her eyelids with each swat that is coming down in rapid succession now.

Scarecrow has no mercy and rains the leather down upon her over and over again. Each strike is harder than the last, and I already see angry red lashes that will surely bruise. Wife Number Two holds position and, though crying out, isn't trying to reach back and protect herself.

She knows better.

It's obvious that she knows better.

I can only stand and watch on helplessly. I know these two men in this room. If I try to stop it, it will just mean more of a whipping for Wife Number Two, and one for me as well. I can't reason with insanity, and that is exactly what Scarecrow is.

This is insanity.

The deepest, darkest, cruelest, and most vile form of insanity.

When Scarecrow finally finishes the beating, he pulls away, loops his belt back into place, and hobbles his way to Wife Number One. I inhale sharply and close my eyes.

She's next.

I open my eyes right as he takes a handful of her hair, forcefully pulls her head back, and says, "Now make us some supper, and don't ever do that again, or Wife Number Two will pay for your transgressions once more."

She nods and rushes to the makeshift cook station she has and begins digging in burlap bags for what looks like rotten potatoes and nearly rotten carrots.

Wife Number Two stands up and fixes her dress as she wipes away the tears from her face. She doesn't make eye contact with anyone but instead makes her way over to Wife Number One and assists in the supper preparation.

Not knowing what else to do, I also walk over, reach for a potato and a knife, and begin cutting away the rot. Swallowing back the impending dread, I busy myself in the now.

All I have is right now.

6

EMBER

I can hear Papa Rich and Scarecrow talking outside the door as they smoke their pipe and drink from a tin cup full of cheap whiskey—which they of course didn't offer to any of the wives. They also ate most of the supper that we had prepared, though I didn't mind one bit. My stomach is still nothing but a ball of nerves, and I'm not sure I could have held down much more than the couple of bites I did have dished up on my plate.

"We need to leave at first light tomorrow," Papa Rich says. "I know we just got here, but I don't like that the pilot knows our general location. He could tell the police where we're at."

"No, he'll stay quiet. He'll be in a shitload of trouble if he admits to helping wanted fugitives fly across state lines," Scarecrow replies.

"And Louisa Davenport? What if she caves under questioning from her son? I can see that happening."

"That rich bitch is going to keep her mouth shut too. Do you think she wants it known she helped us escape? Not only escape but gave us funds that will get us through the winter," Scarecrow prompts.

"Still… I'm not comfortable with the fact. And though we may have stayed away from the authorities up until now, they are going to beef up looking for us even more now that we have Ember. Nevada isn't safe for us anywhere. They will comb every inch of these mountains and deserts, and you know it."

"It's remote here."

"Not remote enough for my liking."

There's a long pause, but then Scarecrow finally says, "So, you still thinking Wyoming?"

"Yes," Papa Rich says. "Montana is an option, but a Ranger buddy of mine once told me of a very old and desolate town in the mountains. It will be in poor condition, but nothing we can't handle."

"And you're positive we can find it? I'm just not liking the idea of having my wives travel through a huge state to hunt for a town we may or may not be able to find."

"Which is why I'd like to suggest an idea I've been stewing on," Papa Rich says as I hear him inhale deeply from the pipe he's smoking. "I say you and I leave for now. It's going to be winter soon, and from the looks of the sky, a storm is brewing. We brought back plenty of provisions for the women to live off of while we're gone. The snow the storm will bring will keep them… securely in place until we return. We go and scout the area, find our new home, then come back and get your wives to start a new settlement."

"I'm not sure how I feel about leaving the women alone up here. The winters are brutal."

"I get that," Papa Rich says. "But I know Ember knows how to survive just fine. I taught her well. I'm also sure your wives know how to make do. And I think you and I have a better chance buying that truck we saw and heading out on our own. Ember being with us could draw more attention."

"The last time you left Ember unattended, she burned down an entire town. You really think we can trust her?"

"She's learned from her mistakes, or she wouldn't have left with us. We didn't have to tie her up and drag her back here. Plus, you have your two wives to look after her. You know damn well those women wouldn't dare anger you by doing something as foolish as trying to leave. Where would they go? What would they do?"

"You have valid points," Scarecrow says slowly. There's a long moment of silence, and then he adds, "We better get moving at first light. I don't want to hike down the mountain in the snow and rain."

"I don't think Husband will appreciate you spying on his conversation," a voice from behind me says, startling me as I spin to face my accuser.

"I—"

Wife Number One motions for me to follow her, fear in her eyes as she glances at the door, expecting it to open any second. "I just don't want you to catch the wrath of Husband."

I follow her to where Wife Number Two is working on masoning the fire pit with the river rock and the bucket of clay.

"Can I help?" I ask, grateful that Wife Number One is only trying to help rather than get me into trouble by telling Scarecrow and Papa Rich that I practically had my ear to the door.

"Snow is coming soon," Wife Number Two says, not looking at me as she continues to build. "If we don't get this hole patched up with a chimney, we're going to freeze." She points to the rocks. If you hand me one at a time, I'll apply the clay. I can move faster that way."

I rush to her side, grateful to have something to do and also for a way to help prove my worth. I'm sure they are wondering who I am and why I'm here.

"I'm Ember," I begin as I hand a rock to her. "Richard is my... father."

"We know who you are," Wife Number One says from behind

me. "Scarecrow told us all about you and what you did... to Hallelujah Junction."

I freeze, scared to look over my shoulder at the woman in fear of the judgement I'd see in her eyes. I wonder what they must think, having an arsonist under their roof.

"My name is Holly," Wife Number One says. "And this is Violet."

"We're sisters," Violet adds. "My father promised our hand in marriage to Scarecrow not long ago, which is how we came here."

What kind of father would do such a vile and cruel thing? One look at Scarecrow says it all—he's not husband material. He's just... disgusting.

Although... isn't that exactly what my own father is doing? Marrying me off to a sick creature?

"I'm Wife Number One," Holly says. "I'm the oldest, and my sister is Wife Number Two."

She makes the statement like it's completely ordinary and I wouldn't find this information shocking in the least.

"It looks like you're going to be Wife Number Three," Violet says. She stops applying the clay to the rock and looks up at Holly. "What do you think her purpose will be?"

"Purpose?" I ask.

Violet looks at me and smiles, but then her face grows grim just as quickly. "Holly's purpose is to provide Scarecrow with pleasure. She's the one in charge of doing her wifely duty in the... bedroom." Violet returns to her clay and reaches for the rock that's in my hand. "My duty is to pay for my sister's as well as my indiscretions. I am the extra, the standby."

My thoughts go back to the whipping she took for not having supper ready.

She shrugs. "I think Holly has it far worse."

I then picture Holly being intimate—no doubt against her will—with Scarecrow. The bile rising in the back of my throat has me 100 percent agreeing with Violet. Holly has it far worse. I'd take a beating every day with a belt over having to have sex with Scarecrow.

"I don't know what her purpose will be," Holly says. "But we welcome you as a fellow sisterwife."

"Thank you," I say, even though I don't feel very thankful. I don't want to marry Scarecrow. I don't want to have a purpose.

"Is Richard your only family?" Violet asks.

I pause as I don't know what to say. Christopher... he was my family, but I suppose I need to accept that it all changed when I hopped on the plane and left New York.

"Yes," I answer, which makes me feel like I'm somehow betraying Christopher.

"We only had our pa too," Violet says. "Our ma died when we were real young. It was just the three of us living off the grid. Pa didn't believe in society."

"I understand." Which I do, considering Papa Rich is the exact same way.

"He met Scarecrow years ago," Violet adds. "They used to trade."

"Until our pa traded us," Holly cuts in, the venom in her voice clear. "And now you get the pleasure of being Scarecrow's wife as well. Congratulations."

Before I can get myself worked up with the thought, Scarecrow and Papa Rich enter the chapel.

"All right, women. We have come to a decision," Scarecrow announces as the loud pounding of his crutches on the wooden floor seems to amplify his voice. "I'm going to marry Ember right here and right now. We don't have any time to lose, since we're leaving at first light tomorrow to find us a new homestead." He glares at me. "Ember here has made our current situation more precarious, and therefore, we don't feel like staying here is wise. Plus, I believe God has spoken to me and told me that our journey to Wyoming is a good one."

Holly and Violet both nod obediently. They don't question,

they don't argue, and they don't show any emotion other than their complete submission.

I consider speaking up, but my mouth remains closed.

"Come on now," Scarecrow says as he walks toward a wooden cross on the wall. "This is as good a spot as any."

I steal a final glance at Papa Rich, silently begging him to put a stop to this. But instead, he follows Scarecrow to the cross, which tells me all I need to know.

My wedding day is today. Right now. No escape.

7

EMBER

"Good Lord, bless us on this day," Papa Rich begins. He's reading from a paper that Scarecrow has written for him. He's reciting the same words that Scarecrow gave when marrying Christopher and me. "Brother Scarecrow and Sister Ember stand before the Almighty to be crowned under the union of matrimony."

He looks at Scarecrow, who is leaning against his crutch, balancing on his one leg as dirty straw falls from his other pant leg.

"I give away this woman—my daughter—to Brother Scarecrow on this day with the blessing of God," Papa Rich says. "I also ask forgiveness from God in my misdeeds and promising her hand to another. I was tempted by the devil and hope to make amends by correcting the wrong now."

Papa Rich raises his arms up toward the ceiling of the chapel, which has now converted into my new home, and I see the sweat stains under his pits, reminding me of the man I'm about to marry. I don't need to look at Scarecrow to know he's in front of me. I can hear his heavy breathing. I can smell his horrific odor of body sweat and onion.

I glance to my left and see Holly and Violet are watching on with deep sadness in their eyes. I wonder what they're thinking. Are they sad for me? Are they sad for themsleves? Why are they so sad... other than the fact that we are all going to be wives of the most disgusting and putrid man possible? Will these women become my friends or enemies? Will they like or hate me? Maybe they don't want to share their husband with me, even though I don't want to be wed to begin with. Maybe they will try to push me out the door just as Louisa had in New York.

Maybe I will never be welcomed by anyone.

Maybe the fate of the ghost of Hallelujah Junction is to be alone forever.

And yet... alone would be better than what is happening now.

I'm marrying Scarecrow.

I have no choice. Not now. Not ever.

This is my life.

Papa Rich looks down at the paper again and reads, "Now you will feel no rain, for each of you will be shelter for the other. Now you will feel no cold, for each of you will be warmth to the other. Now there will be no loneliness, for each of you will be companion to the other. Now you are two persons, but there is only one life before you. May beauty surround you both in the journey ahead and through all the years. May happiness be your companion and your days together be good and long upon the earth. May you both walk under God as dutiful servants. We honor fire and ask that our union be warm and glowing with love in our hearts. We honor wind and ask that we sail through life safe and calm as in our Father's arms. We honor water to clean and soothe our relationship—that it may never thirst for love. With all the forces of the universe you created, we pray for harmony as we grow forever young together. Amen."

It's word for word from my wedding day with Christopher.

Christopher... my husband.

My old husband.

No longer. Never again. *Goodbye, Christopher.*

Scarecrow and Papa Rich both say, "Amen," but I barely squeak out the word, as my throat feels like it's closing.

My heart is shattering, because I truly believed Christopher and I would be wed for life. We gave our vows. We spoke the words.

But then, I remind myself that he was forced to marry me. He was forced to love me. He was forced to care for me after our rescue. He was forced in every aspect. He didn't marry me of his own free will, and even though he said he'd watch over me after we were rescued... did he really have a choice? No. I forced that too.

Force.

This is my punishment for my part in his captivity. This is God's way of righting our sins.

I have to marry Scarecrow.

Papa Rich opens his hands before us, and resting in his palm are two gold bands. I take the larger one, and Scarecrow takes the smaller. It's the same ring I wore with Christopher that Papa Rich had taken from me on the plane. They are recycling the ring. The same ring but a different man.

"Brother Scarecrow." Papa Rich slices through my thoughts. "Do you take Sister Ember to be your bride, to honor, to cherish, and to walk under God's eyes together as one?"

"I do," he says with a smile on his face that shows nearly every decayed tooth in his mouth.

"Sister Ember," Papa Rich continues as I consider running outside and jumping off the ledge of the cliff and putting myself out of the misery I feel and know more will come. "Do you take Brother Scarecrow to be your husband, to honor, obey, and walk under God's eyes together as one?"

"I do," I somehow manage to say. I'm still not sure if it's because the possibility of death by falling to my demise is still on the table.

The gold band slides onto my finger, and I allow the tears that had been threatening to shed cascade down my cheeks.

At least I have the ring. It will remind me of Christopher. It will keep him close to me in a small way.

I swipe at a tear. But is that what I want? Do I want a constant reminder of what I had but what never truly belonged to me to begin with?

"I now pronounce you husband and wife. You may kiss your bride."

Run to the cliff now.

Run and jump.

Run and jump!

Death is better than—

Scarecrow leans forward and presses his chapped and scabby lips to mine. The kiss is brief, but not brief enough. I nearly vomit, but before I do, he mercifully pulls away, beats his cane on the floor, and lets out a hoot.

"Hot damn, I got me Wife Number Three!"

"It's getting late," Papa Rich says, acting as if he didn't just marry his daughter off for the second time.

No big deal, right?

Just take a bride from one husband and have her marry a second.

"True," Scarecrow says, studying me. "Out of respect for Richard being under the roof, we'll wait to consummate the marriage when I return."

His words are as if the angels from above flew down and granted me their grace.

Consummate the marriage...

The very thought....

Thank God for his decision.

I've survived some extremely harsh situations, but I don't believe I can survive having Scarecrow inside me. I can't have sex with the man. I'd die first.

"Holly will be sleeping with me tonight," Scarecrow adds. He points to a corner of the room with a tattered curtain hanging. "Ember, that will be your room. Violet will assist you in finding bedding. We don't have much, but I'm sure she can muster something up." He then looks at Papa Rich. "I'm sure you can make do with your pack?"

Papa Rich nods. "Let's get some sleep. We got a long journey ahead of us tomorrow."

Violet takes me by the hand. "I have an extra blanket from my bed for you, and I know we have some straw." She then leans into me and whispers in my ear, "When they leave, we can take from Holly and Scarecrow's bed, as they have extra blankets and pillows for him. I know Holly will share."

I somehow get my feet to move, which oddly feels as if I'm floating. I'm not sure if I'm shocked by what just occurred, if I'm grieving over my new life, or if I'm ... suicidal. The thought of the cliff outside still lingers in my mind.

The strong stench of onion will forever burn my nostrils, and the vows I made to Scarecrow will forever taint my tongue.

When Violet and I are behind my privacy curtain, she begins making my bed. "I know you don't want to be here," she says. "I don't blame you." She looks up at me and smiles. "But I'm happy you're here. It will be nice to have some extra company around. It's awfully lonely up here on the mountain."

I try to smile politely back, but my face is frozen in misery. I wonder if I will ever smile again.

8

EMBER

IT'S SO COLD. BONE-SHATTERING COLD.

We don't have enough firewood to get us through the night unless we use it sparingly, which sadly isn't enough to keep the chapel warm. The three of us knew Papa Rich and Scarecrow didn't leave us with enough food to survive the entire time they'll be gone, so we spent the next two days foraging for food before the snowfall made it impossible to do so. Which then meant we didn't gather and chop firewood like we should, since something had to give.

Luckily for us, Violet seemed to have good luck when she went into the forest alone. She'd come back with a basketful of mushrooms or berries. She went out this morning, insisting to go alone, and came home with two rabbits and told us she came across them in traps that must have been set by Scarecrow. Violet's eyes sparkled with pride, but she never smiled.

None of us smiled.

Sadness is her permanent, as it is ours.

But no matter how sad Violet appears, a sweetness masters all else. Such a gentle soul. So kind, generous in everything she does, and I truly have fallen in love with her. Even in this short time, it's impossible not to. I never had a sister, and now... I have two.

Holly—though kind—is very different in how she interacts with me. Strong, steadfast, and determined are her characteristics, but they all give me comfort. I know I can count on Holly and her leadership. She knows this mountain. She understands how it ticks, how it breathes. The mountaintop has a heartbeat, and her palm is the one over it.

She collects pine needles and rosehip for teas. She pulls moss and pine branches and carries them back to the chapel to fill in all the gaps in the wood that allows in the cool air. She has also placed containers outside to start collecting water when the storm comes. She's preparing for the storm, and it's obvious this isn't her first time.

Because it's so cold tonight, we all choose to make our beds around the fire rather than our respective corners with our privacy curtains pulled. I've reached a point of comfort with the women, and I figure we'll spend the majority of the approaching winter together with the fire giving us warmth rather than concealing ourselves in coldness.

The fire crackles, and I hear the heavy breathing of Holly asleep beneath a thick quilt. Easy sleep—her reward for the hard work she does in a day. Sleep of my own begins to take over when I feel Violet's body cuddle up behind me. Considering the chill in the room, I don't mind the touch and the need for body heat.

"Is this okay?" she whispers, wrapping her arm securely around me.

I nod, not sure if it's appropriate or not. But I'm cold, I'm on the ground in the middle of nowhere, and at this moment in time, I don't care what is right or wrong. Her touch gives me comfort, and clearly mine gives her the same.

"I love you, Ember. Sweet dreams," she says as she snuggles her face into my hair.

"Sweet dreams, Violet."

We both deserve them.

Christopher

The pilot is lucky I don't turn his ass in. Although he seems the type to keep his head down and just see what he wants to see— as long as there's a paycheck in the end. I don't like the man one bit, but when he got the call from my mother with the orders to fly me to the exact same spot he dropped Richard off at, he obliged. Did he offer me any other information when I grilled him? No. But at least I was in the general area. The man had to be scared shitless now that his idea of fast cash was blowing up in his face.

We land on an old tarmac in a meadow surrounded by pine and redwood trees for as far as I can see. My guess is the runway was once used—or maybe still used—for wild land firefighters and hotshots. I had once done a shoot on the heroes who fought the mountain blazes, and we went to remote places such as this.

"If you're really crazy enough to hike out there in the mountains with no destination in mind, you better find shelter or someplace soon," the pilot says as I get out of the plane. "A storm's coming, and I'm not hanging around."

"I got this," I say, grabbing my backpack, which is fully loaded with every survival necessity I usually travel with on destination shoots.

Biting my tongue so I don't say what I really want to say, I walk away without speaking another word. I don't need his concern, and I don't need to waste my breath telling the man what a piece of shit he is either.

I just need my wife.

He's right, however. A storm is coming. Luckily, I dressed in thick boots, waterproof clothing, and a down jacket that could withstand the arctic. My experience as a photographer in some rugged and freezing locations has truly trained me for this. Ironic to think that my career brought me into Ember's life, then chased her away, and now it's going to help me bring her back into it.

During the flight, I studied the maps and terrain and really tried to put myself into Richard and Scarecrow's minds. Where would they go? They'd have to walk away from the plane just as I am, so they couldn't go too far. No way to have a vehicle to aid in getting away. They also have Ember, and though she's physically in shape, there is only so far she can hike in these conditions. And though they may have tents, something deep inside me screams that they'd try to repeat history. They'd want an old mining town or at the very least a hunter's lodge. They'd want to rebuild another version of Hallelujah Junction. They'd also know the authorities are hunting them down, so they'd need to hide. Which means wherever they are would be remote but in a place they'd see people coming with a way to escape if they were found.

A ridge. A cliff maybe. Some place vehicles couldn't drive to give the authorities the upper hand. Richard would pick a place that any sane man wouldn't want to reach.

But I'm not a sane man. Not anymore.

I'm about as mad as The Hatter due to Richard. And for that... he'll now have to face my insanity head-on. He created this beast inside me. I'm his own creation and will be his undoing.

Now, to hunt down my prey....

"Mr. Davenport," the pilot calls out as I begin my search.

I turn to face him but don't say a thing. Speaking to the man who helped madmen capture Ember is not on the top of my list of favorite things to do.

"You have a satellite phone, right?"

I nod and pat my backpack to show I do.

"I'm removing myself from this situation. I'm going to act like I didn't meet any of you." He clears his throat. "But I'm going to tell a colleague of mine about you and that you're out here. I'm going to tell him to fly you and that woman of yours out of here when you're ready."

"I'd appreciate that."

The pilot looks up at the sky. "But he can't fly during the storms or even the risk of one coming. So, you have windows where he can come and when he can't. Be prepared to wait out the storms if need be. And that phone of yours won't work well or at all in parts of this mountain. Especially during a storm. Just be aware." He hops out of the plane, marches to where I am, and hands me a card with the other pilot's information.

I nod again, turning on my heels to leave, grateful I at least have a way out when the time comes.

"One more thing," the pilot calls out.

I turn to face him, still annoyed but appreciative that the man's conscience is getting the best of him. "They spoke of a chapel. They also spoke of hiking *up*. I don't know where exactly, but they kept mentioning 'up' and 'chapel.'"

I reach for my maps and begin looking at all the terrain and my notes again. Chapel? There's no town anywhere near the area. We are literally in the middle of nowhere. Nothing but mountaintops, ridges, canyons, cliffs, and pine trees for as far as the eye can see.

"I also don't think they were going too far from where we landed. They were lugging a lot of supplies and bags. They were stocked up but nothing but their backs to carry it all with. No way would they have trekked far with all that weight," he adds. "And one of the men only had one leg, so I can't see how that would lend to intense hiking."

Folding the map and deciding to head toward the highest ridge, I say, "I appreciate the added info."

I pick up my pack and look toward the sky. A storm is coming, and I don't have a lot of time to find some sort of shelter. I have a sleeping bag that will keep me warm in subzero temperatures, but I don't exactly want to test how efficient it is.

I've gone on many photo expeditions in my time. I've hiked the most grueling trails, put myself in extreme temperatures, and placed myself in the middle of dangerous situations. All for the perfect photos. And to be honest... I loved it.

But this is different. Hiking this mountain, with no camera in hand, in search of my wife who was taken from me, is anything but fun. I know I'm a skilled survivalist, if need be, but I really don't want the need to be. Not to mention the last time I went out in the wild by myself, I got hit over the head by a madman, held captive in a cellar in a ghost town, and forced to marry a woman who was also kidnapped and held captive. You'd think I'd learn.

Miles and miles, I walk with no destination. I just go "up" and search for any sign of life. Tiny snowflakes begin to fall. They aren't sticking yet, but I know it's only a matter of time until they do. But I won't give up until I find something... anything... Ember. I *will* find Ember.

9

EMBER

I CAN FEEL EYES ON ME.

I'm not alone.

"Hello?" I call out. "Is someone out there?"

I'm on the top of a mountain with only the sisters inside as company, but I'm not alone.

I feel it in my bones.

Someone's watching me as I collect firewood. Someone's out there.

"Papa Rich?" I call out, wondering if he and Scarecrow never left.

Maybe this is a test. They tell us they are leaving to see what I'll do. Will I escape? Will I take the sisters with me? Will I try to burn down the chapel like I burned down Hallelujah Junction?

Are they waiting in the woods, watching my every move?

They did leave easily enough. They didn't even warn me or make threats. They simply left... or did they?

"What are you doing out here?" Holly asks. "It's getting dark."

"I think someone's out there. Watching."

She looks toward the woods. "What makes you think that?"

"I thought I heard something. And it's just a feeling I get."

She studies the dense trees for several moments, then reaches for the pile of wood in my arms and takes some. "We really need to get inside. It could be a mountain lion or a bear stalking us."

As we head back to the chapel, I look over my shoulder and swear I see movement in the distance. "Do you think Papa Rich and Scarecrow really left?"

She pauses her steps for a moment but then continues on. "Why would you ask that?"

"I don't know," I say. "I just get the feeling it was a person out there."

"They left," she states simply.

"I know it might sound crazy, but I really feel like there was a person out there."

"Did you see a person?"

"No."

"Well then...." She opens the door to the chapel and ends the discussion as we enter inside.

I spend the rest of the day uneasy. The incident in the woods didn't sit well with me, and Holly and Violet's reaction to my feeling as if someone is out there doesn't sit right either. It's almost as if they know someone is out there. That they are in on a secret that I don't know.

Did Papa Rich and Scarecrow tell them they were going to test me?

Are they in on the plan to catch me trying to escape?

I've never been good at reading people. I never had practice. And by my most recent experience with Louisa Davenport, with Christopher's good friend attacking, his ex-girlfriend, and the media circus... I don't exactly trust anyone.

Although something inside me tells me I can trust the sisters, which makes their actions odd to me. What do they know that I don't?

"So, what did Scarecrow tell you about me?" I ask, wondering if my voice sounds as suspicious as I feel.

Violet looks up from her masonry that she's nearly

completed. Her head tilts slightly as if she's reading me, but no doubt she's just as out of practice as I am due to her living situation. "He told us that you burned down your home with a man who was your husband. That you fled to live in the evil world. He said you were tempted by the devil and couldn't resist."

"Did they say anything to you when they left?" I question.

Violet shakes her head and returns her attention to her chimney. "Scarecrow doesn't say much to me."

I look at Holly, who shrugs. "His usual," she says. "He warns that I better keep the homestead up, that I better watch over all, and that I better pray to God he returns to find things in order." She walks over to the table and pulls some mushrooms we had collected earlier out of a bag to add to the stew we're making. "He didn't ask me to spy on you, or to test you, or to make sure you don't burn down the chapel. I know that's what you're getting at." She does look up from cutting then. "And even if he did, we wouldn't. We like you, Ember. You're on the same team as us. Trust in that."

"It's hard to trust anyone anymore," I admit.

"Scarecrow did say your husband was a bad man," Violet says.

"No," I nearly spit out. "Christopher is his name, and he's far from a bad man. He's a genuine, kind, and gentle man. He's a protector, caring, and loving. He's not bad."

"Then why did he try to kill your father?" Violet asks. Her tone isn't accusing but simply curious.

"We didn't try to kill him when we started the fire. We just wanted a way out. Christopher was being held captive. We were chained together and knew we couldn't get far without authorities coming to us. Papa Rich was away... or at least we thought he was." I take a deep breath and say the truth, even though it hurts to. "Papa Rich is the bad man. He's always been the bad man." I look at Holly and then back to Violet. "But so is Scarecrow. You both know this."

"Scarecrow is no worse than our father," Holly says, which makes me sad for both girls.

They've never known happiness and comfort. At least I got that for a short time with Christopher. Even though my life was chaos in New York, and there were so many times I was unhappy... I did have happy moments. I did have times of love and affection. I had hope. I had so much hope.

Holly and Violet, however... they've only had darkness.

"Why did you leave him?" Violet asks. "Christopher. If he's such a good man, why come back to... this?"

"For him," I admit. "It wasn't fair for me to stay. He didn't ask for me. He didn't deserve to have his nightmare continue. I did what was best, regardless of how hard it was."

"I'm sorry," Violet says as she stands to approach me. I think she's coming to hug me but stops midway as if she's gone too far as it is. "But I'm glad you're here. We can make a home. We can have a family. I promise."

I hear Holly sigh, and I turn to face her as she says, "Let's just focus on surviving the storm. One day at a time, remember? That's how we live. One day at a time."

10

EMBER

THE POUNDING OF THE DOOR CAUSES ALL OF US TO JUMP. WE STARE at each other wide-eyed, uncertain what to do.

Feeling as if I should be the one to defend us, if need be, I pick up a fire stoker and place my finger on my lips to tell the girls to remain quiet.

Another knock and a rattle of the door that we fortunately have locked has us all jumping again.

I hesitate at first but then pad over to the door, unsure of who could possibly be on the other side. I hold the poker high enough that I can bring it down on someone's head if I need to. Or maybe I should have it in a position so I can stab them...

Or maybe we should just hide and hope no one enters.

Another knock. This one louder.

Is it the person I could have sworn was watching us? Was he just biding his time to catch us when we're least expecting it? But why knock on the door? Why not just force his way in?

And then I hear a muffled voice on the other side. "Open up! Ember! Are you in there? Ember!"

Another knock and then the rattle of the handle.

"Christopher?" I open the door, cautiously, unsure.

Snow swirls around him, the tip of his nose red from the cold, and he's bundled up so much that if I didn't have a close relationship with the man, I may not have been able to recognize him.

"What are you doing here? How? How did you find me?"

Am I imagining him standing before me? Is this all in my head—wishful thinking?

The biting cold hitting my exposed skin is the only thing that is keeping sanity present. It acts like the slap to the face I need in order to remain in the present. I reach out to be sure I'm still awake or alive and touch his arm.

He's here. He's really here.

He remains frozen in place as if the storm is holding him hostage.

"Ember," he says as he pulls a scarf away from his mouth.

Christopher's eyes are wide, flecks of snow on his lashes. He seems as stunned to see me as I am him.

"I was scared I'd never find you," he says, still not moving toward me. It's as if part of us both want to throw ourselves into each other's arms, but something more powerful is holding us back.

"Ember?" I hear Holly call from inside. "Who's at the door?"

Her words seem to free me from my stunned daze, and I reach for Christopher's arm and pull him inside from the swirling snow outside. The church isn't exactly warm, but it's shelter from the storm.

I pause and look over my shoulder at two wide-eyed women who stand terrified by the fire.

"This is Christopher," I say. "He's my husband. Or... he *was* my husband." I lick my lips, trying to soothe the dryness that is causing my voice to crack.

I look at Christopher, whose head snaps in my direction as if I just punched him. "I *am* your husband, Ember. I'm your husband, and I've come to bring you home."

I lift my hand up to silently tell Holly and Violet that

everything is all right and then return my stare to Christopher, who is scanning the room with a clenched jaw and darkened eyes.

"Where are they?" he asks.

I take a step toward him, still wanting to desperately throw myself into his arms and beg him to never let me go. But I can also see by his clamped fists and his stiffened spine that he's in the mood for a confrontation.

He's ready for a fight. A fight he'll win.

"Gone," I say, hoping my answer is all that is needed to soothe his fury.

"What do you mean gone?" He then points at Holly and Violet. "Who are they?"

Holly takes a protective step toward Violet and wraps her arm around her sister's frail shoulders. "Ember? What's going on?" she asks.

All eyes are on me, and I feel as if I'm the only person in the room who truly has no grasp of reality. I don't know what's going on. I don't even know if this is real or if I've somehow mentally cracked and am living some alternate reality. There's no way Christopher can be standing here in our house out in the middle of nowhere.

How did he find me?

Why would he even bother trying?

"Were you outside earlier, watching us?" I ask.

Confusion washes over his face. "No. I've been hiking all day, hoping to find you. Then I saw the smoke from the chimney and ran straight here. I hoped it was you. God, I'm so happy it is."

"How did you find us?"

"The same pilot who took you flew me here," he says. "And a shitload of luck."

"You risked your life—"

"Where is Richard?" Christopher asks, taking his snow-covered backpack off and spinning around the room some more.

"He and Scarecrow left to find us a new home," Holly answers for me. I'm grateful for her, since I can barely swallow my own spit, let alone speak in complete sentences. "They aren't here and won't be for quite some time."

And thank God for that. If they had been here, what would have happened? Someone would end up hurt, maybe dead. There is no way the meeting of the men would end good. I need to get Christopher out of here before they return, because the clash of the Titans would be devastating for all.

Christopher's eyes narrow on Holly. "And you are?"

Holly looks at Violet and then back at him. "We're Scarecrow's wives. We live here."

He takes a moment to analyze both women, who stand barefoot by the fire, wearing thin and worn floral dresses, and I wonder if he sees the old me in them. Does he see the ghost of Hallelujah Junction?

He subtly shakes his head, then closes the distance between him and me and finally takes me into his arms. Pressing my face into his chest, he holds me as if he never plans to let me go. "I was worried I would never see you again."

Wrapping my arms around his back and inhaling his spicy scent even through the wetness of his coat, I whisper back, "I never thought I'd see you again."

He presses his lips to the top of my head. "Why? Why did you leave?"

"I had to" is my only response.

"No, you didn't. You shouldn't have. You belong with me. We belong together."

I want to argue and explain why he's wrong, but I don't have the energy to fight the moment of euphoria I'm feeling from within the security of his arms.

"Ember?" I hear Violet's voice from behind me. "What's going on? Are you leaving?"

I break the hug and see a woman whose eyes are glistening and lip is trembling. I don't know how to answer her, because I don't know what's happening next.

Am I leaving?

Will I leave with Christopher?

Is it as simple as that? Or is it as difficult as that?

I don't know.

I don't know.

"I don't think *he* should be here," Violet adds. "If Scarecrow finds out about this...."

"No one's leaving right now," Holly says as she points to the side window revealing the snow, which is coming down harder and harder by the second. "It's a storm outside that is only going to get worse, and walking out that door will mean death."

Christopher reaches for his backpack and pulls out a large black phone. He presses some buttons and frowns at the screen. He then points it above his head and continues to scowl. "I need to get someplace not within the trees to get a better signal."

I instantly think of the cliff overlooking the canyon, but there's no way we can make our way there in this storm safely. "I know where we can go, but not until the snow stops."

He places the phone back in his bag and returns his attention to me. "Where exactly did Richard go?"

"Wyoming," I answer, feeling an odd sense of betrayal toward Papa Rich for telling of his whereabouts. "They're hoping they can find a small mining town like Hallelujah Junction that isn't so much on the radar as any place in Nevada or California right now."

"Scarecrow is going to be really angry when he finds out you're here," Violet says again, her voice cracking as she shifts her weight from one foot to the other.

I look at Violet and then Holly. I need a moment alone with Christopher without an audience. Luckily, Holly picks up on my need and discomfort.

She takes Violet by the hand and says, "Let's go over here and work on the chimney more. The snow's getting in and will snuff out our stew if we aren't careful."

I take this opportunity to take him to my corner of the chapel and pull the curtain to give us some visual privacy. I know that if Holly and Violet want to listen to our conversation, they can, but at least we have some seclusion. But no matter how much we whisper, the reality is that we are all in one room with no walls separating us.

"You shouldn't have come," I whisper, rubbing my arms to try to heat up my flesh that's gone cold.

"Did you really think I wouldn't?" He notices I'm cold and begins rubbing my arms for me, and though his hands are icicles themselves, they do offer a sense of warmth and comfort.

I don't know what I expected. But did I think Christopher would be able to track me down? Did I ever think I'd see him again?

No. Never in a million years.

"When the snow stops, we're getting out of here," he says.

I shake my head. "It's not that easy."

"It is. I have a satellite phone and a pilot on standby."

"Christopher... there's something you need to know." I want to throw up, and I sit down on my pallet of wool blankets, because if I don't sit, I'm afraid I'll collapse.

He sits down beside me, wraps his arm around my shoulders, and pulls me closer to his body. "We have shit to work out. But we can handle everything once we're in a safe place."

"When I left with Papa Rich and Scarecrow, I never thought I'd see you again," I begin.

"I'm your husband, Ember. I'm not going to just let you walk away that easily."

"But we aren't married. Not really. Your mother was right when she said that."

"Fuck my mother," he snaps. "I know what she did to you. I was fucking blind, and I should have paid closer attention, and for that I'm sorry. I'm so, so sorry you went through all of that alone."

I look up into his eyes. "You know about your mother finding Papa Rich?"

He nods as his jaw stiffens. "I know about everything. She was cruel to you, tried to fuck with your head and attempted to make you feel you were losing your mind. And though I'll never forgive her for what she did, I'm angrier with myself. I was so wrapped up in trying to get my life back. I wanted so desperately to have my normal to return. I kept telling myself that it was so I could care and provide for you, but that was total bullshit. I was being selfish and not focusing on you. I don't blame you one bit for leaving. I would have run for the hills too." He smirks and looks out the window at the falling snow. "Which you literally did."

"You were trying your best," I say. "And you deserved to have your life back. You had every right to want normal." I release a deep breath I've been holding. "Your mother told me that I was holding you captive. That I was just as guilty as Papa Rich in kidnapping you—"

"My mother is a selfish bitch. What she's done to you is criminal," he interrupts, his face reddening.

"But she was right in many ways. I *was* holding you captive. You didn't choose to marry me. It wasn't fair to expect you to remain married and take care of a woman and a situation you were forced into. You deserved better."

"I chose to stay with you," he growls. "Yes, our situation is not ideal. This isn't how I saw my life going, but regardless, the minute we left Hallelujah Junction, I knew I was committed to you. My wife. The woman I love." He reaches for my hand and squeezes it tightly. "And I still feel that way. I don't want you gone. I don't want us apart. I don't want my old life without you in it. I want *you*, Ember. I need you to understand that."

"But it's asking a lot. It's not fair to you. You should have been able to go back to your career without a worry in the world."

He nods again. "But it should have been something we did together. I was insensitive. I put me first. I know this, and I plan to fix it if you'll allow me to. I want us to leave here and start over. I want to be the husband you deserve."

Something is gripping my heart so tightly that I can barely

breathe. I push myself away from Christopher and scurry a few feet away so I can have some room. I want to bury my nose in his chest and never face reality, but I also know I can't.

"I married Scarecrow," I blurt out.

I refuse to look at Christopher after I spit out the words, but I can hear his intake of breath.

"I don't understand."

I steal a glance at him and see the stunned confusion washed all over his face. I'm so ashamed for what I've done, how we got to this place, and for what's still ahead of me in the future. As happy as I am to see him again, I'm also devastated he has to see me in this light.

My true light.

"Papa Rich made me. He said that what happened between you and me was a mistake. That the devil made it happen, but that me marrying Scarecrow would correct the sin."

"This is insane."

"I didn't know what to do. I was so scared of what Papa Rich would do to me for burning down Hallelujah Junction. I felt like I was walking on eggshells, and... I left you. I left any chance, any hope, for a different life. My reality was right here." I point around. "This is my life. It's what my life has always been and what it will always be."

Christopher shoots up from sitting before me and towers over me. His eyes darken, and his entire presence morphs from a man offering me salvation to a man full of fury. "There is no way in hell I'm going to stand by and allow you to remain with that man. They are fucking lunatics who both deserve to be locked up for life. I don't care what they told you or what they forced you to do; there is no fucking way you're married to Scarecrow! Do you hear me?" His entire presence morphs to an almost beast-like creature. "I'll burn the fucking world down to keep you safe and next to me, starting with this place."

The sound of his booming voice rattles the rotting rafters above and dust speckles its way down on us.

"Ember?" I hear Holly call across the room. "Why don't you and Christopher come over here and join us by the fire? He's soaking wet, and it's cold."

"Did he fucking touch you? Did he... did he *make* you his wife?"

I shake my head vigorously, knowing exactly what he's asking. "He didn't consummate the marriage yet. He said he would when he returns." I swallow hard. "I haven't had sex with him."

He inhales deeply and appears relieved. He then looks out the window again. "We need to get out of here. Now."

"There's a blizzard coming," I say calmly. "We won't make it down the mountain. We may not be able to for days."

And that's if I go with him, which I can't see how it's truly possible.

He runs his hands through his hair and lets out a deep sigh.

"Ember," Holly calls out again. "Come sit by the fire and warm Christopher up until the stew is ready."

She's not going to give up, but she's skilled in knowing how to tame the beasts. She's had plenty of practice with Scarecrow.

"We should get you out of those wet clothes," I offer, knowing we need a break from all this for at least a moment.

I do.

I need to breathe. I need to focus. I need to stop the ringing in my ears.

He nods, but I can see he isn't happy.

I don't blame him.

I'm not happy either. But the difference between him and me is that happiness can be in his future. Not mine. I simply need to get him to face that hard fact.

I have. I've faced my dark future head-on. I've seen the red in the devil's eyes, and I've accepted his greeting.

11

EMBER

CHRISTOPHER IS RESTLESS IN THE CHAPEL, AND I DON'T BLAME HIM. I watch his eyes examine the girls and the way they're dressed. I know he has to hate seeing I reverted to my old look as well. He also seems to be looking for an escape route, as if he's expecting Papa Rich and Scarecrow to enter at any moment.

And that fact is a reality.

They could return.

They could hit weather of their own and decide they want to wait until winter has passed to start the journey to Wyoming. They may have also left us as a test. To see if we would indeed try to escape, regardless of how Holly feels that isn't true.

I can see them testing me. See if I'm trustworthy now after the Hallelujah Junction incident.

"How long have you lived here with Scarecrow?" he asks Holly and Violet.

"We don't really pay attention to days," Violet says softly. "Seasons are easier to track."

"Did he kidnap you too?" he asks.

"Our hands in marriage were promised by our father," Holly

says, cutting more vegetables to throw in the stew. She knows we have another mouth to feed, and we barely cook enough for ourselves as it is.

"Your father married you off to *Scarecrow*?" Christopher says his name as if it burns his tongue.

Violet nods. "At least my sister and I could stay together."

"We need to get you both out of here too," Christopher declares as if it's as simple as that. "It's wrong what's been done to you."

Neither Holly nor Violet respond but look at me for answers.

Answers I don't have.

"We can't just leave," Holly finally says.

"Scarecrow would kill us if we did," Violet adds.

"Not if we go to a safe place," I suggest, realizing we really could all leave as one. "If the police get involved—"

"Weren't they already involved?" Holly asks. "And yet, you are here."

"You both don't need to be afraid of those men," Christopher reassures. "We'll get us all off this mountain, and I'll make sure that when they return... well, they won't like what's waiting for them."

Holly huffs. "You have no idea what you're up against. Scarecrow and Richard aren't going to simply walk into a trap. They're smart. Smarter than you give them credit for. Just because we all live off the grid doesn't mean we are inbred, uneducated fools."

I can see Holly is growing more and more agitated by the minute.

"I'm not saying you are," he says gently, most likely seeing her change in demeanor the same way as me.

"He wants to help," I tell her softly. "He only wants to help us."

"I'm going to go out and see if I can get a signal with the satellite phone," Christopher finally announces, not satisfied just sitting by the fire and maybe realizing there needs to be some space between him and the women.

I stand to go with him.

He puts out his hand and says, "I'll go alone. I'll only be a minute. No reason for you to get wet and cold."

He doesn't wait for me to argue but instead grabs his coat and hat hanging by the fire and heads out the front door.

Holly calls after him, "There's a cliff to the right. It's straight down to the canyon below. You may not be able to see well with the snow. I'd be careful not to get too close."

"I'll watch out," Christopher replies as he opens the door and charges into the harsh weather.

"If Scarecrow finds out about this...," Violet whispers as if someone can hear us.

"We'll be gone before he does," I say, though not with much confidence.

I'm just as scared as they must be. I've seen what happens when Scarecrow feels his wives have misbehaved. And sadly, it will be Violet—Wife Number Two—that will pay the price for us all.

I reach for Violet's trembling hand. "We'll be okay. I promise you. No matter what happens, we'll stick together and be okay."

Normally Violet likes my touch, but not now. Instead, she pulls her hand away sharply and shakes her head. "I'm going to get some firewood from the stables. I think we should before the snow buries us in."

I open my mouth to offer to help but then decide she needs the fresh air and the moment alone to process everything.

Or maybe that's what I need.

The front door opens and closes, and now it's just me and Holly. "We don't want to leave," Holly announces as she stirs the stew.

"I know the idea is scary—"

"We aren't like them," Holly adds quickly. "You know that, Ember. You lived out there and saw it for yourself."

"Christopher will help us."

"Even if we left with Christopher," Holly continues, "where would we go? What would we do? We have no money. We have no family other than Pa, who would beat us to death for leaving our husband and going against our vows to God. Leaving here is walking through the doors of hell."

I want to argue, but I don't have valid comebacks to what she's saying. She's right. We are different. Holly and Violet are no different from me. They were raised in captivity as I was, and being brought into the modern world is actually like walking into hell. They're right.

"You know you can't keep your sister with Scarecrow any longer. One day, he's going to beat her to death, and even if he doesn't... do you want your sister abused for the rest of her life? And what about you? I know you're forced to have sex with Scarecrow. You want to be raped forever?" My words come out harsher than I want, but I need Holly to start to see reason.

"We all have our paths in life."

"No," I snap. "That's what you were brought up to believe. You don't know any better. I didn't know any better, and though I didn't like New York... I liked it a hell of a lot more than I do this place. We all deserve better. We all deserve to truly be happy."

She smirks and shakes her head. "Happy is a fairy tale."

"I used to think that too. I still may. But I do know one thing. We can't be here when Scarecrow comes back. We can't be his three wives. It's no way to live."

She doesn't say anything but returns to the stew pot and begins stirring.

"Holly... I won't leave you and Violet."

"You may have to."

Christopher

· · ·

The snow's coming down hard. So hard that walking in it is becoming more of a challenge as I sink into every step. I was warned to watch for the ledge, and with the falling snow, I can see how easily it could be for me to just walk right off.

Ember wanted to come with me, but I wanted her to stay warm, and I also got the sense that she needed some alone time with the sisters to explain what was going on. Plus, I don't want her standing in front of me if I do reach the authorities. I don't want her to actually hear me telling them where to arrest the man she still loves and sees as her father.

The wind is whipping around me, and though we aren't in blizzard conditions yet, we aren't far from it. I know we aren't getting off this mountain anytime soon, but I can at least reach out to the authorities and let them know Richard and Scarecrow are headed toward Wyoming, but more importantly... they will return here for the wives.

The wives.

The very thought of Scarecrow thinking Ember is *his* wife makes me ill and full of rage. If he even dared tried having sex with her... I would have cut off his other leg.

I still may.

"Please don't take her away from us," Violet says, walking up to me on the edge of the cliff as I search for a signal.

I turn to face her, surprised to see her outside without her sister or Ember. Something about her mousy and scared actions tells me this is out of her normal, to be so bold as to approach me.

"We can *all* leave," I say again, trying to reassure her that I meant it when I said we would all go together.

She shakes her head. "That's not what I mean. Even if Holly and I do go with you, I know Ember will be forever gone. With you. I'm asking you not to do that. I don't want to lose her. Please."

"You won't lose her," I assure. I can see the pain in her eyes as her lip trembles. "I see that Ember cares about you and your sister very much. We won't abandon you. I want to help you get a better life. A life that you deserve."

"I don't understand why you think leaving this mountain is a better life."

I glance down at the phone and see there is still no signal. I try to not show my frustration in the fact that I have to remain on the mountain another minute and give a fake smile. "It's better. Trust me."

I'm not giving her my full focus, and maybe I should, but at this moment in time, I'm standing on a cliff on a mountain in the middle of nowhere during a snowstorm that could last God knows how long.

"Did it ever cross your mind that maybe Holly and I wouldn't want to leave?"

I refocus on her, clearly seeing that she wants to have this conversation, and though it's damn cold outside, and we're getting soaked, she's determined.

Taking a calming breath and putting the phone away, I ask, "Why wouldn't you want to leave?"

"This is our home."

"With Scarecrow," I say with a snarl. Even the sound of his name and me having to say it makes me sick.

Her eyes glance down to the snow piling up around her booted feet. "He's our husband." She looks up at me. "And he's Ember's husband too."

Her words slap me in the face, and I clench my jaw not to shout obscenities back at her. "No. He's not."

She nods slowly, her eyes locked with mine. "But he is. You not liking that fact doesn't change the reality."

"Just because he made up vows, forced her to say them, and had some person claiming it so under God does not make it a legal wedding."

"Isn't that how you and Ember got married? So, are you saying she's not your wife too?"

This little pixie of a woman with her too-pale face and hollow eyes is pissing me off. I don't want to stand discussing this in the falling snow anymore.

I begin to walk back to the chapel. "We should get inside. It's really coming down, and we're going to get frostbite or hypothermia."

She reaches out and touches my arm as I try to pass her. She pauses, as if she's surprised she actually touched me—a man—but then she swallows back any uncertainty, straightens her shoulders, and stares back into my eyes.

"Do you want to know why Holly and I married Scarecrow?"

I don't say anything, but I remain standing in place.

"We married Scarecrow, because our pa deemed it so. But it wasn't a bad thing to get away from that situation—with our pa. Did we exchange one evil for the next? Maybe. But you know what? Holly and I welcomed the second evil."

"I'm sorry you had to do that," I say genuinely.

"Did you ever stop to wonder why Ember married Scarecrow?"

I don't answer but know exactly what she's going to say next.

"Because she welcomed the second evil."

I turn to walk toward the chapel, afraid what I may say next to the woman.

She takes a few quick steps so she can block my way. "And you want to bring her back and force her into the evil she was escaping. Is that fair? Is that truly what's best for Ember?"

My face heats regardless of the cold temperature. "Richard and Scarecrow deserve to be in prison. Period. End of discussion."

"And what do Holly, Ember, and I deserve?"

"Peace."

"Then don't take Ember away from us. Don't take her back to your world. *Your* world."

"We've been out here enough." I reach for her arm to assist

her back into the house, but she pulls away from my touch as if I burned her skin.

She doesn't say another word but marches ahead of me back to the chapel.

Back to *her* world.

12

EMBER

VIOLET STORMS PAST ME AND WALKS OVER TO THE FIRE WHERE Holly is, ignoring that I stand right by the door. She's upset, and it's the first time I've ever seen her this way.

"Holly," she snaps, "I think we should go get some wood from the barn. We need—" She looks over her shoulder at me. "—some space."

Christopher also walks into the chapel. He's taking deep breaths, and I know him well enough to know he's doing everything in his ability to not yell. We both step out of the way as Violet and Holly walk outside, and the coldness coming from them is far greater than the chill from the open door.

"She's right," I blurt to Christopher as he enters the chapel more. I heard the entire conversation between Violet and him.

"No, Ember. She's not right. She's scared. I understand that... or at least I'm trying to. I'm trying my best to understand what you are all feeling."

"But you don't, and you never will. That's the problem and will always be the problem. You and I come from two different worlds. We're different. And I don't see that fixing simply because you come up here and demand we all three leave with you."

He peers over his shoulder at me. My heart falls to the pit of my stomach at the hurt I see in his eyes.

"I want to be with you, but I can't just.... I hated New York." I pause and take a deep breath. "I wanted so badly to be the wife you deserve, but that place was swallowing me up whole. I felt trapped there. I felt like I was drowning in thick mud, and no matter how hard I tried to fit in... I didn't. I missed Hallelujah Junction. I missed my old life. I didn't want to tell you that, because I was scared you'd think I was crazy. I mean... maybe I am crazy. How could I possibly miss a place that held me captive? But I did."

"It's normal for you to miss what you've always known."

"It was more than that. It was more than the Stockholm Syndrome the therapist mentioned." I take another deep breath to drum up the courage to finally tell the entire truth. "I fantasized about you and me back in the schoolhouse. I missed our chain around our ankles. I missed the time it was just you and me... connected. I liked that we shared the same air as we took each breath. I liked that I had to walk with you in cadence as the metal jangled around our feet. I missed the warmth I felt from your body at all times because there was never any space. I missed our captivity. I missed you," I confess, unconsciously reaching out a hand, beckoning his touch.

He stares at my hand and then at my tear-filled eyes. His expression is firm, unbreakable, then softly it melts. He turns so he faces me fully, his body taking up the entire space of the doorway.

I stand still, barely breathing, my hand still outstretched. "I do want you. I want it more than anything. I just don't know how to want all that comes with you."

"Do you really feel we can't fix this? Do you think we can't be together simply because of New York? Because I'm here to tell you that we can fix anything."

The weight of my past feels like a hundred-pound brick rests on each shoulder. "I don't know how to be normal. I tried. I hope you saw how much I truly tried. I wore the clothes. The shoes. I tried to go to the parties."

He simply nods.

"When I was growing up, reading every romance book I could get my hands on, I would dream of the day I'd find my own Prince Charming and go to the fancy parties and live in the large house with lavish furniture and chandeliers in every room. And then all of a sudden, I had it. I had it all. But what it really became was a deep, deep hole that I sank into."

"So, we don't go back to the house. I should have found our own place right at the beginning," he says. "And if you hate New York, then we'll move someplace else. Maybe a small town with less noise and action."

"And what about you? That's your home. That's who *you* are. I can't pull you away from everything you've ever known any more than you can pull me away from what I have grown up with. We are who we are."

"And you think we need to do that apart? Be who we are?"

I tense, fighting the devastation that threatens to consume me. I search his face, his posture, for some clue as to what he feels. "Yes," I barely whisper.

"You're wrong." Christopher takes the few steps that separates us and grabs my hand. "You and I have one thing that is stronger than all else. Love."

Tears well in my eyes; pain wells in my heart. "We are the demented love story. Remember?"

He pulls me into his arms, burying my face against his chest. "But a love story, nonetheless. I love you, Ember. I know that with every inch of my being. I also know I can't live without you. So, yes, if we *both* have to start over so we can begin anew, then so be it. The question is if you are willing to."

I nod against his warmth. "I want to. I want to so badly. I'm just scared. And I love you. I love you so much that it actually hurts when I think about it. My chest tightens to the point of pain."

"Then we fight," he murmurs against my hair. "We fight against every single person getting in our way. No one will block us any longer. No one and nothing. You are *my bride*, and I'm taking you back."

"How? There's still a storm outside, and based on what Holly says, it could keep going for days," I counter, clutching tighter to him. "And I know you said we'd call the police on Richard and Scarecrow. But then where does that leave Holly and Violet?"

"We'll figure it all out." He looks out the door at the snow falling and then closes it behind him. I realize the door has remained open the entire time. Maybe giving us both the option to flee. A choice we've both decided against.

He then tips my face up to meet his, his eyes filled with a blend of love and passion. "I love you."

"I love you."

I turn to walk away and put some logs on the fire, knowing Holly and Violet will be back with a fresh pile of firewood soon. Christopher grabs hold of my wrist and pulls me close to him. He leads us to my private corner with nothing but a tattered sheet, concealing what I know is coming next.

"Not yet," he says. "Don't walk away yet."

"But the fire... I should tend to the fire." I turn away again, but he pulls me harder.

I look over my shoulder, down at my wrist that is firmly gripped, and then back into his eyes.

He tugs my arm toward him, giving me no choice but to stumble up against his chest.

"Kiss me," he orders in a gruff whisper.

I follow his direction gladly. I want nothing more than to feel his lips against mine.

Our mouths meet, a pull neither can resist any longer. Our hunger demands to be satiated. Time and distance has kept us apart, but our true love never broke. His heart beats against mine as he arranges my body closer. The single kiss has the power to reunite us forever, forgetting all the wrong by both. The kiss is the period to our run-on sentence that seems to never end. One kiss speaks volumes for what is meant.

I want him.

I want him this very second... regardless of our current location and situation. Regardless that Holly and Violet can enter the chapel at any minute. And regardless that I don't know if we will ever get our happily ever after. But I want him...

Now.

"I need to be with my wife," he says as his eyes seem to darken right before me.

My heart skips, knowing he feels the same way I do. Our bodies are in tune, even though our lives will never be.

Without asking, without pausing, he removes my dress effortlessly, nothing beneath it to cover me. I'm completely naked, standing before my husband.

"I need you too, but...." I can feel the heat of his stare on my naked body, but I don't try to conceal myself. I stand and await his next command.

"Don't fight this. Stop fighting us."

He leans forward, takes hold of my hips, and pulls me closer to him. Kiss by kiss, he lowers us to the makeshift bed, and then lowers further down until his face is inches from my sex.

"I want the taste of you on my tongue." He doesn't wait for permission but rather kisses my pussy, followed by licking my throbbing clit.

I tense at the invasion—thinking I'd never get to feel such pleasure ever again in my life. Part of me wants to stop, and the other part wants the feeling to never end.

He swirls his tongue in circles, lapping up every sign of my arousal. I moan with complete abandon, knowing Holly and Violet could walk in at any minute, but I can't resist.

My body seems possessed by Satan himself—no doubt something Papa Rich would accuse me of. I have absolutely no power against the devil when it comes to what Christopher is able to do to my body.

Lick after lick, he brings my body to another level. Just when I believe I can take no more, he thrusts his finger past the lips of my pussy. In and out, he plunges, pulling gasps and muffled moans from me. I hide my face beneath a pillow in hopes of concealing my rising pleasure.

"Spread your legs wider," he directs, his voice husky.

Suffocated by love at the familiar—yet so very distant memory—command, I do exactly as he asks without any hesitation. Lying beneath his shadow, I peek up from the pillow to see his face. The strong features, the firm lips, the sensitive eyes. The same expression I remember washes over his face... strength, love, passion. These are the eyes of my husband. The man I vowed to love. The man I vowed to spend the rest of my life with.

And yet... I ran.

I broke the vows.

I shattered everything.

"I'm sorry," I murmur more to myself than to him. "I'm so sorry I left."

"Shh," he whispers as he places his lips to my pussy.

His intimate kiss forgives, but does he?

His body is offering amnesty, but does his heart?

He caresses my mound without saying a word, quickly following with a kiss to my belly and then my slit. Once. Twice. The kissing continues as heat ripples over my body in waves, leaving me breathless. "Christopher," I whisper. "I—"

I want to apologize over and over if this is my penance.

Further words are lost as his kisses turn into licks and nibbles. The sting of his bites on my inner thigh makes me want to beg for mercy yet also leaves me wanting more. Moaning, gasping, whimpering, I close my eyes and give myself up to the moment... to Christopher and his show of forgiveness.

He pauses a moment, rubbing his hand along my heated flesh. Dipping his finger down the crease of my butt, he presses past and rests his finger at the entrance of my tight rosebud, teasing me with the unknown of what's to come. Slight pressure is added, but not enough to break past and enter fully. Slowly, he lowers his other hand to my silky folds, wet with desire.

A deep moan rumbles in his chest and escapes as he thrusts his finger into my hungry sex. I buck against his hand, moaning in pleasure. Dizzy with the need for more, I do everything I can not to beg to be fucked right then and there.

I don't want Holly and Violet to hear from outside, but at the same time, my body doesn't care. I need Christopher. I need him now, and my body and soul nearly scream out in desire.

His finger is soon followed by a second as he pumps in and out of me, demanding my complete surrender to his touch. Trying my best to remain quiet but failing miserably, I can do nothing more but allow the climax to build. And when he removes his slick finger and presses it into my anus without warning, the orgasm rocks my body at an intensity that has me screaming out.

Submission, passion, and animalistic need for more explodes through my body like the crack of lightning during a desert thunderstorm. Moaning, I press against his hand, driving his finger deeper into my forbidden channel, his touch entrenched within me as I melt against him.

With one finger buried in the taboo, he places the palm of his other hand on my wet and needy pussy, continuing on with the stroking and caressing. One, two, three fingers are pushed inside my pussy, and I mewl as the erotic bite sends me to the edge once again. My breath catches in my throat as I hold back a cry of lustful yearning. I can't focus, lost in a fog of bliss. Pleasure and pain weave themselves together, escalating until I cry out his name in a husky whisper that doesn't sound like my own voice.

After the final orgasmic wave leaves my body, he cups his hand over my pussy, using it to adjust my body until I'm tucked snuggly into his arms. Instinctively, I nuzzle my face against the warmth of his neck, and my body melts to his. The feelings, the emotions... nothing can describe them.

Other than safe.

I'm safe with Christopher.

It's the only time in my life I truly feel this way.

Safe.

"Tell me that you'll never leave me again," he whispers into my hair as he follows the command with a kiss to my head.

I pause, because I don't want to promise things I can't keep. I don't know what happens next. I don't know if I can do what he wants.

Can I simply leave?

Can I walk away from Holly and Violet?

Can I go back to the life in which I didn't belong?

Instead of saying what he wants to hear, I pull away enough so I can kiss him.

The only thing I can promise right now is to always love him. That much will always be true.

"I love you, Christopher. I love you so much."

I kiss him again, driving my tongue into his mouth, hoping my answer will do for now.

13

EMBER

I'VE WANTED THIS.

I've lied to myself, pretending that I didn't.

I want Christopher.

I've always wanted Christopher.

And now that I have him, I'm never letting him go.

"Take off your clothes," I say, my strong will coming back.

I feared I lost this part of me. The strong woman who asks for what she wants.

He does as I demand, his eyes locked with mine the entire time. He then slips his hand around my waist, repositioning us so he's on top of me fully. Fingers laced, thighs rubbing against thighs, my breasts molded to his torso, his cock resting at my entrance—heavy and hot.

Not wasting another moment, he moves to kneel before my face and places his hard dick to my lips. I look up and into his eyes. No words need to be said. I open up my mouth and allow his cock to lie against my tongue. My natural instinct is to pleasure him. It's always been the one thing I want to do to him more than anything else.

Pleasure him.

I'm good at this.

I thrive at this.

I'm proud that I can do this so well.

Watching bliss blanket his face fills me with a purpose I didn't know existed before I met this man, and I wonder if I will ever get to experience it again in my lifetime if indeed Christopher and I have to part ways. As I suck up and down his ready dick, I fully submit to an old hope for the future that now renews.

Maybe... just maybe... we can have a happily ever after.

Maybe he can rescue me from this mountain, and we can have it all.

Maybe I can truly be free and not captured in Papa Rich's web.

Maybe... just maybe.

Up and down, I move my mouth until I'm rewarded by my name escaping his lips in the most passionate of ways. My name never sounded as good as it does the moment it slips from his mouth.

I add my hand and begin to pump his cock while licking all around it. His body shakes and tenses, and he pulls me away as he takes a deep breath.

"I've missed your kiss," he says, his gaze dipping to my lips. "I've missed everything about you and what you do to me. But mostly, I miss the way you make me feel. I was so scared I'd never be able to tell you this. I was so scared we'd never be like this again."

His moment of vulnerability only spurs me on. I need it. I need it to regain my strength, to take hold of my confidence, to return to the Ember I was working so hard to be.

Reflexively, I slip my tongue across my mouth, waiting for his to make contact.

Slowly, he pulls me up to him.

We kiss, soft, romantic, and pure.

Husband and wife blocking out all the bad around us.

He slides his hand to the wetness of my sex, driving my thirst for him to be inside me to a whole new level. I approach the edge, wanting desperately for more. "Please, Christopher. I need you."

Christopher cups my face and plants a slow, deep kiss on my lips. His mouth blazes a path from my lips to the base of my neck. I let a sensual moan escape regardless of how quiet I've been trying to be, hoping to encourage him to keep going.

Skimming my fingers down his rippled stomach, I simply moan and wait. I know he'll give me exactly what I want if I just wait. I can count on him. I can rely on him. Always.

"You're mine, Ember. Mine forever, no matter who tries to get in the way of that."

I gasp at the sensation of his cock pressing against me at the end of his declaration.

Closing my eyes in ecstasy, I dig my fingers into his shoulders as he presses beyond the tightness, entering me completely. The delicious sting is quickly replaced with an erotic pleasure that captures my breath.

He continues to place gentle kisses all over my neck and face while his thick shaft probes deeper within. The contrast of soft and hard manages to push me toward that familiar edge. Sparks, electricity, pure primal need washes over me, drowning me in pleasure as we both rock each other into completion.

There is nothing else but us.

Christopher and Ember.

I don't know how long we lie there, but I take the time of silence to focus on his breathing and the beating of his heart. I touch the tiny curls on his chest and trace my fingertip over the ridges of his stomach. I'm hypnotized by the feeling of contentment and security, but I also know we can't stay in this little euphoric bubble forever.

"I've missed you so much, Ember. I've missed the feel of you in my arms," Christopher murmurs into my hair.

"I missed you too. More than I thought possible." I smile at him as I pull away from his warm embrace, and I put on the last of my clothing, wishing we could be naked in each other's arms forever. But I have Holly and Violet to think about. Not to mention the storm is still raging outside, and the biting wind is forcing its way inside the chapel. They'll be back from the barn soon simply because they will have no choice.

"I want us to leave the minute this storm allows," he says, the determination in his eyes as unrelenting as the tone of his voice. It's clear the reality of our situation has hit him again, and his moment of sex-induced amnesia is gone. "I want you back in my life, and I want us to forget this place and any future places Richard offers."

When I open my mouth to protest, Christopher cuts me off. "And I don't give a fuck what wedding vows Scarecrow made you say, or the fact that they think you are now his wife. No fucking way. Do you hear me?"

"It's just…"

I look at the pulled curtain offering us the limited privacy we needed—faded and worn—knowing what's on the other side.

My new life.

A life that now involves other people. Though I have just met them in actual days, if feels like a lifetime. They get me, I get them. We walk the same path in life and always have. When I look at them, it's like looking in a mirror.

"It's not that simple," I finally say.

"Yes, it is," Christopher says, sitting up and reaching for his shirt. "This isn't open for discussion, Ember. I don't want to be an asshole, but I will if I have to be. We're leaving this place, and it's final." He then stands and puts on his pants. "I get it. We have shit to work out, but we'll work it out together. I'm going to get you as far away from this madness, and I'm never going to let you come this close to those sick fuckers again."

"Except this 'madness' also includes two women who I've become close to. I can't just leave them here. And I get the feeling they are determined to stay."

"Then we'll allow them to do what they want. But *you* will not stay. Period."

"I can't leave without them. It's not an option. What do you think Papa Rich and Scarecrow will do to them when they return and find me gone?"

"What Richard and Scarecrow will come home to find is the police waiting to arrest their asses."

I sigh deeply. "You say that. But the police haven't exactly been much help since the day we left Hallelujah Junction. I don't really have faith in them."

The truth of the matter is I don't really have faith in anyone. Which I suppose is sad. Funny how I saw life in such a happier way when I was being told lies and mentally being held captive in a schoolhouse in a ghost town with a serial killer as a "father."

Maybe Louisa was right about me—I'm broken. Just a freak. And the reality is... I belong here with Holly and Violet. They get me. They *are* me in a sick and twisted way.

"Ember...."

I lean forward and give him a quick, avoiding-the-topic peck. "I hear footsteps in the snow outside. Holly and Violet are here."

14

CHRISTOPHER

IT'S BEEN TWENTY-FOUR HOURS SINCE I ARRIVED, AND I'M GOING freaking crazy. Cabin fever is truly a real thing. The snow is falling softer now, but it dumped overnight and most of the day, and I'm not sure how easy hiking down the mountain is going to be for any of us. The women don't have warm clothing, or at least not warm enough. They go out into the elements to collect wood with nothing but crocheted shawls over their thin dresses that hang off their narrow shoulders. At least they all seem to have rainboots to slip on and off when they do go out, but even those may not be good enough if we are sinking to our knees with every step.

Holly and Violet also seem to be malnourished, and though their strength and energy seem to be up, I still worry if they will have the stamina it will take to make it to the makeshift tarmac in the valley I was dropped off on.

The other concern I have is their respiratory system. Both women have a hack when they cough. Neither seems sick, but after staying in the chapel for one night, I clearly see the culprit. The fire is releasing too much smoke in the chapel. Though they have worked on a chimney of sorts, it's neither completed nor all that effective. It's blocking the snow from extinguishing the flames, but the amount of smoke now being trapped inside is downright dangerous. And based on their coughs... this is something they have been dealing with for a while.

Violet stands from where she's been sitting and staring at the fire in silence for the entire day. "I'm going to get us some more wood."

The rate we've been burning the wood to keep warm is keeping us up all hours and having to recollect to stoke the fire. And it's going to be another cold one tonight.

"I'll go," I offer, needing to get up and stretch my legs anyway. Plus, my eyes are starting to burn from all the smoke.

She pauses, nods, then sits and stares at the fire some more. She has barely spoken since her conversation with me near the cliff. It's very clear I am not one of her favorite people, and though I feel for her situation and am trying to be sensitive to her feelings, I will pick her up and carry her down the mountain if I have to if it means Ember agreeing to leave with me.

Ember has agreed, but I see her wavering. I think it depends on the moment for her. One second, she wants to run away with me this instant, but the next minute, she wants to stay with the sisters and feels obligated to keep them happy with whatever they need.

I'm scared that the longer we stay, the harder it will be to convince any of them to leave.

I walk over to Ember, who is peeling some potatoes, and kiss the top of her head. She stops to look at me. "Do you want some help?"

"I'm fine. It's too cold for any of you to be out there without the proper clothing," I say, reaching for my coat and hat hanging by the fire. "I'll be right back."

I need to check out the path I took up here to see if it's even possible for us to leave anytime soon. I also reach for my satellite phone again in hopes that maybe, just maybe, I can get a signal.

I'm right in worrying about us sinking to our knees in snow, because the minute I walk out of the chapel, that is exactly what I do. I suppose it could be worse—it could be to our thighs.

Trekking through the snow, I walk all around the area with my arm up, hoping I can catch a signal if I just turn the right way. The snow has stopped falling for the time being, and the evening sky is peeking out from the clouds. Maybe it will warm up some, and the snow will start to melt tomorrow. I can't even see where I hiked up, so I'd have to carve a new path for us, which I'm prepared to do.

Giving up on the phone, I pocket it and head toward the barn that is holding the firewood. When I make my way in that direction, I hear a rustling in the dense forest to my left. I freeze, wishing I had brought a weapon with me so I could hunt whatever animal is nearby. But when I steal a glance, I swear it's not an animal I see. It's human.

Whoever it is quickly scurries away, but I know without a doubt it isn't a deer or a bobcat or any other woodland creature.

It's them.

It has to be them.

They are watching. Waiting. Planning.

I run toward the edge of the forest, not truly thinking my actions through. I have absolutely nothing to defend myself with, but if it's Richard or Scarecrow, I'll kill them with my bare hands if I have to.

"Richard!" I shout toward the forest. "You fucking coward. Come out and face me! I know it's you. Scarecrow? Can you hear me? I'm here with your wives! They're mine now. Mine. Do you hear me? How does that make you feel? Get your one-legged shithead self out here and fight for what's yours!"

Silence.

"Fucking cowards!"

Silence.

I run toward the exact location I saw the movement and don't see any footsteps in the snow. But I do see disruption. They're covering their tracks behind them as they run away. I know I can follow the tracks... and I may, but first I need to get back to the chapel and prepare the women. I also need to grab my gun that I packed. I didn't plan on using it unless necessary, but if those assholes are here... it's necessary.

Ember must have heard me shouting, because she comes running out of the chapel, wide-eyed and calling my name.

"Go back inside," I say as I run toward her.

She doesn't do as I ask until I reach her, but we both run inside together as I slam the door behind me.

"Richard and Scarecrow are here. They're in the forest," I say, winded from my run in the deep snow.

Holly and Violet both stand up quickly, panic on their faces.

"What? You saw them?" Ember asks, her hand over her mouth, terror in her eyes.

"No," I say. "I didn't get a good look, but I know there was someone."

Holly and Violet look at each other and then back at me. "It could be an animal," Holly suggests.

I charge toward my pack and pull out my gun, turning off the safety and preparing to use it. "It was a man. I know it was."

"I swear I saw someone watching us too," Ember says. "I worried it was them as well."

"It just doesn't make sense," Violet says. "If it's Richard and Scarecrow, why wouldn't they come inside? Why would they stay in the woods with no shelter? Especially all night in a storm."

"Because they're insane! They're sick motherfuckers with no rhyme or reason to what they do!" My voice booms throughout the chapel, and I realize I'm losing control.

I have to keep my control and wits about me to defeat them. I can't let them get inside my head so that I make poor decisions. They're playing a game of cat and mouse, but this time the mouse will tear the cat to shreds.

Violet runs to the window by the door and peers out. "I don't see anything."

Ember joins her to look. "I don't think you should go out

there. What if that's what they want you to do? They might have guns too."

"If they wanted to shoot me, they had the opportunity," I say, marching to the door. "And if they were wise men, they would have. I'm not going to be afraid of those men and hide in this chapel. If they want a fight, I'm ready to give it to them."

I run back toward the forest's edge. My trek is easier this time with the adrenaline as well as running back across packed snow from where I was before. I run into the forest and follow the trail for as far as I can. I'm getting farther and farther into the thickness of the trees until I reach a creek, and then just like that, the trail is gone. I can't tell where they went.

Gone.

The motherfuckers are gone.

I spin around and call out, "Are you watching me? Get a good look, fuckers. Look at the man who is going to bring you down. You can hide like the rats you are. But I'll find you. I'll find you!"

My voice bounces off the trees and seems to echo back at me.

Complete silence after that.

I don't even hear a chirp of a bird.

"Christopher! Christopher!" I hear Ember's voice calling from up near our shelter.

I know she's got to be terrified, so without wasting another second taunting men who may or not be within earshot, I run back toward her.

When I see her, she appears frantic as she trudges through the snow toward me.

"They're gone," I say as I approach and take her into my arms.

She glances around me at the forest. "I swear I saw them too." She's winded from her run. "But why? It makes no sense that they'd stay out there. They could freeze to death."

"I don't know," I reply as I lead her back to the warmth of the chapel. "But we need to get out of here as soon as we can. They're planning something. I'm not going to just sit here and allow them to hunt us like prey."

"Did you see anything?" Violet asks as we enter.

I shake my head. "They ran off."

"How do you know it wasn't an animal? We're surrounded by them here."

"I just know," I answer.

"I agree with Christopher," Ember says. "I still feel like I saw someone as well. My gut tells me it isn't an animal out there."

"You both don't know this mountain," Holly says. "We do."

"And we know what is and what isn't out there," Violet adds.

They both look at each other, which sends alarm bells off inside me. It's the second time they've given a knowing look to each other.

"What the fuck aren't you telling us?" I ask firmly. "I can tell there's something."

Holly snaps her head toward Christopher as if prepared for an attack. "Excuse me?"

"I've seen you both looking at each other," I say.

"I've felt like you may be keeping something from me as well," Ember confesses. "You were quick to tell me what I saw was also an animal."

"We just know Scarecrow wouldn't stay out there. He doesn't like to be uncomfortable. He wouldn't allow us to be sitting by the fire while he's out in the cold," Violet cuts in.

She has a point, and it truly doesn't make sense how Richard and Scarecrow could have survived last night in the snow. But maybe there is a hunting shack they know of and are hiding there. Regardless of their reasons, their thinking, or their sick plans, I know what I saw, I know what I feel, and I know there was a man watching. Not an animal, but a man.

And though I'm not going to push the issue anymore for right now, I also feel that Holly and Violet know something and are keeping it secret.

Holly hasn't stopped glaring at me, and Violet is biting her nails so hard there may be nothing left when she's done. I'm not going to apologize for my actions or my beliefs, and if I have to stand here watching them all day to get some answers, then I will. Eventually I'll be able to read them and figure out what's going on.

Ember must be picking up on the tension in the room, because she suggests, "It's getting dark. Why don't we settle in for the night, eat some potato soup I made, and go to sleep early."

"You never got the firewood," Violet says with a scowl. "I'll go get it."

I consider stopping her to go get it myself, but Holly adds, "I'll help. We can chop some wood while we're out there."

Frankly, right now, I need them out of the chapel. I need a minute to breathe. I need a minute with Ember. And I need a minute to just process the madness that is presented before me.

15

EMBER

"They're just scared," I try to defend. "Holly and Violet live a life that no one can understand."

"I know," he says. "I don't understand. Just as I didn't truly understand all you were struggling with. I won't make the mistake of thinking I do again."

"But they are keeping something from us," I concede.

"They are," he agrees. "But I'm not going to push anymore. I'm just going to watch and keep my eyes open."

"They wouldn't hurt us," I say, truly believing the words.

"I believe that. I don't think it's in their nature to hurt anyone. But I also think they will do whatever Scarecrow tells them. They will also do whatever they can to survive. If lying to you and me about a bigger plan is what it takes for survival, I don't think they'll have a choice."

"I'm so sorry," I murmur as I place my hand gently on Christopher's shoulder. "You're here because of me, and I'm sorry."

"We both have things to be sorry for," he says, releasing the breath he seemed to be holding. "But I wouldn't want to be anywhere else without you. This is temporary, and we will get out of here. Regardless of whether Richard and Scarecrow are out there or not, we're leaving tomorrow if the snow lets up. We'll let the authorities deal with them."

"Do you think they'll come tonight?"

He holds up his gun. "I hope they fucking do. I'd like to end this right now."

"You aren't a ruthless killer," I say as my heart skips at the idea of him doing something so violent as to kill another human being. I know he wanted Papa Rich to burn in Hallelujah Junction, but setting a fire and running away is a far cry different than staring a man straight in the eye and then pulling the trigger.

"Just like Holly and Violet, I'll do whatever it takes to survive and to protect you."

My eyes go to the gun, to his dark eyes and tight jaw, and then back to the gun. "This wouldn't have happened if I didn't leave. I put us in danger. It's all my fault."

He clicks the safety on the gun, puts it on the table, and takes me into his arms. "Let's focus on the future and stop beating ourselves up for what we did or didn't do in the past. There's no need to keep punishing ourselves." He kisses the top of my head. "I think we've both gone through enough for one lifetime. This will all be a distant memory soon enough. When we leave here, it will just be you and me. We'll block out all the bad, all the resistance, and anything and anyone who is trying to keep us apart. I promise you, Ember. It'll be better. I swear."

I pull away just enough so that I can kiss him. I need his affection more than I've ever needed anything. I need his taste. I need his smell. I need him.

"I should have trusted in your love for me," I whisper through our kiss.

"Yes, you should have," he says and then kisses me deeper.

We should wait. We shouldn't be doing this here. Not here.

We have an entire life to do this.

A new home to create, where we can be together over and

over again, in the privacy of our own space, but I just can't get enough of this man. And with how much he's constantly touching me, kissing me, and giving me the hungry look that makes my knees nearly melt... he can't get enough of me either.

We try to be discreet, but the sisters know.

And I feel guilty for it. Maybe because I'm getting happiness and love when they aren't.

Or maybe...

As sick as it sounds, I may feel guilty because deep down I worry they are judging me for committing adultery on Scarecrow. Maybe they don't understand that Christopher is my husband in all ways that matter and always has been. Maybe they think what I'm doing is wrong. Dirty. Sinful.

Yes, I fear the sisters think I'm a sinner.

And I do care what they think. I desperately want them to approve of me and Christopher. I want them to see in him what I see. I want them to trust him when he tells them he will keep them safe. I want them to believe when he says he will help them start over and have a better life. I want them to have faith that all will be well, and we can all be a family... in our own demented way.

But I don't think they do.

They watch. They're quiet. They go about the hours that pass in a silence that makes me uneasy. Violet seems hurt. Almost as if I've betrayed her by allowing Christopher to reach out and hold my hand.

I wish I could make it all better.

I wish I could make *them* better.

I also wish I could resist Christopher right now... but I can't.

He doesn't hesitate, and I'm thankful when he guides us to my private nook, shedding me of my dress as he does. If the sisters enter, at least we won't be in plain sight, but I still hope they stew outside in the barn for a little longer.

He lowers me to our poor excuse of a bed, but I've never been happier to make contact with the rough wool.

I know what's coming next.

Christopher sucks my breast, then moves to the other to give it equal attention. Lowering his hand to my mound, damp with fresh arousal, he dips a finger to my clit and applies pressure as he rouses an overwhelming longing that has me gasping for air.

Moving from my clit, he presses his fingers past my silky folds and pushes one, then two digits into my sex. I force my hips up to drive them inside my pussy even deeper.

They aren't enough.

I want to feel the small bite of pain as his cock stretches me while he claims what is now his. I want to feel him so badly that the hunger changes who I am.

I'm not Ember—the timid, scared, and broken woman.

I'm an animal.

Primal.

I'm a stalker in search of its victim.

I'm a woman who needs to be fucked hard by her man. Her man who nearly slipped away but now will forever be in her grips.

This is me. Powerful, knowing, willing to fight for what I want.

I want Christopher.

I want to be married to him and spend the rest of my life with him.

But right now...

Right now, I want his cock, and I'm not ashamed to admit it. It's natural, it's right, and there isn't anything sinful about my needs and desires. I'm learning this. I'm growing, and as I do, I will take what's mine. Mine.

Christopher is mine.

Unable to hold back the fever that scorches me, I beg, "Please, Christopher. Please..."

"Please what?" he teases as he dances his fingers inside my core. "Say it, Ember. Tell me what you want. I want to hear the dirty words come from this perfect mouth." He nibbles on my bottom lip and then pulls away, staring into my eyes.

I want to look away, because the familiar timid girl still lurks inside me, but his eyes demand that I keep them in place. My body obeys. My mind obeys. I obey.

"I want you," I pant, desperately wanting to feel the orgasm that rests just beneath the surface, begging to be set free. But I need my husband's heavy dick spreading me to make that happen.

"Not dirty enough." He pulls his fingers out of my pussy as punishment.

"Fuck me!" I blurt out as a moan follows my frantic command. "I want you to fuck me hard and make me feel you between my legs tomorrow. I want it to be rough. I want it to sting. I want to feel the pain that is followed by pleasure. I want your cock to stretch me and fill me. Fuck me!"

I am absolutely thirsty and ravenous at this point as his fingers hit a spot inside my pussy that has me uncontrollably twirling in ecstasy. There isn't anything I wouldn't do to have him enter me deep and hard. The power this man has over me....

Sparing me of my uncontrollable desires, he finally grants me my filthy wish. He sheds his clothes as fast as possible and mounts me. Feeling his weight on top of me, I'm soon rewarded as his cock presses up against my opening and easily slides in with the aid of my soaking wet pussy. Wrapping my legs around him, I hold on in fear that he'll change his mind and torture me some more.

And with a forceful shove of his hips, he drives his thick cock all the way in, claiming me completely. So deep. So fucking deep.

I want to stay like this always. Connected. Always connected.

Yes, yes, yes... I am his. I should have never left. I should have never allowed anyone or anything to get in the way. I should have resisted the voices in my head that tried to take over. I should have run away from the darkness and only looked toward the light.

Christopher—my light.

In and out, he thrusts, deeper and deeper with each pounding action. My moans blend with his as our bodies merge as one—as *only* one, like we are meant to be. Fate—she has brought us together more than once, and it's about time I fucking listen to her.

"This pussy of yours is mine. Only mine," he growls as he powers into me, his muscles taut, his eyes glazed over with a fierce intensity that only drives me closer to the edge. "I want to hear you moan my name," he demands. "Moan."

As if I can do nothing else but obey, I do just as he orders.

Moaning with each vibration of wantonness that attacks my pussy, I truly collapse into an encompassing hole of sexual bliss.

With a few more thrusts, Christopher's groans blend with the sounds of my completion, and he too joins me in our own world of lust.

Slipping my arms around his neck, I pull away enough to stare into his eyes. "I'll never run away from you—from us—again." Choked by emotion, I rest my head on his shoulder and close my eyes, wishing the moment of connection could last forever.

"I should've never given you reason to leave," he murmurs, drawing my lips to his. "You're everything—" But before he can say more, the door to the chapel opens, and the sound of booted feet breaks our privacy.

"Ember? Christopher?" Holly calls out.

We both stand and scurry for our clothing, dressing as fast as we can. I don't think they will move the curtain, but maybe they will.

Scanning each other quickly to make sure we're appropriately dressed, we both walk out from the curtain to greet the sisters.

Caught in the act, but an act I hope to do again, and again, and again, I wonder if I'll ever get enough of this man.

16

EMBER

WE'RE ALL SITTING AROUND THE FIRE IN SILENCE, EATING LEFTOVER soup from last night. It's awkward. We've been coexisting in a suffocating tension that I can barely stand. I look at Christopher with pleading eyes. I want this to be better. It has to get better.

Christopher must read my mind, because he clears his throat and says, "I'd like to apologize for my aggression last night. I really feel as if Richard and Scarecrow are out there, but regardless if they are, I feel I may have scared you with how I acted. I'm also sorry for accusing you both of keeping something from us."

Holly looks up from her soup and gives him a small smile. "It's a stressful time," she offers. "We understand."

Violets shoots daggers at Holly, clearly not appreciating having her sister speak for her.

"I know the topic of us all leaving is a sensitive one, but it's still one we need to discuss," Christopher continues, putting down his bowl. "The storm has passed, and I feel like we have a very small window to act. We need to get down the mountain to where I can reach a pilot to fly us out of here. We need him to reach us before he can't due to more weather."

I look at Holly and Violet. "Please come with us," I beg. "I know you're scared. I am too. But we'll get through this together."

"No," Violet says. "My answer is no." She gets up without another word and storms out of the chapel.

"We need a little more time," Holly says, grabbing all our empty bowls and bringing them to a large barrel we use for dishes. "Just give her time."

"I'm going to go check on her," I say, getting up, feeling like I need to.

"Do you want me to go with you?" Christopher asks.

"I'll be right back. I need to talk to her in private," I reply.

I walk outside, happy to see the sun is out and the snow is indeed melting as Christopher was hoping it would do. I walk to the barn, which is the only form of real shelter other than the chapel on this property. When I don't find Violet inside, I walk out and see her standing outside near the cliff.

"Violet? What are you doing out here?" I ask as I approach her. The snow has stopped falling, but the temperatures are still near freezing, and being close to the cliff isn't safe at any time, but definitely not now.

She doesn't turn to face me but instead looks out over the canyon. The clouds hang low, and all the treetops are covered in white.

"Did you convince Holly to go with you?" she asks softly. If the air wasn't so eerily still, I'm not sure I'd hear her.

"She hasn't decided yet."

"But you have?"

"I have. I'm leaving with Christopher. I love him."

I take a step toward her, noticing she's dangerously close to the ledge. "Violet, why don't you step away from the edge. It's icy. I don't want you slipping."

"I thought you loved us."

"I do. Which is why I want you and Holly to come with me. We can figure out our next chapter together." I keep repeating this over and over in hopes that eventually she'll believe me. I take another step toward her, not liking that she refuses to turn and face me. "Violet. Please, come away from the cliff. I'm worried you'll fall."

"I've seen what men do," Violet says, her eyes on the canyon below. "They're cruel. They're ruthless. They truly are the devil in human form."

"Not all men."

She nods. "Yes, all men."

"Violet..." I take another cautious step toward her, but I don't want to get too close and startle her or have her try to take a defensive step away from me, causing her to fall. "Please come to me."

"You hated it out there," she says. "You hated it and didn't fit in. You told us about the stories around the fire, and now you change it? You can't take back what you said. You hated it! You told us so." She still doesn't step away from the cliff nor look at me. "You know Holly and I won't fit in either. But Holly's strong. She's so much stronger than me. She may be able to adapt. If anyone can, it's her." She pauses. "But not me. I'll never belong anywhere."

"You belong with me."

She shakes her head. "No, Ember. I don't."

"Do you want to stay here?"

"No. Scarecrow is a cruel man. And an evil man." She looks over her shoulder at me for the first time. Her eyes are dark and appear sunken in. "Don't you see? I have no home. I have nothing."

"You have Holly. You have me. You also have you."

I take one more step toward her, but this time she does move closer to the edge as a warning for me not to come any closer.

Fearing what she might do, my heart stops, and I struggle for the right words but decide I can only speak my truth. "You're right that I was miserable out there. You're right that I hated being away from Hallelujah Junction. We're different people—outcasts. We've lived different lives than the masses, and no matter who I met, no one truly got me. Even Christopher. He sees me the way he wants to see me but refuses to see the damage inside. He doesn't want to see the ugly, the pain, and the vileness that surrounds me. My past is suffocating and my future dim. He doesn't want to see that. But I need to move forward for me. For *me*. Just as you have to move forward for you. You."

"Move forward where?" Her voice is shrill, and I realize this is the first time I've truly heard her raise her voice. There isn't a shred of timidness laced within the words she speaks.

"I don't know. But I do know we can't stay here. We have to escape Papa Rich and Scarecrow, and we have to stop being held captive. It's time we're free."

She faces the canyon again and nods, taking a step toward the edge. "Yes, I want to be free."

"Violet!" I stop myself from lunging toward her, fearing that my action could push her over the edge. "Don't do it. I know you think all will be better, but don't. Please. Think of Holly. Think of anything but what's at the bottom of that cliff."

"Go inside, Ember," she says.

"I'm not leaving you. I'll never leave you. Trust me on that. Never."

She lifts her head and looks up at the sky, taking a deep breath. She extends her arms and says, "I've never been free. I've never truly been happy. It's time I stop the suffering. It's time. I have to escape the darkness, Ember. I hope you understand. I have to escape."

"Violet, I love you!" I shout, hoping I'm loud enough that Holly and Christopher will hear and come running. I need reinforcements. I need help. But I'm too scared to scream for help, because I feel it's all it will take for Violet to jump before Holly can see her do it. "Don't do this. This isn't your way out. It's not your way out!"

She looks over her shoulder and gives me a warm smile. "But it is."

Without hesitation, she flings herself over the cliff,

disappearing into the mountain fog.

17

CHRISTOPHER

Never in my life have I heard such a blood-curdling scream before.

"Violet! No! Oh God, No!"

It's Ember's scream. Ember is screaming!

I bolt out the front door with Holly close behind. I know I'm running, but I can't feel my feet, and I'm not sure how I actually reach Ember at the cliff's edge. It's as if I somehow teleported at a hyper-speed. My heart beat once inside the house and then not again until I reached Ember and knew she was all right.

If you call the out-of-control, screaming woman I love all right.

"She jumped! Violet jumped off the cliff!"

Ember's lying on her stomach in the snow, her arms outstretched over the edge as if she can somehow pull Violet back to land.

I start to reach for Ember and take her into my arms, but then I see Holly charging toward us, her own horrific scream howling through the frigid air. I intercept her run, feeling as if she would also fling herself over the edge, following her sister to her death, if I don't hold her tightly.

"I tried to stop her! I tried to stop her!" Ember is clawing at the icy earth, madness taking hold.

"No! No! Violet!" Holly is beating against me with her tiny fists as she tries to free herself. "No!"

The sound of pain shattering through the sky stabs at every nerve in my body.

I'm rooted in place. I want to fall to my knees and help the woman I love, but Holly needs me more right now. And Violet... oh, God, Violet... there is nothing I can do to help her, but I can't help but feel if I lie on the ground and claw at the earth like Ember that I too can miraculously bring her back.

But there's no bringing her back.

She's gone.

Violet's gone.

I'll fight with Holly for hours if it means she won't follow her sister, but suddenly her pummeling of fists stop, and she wiggles out of my arms and charges away from the cliff, back toward the house. I see an extremely large man dressed in flannel and furs sprinting out of the thick woods, and Holly is headed straight toward him.

"Violet!" she screams. "She jumped. Oh my God, she jumped!" Her words turn to howls as she crumbles to her knees right in front of the stranger who swoops her up and cradles her in his arms.

He continues toward me, and I'm not sure if I should welcome this stranger or feel guarded. He's larger than me, thicker. He has a full beard, long hair, and is rugged, but he's not exactly dirty. It's clear from his appearance that he is not just a hiker or a camper. This is a man who has been living off the land. He has a deer hide around his shoulders, providing him warmth against the storm. Furs are underneath the leather, and flannel beneath that. He is layered and warm, prepared for the mountain as only a man who lives and breathes it can be.

"No... no... no..." Ember's cries bring my focus back to her. I bend down and pull her off the snow-covered ground and into my arms.

I don't say anything, because what can I say? But instead, I hold her shaking body close to my chest and place kisses on the side of her head. I want so desperately to take away her pain, but I'm completely at a loss as to how I can.

The mountain man reaches us and places Holly on her feet next to me. Holly stands in place and watches the man walk toward the edge and peer over the side. I'm nervous for him, since the snow and ice all around doesn't make the ledge a safe place for anyone to be. He falls to his knees and leans over more—so much so that I prepare myself to pull him back from his own death if I have to.

Holly—who hasn't moved—cries out, "Violet, why? Why?"

Ember clings to my shirt and sobs even louder.

"I think I see her," the man calls out. "She's down there. I see her."

I release Ember and charge toward the edge myself. "Alive?" I ask.

"I don't know... but she didn't fall all the way. A tree branch stopped her. She's caught in the tree."

Ember and Holly both start toward the edge, but I turn around and put out my hand to stop them. "Don't come any closer. It's slick here!"

"Is she alive? Oh my God! Is she alive?" Ember asks, her hand over her mouth, her eyes wide as she trembles in place.

It kills me to see the woman I love appear so unhinged. I want Violet to be alive for her own sake, but also for Ember's. I'm not sure she'd survive this if Violet truly is dead.

"Please tell me you can see if she's breathing," Holly calls out.

I lean myself over the edge, and the mountain man holds onto the back of my shirt to make sure I don't slip off. He's right. Violet is about twenty feet down or so, stopped by the large limbs of a cedar that has grown from the mountain.

"I see her!" I say as I try to focus on if she's moving at all or if I can see her chest rising. "I can't tell if she's breathing."

But then I hear a moan and see a slight movement of Violet's head.

"She's moving! She's moving!" I shout, turning my head to look at the man. I then refocus my attention on Violet. "Violet! Don't move. If you can hear me, you stay still! Don't move an inch. We're coming for you."

"She's alive?" Holly screams, running to the edge of the cliff, regardless of my warning. Luckily, Ember has regained some sense and is pulling Holly back to a safer distance.

"We'll get to her," I say, not sure exactly how we will, but no fucking way will I allow her to die down there alone.

She may have every single bone in her body broken, and death may be inevitable, but she'll die in her sister's arms, knowing she's loved. Not alone. Not cold. Not on the side of a cliff.

The stranger, who has yet to give me any indication as to who he is, says, "Go get us some rope. Quick!" His voice is gruff, as if he hasn't used it in years.

Holly spins on her heels and charges toward the house. I look up at Ember and tell her, "Don't worry. We'll get her."

Tears are flowing down her face, but for the first time since running out here, I see some sanity returning to her expression. Hope is soothing the madness away.

I turn to the cliff and scoot my belly a little closer so I can get a better look. I'm not sure how we're going to reach her, and I hope Mountain Man has an idea. I already know my phone isn't working, and the hike out of here will take too long. So, any chance of rescue will rest solely on us. Holly returns quickly with an armful of thick rope. It's dirty, tattered, and frayed in some places, but it does appear intact.

The stranger takes the rope from her and runs toward the nearest tree, which sadly is only an aspen, and not even a fully matured one at that. The thick-trunked pine trees are too far, and no way will the rope reach them. I'm not sure the aspen is strong enough to hold Violet's weight, let alone the stranger's or mine, but we don't really have a choice.

The mountain man must be thinking the same as me, because he calls out, "I'm not sure this tree will hold my weight. I'm going to need you to also hold the other end and try to bear the majority of my weight." He continues to tie the rope around the tree and looks up at me for confirmation that I'm on the same page as him.

Jesus Christ, we're doing this.

This man is going to throw himself off a cliff to rescue a woman who is barely alive, and I'm going to hold him with nothing but my weight and hopefully a well-rooted aspen tree.

Ember and Holly both run over to where I've just gripped the rope and take hold as well. We can use all the help we can get, because he is not a tiny man.

With the skill of a true outdoorsman, the man wraps the rope around his torso and begins to rappel off the edge without the slightest hesitation. The tug on the rope burns my hand, but I hold firm as I glance at the tree, which is also remaining steadfast.

"If this tree breaks, let go of the rope," I order the women. But I already know they won't, just as I won't. If Mountain Man goes down, we all do.

"I'm almost there," the man shouts from the other side. I appreciate his feedback, because not knowing makes this harder.

I scan the length of the rope and am happy to see that so far it's holding his weight as well.

"I've reached her," he yells up. "She's alive and conscious. I don't think she can make it up the cliff alone. She's pretty hurt. So, I'm going to have to tie her off with me. It might be too much for the rope—"

"We got you, man," I shout out, sweat beading on my forehead. I want to take as much of the weight as we can so we don't tax the tree until we absolutely have to. I'm terrified to hear the snapping sound of the bark.

"Please be okay. Please be okay," I hear Holly chant under her breath as she digs her heels into the snow and holds the rope with a strength that only a sister trying to save her sibling can do.

"Go ahead and start pulling," he orders from down below.

I can tell the minute Violet is added to the rope and the mountain man is climbing back up. I begin to pull with all my might, tearing at the flesh of my hands. Ember is yanking, Holly is as well, and slowly we are pulling them to safety.

Fresh snow begins to fall from the sky, but luckily it seems to not be sticking. The only sound is our heavy breathing and groans of exertion.

"Almost there," the man calls out. "I can almost reach the landing."

I pull harder with his words, knowing he'll need that extra heave to get Violet to the top.

"Ember, you let go of the rope on the count of three, go to the edge, and help pull Violet up when you see her. One. Two. Three!"

I dig my feet farther into the wet snow as I feel the rope give when Ember follows my command. For such a small woman, it's clear how much of the weight she was holding, because I feel my feet slipping a bit, and Holly and I both have to readjust our stance to pull even harder.

"I see them," Ember calls out. "Violet's eyes are open! She's alive. Alive!"

"Be careful!" I shout between clenched teeth. "Get down on your belly to reach out. Don't let their weight pull you over."

Grateful that Ember doesn't question my command, I watch her do exactly as I say. And within seconds, Violet and Mountain Man are cresting the impossible. His thick fingers grab the edge, and he climbs the rest of the way up, pulling Violet alongside him with Ember's assistance.

Holly and I both release the rope and run toward them.

"Violet! Oh God! Violet!" Holly is nearly hysterical.

Ember sits back on her butt, winded from the exertion. She's watching the sisters hug as tears run down her face.

Violet is weak, cringing in pain with every movement, but still able to give her sister the affection that none of us believed would happen again.

Feeling as if I can breathe for the first time since running out of the house, I walk to the stranger and extend my hand, helping him off the snow-covered ground.

"I don't know what to say, man. Thank you." If he hadn't come out of the woods... Violet wouldn't be alive. No way in hell could I have done that myself.

He nods, looks at Holly and then Violet, and starts to walk away.

"Wait!" Holly calls, jumping up and reaching for him. "You can't leave. Please stay. Please. Violet needs you now."

I get the feeling she knows the man—the way she ran up to him and now begs for him to stay. But at the same time, she knows it's unlikely he'd stay without her begging him to.

Ember is looking at Violet's leg. "I think it's broken," she says.

The man's face appears pained, and he kneels where Violet is lying and takes over examining her leg. When he moves it, she cries out in pain.

"We need to get her inside," I say, knowing she's been outside in the elements for too long, and aside from broken bones, we'll have to deal with hypothermia.

The mountain man reaches beneath Violet, swoops her into his arms, and begins trudging through the snow as if her body doesn't weigh a thing.

I reach down and assist Ember up. Her body is frozen, and I worry about her as well. I wrap my arm around her and say, "We need to get you warmed up too."

"Thank you," Ember says as we head back to the house. "You saved her life. You saved her, and you saved me. I couldn't have lived with myself if—" Her voice cracks, and a sob escapes her chattering lips.

I pull her closer to me and speed up our pace as the snow falls around us a little harder now. "She's safe now. All will be fine."

"Because of you," she chatters. "Everything will be fine only because of you."

18

CHRISTOPHER

"I DIDN'T CATCH YOUR NAME," I SAY TO THE MAN AS WE ALL STAND around the fire, trying to warm our soaking-wet bodies.

The man looks at me but doesn't say anything. His long beard is wet, his clothing as well, but he seems steadfast and strong. I don't see a shiver in his body. His only concern and focus is Violet, who he's placed on blankets laid out by the fire by Holly in a mad dash when we entered the chapel.

"Do you live around here?" I press. I feel the need to get to know this man. Not because I don't trust him, but because there's a deep curiosity to find out who he truly is.

Ember is studying the man intensely as well. "You've been watching us, haven't you?" she asks. "It was you who I called out to, wasn't it?"

Ember's right; it's been him in the woods all along. "I saw you too, right? It was you who I saw and was yelling at."

He doesn't say anything but nods. It was never Richard or Scarecrow. It was this man... watching.

"You watch us and have been. That's how you knew Violet went over the cliff?" Ember adds. "You were watching the whole time."

"The mountain is no place for women to be left alone," he says as he runs his fingers over Violet's other leg and arms. "I think the only broken bone is your leg," he tells her. "I'll splint it if you'll let me."

Violet nods as she reaches out for his hand. "Thank you. Thank you for saving me... again." She then looks up at Holly and begins to sob. "I'm so sorry. I'm sorry I did that."

Holly kneels beside her and takes her hand in hers. "Shhh... you don't need to worry about that now."

Violet looks at Ember. "I'm sorry, Ember. I know I can never take back what I did. Why I did it... I'm sorry."

Ember takes her other free hand. "Promise me you'll never do this again. We love you, Violet. Nothing is ever so awful that you have to.... Promise me."

Violet nods but continues to cry.

I stoke the fire as Mountain Man begins to work on splinting Violet's leg, noticing the storm isn't letting up as I had hoped. I really thought I'd be hiking down the mountain soon, but now with Violet's condition, this plan is definitely going to have to be modified.

Ember returns her attention to the mountain man, then looks at Holly and Violet and clearly sees what I do. This man isn't exactly a stranger to the sisters. "Do you know this man?" she asks Holly.

Holly glances at him and nods. "We do."

"He saved me from a mountain lion," Violet says. "And he's been watching over us ever since."

"Why didn't you tell me it was him out there watching us?"

"He likes his privacy," Holly says, shifting her weight and avoiding eye contact with Ember.

"Scarecrow would kill us if he knew we've spoken to another man," Violet says. "So, we kept him secret." Her eyes look up at him lovingly. "But he's always looking out for us. If it weren't for him, we would have starved when Scarecrow and Richard left to find you. They didn't leave us with any food or means to hunt for any." She hisses in pain as the mountain man secures the splint tighter.

Ember smiles and shakes her head. "Was it you giving the rabbit and mushrooms to Violet a couple of days ago?" She shakes her head. "I was wondering how Violet could be so lucky to find all that."

"Do you have a name?" I ask again, liking the man but uncomfortable not knowing his name.

"Isaac." He sits Violet up and asks, "Do you mind if I run my hands up your spine and on your ribs? I want to make sure you didn't do any harm to them."

She looks toward Holly to make sure she's doing the right thing by allowing him to touch her even more than he already has.

"Go ahead," Holly says for her.

Violet cringes in pain when he touches her, but Isaac seems happy as he nods. "Nothing looks broken. Just bruised, which will still hurt like a son of a bitch."

Ember stands from her crouched position and walks over to me. She doesn't say a word but rests her forehead against my chest. I wrap my arms around her and pull her closer to the fire.

"I've never been so scared in my life," she says quietly to me. "I don't know what Holly and I would have done without you and Isaac." She tilts her head up at me. "But we can't leave. I know you want to. But with Violet hurt... and the reason she jumped was... it's my fault for her fall."

"No," Violet calls out, hissing when she moves too quickly, overhearing what Ember is saying. "Don't you blame yourself. Please don't. I don't know what got into me. It's just that sometimes I'm so sad. So... it feels like blackness covers me. Like a thick tar. I can't see hope. I can't see good. But this is not your fault, Ember. It's not. Please, please don't think that. I was stupid. Reckless. And God gave me a second chance that I will not take lightly."

"Why did you do it?" Holly asks, new tears falling from her eyes. "Why?"

"The thought of leaving was too much for me. I didn't want to go. But I didn't want to stay."

I notice Isaac look up at her and scowl, but he doesn't say a word.

"I feel lost in the woods with no trail," she adds.

"Well, right now, you don't have to worry about anything but healing. You'll have to stay off this leg for a while. No chores. No firewood gathering, and absolutely no hiking down the mountain," Isaac interrupts, still frowning.

Ember looks at me, and I nod in understanding.

We may be here a while.

But at the same time... we have to leave before Scarecrow and Richard return. We have a time limit, and my gut tells me we're running out of that time. Those men won't stay gone for long.

Isaac stands up, warms his hands by the fire, and says, "I'll be heading home. But if you need anything—"

"Please don't go," Violet says as Holly wraps a quilt around her shoulders. "It's snowing outside and getting dark. I can't live with myself if someone gets hurt because of my actions. Please stay with us. We don't have much, but we can make up a bed. Please."

"Yes, stay," Holly adds. "I don't know where your home is, but since we've never seen it gathering wood or foraging for food, I know it has to be far enough away that walking in the snow and at night isn't safe. So please. I'll start supper too. Stay."

Isaac looks at me, and I simply shrug. "Women have spoken. As you can see, I'm not going anywhere either. I think we're stuck here for at least the night."

For the first time, I see Isaac smirk as he nods. "You may need my help lifting Violet," he says, not saying yes but not saying no.

"Then it's decided," Holly announces, turning her attention to making supper.

Violet reaches out for Isaac's hand again. "Thank you, Isaac.

I'm so happy to have you in my life. If it weren't for you—twice—I wouldn't have one."

He squats next to her and with his free hand swipes her hair away from her face. "Never again, little one. Do you understand? Never again."

She nods and swallows hard. "I'm sorry. I don't know why...." She begins to cry, and Isaac pulls her into his chest. "I don't want to leave. I don't want to stay. I don't want this life anymore. I don't know what to do."

"Shh," he says. "Everything's going to be okay. Just rest right now. Rest."

I watch Ember walk over to Holly and take her into her arms. Holly breaks down and begins crying into Ember's shoulder. And for the first time since arriving, I really see why Ember has been so torn about leaving. She truly loves these women. They truly are her family. And after what happened, after doing everything within my power to save her family and the tiny and broken woman lying on the floor... I can actually picture them as my family too.

Ember walks over to me eventually when Holly returned her attention to the supper preparation. I don't know if it's because everything was so bad, so awful, and so dark, but when Ember reaches for my hand and holds it tightly, I get an odd sense of warmth and comfort. Almost a sense of home. A glimmer of light shines through the black. At least for now. Right this second.

I have Ember, my wife.

I have shelter and a fire to keep me warm.

I have people around me who are only good and genuine.

I have simplicity.

For now... I can breathe again.

19

CHRISTOPHER

"Looks like the storm fizzled out last night," Isaac says from behind me.

It's first thing in the morning, after a long, sleepless night, and I'm questioning if today is the day for the descent or if tomorrow is a better day. I also can't figure out how we go about moving Violet, and I'm wondering if I need to go down by myself, get help, and take it from there. I don't want to leave Ember, but at the same time, I know she won't leave without Holly and Violet.

"I don't think it will last, however," I say, looking up at the sky and trying to judge if the clouds in the distance are storm clouds or not.

"Those clouds will bring snow," Isaac says, answering my question.

I sigh loudly, not sure what our next step should be. "It's refreshing here," I say. "Too bad this place is laced with evil."

"They don't want to go," Isaac says. "I think Violet's desperate act yesterday proved that."

"I understand," I reply, turning to face him. "I really do. But you don't know Scarecrow and Richard like I do. I can't in good faith leave those women here. And I also can't allow Scarecrow and Richard to leave for Wyoming and be free men. They're sick and belong behind bars. Which then leaves those women alone."

"I moved to these mountains about ten years ago," Isaac says as he looks out into the forest. "I live down the mountain some and near a river with a waterfall and large slabs of granite. It's my paradise, even though you may disagree. Violet and Holly see the beauty in this land like I do."

"It is beautiful," I agree. "But as you said last night—no place for two women to survive alone."

"True."

"You couldn't even leave them here alone," I point out. "You were helping and watching over them."

"True."

"So, you understand why I feel responsible for them."

"I do."

"And I have my wife to think of," I add. "Ember loves those women and will not leave without them."

"She wants to know they're safe," Isaac says.

"Of course. I do too."

"Do you have a plan? Where will you take them once you fly away from here?" Isaac asks, though I don't get the feeling he is drilling, judging me, or even accusing me of doing something reckless. I get the feeling he generally cares and wants to help.

"I don't know. I wish I had a concrete plan in my head, but I don't. I impulsively hopped on a private plane to get my wife back. I didn't have any idea what would happen after. And then when Holly and Violet were thrown into the mix." I release a deep breath. "I don't know."

"I think the women are picking up on that. I think they know you don't know what happens next. They sense it."

"But again, whatever we do is better than what's happening to them now. Those poor women... and no way in hell will I let Ember be here for another second without me."

Isaac takes a deep breath, inhaling the crisp mountain air. "When I sold everything I had to move up here, people thought I had lost my mind. I was crazy for wanting to leave a lucrative business, a lavish lifestyle, and basically the American dream realized. But you know what? I was miserable. Absolutely miserable. From the little I spoke with Ember last night, it sounds like her experience in New York was the same. I can relate to that. I hate New York with a passion."

I nod. "I won't be going back. Everything there and the people are dead to me. I'm here cleaning up a mess caused by *New York*, and I won't be repeating that mistake again."

"I understand that feeling. I left everything behind," Isaac says. "My past is dead to me as well."

"Christopher?" I hear Ember's voice call from behind me.

I turn to face her. "I'm out here talking with Isaac."

"Can you come inside? Holly and Violet want to speak with us."

I nod and all three of us go inside, where Holly is sitting next to Violet, who is propped up and already has renewed color in her face. She appears more comfortable and at ease, and it's obvious that a good night's sleep served her well. Holly also seems better. Last night, she fretted for hours, unable to settle and jumping every time Violet moved.

"We know you want to leave today," Holly begins as we all circle around the fire where they are. "And we know why you do and can understand that. But Violet and I spoke for hours last night while you were all asleep, and we came to a decision."

"We aren't going with you," Violet blurts.

Ember gasps, and I see tears well in her eyes instantly.

"But before you get upset or try to talk us out of it, I want you to hear us out," Holly cuts in, walking over to Ember and placing a hand on her arm. "Listen. Please."

"Our mother and father made a decision when we were children to live off the grid. They homeschooled us and taught us to live off the land. Our pa wasn't always a bad man, but when our mother died, he died too... or at least his spirit did. It got ugly then. Our life got really ugly. But the one thing Violet and I had

44

was the beauty around us. We could see what our mother saw. We could love what she did. We could live the life she always dreamed of. She wanted us to live like this, and for the most part, we loved it too."

"But Scarecrow," Ember interrupts.

"Yes, he's awful," Violet says. "Which is why we aren't going to stand in your way of reporting him and Richard to the authorities. We actually hope you do so we never have to see him again. We want him to rot in jail for everything."

"So, what we are going to do is leave and find a hunting shack we know exists nearby. We will hole up there until after Richard and Scarecrow return and are hopefully arrested. In which time, Violet and I will return to the chapel—our home—and live off the land. We know how. We *want* to know how."

"Then I stay too," Ember blurts, which rips at my soul.

Holly shakes her head. "No, Ember. You belong with Christopher."

"We see that," Violet says with a warm smile. "We see how much you both love each other."

"But I love you both too," Ember argues, tears falling freely now.

"Then you come and visit," Holly offers. "Once everything settles and it's safe for you to do so. And who knows, maybe someday, Violet and I will want to leave this mountain, and it will be nice to know we have a place to visit as well."

"What if I find us a place in the mountains?" I suggest. "I could buy us some land, build a house—"

"We want to stay here," Violet says, her eyes stealing a glance at Isaac, who stands by and watches. "We have a good friend nearby, and we don't want to leave him."

"You're injured," Ember points out, swiping at the tears on her face. I can see her sadness is morphing into anger. "You both just experienced an awful ordeal and aren't thinking straight. It's winter! You don't have enough supplies, you can barely keep up with the firewood, and this chapel doesn't even have a completed or functioning chimney! I need you both to stop and think with your minds... not your hearts. I get it. You're scared."

"We're not leaving this mountain," Holly presses. "I'm sorry."

Ember whips her head toward me and then to Isaac. "Say something! Convince them that this is just another suicide attempt. You will die in some hunting shack while you wait out the winter!"

Isaac nods. "Ember's right. You can't leave here and go live in a shack. I know this mountain, and the closest hunting shack is still two miles away from here, and there's no way Violet can make it in her condition. Not to mention, there are no resources to live off of during this time of year."

"See!" Ember squeaks as she returns her attention to Holly and Violet. "Even Isaac believes you should leave with us."

"No," Isaac says calmly. "I didn't say that. I understand why they don't want to leave. I get why they want to keep this chapel and this land, but I don't agree with hiding out in the hunter's shack." He walks to Violet and squats down next to her so he can look her directly in the eyes. "I'd like to suggest that you and your sister come stay with me. At least until Richard and Scarecrow are no longer a threat. I have room, and I have the supplies to last us through the winter. I can also care for your leg during your mend."

Tears form in Violet's eyes, and she shakes her head. "I can't ask that of you. You've already done so much for us."

"I wouldn't be offering if I didn't want to."

"We know you like your privacy," Holly says. "We can't impose."

"You can, and you will," he says more firmly. He then turns to look at Ember and me. "I can take good care of them until we get the news that all is safe and those men are gone."

I nod and look at Violet, who is staring at Isaac as she silently cries. I then look at Holly and ask, "Is this something you would want? I'd feel better leaving you with Isaac. In fact, I think it's the only way I'll agree to not taking you both with us."

I walk over to Ember and take her hand in mine. I squeeze gently, knowing she needs my connection to help her get through this. I know she doesn't want to lose her friends, but at the same time, she has to understand what they're going through and why they're considering other options.

"Violet?" Holly asks. "What do you think?"

Violet keeps her eyes on Isaac. "It's too much. You're being too nice."

Isaac pats her good leg and smiles. "The way I see it, it will save me from having to hike in the snow every day to come up here and check on you ladies. You'd be doing me a favor."

Violet smiles warmly and then looks up at Holly. "What do you want to do?"

Holly glances at me and then at Ember. "Would you agree to leaving us with Isaac?"

I nod, then wait for Ember to finally answer, "I don't want to leave you. I'll miss you every day, but I also understand." She looks at Isaac. "Thank you for being here. Thank you for being there for them."

Holly then places her hand on Isaac's shoulder. "Thank you for your generosity. My sister and I would love to stay with you until the chapel is safe."

Isaac pats Violet's leg one more time and stands. "All right then. I have plenty of blankets, food, and supplies, but you ladies better pack your clothing and any other items you want. It's going to be awhile until you can return." He then turns his attention to me. "Do you mind helping me get Violet to my place before you and Ember make your journey down the hill?"

"It's the least I can do," I reply, more than happy to be of some use.

The man has become all of our savior. He gave a solution to a problem I didn't feel could be solved.

"Let's get a move on. We have a lot to do before it gets dark. My place will take about half a day with Violet."

As everyone scrambles to get to work, I take a minute to pull Ember into my arms and ask, "Are you all right with this?"

"It's what they want," she says, her voice cracking. "I want them to be happy. They deserve that."

"And I want you to be happy. What will it take to make that happen?"

She pulls away and looks into my eyes. "You," she states simply. "I just need you to make me happy."

20

EMBER

IT HAD BEEN A LONG DAY AND A GRUELING HIKE GETTING THE sisters to Isaac's cabin. Christopher and Isaac were able to carry Violet the entire way, while Holly and I carried the supplies. Once we had them settled into the cabin, Christopher and I decided it would be best to come back to the chapel before dark, spend the night one last time, and then head out for the meadow at first light. Though Isaac offered his place for us to stay, both Christopher and I felt we needed some privacy so we could figure out our own future. We still have so much to discuss, and we really need some time to just be us... one last time before the craze of starting our new life begins.

Goodbyes were hard, but we all promised to stay in touch. Isaac promised to watch over Holly and Violet until we get word to them that Scarecrow and Papa Rich have been arrested, and knowing this made it possible for me to walk away. As hard as it was to leave them, I know deep down that they are happy now. They are living their lives the way they want to and on their terms. I could never force them to do anything but.

"It's just me and you now," Christopher says as we enter the chapel.

"It's so quiet," I say, walking over to the fire that is only embers now. It won't take me long to get it raging again, and I get to work quickly before the room gets any colder.

Christopher comes up from behind and wraps his arms around me, kissing the side of my neck. "I know today was rough on you. But I'm proud of you. You put their needs before your own, and I'm proud."

"It was hard. I want them with us, but I also know how hard it is out there... in society."

"Which is why we need to come up with a plan so it isn't so hard for you. Starting with the fact that we aren't going back to New York. You won't ever have to see my mother again or have the media hounding you. Wherever we go, we're going to keep it secret. It will take a damn good private investigator to hunt us down, and if they do... we'll leave again."

His words fill me with so much hope for the future. "What about your job?"

"I'll get another job if I want. Money isn't an issue for me, as you know. I love taking photographs, and that doesn't have to stop just because I don't work for *The Rolling Stone*. I can take freelance down the road if we decide it works for us, or I can take pictures for pleasure. Regardless, as long as I'm with you, I'll be happy."

"And your mother? Can you really walk away from her?"

He counters my question with one of his own. "Can you really walk away from Papa Rich?"

"It'll be hard," I admit.

"And it will be hard for me. But it's something we have in common. We won't be the first couple to have to deal with toxic parents and figure out how to handle that. They both deserve to be in jail, and hopefully that happens."

"So where do we go?" I ask.

"Do you still want the desert?" he asks, clearly thinking of locations.

I shake my head. "No. I like what you said earlier about living in the mountains. Being up here in the trees... this place makes me happy. Could we maybe find a place nearby? I don't mean living off the grid, but maybe a small mountain town?"

He tightens his hold on me and kisses me on the neck again. "I love that idea. A cabin with a wood stove and a carved bear out front."

"Just ours."

"Yes," he agrees. "Just ours."

"Someplace that they can't reach us. Never again."

"Never again."

I spin around and press my lips to his, instantly feeling the fire ignite inside me. Funny how hope for a good future acts like an aphrodisiac.

"We're all alone," I whisper seductively. "Just you and me. We don't have to be quiet." I nibble his lip and lower my hand to his crotch, which is already hard to the touch. "We can be loud. We can be very, very loud."

"Careful," he playfully warns. "You're awakening the beast."

"Maybe I don't want to be careful," I say as I dip my fingers down his pants and lightly caress his pubic hair. "I happen to like the beast."

"Take off your clothes," he orders.

Without hesitation, something I know the alpha in him expects—immediate compliance—I stand back and, with as much grace as I can muster, remove each item as seductively as I can. I know we aren't in the sexiest environment, but I want to please him. I want him to feel the desire I have inside for him. I can't give him lingerie and high heels, but I can give him complete surrender.

Christopher sits back on the wooden table, crosses his arms against his chest, and gives a wolfish grin. I get the feeling he's enjoying what he sees.

"Stand naked before me," he commands once all my clothes are removed.

I do so without protest, loving the sense of seductive power I feel from doing such a simple act.

"Turn in a circle and allow me to see that ass of yours."

I do as he says, turning my back to him, feeling his eyes burn against my skin.

"Spread your legs wide." I comply. "Bend over so I can see you on full display."

I pause for a moment—forcing myself to block out the dark memories of what that command would bring in my past—but do as he asks, knowing my future is so much better.

"Spread your cheeks for me. I want to see the hole that I plan to claim."

My heart beats hard against my heaving chest, but I reach behind and pull apart the fleshy mounds of my ass. The cold breeze of the chapel caresses the most intimate of spots, sending shivers down my spine and over every inch of bare skin.

I remain in position and feel a drop of arousal run from my pussy to my thigh. I can smell my desire, and though I know his eyes are feasting on the sight before him, I can't help but feel a mixture of humiliation and desire in my stance. The push and pull of the two emotions seems to drive my need for more even higher.

I hear his footsteps approach. I remain in position, determined to stay that way until he gives the command to move.

I flinch slightly when I feel his palm on my ass. "Keep them spread," he growls.

I've come to recognize the sound of his voice that means my body will pay the price in the most wicked and delicious of ways. He morphs into a beast, and I know exactly the tone.

I hear it now.

"I want to fuck your ass. I want my cock buried in this tight little hole."

My heart beats so hard I can feel the pulse in my temples. I swallow back the lump in my throat, trying not to break the position I know he wants me to hold.

"I don't have lube," he says. "So, I'm going to fuck this ass with your juices alone."

Panic mixed with a forbidden desire to have him do just as he pleases rumbles within me.

He swipes his fingers along my pussy, collecting the wetness, and presses them past my puckered hole. He coats every inch of my hole, preparing it for entry with my desire only.

He moves me to the edge of the wooden table and presses me down to lie on my stomach against the cold surface. "I'll go slow, but this is going to have more friction and won't be easy."

I tense but nod. I want this. I want to feel him inside me in the most intimate spots of my body.

"I'll be gentle, but this will take some time for you to adjust. I can't slide in with as much ease. I need you to relax, submit, and open up."

"Is it going to hurt?" I ask.

"Yes. Just the way you like it."

I nod again. Yes, just the way I like it. Only Christopher truly understands my need for a darker touch. My hunger for a little edge.

He lowers himself over my back and begins to softly kiss the side of my neck, my shoulder, my earlobe—each kiss sending tingles to my throbbing pussy. His cock presses against the crease of my ass, and I know the soft caresses are only a ruse to trick my body into relaxing before the rough claiming of my ass begins.

"I'm scared," I finally admit.

"Breathe...."

"I'm scared it will hurt too much. It will be too dry," I admit, fearful of the unknown. "But no matter how much I cry out, don't stop," I direct. "I want it. I want to feel you fuck my ass with nothing preventing the friction. Make my ass raw," I murmur, knowing that my own primal beast inside has finally been unleashed.

He reaches down with his hand and guides his cock to my tight back entrance. Very slowly, and with so much control, he presses the tip of his dick past the tight ring. He pauses so I can get used to the initial shock, the spread, and the burn from only having my own slickness as lube.

"Relax. Open yourself to me," he groans in my ear, following the words with soft kisses to my neck.

He pushes farther, causing me to gasp. The bite, the stretch, the erotic feeling, it all becomes too much. I miss the lube. I miss the ease.

I shake my head. "You're too big for me. I think I'll tear without lube."

Christopher whispers in my ear, "Take a deep breath." I do as he asks. "Take another one, and relax your muscles. You need to trust that once I am fully inside you, it will feel good. Submit yourself, your apprehension, and your complete body to me."

He reaches a hand around my front and finds my clit. He expertly circles his finger around it, giving me the exact sensation I need to allow my ass to fully take him. I focus my attention on the pleasure his finger gives me and am able to ease the muscles of my anus completely, pushing back against him to drive him even deeper. Doing so allows his dick to fully be rooted in my ass balls-deep as I cry out his name in pain and in pleasure.

I've come to realize I love and crave the two feelings combined above all.

"That's it, Ember," he praises as he slowly pumps his thickness in and out. "Let me claim that ass of yours. Let me make you mine."

My bottom hole stretches to impossible levels and is dry without the lube, but I enjoy the stinging friction and look forward to every biting thrust he gives me.

His gentle thrusts become a little more aggressive. Each push drives slightly deeper than before. Tingles in my ass become sparks of ecstasy. My dark channel pulsates around his massive dick, and I scream out his name. Tears of surrender course down my face as I allow every sensation to swamp my body. I don't resist. I don't fight. I don't think. I simply am.

My mewls and whimpers bring on a few more driving thrusts,

and Christopher finally ends the ass-fucking with a roar as he shoots his seed in my dry hole.

We remain frozen, bent over the table, our life still in flux, Papa Rich and Scarecrow still out there. But right now... this very second, we have calm. We have us. And I realize that is all I need.

21

EMBER

"They caught the sonofabitch!" Christopher announces, his eyes full of excitement and body tense with emotions as he hangs up the phone. "They have both Richard and Scarecrow in custody."

"Oh my God," I barely squeak out. "They found them?"

"They came back for you as we knew they would, and the Feds were waiting." He walks over to the television and turns on the news.

I stare in disbelief as I watch Papa Rich in handcuffs being escorted by police into a building. His head is up, shoulders proud, and not an ounce of remorse is present in his face. Commentary about capturing the Ghost Town Killer rings in my ear as I watch the man I believed I loved walk toward his end of destruction. No one can die from his hand any longer. No more misery can be cast down upon the poor, unexpected trespassers.

He'll never get to be a ranger again. Only a prisoner.

They cut away and show Scarecrow in a wheelchair being pushed through a media storm and surrounded by police. He looks pathetic with his one leg. They've removed the straw stuffing of his other leg, which I'm sure has him pissed off. They took his identity and his dignity by forcing him to be pushed in a wheelchair by someone else. I feel for the person escorting him. I wonder if he still smells like onions, body odor, and feces.

"Watching them both, so far away, almost seems like being cheated. I didn't get to see them arrested for myself," I confess.

"I know," Christopher says. "It took everything in me to not be up on that mountain waiting for their return. But at the same time, we have to move on. We can't be held captive by them forever. They aren't part of our story anymore."

"This doesn't seem real," I say under my breath. "I thought they'd never catch him. Never."

Christopher walks up behind me and places his comforting hand on my shoulder as we watch together. "Agent Martinez told me that they're going to want us to testify. I'm going to get an attorney right away to handle everything for us and help guide us through this storm."

I look up at him, instantly in a panic. "But what about our home? Will the media find us? You said where we're at is secret. It's ours. Only ours."

I love being in our cabin with no reporters waiting outside. Is that all going to change?

"We're going to stay hidden the best we can. I'll have our lawyer be our point of contact, and though we may have to travel to testify, we'll deal with the media and authorities *away* from our house. Our home will be our sanctuary always." He leans down and kisses my forehead. "I promise. I like the peace and quiet here just as much as you do."

Christopher had kept his word the minute we flew off the mountain. We didn't go back to New York, we had no interaction with his mother, and he found us the cutest cabin in a small mountain town called Pinesville. The town consists of one market, a post office, a pet store, a barbershop, and some other small businesses. It's quaint, charming, and already feels like home. We've met a couple of the people who live in the town, but they all seem to keep to themselves as we do. It's friendly, but not overly so. And if they know who Christopher and I are due to the media, they aren't letting on that they do.

Christopher is taking nature pictures and seems to love it. We go on hikes, and he gets lost in snapping one photo after another. We've settled into a routine of love, happiness, and contentment that I never thought possible. But I always knew in the back of my mind it was temporary. We were working on borrowed time because Papa Rich would enter my life once again.

And here he is.

On the television, so far from me but also so close.

"I'm not sure I can face him," I confess, staring at the man who at one time was my only family. The only person in my life who meant anything. The man I believed to be my Papa Rich.

I don't recognize the man anymore.

And not because he changed. No... he's the same man. The same *evil* man.

I just have my eyes open now. I can truly see the truth.

He's not *my* Papa Rich anymore.

He's Richard. He's the Ghost Town Killer. He's a bad, bad man and was my kidnapper.

Christopher lets out a deep breath and begins rubbing my back. "I wish I could tell you that you don't ever have to see him again. But I know you and I will be key witnesses in his trial. He'll be in the courtroom when you have to take the stand."

"What about your mother? Will we have to see her?"

He continues to rub small circles on my back. "It's likely. She's now a part of this court case as well. There's no way she'll be able to walk away from this with her hands clean. No matter how much money and how many fancy lawyers she throws at this, she aided a wanted felon. It's a crime, and I don't see her not having to pay for what she did to you. But my mother is no longer my concern. She gets to deal with her legal issues on her own."

"Are we going to tell the authorities the truth about what she did?" I ask, prepared to lie if that is something Christopher wants.

Louisa is his mother, and I completely understand the pull of family and what they can make you do or not do.

"I've already told Agent Martinez everything. I'm not going to lie for that woman, and I don't expect you to either. She'll have to pay for what she did one way or another. Knowing her, it will just be through her pocketbook. She has a way of getting out of everything bad. But regardless, she lost me in the process. She's dead to me, just as Richard is to you."

I reach for the remote and turn off the television. I don't want to see his face or hear the grating voices of the reporters any longer. "It's been so nice the last couple of weeks here with you. I just don't want to see it end."

Christopher walks around me and sits next to me on the couch. He takes both my hands into his and looks me straight in the eyes. "It won't end. We may have to take a small detour, but we'll return to this. I love it just as much as you do."

"I'm afraid that once we go back to that life, you may realize you miss it all. City life could pull you back."

Christopher smiles. "I haven't missed a thing. I've been asking myself why I waited so long to do something like this. I've always loved the mountains and vacationed near here often. So, to be able to live here every single day... it's like a permanent vacation." He leans forward and kisses me. "I'm making this change for me just as much as I'm doing it for you."

"We need to let Isaac, Holly, and Violet know that the chapel is safe," I suddenly realize, wondering how long it will be for us to get out to see them all.

"I already made sure that happened," Christopher says. "The Feds want to keep us happy right now so we cooperate with everything they need from us. I asked them to send one of their men to Isaac's immediately. Once the dust settles, we'll head out there and visit. See how they are settled in and if they need anything from us."

I've missed the sisters like crazy and can't wait to see them again, but I also know it was impossible to go back before they captured Richard and Scarecrow. We had to remain in hiding for our safety as well as theirs. Plus, we didn't want to give any clues to Richard and Scarecrow that we had already fled the mountain.

"Christopher..." I begin, not sure I want to actually speak my thoughts out loud. "Do you think it's possible to see Pap—Richard before we are in the courtroom? I don't want to see him, but there's a part of me that feels I need the closure. I need to be able to say goodbye to him and that part of my life. I won't be able to do that if I'm on the stand and he's staring at me from across the room."

"I'll have our lawyer work on it first thing. I'm sure it can be arranged if it's something you really want."

"It's not something I want but something I feel I need to do."

"I understand," Christopher says as he stands. "I'll make the calls now and make sure we have the best lawyer in the country handling us."

22

EMBER

I used to be a scared girl. Actually... I used to be a terrified girl.

Everything made me worry. Every shadow haunted me.

I hid in a schoolhouse, not just because I was forced to, but because I didn't know how not to hide.

It was safe there, and I craved safe.

I still regret that I was too weak and too cowardly to help Christopher when he first arrived in Hallelujah Junction. I didn't have the strength it took, and no matter how badly I wanted to step in and do the right thing... I couldn't.

I will forever be haunted by all the poor souls Richard killed in the acid pits. I wish I could have saved them. I wish I could have prevented their deaths somehow. I wish I could have been a different person.

But somehow, with Christopher by my side, and with time, I've become the person I always thought it was impossible to be.

I'm not the scared little girl who was kidnapped at age five.

I'm not the terrified ghost hidden away in a dilapidated building.

I no longer look out from the inside, wishing for a life I'd never have.

I've risen from the ashes of the town I helped burn down.

I'm stronger for it. I'm better for it.

I am no longer the Ghost of Hallelujah Junction.

I'm Ember Davenport, and nothing and no one will crush my spirit again.

Yes, I considered not having this meeting over and over again. But I know it's something I have to face head-on if I'm ever going to be able to let go of Richard. No amount of therapy will be able to cure me of the darkness he brings and the suffocating grip he has over me. It's on me. I have to do this. I have to take the control back.

Christopher and I have been traveling hours to get to the jail that is holding Richard until trial, and though we're both exhausted from the drive and the rush of different emotions, I insist that we come straight here. I need this to stop lingering over me. I need it to come to an end now.

And as I sit down in a plastic chair facing a glass divider, waiting for Richard to be escorted into the room on the other side, I release the breath I've been holding. I know it's going to be hard, but I have no idea just how much until I see him in his orange jumpsuit take the seat in front of me. Even though I know there is no way he can reach me, and the only way he can speak to me is by picking up the phone, and that police are all around us, I still have a moment of wanting to flee. I still feel terror that this man can take me again and I'll have to live my life in captivity once again.

But I fight back against the urge to run, and I also refuse to let him see the flurry of emotions raging through me.

We both pick up our phones and bring them to our ears, our eyes locked together.

"Ember," he begins. "I was hoping you'd come."

"Why?" I ask.

Is it so he can try to control me from afar? Is it because he wants my help to secure better legal counsel? Is it because he wants to yell and blame this all on me? Or is it so he can make me feel guilty for being free when he isn't?

"I'm going to be in here for a really long time," he says calmly. "You're going to have to be a strong girl and live without your papa."

I slam my hand on the table and lean toward him. "No," I seethe. "Don't you dare treat me like a weak little girl. You are not my father. You've never been my father. Do you understand that? I'm not going to sit here and let you speak to me as if I'm nothing but a scared child. Those days are over. Over!"

Richard leans back, licks his lips, and gives me a smirk. "I see Christopher has gotten into your head. You've allowed the devil inside."

"You're the devil," I say, regaining my calm. "You always have been."

He shakes his head. "No, Ember. I saved you. I raised you. It's because of me that you're even here breathing."

I take another deep, calming breath. "It's because of you that I missed out on life. You held me captive in a schoolhouse, tricking me into believing that it was all there was. You made me believe I had no other choice. You kidnapped me. That's the reality. You kidnapped me and trapped me in your own version of hell, just like you did to Christopher."

"I should have never brought that man into your life," Richard spits. "I'm paying my penance for that mistake now."

"You're paying your penance for all the people you killed and for all the bad that you did."

"Hard decisions have to be made in life," he counters. "You'll see this soon enough."

I nod. "Yes, I know all about the hard decisions. Coming here to face you was a hard decision, but I had to come. I had to look you in the eye and say goodbye. You won't see me or hear from me again after today. Not until I take the stand and help put you away for life, or to aid in giving you the death penalty if that's what's decided. I'm not your daughter. I'm not that barefoot little girl in Hallelujah Junction anymore. I never will be again."

"Christopher Davenport has corrupted you. I know this. I know this isn't really you speaking. You'll come around."

He's trying to act like my words mean nothing and aren't bothering him, but I can see in his eyes that they are. He's losing. He sees this. He hears it. And soon, he'll have no choice but to face it.

I shake my head and give my own smile. "No, Richard. This is not him speaking. It's me. All me. And I want you to know that you did one good thing for me. One. You gave me Christopher. He's a good man. He's my husband in all ways and forever will be. I have you to thank for that, but only for that one act."

"Don't let the devil stay inside you, girl."

Irritation prickles my skin. He'll never hear me. Not really. He'll sit there behind the bars of his cell and never see me for the new woman I am. No matter how much I try, I'll only be wasting my breath. I see this now. And the truth of the matter is...

I don't need him to see me for the strong and resourceful woman I've become.

I don't need his approval or his blessing.

I don't even need his understanding that I will never be in his life again.

I don't need anything from this man.

"You're going to spend the rest of your life looking out a small window at a freedom you will never have. You are going to be held captive. You are going to be at the mercy of your jailer. You are going to die knowing exactly how I felt. You are the captive now. Not me. I'm free. I'm finally free."

I hang up the phone and stand up to leave. I see his lips moving in rebuttal, his face red that I have the audacity to end the conversation before he's finished, but I couldn't care less what he's trying to say. I'll have the last word.

Me.

I'm in control. Not him. Never again will I hand my strength over to another person.

I walk out of the jail to join Christopher, who has anxiously been waiting for me. He doesn't see me when I first arrive, and he's pacing back and forth. The minute he does see me approaching, he runs up to me and takes me into his arms.

"Are you okay? How was it?" He pulls away so he can study my face.

I release the last breath of tension that is locked inside me and smile reassuringly. "He's a sick man. He's an evil man. But I know now that I'm free from all that. I never have to have him in my life again. It's over. It's finally over."

Christopher pulls me into a hug and kisses the side of my head. "Yes. You're free now, Ember. And I swear to you that you'll never have to go through that again. I love you; I'll always love you, and nothing and no one will ever change that."

Yes, I'm finally free. The Ghost of Hallelujah Junction no longer haunts the town.

EPILOGUE

EMBER

"They're here!" I hear Violet scream from the doorway of the chapel. "Holly! Isaac! Ember and Christopher are here!"

We reach the top of the mountain, winded from our hike but thrilled to finally see our friends again. Winter has passed, as well as spring, and the signs of summer are all around us. New life, new birth, a new beginning. The hike up to the chapel was far harder than the hike down, but I had the excitement of seeing them driving me forward.

Holly and Isaac follow Violet as they meet us halfway. I've never seen the sisters look so happy. They have put on some weight, don't appear hollow and sad in the slightest, and I see smiles on their faces until their cheeks run out. Violet is the first to reach us as she throws her arms around me and pulls me into a tight embrace. She shows no signs of her once having a broken leg and in fact looks to be in perfect health and fitness.

"I've missed you so much," she squeals.

I see Isaac extend his hand to Christopher, and they shake and then hug like long-lost buddies. A bond has been forever formed between them, and it's obvious to see.

Holly forces Violet out of the way and gives me a hug herself. "It feels like forever since we've seen you," she says. She pulls away and scans my body from head to toe, smiles, then looks at Christopher. "Come on inside, out of the sun. Let's get you something to drink and eat. I'm sure the trip up here wasn't easy."

"That sounds great," I say, looking at the chapel with new eyes.

It doesn't have the haunted, evil, ominous look it did when I first laid eyes upon it. It's obvious that repair work has been done to the exterior. There are no longer gaps between the weathered wood. Dead weeds that used to kiss the edges of the foundation are now colorful wildflowers.

When we enter inside, I almost don't recognize it. Log walls have been built, sectioning off rooms, instead of the tattered sheets we used before. The floors are clean, the windows sparkling, freshly cut flowers are in a mason jar in the center of the large table, and the chimney is complete. It feels like a home rather than a prison. It smells of Holly's stew, but this time it's being cooked over a hearth that appears expertly built.

"You've done so much to the place," Christopher says, spinning around and taking it all in. "It doesn't look like what I remember at all."

"It's beautiful," I add. "It really feels like a home."

Violet nods, walks up to Isaac, and takes his hand in hers. "Isaac helped us fix it up. We even have a well now with the freshest mountain water!"

Holly walks over to a pitcher of this water and pours us some glasses. "We couldn't have done this without him."

Isaac pulls his hand out of Violet's but replaces it by arranging his arm over her shoulders in a possessive embrace. I notice how Violet's cheeks pinken as he does so, and her smile beams even brighter. "I'm not taking any of the credit. These ladies know how to work hard. Once Violet's leg healed, she was up and at 'em like a tornado. I couldn't keep her down."

My heart warms as I watch Violet press her body to Isaac's. Holly doesn't seem to notice or care, which tells me this act is part of their normal day. Something has happened—a connection and closeness between Isaac and Violet—and I can't wait to get Violet alone so I can hear all about it.

We all settle in around the table and have small talk at first, but then it's Holly who finally says what we have all been waiting to discuss. "I can't believe they found both of them guilty. It almost seemed too easy."

"This nightmare is over," Christopher inserts. He reaches under the table, puts his hand on my thigh, and squeezes. "It hasn't been easy and nearly broke us at times. But it's finally over."

"It almost doesn't seem real sometimes," Violet adds. "I still keep expecting Scarecrow to walk through that door at any moment, demanding his supper."

I watch Isaac place his hand over hers and pat reassuringly. The brief moment of sadness that washed over her face vanishes the minute he touches her. All I see is pure happiness and bliss. I've never seen Violet look so alive.

"We can move on with our lives now," I say, happy that the trial is finally over.

Though our bulldog of a lawyer managed to shield us from a lot of the media madness, it still was a lot to take. Our privacy, however, remained intact, and our home is still our secret. It's pretty obvious that the townsfolk know who we are now if they didn't already, but they don't bother us about it. And with time, I'm sure they will move on to another's gossip. But we've started to make friends and settle in. Roots are growing, and I actually use the term "home" and mean it when I say it.

"Violet," I say, standing from the table. "Why don't you and I go get some firewood." I look to the full stack by the fireplace and smile. "For memory's sake."

Violet hops out of her chair and readily follows me. When we shut the door behind us and head to the barn, I get straight to the point.

"What's going on between you and Isaac?"

Violet blushes and looks down at her feet. "I like him. I like him a lot."

"It appears he feels the same way."

Her eyes dart up at me. "Really? You think so?"

I nod and smile. "I do. It's pretty obvious there is something there between you two."

"He took such good care of me when my leg was broken. Holly and I couldn't have survived without him. He's such a good man."

I gather an armful of wood and head back to the chapel. "He truly is. I owe him everything."

Violet reaches for some of the wood in my arms to lessen the load. "I know I wouldn't be here with my second chance at life if it weren't for him."

I pause before the door and turn to her. "Then take hold of what makes you happy. You deserve it. If Isaac is who you want, then grab on and never let go."

"I will," Violet promises. "I know what a gift I have now that I get to live life... and be happy. I won't throw it away ever again."

We both enter the chapel as if nothing of importance was discussed and easily join the group conversation as if we hadn't even left.

"Are you all still happy living up here?" Christopher asks, although we both already know the answer to that question. We can see it in how they look and how much work has already been done to the chapel. "My offer is still on the table to move you wherever you want. Pinesville is a great mountain town that Ember and I love calling home. You could join us there."

Violet's eyes dart to Isaac and then to Holly. "We've never been happier."

"Yes," Holly says. "We appreciate your offer, but we're really turning this place into our home."

Isaac chimes in with a proud sparkle in his eyes. "I've managed to purchase the property the chapel sits on. It connects to my own land, and so it was easy to just expand."

"What about you two?" Violet asks. "What are your plans? You just mentioned living in Pinesville. Are you going to stay? Raise a family someday?"

"Well, that's one reason why we're here," I answer as I reach for Christopher's hand. "I know you don't want to move from here, but we were hoping you'd at least come visit us in Pinesville for our wedding. Christopher has officially asked for my hand in marriage, and we're going to make our wedding vows legal. It's the last step of erasing our past and what was forced upon us. We are choosing to be married now. I want our vows to be made without an actual chain around our ankles."

"It would mean a lot to have you three there," Christopher adds. "You're our family."

"We wouldn't miss it for the world," Violet announces. "Oh, what amazing news."

When both Holly and Violet squeal in joy and pull my hand out of Christopher's so they can see the large diamond ring he bought me, Christopher and I both laugh at their excitement.

"You both look really happy," Isaac says. "It didn't come easy, but well worth the wait, it seems."

"I wouldn't want to go through this journey with anyone else —hard or not," I admit, looking at Christopher with so much love in my heart that it actually physically feels tight.

Christopher puts his arm around me and pulls my chair closer to him as he says, "It's about time I *truly* make Ember my bride. She was my captive bride, then my kept bride, and then my taken bride. But it's about time for her to be my forever bride."

· · ·

The End.

What's next? I have some secrets of what book is coming soon...

Be sure to sign up for my newsletter so you can be the first to know.

Alta's Newsletter

SNEAK PEEK

What do you think of Papa Rich?

Would you like to get a sneak peek of where The Secret Bride Series all began? Richard plays a part in a book I wrote a few years ago called CAPTIVE VOW. Let's just say that he learned all his wicked ways from the best.

CAPTIVE VOW
CHAPTER ONE

Jack and Jill went up the hill to fetch a pail of water.
Jack fell down and broke his crown,
And Jill came tumbling after.

My momma used to hum that nursery rhyme. She used to hum it a lot. And on days she was stressed, anxious, or short fused, she would even sing it with a high-pitched, haunting voice over and over again like a stuck record. It was the sound of my childhood. I hated that song.

I still remember the day I asked her why she loved it so. I wanted to know why two people climbing a hill and then falling off it was so important to her. Who was Jack? Who was Jill? She had looked at me stunned, as if surprised I had noticed and had paid attention to her humming and singing it all these years. Or was she shocked I didn't know the answer to my question? Whatever it was, she studied me for several minutes before answering me.

"It was your father's and my song. It reflects us. Our love we once shared."

My mother never spoke of my father. I had never met him nor ever saw a picture. Whenever I asked about him, for stories describing who he was, my momma was quick to shut it down. She said he was 'gone' and that was the best answer I would ever get.

"A nursery rhyme?" I had asked. "*That* was your song?"

"Yes. It's about two lovers who beat all the odds holding them down. They climb above it all, but only to be crushed again."

"I don't understand. Why do they have a pail of water?"

"A pail of water is a euphemism for having sex. For finally being in love and able to be together. But then Jack dies... and Jill soon follows."

"They die?"

She nodded, appearing so deep in thought. "Yes, they both eventually die."

The sound of the phone ringing in the middle of the night was never a good thing. It's always the sound of bad news, an emergency, or even death. The shrill resonance cutting through the night's air is like a town crier announcing impending doom.

My heart thumped against my chest as I reached for my cell phone sitting on the nightstand beside my bed. The number on the screen showed unknown, which only intensified my panic.

I cleared my throat, not wanting to sound as if I had been woken from a deep slumber and answered, "Hello?"

There was an operator's voice on the other end. "This is a collect call for Demi Wayne from The Eastland Women's Correction Facility. Would you like to accept the charges?" I had heard this question many times before.

"Yes, I will accept the charges." I sat up in my bed and turned on the bedside lamp, rubbing the sleep out of my eyes.

A clicking sound was followed by, "Demi?"

"Hello." I felt sick. I wanted to vomit. Her voice on the other end always made me feel ill, but tonight was worse. So much worse. I scanned my nightstand, wishing I still had the emergency pack of cigarettes I kept for an occasion such as this. Why the fuck did I decide to quit?

"How are you?" she asked.

What did she expect me to say? How was I supposed to be when I was getting a call from my mother in the middle of the night from a prison where she'd been incarcerated for the past six years? I needed a goddamn cigarette is how I was.

"Fine," I lied.

"Have you been watching the news?"

"No." Ever since my mother was arrested for blowing up a building and killing the five guards on that night's duty, I avoided the media completely. I couldn't take it. The pictures of her. The pictures of me. The pictures of us together and how the media would say I was a spitting image of my mother. They would say we looked like angels with our blonde hair and blue eyes, but then in the same sentence, say my mother had nothing but the devil inside of her. I didn't want to look like her. I didn't want to be the devil. I hated the media. I hated them all. I couldn't handle all the awful things being said about my mother.

Demon.

Murderer.

Monster.

And they were all true. Everything they said was true.

There was a long pause of silence. "I'm calling to say goodbye," she said with a wavering voice.

Bile built up in the back of my throat. "Goodbye?" We had already said our goodbyes when she was handcuffed and escorted off to prison. So what could she possibly mean by saying it again?

"I lost the final appeal."

I remained silent. I struggled to comprehend the information being fed through the phone line. It was as if my body was protecting me from processing the words threatening to shatter my soul. *Lost. Final.*

"I'm being sentenced to death tomorrow. Lethal injection. The lawyer says today was my final attempt at overturning the guilty verdict. I lost again."

Guilty.

The judge and jury had deemed her guilty.

She *was* guilty. She had placed the bomb in the building. She had killed those men. When she was asked why, she had said it was for the cause. The company housed in the building was testing against animals. *She* had been the judge and jury in that case, deciding that the experiments they were conducting deemed them worthy of being destroyed. 'A cause,' she had stated over and over. She was proud of her cause. She was proud of what she did. Not once did she say she was sorry. Not once did she glance over at the wives and families of the men she killed and beg for their forgiveness. Not once did she look at me and tell me she had made a huge mistake and wished she could take it all back. Not once did she show even an ounce of decency in her actions. When I had asked her why she would kill those innocent men, praying to God it was an accident, she simply shrugged and told me it was collateral damage. The price to pay for a bigger and better cause. So yes, what the media was saying about her was true.

Demon.

Murderer.

Monster.

My momma.

Yes.

So, I had no choice but to carry the shame for the both of us, and what a heavy weight it was. On my eighteenth birthday, I sat in the crowded courtroom and watched my mother stand with an aura of defiance and pride while the judge sentenced her to death for five counts of murder.

Happy Birthday to me.

"Demi?"

"Yes?" My voice cracked. I glanced around my bedroom at the piles of dirty clothes strewn about as my heart threatened to beat out of my chest. My room reflected my life. Dirty, neglected, disarrayed, shambles. My life was in chaos, and all I wanted right now was a fucking cigarette. This couldn't be real. This couldn't be real. This couldn't be real... yet, it was.

"Did you hear what I said?"

"Yes."

There was a long pause as darkness suffocated me. As darkness stabbed at my heart over and over. As darkness bludgeoned me to a bloody pulp. Darkness destroyed me as I sat there with the phone to my ear.

Dead man walking...

Correction.

Dead *woman* walking...

"It's okay, Demi. I'm at peace. I finally get to be with your father."

I said nothing as I struggled to breathe. The small room of my one-bedroom apartment shrank in size as the walls appeared to be closing in on me. I was trapped in this nightmare that I couldn't elude. There was no escape from my life.

"Jack and Jill went up the hill to fetch a pail of water. Jack fell down and broke his crown. And Jill came tumbling after," she sang softly as she had done so many times in my youth. She paused, as if she were waiting for me to say something. As if wanting me to ask for clarification.

I wanted to scream for her to stop. I didn't want to hear that awful nursery rhyme ever again. I wanted her to shut the fuck up! Yet, I didn't want those to be my last words to her. No matter what, she didn't deserve that. I didn't want her to die hearing my cruel—but honest—words ringing in her ears. A daughter's truth to a mother who had done her wrong... so very wrong. So, I remained silent. Silent like all the times I watched her and others meet in my living room planning to take down a government agency or corrupt company. These strangers plotting and planning in my childhood home all spoke as if they were the good guys, and everyone else were the villains. I had grown up to distrust our government due to all the conspiracy theories I heard growing up. I never questioned. I never disagreed. I never told a soul of their plans. I only remained silent as a good little girl would do.

"I'm proud. Your father died for his cause, and now I get to tumble down after him."

I had finally learned all about my father after my mother was arrested. Not from my momma, but by the television. The media had informed me that my father—who I was simply told was 'gone'—had died in a blaze of police gunfire when he refused to surrender after trying to blow up a nuclear power plant. He was a leader of a terrorist group. He had died that day, leaving behind a grieving widow and a three-month-old baby. I can still remember the news anchor who stared into the camera while video of my father played behind his profile. The anchorman's gray hair, perfect suit and blue-striped tie, his firm, emotionless expression as he spoke into the camera were still so clear in my memory. Did he know that behind his head on the television screen was a gruesome image playing of a man losing his life as he was gunned down? A man who was my father? Did the news anchor have any idea there was a young woman watching her father— who she knew nothing about—for the first time while he died on old video footage? I often wonder if that news anchor had any idea a piece of me died that day. I had to meet my father, watch them describe my mother as the devil, and come to terms with the fact that I was nothing but an orphan with a dark and twisted family tree. I was a fool. Fooled by my past.

"When?" I asked, swallowing the lump in the back of my throat. "When do you die?"

"They said two o'clock tomorrow."

Two o'clock.

Two o'clock and my mother would be dead.

How odd it must be to know the exact time you are going to die.

Was she afraid? I would be afraid.

The first hot tear fell from my eyes. "So this is it? The last time I get to talk to you?"

"Yes."

"Momma..." The rest of the tears followed as I slipped into a deep hole. At that moment, I wanted to be a little girl with her mother's soothing arms around her, comforting her, telling her it was all going to be okay. But nothing was going to be okay. Nothing at all.

"Promise me one thing," she said. "Promise me you'll find your Jack, and you will climb that hill. You deserve happiness and love. You deserve so much more than I was able to give you." She cleared her throat. "I have to go now."

Panic attacked. "Wait! Now?" Oh God! Was this the last time I would ever hear my mother's voice? Would these be our last words? "Is there anything we can do? Can we hold it off a little bit longer? Maybe hire another lawyer? Get a new judge? Anything? There has to be something!" I felt as if I was hanging on a cliff by my fingertips and the weight of my body was just too much. I was about to fall into the abyss.

"No. The time has finally come. Just know that though you may not have agreed with my cause or what I did, I at least stayed true to myself. True to what your father and I believed in. All I ask is you stay true to yourself, Demi."

"Momma..."

"Goodbye."

With a short metallic click, the phone went dead, and *Jill came tumbling after.*

Day of death. How do you start a day like that? Do you get up, shower, dress and go to work like any other day? How do you face the hours? The minutes? The seconds? How do you breathe when your soul is dying, but your body is too cruel to allow the sweet release of death? How does a daughter live as her mother prepares to die?

"Demi? Did you hear me?"

I turned to see Maria standing in the small break room, looking at me with concern. Her long black hair was set in a low bun like she always wore it while on shift, but the wayward hairs that framed her face revealed she had already worked several hours. The breakfast shift at *Blossoms Diner* could be a real bitch, and no doubt she was anxious to be relieved by me so she could go home and get some rest.

"What?" I hadn't even heard her come in, let alone say anything to me. Ever since the phone call, I felt as if I was wading through a dream cloaked in a thick fog.

"I asked if you were all right. You look a million miles away."

"Just a long night. I didn't get much sleep."

Maria was my friend—the only person I would really consider a friend—but I'd never told her about my mother. I hadn't told anyone about my mother. It wasn't exactly something I was proud of or wanted to relive by retelling the nightmare I tried desperately to keep locked away in the far corners of my mind. I had murderess blood that ran through my veins, and that was a secret I didn't want to reveal. Not to anyone.

Appearing satisfied with my lie, she said, "Story of my life. I swear, if Luis doesn't start sleeping through the night soon, I may die of sleep deprivation. He's just so darn cute that I can't help but pick him up from his crib. I know they say you are supposed to let them cry it out, but that just seems cruel to me."

I tried my best to give a smile and slight nod as I reached for my apron and tied it around my waist. Normally, I loved hearing stories of her sweet little baby, but the fog I was in nearly smothered me in despair. I was afraid Maria would know something was wrong by looking at me, as she always did. I just hoped today she'd write this one off as me being tired.

When I looked up at her after putting on my apron, I found her staring, appearing more concerned than before. "Hey, are you really okay? Are you sick or something? Do you want me to work your shift for you? I can call the sitter and have her stay longer. It's really not that big of a deal."

Having Maria work my shift would have been wonderful so I could just go crawl in bed and hide from all the emotions flooding me, but I didn't have the luxury. Missing even one shift meant me not being able to pay all my bills that month, and it was tight as it was.

I shook my head and gave the best reassuring smile I could give. "I'm fine. Once I get some coffee in me, I'll perk right up."

Maria seemed convinced with my answer, and she reached for the tie of her apron to remove it. "Table five is waiting for you."

"She's here today?"

"Every Tuesday and Thursday, and now Friday it seems. She's making a habit of eating here. Quite the regular. I already placed her order for her."

I let out a big sigh. Not that I minded our usual customer, in fact, she had become someone I actually cared for, but today I wasn't sure I had the patience or the ability to be kind to anyone. Viv Montgomery was a sweet old Asian lady with a heart of gold, but she did take a lot of my time and attention. "Any chance you can stay a bit longer? I know she'll need my help."

"Girl, you can't be expected to stop what you are doing and feed her every time she comes in."

Even though Maria said the words, I knew that if I didn't help Mrs. Montgomery eat her meal, Maria would most definitely step in and fill my shoes. She liked to play the hard ass, but I knew the real her. Maria wouldn't allow a little old lady to fend for herself, and I knew it.

Mrs. Montgomery had Parkinson's so bad, that bringing a spoon to her lips by herself, usually left her covered in whatever food she ordered. Seeing the poor woman sitting alone in the diner's booth, shaking and struggling a few weeks back, I had taken it upon myself to help her. It was the least I could do. And the truth of the matter was, I enjoyed it. I liked the lady, and I liked the feeling that I was being of some use to someone in need.

"Just stay long enough for me to get her started. Can you cover me?"

Maria nodded with a tender smile as she went to put her apron back on. "Softie."

"Yeah, I guess I am," I said as I reached for a ponytail holder in my pocket and pulled my hair into a messy bun, preparing for another long day on my feet serving greasy food to patrons. Hopefully, I would be busy enough to keep my mind off of the nightmare in which I was imprisoned.

When I walked into the dining room, I went straight to table five where Mrs. Montgomery sat staring ahead. Her short grey hair rested on the top of her shoulders, curled to perfection, with tiny, pearl pins right above her ears. It was still possible to see the remnants of what must have been rich black hair in her youth. In this redneck, piece of shit town in South Carolina, an exotic, mature, beauty such as Vivian Montgomery was a rarity. I had also come to realize that she dressed up for her special lunches each and every time. She treated lunch at *Blossoms Diner* like someone would treat a meal at a fine dining establishment. She always wore a dress or skirt, shoes with a stubby heel, nude-colored pantyhose, and carried a different purse that matched her outfit each and every time. She never wore garish jewelry, but she would wear a strand of pearls or a necklace made of some type of semi-precious stone. Though her hands were covered in age spots and wrinkles, her nails were always painted a pretty pink or coral, manicured to perfection. It was obvious the woman took pride in her appearance, and wanted to be at her very best, even if it was for lunch in a small local diner.

"Mrs. Montgomery, don't you look marvelous today," I said as I placed the Cajun chicken pasta she had already ordered from

Maria in front of her shaking hands and sat in the booth opposite to her.

She looked at me with the sweetest eyes and the warmest smile. "You are so kind, dear." She reached across to touch my hands that rested on the table. I could see she was shaking more than normal. She had told me that, with her Parkinson's, she had good days and bad days, but by the intensity of the tremors now, I would say she was having a bad day. I noticed the skin around her wrists looked raw and bruised. So, I made a mental note to ask her about it later, but didn't want to start off the meal by talking about her sickness and injuries due to it. "You look so pretty too."

I smirked, feeling anything but pretty. I couldn't remember if I had brushed my hair. The fact that I was even dressed was a feat within itself.

"Don't give me that look," she playfully scolded. "When I was your age, I envied women like you. Tall, big blue eyes, long light hair, and the perfect cherub face. Like a doll. You are such a lovely young lady."

I smiled and shook my head, feeling uncomfortable hearing her kind words. I never handled compliments very well.

"Thank you," I mumbled as I glanced over at Maria who was taking an order at one of the tables I was supposed to cover myself.

Mrs. Montgomery looked down at her meal and reached for her fork. I always allowed her to start, judging if she needed my help or not. She always did, but I would still watch for a short time to gauge how much. Today she could barely grab the fork, knocking the other silverware to the side as she struggled for the handle of the utensil.

Without asking, I took the fork and poked it into a piece of pasta and chicken. "Why don't I help you with that?"

She nodded and smiled. Her eyes made contact with mine, and we connected like we had done many times before. "Thank you. I don't know what I would do without you."

I fed her the food and returned the smile, poking the pasta for the second bite. "And I don't know what I would do without you, Mrs. Montgomery. You are the sunshine to my day."

"I wish you would call me Viv," she said as she finished the bite of her food. She then took another bite the minute she was done chewing, her entire body quivering lightly as she did so.

"I was taught by my momma to always address my elders in the proper fashion." I gave her a wink, trying to hide the stab in my heart which occurred by bringing up my mother.

Fuck! Why did I say that? I didn't want to think about her. I didn't want to remember a single thing. I just wanted to feed this nice woman and go about my day. One meal, one hour, one minute at a time, and I would survive this day. I had to survive the day my mother would die.

"You must have had a very good momma. She has taught you to be a kind and generous woman." Mrs. Montgomery continued to eat, opening her mouth in a child-like fashion each time I brought the food to her lips.

A dull ache attacked my head, and a ringing filled my ears. I didn't want to talk about my momma. No, she was not a good momma. A good momma would not have done what she did. A good momma would not have left her child to fend off the cruel world by herself. A good momma would not die for a cause that did not matter. I did not have a good momma. I did not have a good momma at all.

"But I still wish you would call me Viv. Friends should be on a first name basis; don't you think?"

Trying to snap out of the spiraling fall from the cliff where I was so precariously balanced, I gave a smirk. "I suppose you are right. We are friends, and we should call each other by our first names. But that goes for you as well then. You call me Demi." She had only called me 'dear' since we first met.

Feeding Viv another bite, I noticed her eyes seemed to glisten as if she were struggling holding back tears. "I don't have any friends," she said.

"Oh, I'm sure you have friends."

She shook her head. "No."

I placed the fork down on the plate, reached for her glass of water, and helped her drink from it. "Well, I'll let you in on a little secret. Other than Maria who works here, I don't have any friends either. I pretty much keep to myself." I picked up the fork and once again stabbed at a piece of spiced chicken. "And the truth is, I often am suspicious of people who have lots and lots of friends. I mean, how can you be best friends with everyone? I think it's impossible. There's only so much of your heart you can give. I would much rather give more of me—the real me—to those select and special people than just a little of me to a large group simply so I can say I have a lot of friends."

Viv turned her head to look at Maria who was behind the counter getting drinks ready. "And Maria is your friend?" she asked.

"Yes. She's really nice and fun to work with. She has a new baby who is just about the cutest thing you've ever seen. We both don't have any family around, so we spend the holidays together... so, I guess you could say we are more than friends."

She looked surprised. "No family?"

I shook my head, hoping to God she would drop the subject. I was not going to go into my awful situation with her or anyone. "No."

"And you don't have a special person in your life?" she asked as she reached for her napkin to wipe at some white cream sauce that stuck to the corner of her lip. Her hand shook the entire time, but she had managed to do it herself.

I shrugged. "Not interested in having a someone special right now."

"Why?"

I didn't usually like talking about myself to anyone, but this little old lady and I had spent many hours chatting as I fed her. I felt comfortable talking to her which was odd, but, at the same time, I liked it.

"All the good ones are taken, I guess." It was a canned answer, and one I really didn't mean. I had found it was a sufficient answer to give when people asked why you weren't in a relationship. It was a much better answer than 'I'm too fucked up to be with anyone.'

"Oh, I don't think so. You should meet my son. He's a good one. I raised him well." She smiled wide, intensifying the wrinkles at the corners of her eyes as her entire face seemed to light up. "But I could be biased since I am his momma."

"I didn't realize you had a son. You never mentioned him before." I had always gotten the impression Viv Montgomery was a widow and all alone. She had mentioned once that her husband had passed away many years ago, but that had been the only mention of family.

"I do. He's a handsome boy. He looks like his father did at his age. Thick black hair, hypnotizing brown eyes, firm jawline, muscular build. His Korean blood gives him a rich caramel-colored skin." She giggled. "Can you tell I am a proud mother? Yes, he looks just like his handsome father. My husband always had that powerful hold of my heart. Do you know what I'm talking about? That crazed, all-consuming love you can't live without." She paused, and a look of sadness washed over her face, but then was quickly replaced with a tender smile. "My son reminds me of him so much. Anyway, he's picking me up after my lunch today."

I tilted my head and studied her expression. I saw so much love and pride on her face. But if she truly loved and adored her son so much, why had she not mentioned him before? "I thought you took the bus here and home."

"I used to. But my son told me that, from now on, he would be driving me to the places I needed to go. Such a kind boy."

"Does he live here in town?" I still found it odd Viv had never mentioned him before, and he was just now stepping in to care for her by providing transportation. I couldn't quite silence the warning bells going off in my head.

"Yes. He lives with me for now. He just returned, and it will take him a bit to get on his feet. But I'm in no rush for him to move out. I like having him around."

Ahh, a deadbeat son taking advantage of his mother is what this sounded like.

"What does he do for a living?"

"He's a pilot. He's loved planes from the time he could barely walk."

"You said he just returned. From where?"

Maybe I was being too nosy. But I heard the stories all the time of lazy and greedy family members taking advantage of their elders. I had no knowledge of Viv's financial situation other than the fact that she always paid in cash and would leave a very large tip. Sometimes too large, and she and I would argue about her overpaying me, but she always won out. I hated to think that her own flesh and blood could use her, or that anyone could take advantage of an elder, but I still found it a bit disturbing he was just *now* popping into her life. She had been coming here for months, me feeding her for an hour on those days, and not once did she mention any family at all.

Viv shifted in her seat, appearing uncomfortable. She didn't say anything, but rather opened her mouth to take another bite. I had overstepped it seemed.

"I'm sorry. I didn't mean to... I'm sorry. I'll mind my own business from now on."

Viv finished her bite. "Oh no. I don't mind. It's just hard to answer that question. I always worry he'll be judged and thought poorly of. He's such a decent and fine man, that it's a shame he has this mark on his past." She took a deep breath and continued chewing the food in her mouth.

Feeling guilty for doing exactly that—judging, I said, "Well, I'm the last person who has any business judging people. And we all have marks in our pasts. Some more than others."

Her tiny, frail body leaned inward. Lowering her voice, she

asked, "You promise you won't think badly of him? He is such a good man. I would hate for you to think otherwise."

"If you say he is a good man, then I'll believe you." I gave her a reassuring smile. "I can't imagine you raising anyone but a fine, upstanding man anyway."

"He just got out of prison," she blurted, looking terrified the minute she said the words.

The word 'prison' hit too close to home, and I instantly felt sick to my stomach. I didn't want to think of prison. I didn't want to think...

"But he didn't do it!" she said in a hushed, yet aggressive tone. "He would never do the things they said. A man like my son would never kill a girl. They had it all wrong when they said he was guilty."

Prison.

Kill.

Guilty.

I couldn't cope. I couldn't hear these dark words that followed me wherever I went. Not today. Not today!

I put down the fork. "I really need to get to work, Mrs. Montgomery. Maria is covering for me, but she really needs to get home to her baby."

Viv reached out a shaky hand to me. "Oh no. Please tell me I didn't scare you off with the news of my son. Please. I can see I have upset you. He was found guilty of manslaughter, not murder, but I swear to you, he didn't do it. And I feel awful now. I can see you are uncomfortable." She appeared to be broken-hearted, and I had never seen her so upset before.

"It's not that... I have a lot to deal with today." I struggled to hold back the tears threatening to fall. "It's not a very good day for me is all." I took her trembling hand and held it firmly. I wanted to reassure her that my demons were not due to her or the news of her son. My demons only needed the slightest push to be knocking at my door once again.

"I worry you are going to get up from here thinking my son is a bad person." Her lower lip began to quiver. "And he isn't. He really isn't."

I nodded and squeezed her hand again, not wanting my own morose thoughts to upset the woman. "I believe you, Viv. I do. I'm glad you have your son back." And I meant it. I'd always hated the thought of her having to deal with her illness all by herself. Now that her son was home, she wouldn't be alone. I scooted out of the booth and stood. "Bring him in next time, and I'll give him a free piece of Blossoms' famous cherry pie."

Her lip ceased trembling, a warm smile to replace it. "Oh I will. He would love that. You are such a kind girl. He will just adore you."

"Okay, well I really need to get to work," I said. "Are you coming in Tuesday?"

She nodded. "Of course." She clutched her hands together to her chest. "I can't wait for you two to meet. I promise you will see what a wonderful boy he is. He may be a bit of a momma's boy, but he is such a good, good boy."

One Click the rest of CAPTIVE VOW now.

ABOUT THE AUTHOR

Alta Hensley is a USA TODAY bestselling author of hot, dark and dirty romance. She is also an Amazon Top 10 bestselling author. Being a multi-published author in the romance genre, Alta is known for her dark, gritty alpha heroes, sometimes sweet love stories, hot eroticism, and engaging tales of the constant struggle between dominance and submission.

She lives in a log cabin in the woods with her husband, two daughters, and an Australian Shepherd. When she isn't battling the bats, and watching the deer, she is writing about villains who always get their love story and happily ever after.

As a gift for being my reader, I would like to offer you a FREE book.
DELICATE SCARS

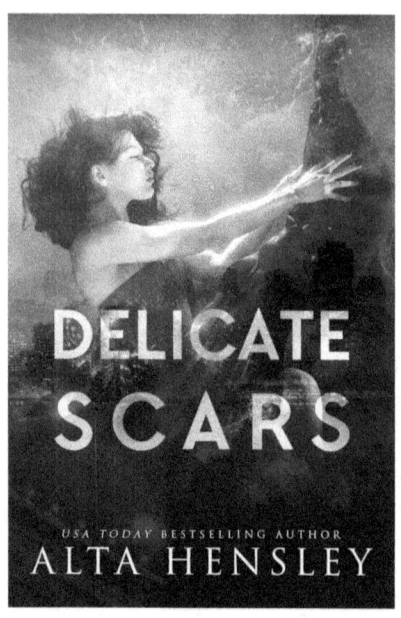

Get your copy now! ~
https://dl.bookfunnel.com/tnpuad5675

I was going to ruin her.

I knew it the moment I laid eyes on her. She was too naive, too innocent.

I would wrap her in the darkness of my world till she no longer craved the light... only me.

I should walk away, leave her clean and untouched... but I won't.

I hold her delicate heart in my scarred fist and I have no intention of letting go.

It all started with a book... doesn't that sound crazy?

For your entire world to come crashing down around you over research for a book?

But that is what it felt like the moment I met him.

My world tilted. Nothing made sense any more.

I only know he became like a drug to me... and I shook with need till my next fix.

Join Alta's Facebook Group for Readers for access to deleted scenes, to chat with me and other fans and also get access to exclusive giveaways:

Alta's Private Facebook Room

Facebook: https://www.facebook.com/AltaHensleyAuthor/
Amazon: https://www.amazon.com/Alta-Hensley/e/B004G5A6LI
Twitter: https://twitter.com/AltaHensley
Website: www.altahensley.com
Instagram: https://instagram.com/altahensley
Bookbub: https://www.bookbub.com/authors/alta-hensley
TikTok: https://www.tiktok.com/@altahensley
Goodreads: https://www.goodreads.com/author/show/4491649.Alta_Hensley
Join her mailing list: https://readerlinks.com/l/727720/nl